SAILOR'S HOLIDAY

S A I L O R ' S
H O L I D A Y

*To Bill Benge
with Best wishes
for a wild life —
Barry Gifford
4 April 91*

T H E

W I L D

L I F E

O F

S A I L O R

A N D

L U L A

B A R R Y   G I F F O R D

THIS BOOK IS DEDICATED

TO THE MEMORY OF LARRY LEE

1942—1990

Copyright © 1991 by Barry Gifford

All rights reserved under International and Pan-American Copyright Conventions. Published in the United States by Random House, Inc., New York and simultaneously in Canada by Random House of Canada Limited, Toronto.

Library of Congress Cataloging-in-Publication Data
Gifford, Barry
Sailor's holiday / by Barry Gifford.
p.   cm.
Contents: 59° and raining—Sailor's holiday—
Sultans of Africa—Consuelo's Kiss
ISBN 0-679-40149-0
I. Title.
PS3557.I283S25   1991
813'.54—dc20   90-9085

Manufactured in the United States of America
24689753
First Edition

CONTENTS

59° AND RAINING

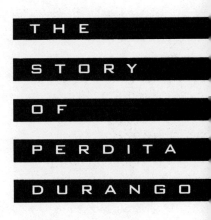

THE STORY OF PERDITA DURANGO

*"Pleasure which vanishes vanishes for good . . .
Other pleasures come, which replace nothing."*

ROLAND BARTHES

III

Perdita met Manny Flynn in the San Antonio airport restaurant and bar. He was gobbling chicken fajitas and she was smoking a cigarette, an empty glass in front of

her on the table, which was next to his.

"You wanna 'nother one?" Manny asked.

Perdita looked at him. Fat but neat. He wiped his thin lavender lips with a napkin. A waitress came over.

"Sweetheart, bring me another Bud and give that girl there whatever she wants."

"Wish somebody'd make me an offer like that," said the waitress. "What'll it be, honey?"

Perdita took a long drag on her Marlboro, blew out the smoke and killed it in an ashtray.

"Coke," she said.

"Diet?"

"Not hardly."

The waitress looked hard at Perdita for a moment, then wrote on Manny Flynn's check.

"One Bud, one Coke," she said, and hurried away.

Manny forked down the last bite of fajita, wiped his mouth again with the napkin, stood up and redeposited himself at Perdita's table.

"You live in San Antone?" he asked.

"Not really."

"You sure do have beautiful black hair. See my reflection in it just about."

Perdita withdrew another Marlboro from the pack on the table and lit it with a pink and black zebra-striped Bic.

"You catchin' or waitin' on one?" asked Manny.

"One what?"

7

"A plane. You headin' out somewhere?"

"My flight's been cancelled."

"Where you lookin' to go?"

"Nowhere now. About yourself?"

"Phoenix. Four-day computer convention. I sell software. By the way, my name is Manny Flynn. Half Jewish, half Irish. What's yours?"

The waitress brought their drinks, set them down quickly on the table without looking at Perdita, and left.

"Perdita Durango. Half Tex, half Mex."

Manny laughed, picked up his beer and drank straight from the bottle.

"Pretty name for a pretty Miss. It *is* Miss, isn't it?"

Perdita looked directly into Manny Flynn's eyes and said, "You want me to come to Phoenix with you? You pay my way, buy my meals, bring me back. I'll keep your dick hard for four days. While you're at the convention, I'll do some business, too. Plenty of guys at the hotel, right? Fifty bucks a pop for showin' tit and milkin' the cow. Quick and clean. You take half off each trick. How about it?"

Manny put the bottle back down on the table, then picked it up again and took a swig. Perdita turned away and puffed on her cigarette.

"I gotta go," Manny said. He threw several bills on the table. "That'll cover mine and yours."

He stood and picked up a briefcase and walked away. The waitress came over.

"I'm goin' off duty now," she said to Perdita. "You finished here?"

Perdita looked at her. The waitress was about forty-five, tall and skinny with bad teeth and phony red hair that was all kinked up so that it resembled a Brillo pad. She wore one ring, a black cameo with an ivory scorpion on the third finger of her right hand. Perdita wondered what her tattoos looked like.

"Just about," said Perdita.

The waitress scooped up Manny Flynn's money. Perdita nodded at it.

"Gentleman said for you to keep the change."

"Obliged," said the waitress.

Perdita sat and smoked her Marlboro until the ash was down almost to the filter.

"Dumb cocksucker," she said, and dropped the butt into the Coke.

"Mummy says he has more money than he knows what to do with."

"Why does he work, then? He still works, doesn't he?"

"Oh, he's just so greedy, that's why. Mummy says he needs to work just to have something to do, which doesn't make any sense at all. At least not to me. I mean, he has all kinds of stocks and everything, lots of property all over the country. He's just so cheap I can't stand it, and neither can Mummy."

"So why does she go out with him?"

"It's just someone, I suppose, until she can find a man she really likes. Could be he's hung like an Australian crocodile, for all I know. Mummy's always had a weakness for big cocks. She told me."

"She *told* you that? My mother's always acted like babies come from a stork."

"You mean like dropped down a chimney?"

"Yeah, I guess."

Both girls laughed.

"She'd never talk to me about sex. Once I asked her if they had Tampons when she was a girl and she said, 'When the time comes, young lady, we'll discuss all that sort of thing.' Then, when I got my period in March, remember? The week before my birthday?"

"I remember."

"She gave me a box of Kotex sanitary napkins and a can of cunt spray and said, 'More of each of these will be on the second shelf of your bathroom closet.' "

"So she never discussed anything?"

"Get real. My mother would drop dead if she knew half of what I've done."

9

"Mine, too, probably, even though she's such a slut herself."

"Come on, I need to get some boots to go with that cowgirl skirt Kristin gave me."

"Sounds good. Oh, do you have your credit cards? Mummy took mine away for a month and I might see something I like."

"Yeah, no prob."

Perdita watched the two girls as they walked out of the coffee shop. Neither of them was more than twelve years old. Both had long blond hair, wore tight, short, black skirts, expensive-looking blouses and large gold hoop earrings. Perdita felt for a moment like stabbing them each in the back and chest and throat dozens of times. She imagined their blood running black, dripping down their smooth golden legs. Just as suddenly the feeling passed, and she forgot about them.

That evening, when Perdita was driving along Tres Sueños, she saw two little girls, eight or nine years old, sitting on the lowered tailgate of a parked pickup truck, petting a fuzzy brown puppy. One of the little girls had long, dark hair cut into bangs in front; she reminded Perdita of herself when she was that age. This sight made Perdita sad because it made her think also of her twin sister, Juana, who was dead. Juana had been shot and killed by her husband, Tony, who was drunk, during an argument. Tony had then murdered his and Juana's two daughters before putting the gun in his own mouth and blowing off the top of his skull. Perdita missed Juana, and her nieces, Consuelo and Concha, too. She guessed she might forever. Tony she always could have lived without.

When Perdita first saw Romeo Dolorosa she thought
he was very ugly. He was drinking a papaya milkshake
at an outdoor fruitstand on Magazine Street in New

THE NAME OF

SCIENCE

Orleans. She ordered a large
orange juice and avoided
looking at him, staring across
the street at a Shoetown.
When she turned back to pay, the fruitstand operator, a
bent-backed, dark gray man of indeterminate age or
race, said, "The gentleman there already done, sweet
thing."

"It's your lucky day, señorita," said Romeo. "And
mine, perhaps, too."

"What's that supposed to mean?" asked Perdita. "I
don't need a new friend."

Romeo laughed. "Oh, but you do," he said, and
laughed again. "What a charming manner you have,
Señorita Spitfire. Are you the daughter of Lupe Velez?
My name is Romeo Dolorosa."

Perdita looked more closely at Romeo. He was really
quite handsome, she realized, with long, wavy black
hair, deep brown skin and blue eyes; perhaps an inch
under six feet tall, but substantial looking. He had beau-
tifully shaped, very muscular arms that tapered grace-
fully down from the short sleeves of his blue and red
Hawaiian shirt. It was odd, Perdita thought, that her first
impression of him was so unflattering. She wondered
what she had seen in Romeo to have made him appear
that way.

"I don't know what you're talking about," she said.
"Thank you for the orange juice. My name is Perdita
Durango. Who is Lupe Velez?"

"Better, much better. Lupe Velez was an actress, a movie star from Mexico sixty years ago, who was famous for her hot temper."

"Why should I have reminded you of her? You don't know me."

"I am trying to make a beginning. Please, I apologize for my presumptuous behavior. Do you live in New Orleans, Perdita?"

"I've only arrived this afternoon. I'm looking around."

Romeo nodded and smiled broadly. He had very large white teeth.

"If you will allow me to buy you dinner," he said. "I'll be happy to show you the town."

As Perdita sipped the orange juice through a straw, she raised her 8-ball black eyes to Romeo's, smiled, and nodded slowly.

"Now we're getting somewhere," he said.

At Mosca's that evening, Romeo asked Perdita if she knew what a "resurrection man" was. She shook her head no.

"A hundred years ago and more," said Romeo, "doctors at medical colleges paid men to rob graves, mostly in nigger cemeteries, and deliver the corpses to them to be used for dissection by students. The doctors soaked the bodies in whisky to preserve them. It wasn't until almost the twentieth century that laws were changed to permit dissection of humans."

"Why you tellin' me this?" asked Perdita, licking salad dressing off her fork.

Romeo grinned. "Science is everything," he said. "The most important thing, anyway. Often it's necessary to go against what is the popular thinking to achieve discoveries. I think about things this way, scientifically. There's nothing I would not do for science."

"About those people saw the Virgin Mary at Tickfaw?" asked Perdita. "And the woman in Lubbock took the photo of St. Peter at the gates of heaven? How's science deal with that?"

"Need funds to research," Romeo said. "Like the $1,925 some fundraiser withdrew without permission this morning from the First National Bank of St. Bernard's Parish on Friscoville Street in Arabi. Science needs money, just like everything else."

"You tellin' me you're a grave robber or a bank robber? I ain't totally clear."

Romeo laughed and stuck a fork into his stuffed catfish.

"Scientists gotta eat, too," he said.

"I knew a guy once named Bobby Peru," said Perdita. "You know, like the country? Thought he was a bad dude, and he was, kinda. Coulda helped us out here, I think, but he got himself killed."

"Know what soothes me?" Romeo said.

Perdita laughed. "Yeah, I sure do."

"That, too," said Romeo. "But I like to read the weather reports in the newspaper. Like for other places than where I am. 'Ten below with snow flurries in Kankakee.' 'Fifty-nine and raining in Tupelo.' Never fails. Calms me."

Perdita Durango and Romeo Dolorosa were sitting facing each other in a bathtub filled with smoky gray warm water in the Del Rio Ramada. Romeo was fondling an H. Upmann New Yorker and flicking the ash into the bathwater.

"Wish you wouldn't do that," said Perdita.

Romeo laughed. "Why not? Keeps away the evil spirits, don't it?" He laughed again, showing off his perfect Burt Lancaster teeth.

"How long you suppose these guys are gonna go for this voodoo shit, Romeo? They ain't all all the way stupid."

"Makes you say that? Could they might be. Besides, it ain't voodoo, neither. *Santería, chiquita*. That's hocus-pocus, Latin-style. But you're right, we gotta do somethin's gonna make 'em pay better attention."

"I know what'll do it," Perdita said.

"Yeah?"

Perdita nodded, her thin black eyebrows uncoiling like cobras.

"Kill somebody and eat him."

"You mean like cannibals."

"Sure," she said. "Nothin' can be more horrible than that. It'll stick in their brain."

Romeo laughed and puffed on his cigar.

"You bet it will, okay," he said. "Stick to their ribs, too."

Perdita smiled and tickled Romeo's penis under the water with the big toe of her right foot. The cobras on her forehead flattened out like reptiles on a rock in the sun.

"You know how to help a man in both mind *and* body, *mi corazón*. What I like about you. It's the good life, okay."

"Let's do it tomorrow," Perdita said.

At three-thirty in the morning Romeo woke up and lit
the half of the cigar he'd left in the ashtray on the table
next to the bed. The smoke woke Perdita up.

"What's the matter, hon?"
she said. "Can't sleep?"

"Thinkin'."

"Anything in particular?"

Perdita had her eyes closed; her long black hair was
strewn across her face.

"Once read about how just before the Civil War
ended, rebel soldiers buried the treasury of the Confederacy within one hundred paces of the railroad tracks
between McLeansville and Burlington, North Carolina."

"How come nobody's dug it up?"

"Good question. It was all gold coins kept in iron
cooking pots. Some farmer found one of 'em, but there's
supposed to be about fifty million dollars worth still in
the ground there. Somethin' to think about."

"For after we get done here, maybe."

Perdita fell back asleep. Romeo finished off most of
the Upmann, imagining himself overseeing a crew of his
disciples digging up pots of gold along a stretch of railroad tracks next to a tobacco field. The disciples could
then be shot and buried in the holes. This was not impossible, he decided.

Perdita woke up and turned on the radio. She lay in bed listening to the news with her eyes closed.

"Finally," said the broadcaster, "from China today comes the announcement that seventeen convicted felons

were sentenced to death and executed before a crowd of thirty thousand people at a stadium in the southern city of Guangzhou. The public trials and executions were carried out, according to the *Legal Daily* newspaper, 'in order to allow the masses to celebrate a stable Chinese Lunar New Year.' How's that for Southern justice, folks?''

Perdita switched it off. She looked over at Romeo, who was still asleep. His mouth was open and his mustache drooped over his upper lip, the long black hairs fluttering as he snored. Romeo might be part Chinese, thought Perdita. The way his face hairs hung so limp, not like on Mexicans. Or Spanish, she reminded herself. Romeo insisted on identifying himself as Spanish, no belly-crawling Indian blood in *his* veins. Perdita snickered. No matter what Romeo said, he didn't look like no white man. He even talked like a Chinaman sometimes, so fast you couldn't follow what he was saying.

They were heading back to the ranch today, which was good. She needed to build a new altar for the sacrifice. This would be something different, really special. Not like with the chickens and goats or dogs. Romeo was a good organizer, he knew how to get the shit across the border, how to get the money. Perdita smiled, thinking about the one time Romeo had tried to smoke marijuana himself. He'd gotten dizzy and had to lie down until his head cleared. Wouldn't touch the stuff for nothing now. That was cool, though, she figured. The dope didn't get in the way of doing business. Perdita made a mental note to buy more candles, they were almost out. Also some grain alcohol. They could use a new sledgehammer, too.

Perdita stuck the index finger of her right hand into Romeo's mouth and pushed down on his tongue. He gagged, coughed hard, and sat up.

"What!? What the fuck?" he said, and worked at clearing his throat.

"*Vamonos*," said Perdita. "We got lots to do today."

Caribe 2.14.1989

Hello Romeo.

Jest these few lines to let you know that everything at

your house is fine. Well Mr Dolorosa sir there is a tolk out in Caribe that you wants to sell your house. People had been asking me about the sale on the house but all I can do is to gave them your phone number so that they can call you and talk with you about it. Well I hope that you will bee back some day jest so that the people wood stop tolking so much shit. Mr Romeo this time I had seed some bad days because in December my dorie brook down cood not even get out to fish can't fine no woor here and most of the time I wood only eat one male per day. So last month the lady at Caribe Keys that bys the fish seant me up her boat so that I can make some money but the first week out fishing was good but the monny was so small. She gets half of the monny an the other half is in between me and another. Look the first 4 days we sold 1,500 Caribe dollar and so far we cant get out for the winds the winds has been from 10 to 20 knots from the eastnortheast an from east for allmost two months that my boddy can get out to fish. I had been a little sick the last pass few week so I went to an Amarican docter here an he told me that my boddy was ran down a lot so he put me on some toneck a madacen and I feale a little better these last few days. But Nelmy had been on an off with her Hedakes. Well yesterday school open for the kids but Alix had healp us a lot with them gatten them most of what they need. Kenny want even come down so that I can get a few days woor with him

I jest dont know watt I will do if this wind dont stop I needs to get out fishing for atlest one more week before you gets here. Mr Rome Nelmy sent to say hello an she hopes that you is fine an she wants you to tell Perdi hello for her. And not to forget her T-V. Mr Dolorosa sir I dont know for shore but some people was saying that Rocky James was senten to jail for 20 years an if Reggie San Pedro Sula ever came back to Caribe he wood go to jail for 15 years. Well the people was at first was saying that you and Mr San Pedro Sula wood go to jail when you ever all got back from the USA but Mr Reggie was here about a week ago and he did not have any problem at all. Mr Romeo if I was you I wood keep away from Reggie San Pedro Sula ontell everything is normal again. Virgil Fredrex is a little up set because Woody Hall took all of his stuff out of the room on the hill an carid it down to his house that is about all for know ontell another Mr Rome take good care Love from my hole fam Nelmy Danito Chonge Nansy Branny and my sister an brothers mom & dad Your good fren

Danny Mestiza

"Do you think some people are born wanting to travel?" Romeo asked. "Or do you figure it's a kind of thing comes over you?"

TRAVEL PLANS

"You mean like in the blood," said Perdita.

"Sorta, yeah."

They were bouncing along in the Cherokee on the dirt road between Zopilote and Rancho Negrita Infante. Perdita had purchased everything she required in the hardware store in Del Rio and she was excited. Romeo's babbling usually made her uneasy but today she didn't mind listening, giving him the feedback he needed to process his thoughts.

"When I was a kid in Caribe, you know," he said, "my family used to go to the harbor when my Uncle Roberto went to sea. I was seven years old the first time I remember it clearly. There was a big gray boat tied up at the dock. 'Margarita Cansino' was the ship's name, in giant black letters. And underneath that was painted the port of origin, 'Panama.' We were there to hug Tio Roberto and wish him a safe journey, which, of course, I did. But I was so impressed by the size of the ship and the thought of it sailing out into the ocean beyond the Gulf, beyond the Caribbean, that the idea of traveling entered my dreams. From that moment I knew I would voyage out far into the world beyond Caribe."

Perdita, who was driving, did her best to avoid the ruts and large rocks in the road. She lit a Marlboro with the dash lighter.

"But yet here you are," she said, "still not so very far from there."

"I've come back, of course. After all, this is my home.

I told you about when I lived in New York, in Paris, in Los Angeles. I was in Buenos Aires and Montevideo, too. In Caracas, Miami, La Paz. One day I'll go to Egypt, to China, to Madagascar to see the fabulous monkeys. I am already twenty-seven years old, but I have plenty of time to travel. Soon there will be enough money for us to travel whenever and to wherever we want."

"It makes me happy to have you include me in your plans," said Perdita.

Romeo laughed. "And why not? You're the proper one for me. Four years younger, beautiful, smart, strong. Someday we'll have children."

"You'll inform me, of course, when the time for that is appropriate."

"Of course, *mi amor*. You'll be the first other than me to know."

"*Bueno, jefe.* And what other plans do you have for us?"

"It's enough for now to finish this business we have."

"I've been thinking about it, Romeo. I think what we have to do is take someone off the street. An Anglo."

Romeo looked at Perdita through his brown-lensed Body Glove glasses.

"An Anglo?" he said.

"That would make the most impression."

Romeo turned his head and stared out the open window at the desert. The hot breeze caused by the Jeep's passage plastered his black hair to his forehead.

"Kidnapping," he said.

"What?" said Perdita. "I couldn't hear you."

Romeo gritted his teeth and let the wind hit his face. Believe it, he told himself. Life with this woman will be without apologies.

Perdita stopped the Cherokee at the entrance to the Rancho Negrita Infante. She cut the engine and got out, leaving the driver's door open. A few feet from the Jeep

she squatted, coiled her skirt around her and urinated on the sand. Romeo watched Perdita from the passenger seat and grinned.

"Always liked it that you don't never wear panties," he said, as Perdita climbed back in.

"Easier that way," she said. "Used to I wore 'em, but one day I just left 'em off. Now I don't think I own a pair."

Perdita started the Jeep up and proceeded toward the complex. She liked this drive, the dust and white sun. It was like being on another planet.

"You know I never asked you," Perdita said, "about how the ranch was named."

"Story is some local woman got pregnant by a black American soldier, and when the child was born it was black, too, a baby girl. So some of the villagers—they're called 'Los Zarrapastrosos,' the ragged ones—took the baby and killed her and buried the body out this way in an unmarked grave."

"Why'd they do that?"

Romeo shrugged. "Ashamed, I guess. Surprised they didn't kill the mother also and bury them together."

Perdita wiped the sweat from above her upper lip and pulled the hair out of her eyes.

"Jesus but I hate that kind of ignorant shit," she said.

There was a main house, a large shack, really, about twenty-five feet by thirty feet, made of tarpaper and wood. The windows were rough squares cut to accom-

THE CAUSE

modate removable boards, but they were nailed shut. There was a smokehole above a black cauldron that at the moment contained a boiled hog brain, a turtle shell, a horseshoe, the spinal column of a goat, and dried blood. On the otherwise bare walls were cheap representations of Our Lady of Guadalupe and Jesus Christ. On the floor next to the crudely built altar was a *Book of Rites* from La Iglesia Lukumi Babalu-Aye.

"Leave the door open, honey," Romeo said to Perdita. "Get some of the stink out."

"We have to clean this place up, Romeo. Get your boys in here with some brooms. Dump the garbage. They leave their goddam empty bottles and cans everywhere."

"*Si*, señorita. I will see to it immediately."

Romeo laughed and grabbed Perdita, pulling her to him and kissing her. She shoved him away and began emptying her bags of candles.

"Hey, *santero*, let's do this, okay?"

Romeo and Perdita cleaned up the house themselves, and then Romeo hauled the debris away in the Jeep. He dumped it in a trench his men had dug about a mile away. Gray shit swirled in the brown air. It reminded Romeo of the August day he came back to Tampa after completing the year he'd been stationed in Lebanon with the Marines. Maria-Jose, his grandmother, had asked him, "They let you visit the Garden of Eden?"

Adolfo Robles drove up in his 1950 Dodge pickup and leaned out the window.

"What we up to, Romeo?" he asked. "We got something going later?"

Romeo took a black kerchief from his back pocket and wiped the sweat and dirt from his face and neck.

"Something big, Adolfo. Meet me back at the house."

Adolfo nodded and grinned, jammed the Dodge into gear and drove slowly away. Romeo kicked some dirt into the trench. He'd been one of the lucky ones, having survived the bombing of his Marine barracks in Beirut. More than two hundred sleeping men had died and Romeo had been barely roused by the noise of the explosion. Standing and sweating next to a garbage pit in Mexico, he was convinced there was a noble reason he'd been spared. Romeo pulled out his cock and pissed into the pit. He stood there after he'd finished, fondling himself, watching the steam rise. The air smelled burned.

"The island of Petit Caribe, where I was raised," said Romeo, "is approximately one mile long and three miles wide. There were only two automobiles on Petit Caribe

THE HAND

back then and of course one day they collided with each other."

Adolfo laughed. "But how could that happen?" he asked.

"How everything happens, Adolfo. It was in fact impossible for it *not* to happen. This is the working of the world."

Romeo and Adolfo were sitting on the bottom step of the porch drinking Tecates. Perdita was inside arranging the chairs and candles.

"Look, here is a letter I just received from Caribe, from my cousin, Reggie, who takes care of the old family property."

Romeo took an envelope out of his back pocket, opened it and removed a piece of paper. "Listen," he said.

" 'Dear Cousin Romeo. I hope this Letter finds you doing the verry bes for your self. I talked to your Lawer on how much it would cost to bring the people to move the two men on the land and he Said 3000 Caribe dollar he mus be out of his mind I then call the Aterny Generald office to my fren Teresa. She is the secon to the Boss. Teresa said nothing can be done so I took the mater in my owne hand and the problem is solve. The only thing is to tell you the sharks are have a feaste day. So Good News.'

" 'The weather gets good now I hope we are now in our third week of Bad Weather Romeo. Can you send som monie for fishing wire and the wood turnin lathe an som tools an som buckets also sheet rock screws. I am try to *buy a mud Hog pump too for workin the Swamp Land joining the North Line by Rockys property. My daughter Halcyan almos drown in the Lagoon las week but she is fon now. All we here wish you well an you send us som thing now Okay? Your cousin an pal—Reggie.'*

"There are constant difficulties on the island," said Romeo, "the same as anywhere. There is no more sense made there than here. You must control your own hand, Adolfo, remember! The rest is unimportant."

Adolfo nodded and studied his left hand. After a few seconds he drained the Tecate and, with his right hand, tossed the can as far as he could.

"I had a friend in Tampa a few years ago," Romeo told Adolfo as they rode in the Dodge truck toward the border. "Eddie Reyes, a Cuban from Marianao. He lived

for a while with my family, even after I left there. I don't know where he is now. Eddie had been a cop but quit the force and was going to law school at night when I met him. He worked during the day in a meat packing plant.

"This Eddie would take several showers each day, very long showers during which he would scrub himself all over many times and use great quantities of soap and shampoo. Then he would spend an equal amount of time drying himself. Eddie had much hair on his body and lots of curly black hair on his head, and of course he had a beard. I do not exaggerate when I tell you that this bathing and drying process took up most of his time."

Alfonso, who was driving, shook his head and laughed.

"He sounds like a crazy man," he said.

"Yes, he was probably a little crazy," said Romeo, "but let me tell you why. One night when Eddie was a cop he was sent to investigate a burglary in progress and a junkie got the drop on him. The junkie made Eddie lie down on the ground on his back and stuck the dangerous end of a forty-five automatic between his eyes. The junkie told Eddie he was going to kill him and pulled the trigger. Eddie shit and pissed in his pants and the gun jammed. The backup cops arrived and the junkie panicked, dropped the forty-five on Eddie's chest and tried to run but the other cops caught him.

"The junkie never went to jail. He gave the cops some information they needed about some other scam and he was allowed to plead guilty to a charge of firing a weapon in a public place. Even though the gun never went off! He got away with a suspended sentence. When Eddie heard about it he quit the force and got the job in the meat packing plant. Eventually he started taking law courses. I always figured all the washing he did was connected to the junkie trying to shoot him. It made Eddie a little strange, I guess, still trying to clean off the shit and piss."

"Maybe it would have been better if the gun had not jammed," said Alfonso. "It must be difficult to live in such a desperate way."

Romeo stared out the window at the passing desert. There was nothing moving other than the heat waves.

"Maybe," he said, "but still, it's better to be desperate than dead."

Perdita and Romeo watched the people pass. They sat at a table behind the front window of the South Texas Barbecue, drinking Lone Star. Perdita's idea was to iden-

PIGEONS

tify a likely prospect, follow him and in some way lure him back to the Rancho Negrita Infante.

"What are you gonna say, honey?" asked Romeo. "Come with me to the Casbah?" He laughed. "We ain't exactly Charles Boyer and Hedy Lamarr, you know. Or, I tell you everything you ever want to know about Lukumi Babalu-Aye? Introduce yourself as a Python Priestess of *Palo Mayombé* and you'd appreciate his allowin' Adolfo to lop off his head with a machete so's we can drain the blood from his body, then hack it apart, cook it up and serve him at the Zombie Jamboree?"

Perdita puffed desultorily at a Marlboro.

"Better you point, I'll follow, club him down, dump him in the Jeep and take off. No tricks."

"That's a nice one," said Perdita, pointing to a young guy crossing the street toward them. "Blond, tan, good shoulders."

"You gonna fuck him or eat him?"

Perdita raised a cobra eyebrow. "Both, maybe."

"He's not alone," said Romeo. "There's a girl with him."

"Could be we'll both get lucky, *macho*. Let's go."

Romeo and Perdita got into the Cherokee and cruised slowly along the Boulevard Botánica, keeping a close eye on the young couple, who were taking in the tacky bordertown sights.

"College kids," Romeo said. "Down from Austin, or maybe just Southmost."

The couple went into a bar and Romeo parked the Cherokee in front of it. When the couple didn't come out after ten minutes, Perdita said, "Let's go inside."

The place was called El Loco's Round-Up, and the young couple, along with several other people, were gathered around a tall, white-haired gringo who was leaning against the bar and talking. Romeo and Perdita went over to listen.

"Everybody who becomes involved with the movie business learns about it the hard way," said the man. He looked familiar to Romeo, but he couldn't quite place him. "When I went out to Hollywood I was fresh from my daddy's insurance company," the man continued, punctuating his speech with sips of J.W. Dant. "I didn't hardly know which hole a woman peed out of. Pardon me, ladies," he said, smiling, "but that's the truth."

"Who is this guy?" Perdita whispered.

"Ssshh," said Romeo. "I know I seen him somewhere."

"I was a good-lookin' kid in those days, though, the kind they were after, like Coop, McCrea, Johnny Mack, Randy Scott. Didn't matter I was out of a Boston insurance office. I looked the part, so they stuck me on a horse and I fit. I did all right, saved my money and didn't forget everything they taught me at Harvard, just the things I never could remember. Trained me to talk like I was bred to take my meals from a Montana Hereford. Some of the others, though, didn't do so well. Lash was makin' pornos last I heard. At his age it's more a credit than a discredit. And Sunset's a doorman at the Thunderbird in Vegas. Saw him there myself. Duke, of course, you all know what he did. Licked everyone and everything except the Big C. And Randy didn't die broke. Only real mistakes I made was to marry a couple of American women. Shoulda stuck to Mexican and Japanese, or somethin'."

When the man paused to pour himself a fresh shot and knock it down, Romeo said to Perdita, "Happy Pard, Protector of the Pecos! That's who he is. Man's a legend."

"I heard you, pardner," Hap said, nodding his head at Romeo. "You're dead right. Made over one hundred westerns before I got my own TV series. They just churned 'em out over at Republic and Monogram. Started the series when I was forty-five, and it ran nine years. Still on in parts of Asia and South America. My real name is Winston Frost, but everybody's called me Hap for so long I finally had it changed legal. The wiseguys even made me sign my IOUs that way!" He laughed. "That was a mean road for me, folks, that gamblin'. For years I'd bet on anything. Why, I'd wager on which cube of sugar a fly'd land on. I tell you, that Russian sonofabitch, Fyodor Dostoyevsky, had it pegged natural. Just read that story of his, 'The Gambler,' and you'll see what I'm gettin' at. Man was the greatest writer ever lived. Had himself the same problem as me."

"What's he talkin' about?" Perdita whispered.

"Don't matter," said Romeo. "There go your pigeons."

The boy and girl, neither of whom were more than nineteen or twenty, walked out of El Loco's followed closely by Perdita and Romeo. Perdita caught up to the boy on the street and put her arm through his. Romeo came up next to the girl and showed both of them the nose of his .38.

"Amigos," he said, "we're goin' for a little ride."

"So what is this? Where are you takin' us?"

"Relax, amigo," Romeo said. "Just a ride in the country. And hey, *mil gracias*, by the way, for not makin' a fuss back at the border."

FACES

"Said you'd shoot us if we did," said the girl.

"Now, sweetheart, I might've, that's right. You can't never be certain a man means what he says, but I've always made sure there's plenty of meanin' in my life. Ain't that right, honey?"

Perdita rode shotgun. She didn't answer, remaining stonefaced, thinking about how best to get the job done. Better to kill them before they got to the ranch. But the boy was cute. She could use him, maybe, then kill him. Romeo'd stick his thing in a keyhole if he thought it'd feel good. He could jump the little white whore if he wanted.

"We'll just be *compañeros* now for a while, if it's okay," said Romeo. "Now, my name is Romeo and the mystery woman here is Perdita. What can we call you?"

"Don't say anything," said the girl.

Perdita stuck her head out the window and let the wind blow through her hair. This is the right girl, she thought. They'd snatched them the perfect platinum bitch. Be easy to smack her, that's for sure.

Romeo laughed. "Better to be friendly, little lady. Easier all the way around."

"Why should we make anything go easy for you?" the girl said.

"You figurin' on ransomin' us?" the boy asked. "If you are, my folks don't have much money. Dad manages a Luby's in El Paso. My mom's a typist for a real estate office. Estelle's folks ain't any better off."

"Estelle?" said Romeo. "Is that your name, princess? Estelle. Almost like Estrellita, little star. I like that better, much better. Estrellita! That's what we'll call you. You like that, Perdita?" He laughed. "And now you, boy. *Cómo se llama?*"

"It's Duane."

"Okay, okay," said Romeo. "I'll take it. Regular name for a regular guy. You look like a regular guy, Duane. You *are* regular, aren't you?"

"I guess."

Romeo smiled his big smile. "Now, yeah! We all know each other's names, and that's a step. Duane and Estrellita. Romeo and Perdita. Mix 'em any way you choose. Duane and Perdita. Estrellita and Romeo. How about Estrellita and Perdita? There's a pair. Or Romeo and Duane. Ha! There they go, hand in hand, the good little boys. We could do this one up right, use some brainpower."

"Where are you taking us?" asked Estelle.

"Show you where the people live, Little Star. Be a place to tell about, you get the chance the next family picnic, all the little Estrellitas and Duanes and things are there, drinkin' bug juice, eatin' pie, honeydews. Fourth of July, could be."

"Only it won't," said Perdita, not turning around.

Romeo laughed. "Oh, Duane and Estrellita, you've heard of 'voices'? You know, like, from the air, not from a person."

"Like disembodied?" Duane asked.

"I think so," said Romeo. "Not a body, just a voice. Like from God."

"Yeah?"

"You're gonna hear it." Romeo turned quickly, looking around at the boy and girl tied up in the back seat.

"Won't be no Fourth of July, baby," said Perdita. "No Thanksgivin', neither."

"How about *Cinco de Mayo?*" Romeo asked.

Perdita smiled at him, showing an even dozen of her tiny white teeth. "What you think of Christmas in hell, Chico? Think your honeycunt here can handle that?"

Romeo banged the steering wheel with both hands, howled and rocked back and forth as he drove.

"Holiday in hell!" he shouted. "Happy fuckin'-A holiday! Whew! You make it right, sugar. Make it fuckin'-A, hard-as-a-rock, crazy-baby okay!"

Perdita laughed. "Well, I guess I love you, too," she said.

Tyrone "Rip" Ford had been born and raised in Susie, Texas, and in the forty-three years of his existence had never, excepting his time in the service, lived beyond plain sight of the Rio Grande. Rip became a deputy sheriff of Larry Lee County when he was twenty-one, three years out of high school and three weeks out of the U.S. Army. He became sheriff of Larry Lee County ten years later and had held the job ever since.

Rip Ford's father, Royal Ford, had nicknamed his son after his own paternal grandfather, Colonel Rip Ford, an early member of the Texas Rangers. After rising to the rank of captain in the Rangers, Rip Ford, elevating himself to colonel, had subsequently recruited a fugitive company of men from South Texas to fight under his command during the War Between the States. Composed mostly of wanted men and men considered too old or too young to be conscripted by the Confederate Army, Ford's irregulars united primarily for the purpose of resisting an expected invasion of South Texas by a Union brigade of Negro soldiers.

Colonel Ford's raggedy group maintained a peripatetic camp along the Mexican side of the border, dodging hostile Kickapoos and Apaches and staging supply raids on isolated settlements on both sides of the river. Declared an outlaw by General Robert E. Lee, his followers branded as criminals and lowlifes, the original Rip Ford attempted to construct a deal just prior to the surrender at Appomattox whereby his company would have switched their allegiance to the North and assisted the Union in a campaign against Mexico. This realignment did not come to pass, but Colonel Ford did succeed in acting as agent between Yankee merchant ship owners and Southern cotton growers, convincing the shipping magnates to place their boats under Mexican registry and transport cotton to the fleet of European ships, mainly English, sitting in the Gulf of Mexico and the Caribbean Sea.

Royal Ford had always admired his grandfather's resourcefulness, and hoped his son—whose Christian name, Tyrone, was given him by the boy's mother, Louise, an ardent admirer of the movie star Tyrone Power—would exhibit a similar tenacity and sense of purpose. Royal was killed during a robbery at the Gulf gas station he'd owned and operated in Susie since his discharge from the army following World War II. A drifter named Ulysses Neck had shot Royal Ford in the back of the head while Royal lay face down on the floor of the office of his Gulf station. Ulysses Neck had exactly thirty-two dollars and eight cents in his possession when he was apprehended by two Texas Rangers an hour later less than ten miles away in the town of Fort Dudgeon. Neck took his own life that night by hanging himself by a belt from the high bars of his cell in the Larry Lee County jail, the same jail that Royal's son, Rip Ford, now commanded.

Rip had never married. His life was his work; no citizen of Larry Lee County could question Sheriff Ford's dedication. From Fort Dudgeon to Susie to Madre Island, Rip Ford was well-known and, at the very least, grudgingly respected by Anglos and Hispanics alike. Throughout its century-long history, there never had been a permanent black resident of Larry Lee County. Those Negro Yankee troops so feared by Louise Ford's son Tyrone's great-grandfather never did materialize.

The moment Rip Ford learned of the disappearance of the two college students, Duane Orel King and Estelle Kenedy Satisfy, he felt a sharp pain in his lower back.

"What's wrong, Rip?" asked First Deputy Federal Ray Phillips, noticing the sheriff's grimace.

"Like as somethin' just poked me with a pitchfork above the right buttock, Fed," said Rip. "Never felt nothin' like it before."

"Better hope ain't nobody down in the Mud Huts stickin' no pins in a doll got your name on it," said Federal.

Both men laughed.

"Nothin's happenin'. *Yet!*"

Fed Phillips looked over at the man who said this and I.D.'ed him. It was Ramon Montana, one of the county's more prominent drunks.

"You can hear me, Señor Fed! You know I mean what I'm sayin' when I say somethin'. I *said*, nothin's happenin'. *Yet!*"

"Heard you, Ramon. Havin' a good weekend already, I can tell."

Ramon Montana staggered to the curb where he fell on his knees and regurgitated into the gutter. He shook himself like a wet dog, got up, cleared his throat, threw back his shoulders, put one foot in the air as if he were about to climb a flight of stairs, listed to starboard and toppled to the sidewalk.

"C'mon, there, Ramon," said Fed, helping him back to his feet. "Let's see we can get you home before you get so scarred up your sister can't recognize you."

"Ain't *goin'* home!" Ramon shouted. "Can't make me. My sister's dead, anyhow."

"Better'n takin' you to jail."

Ramon grumbled but allowed Fed Phillips to escort him the half-block to his rooming house, where Fed led Ramon up the stairs and in the door.

"On your own, now, *amigo*. Sleep tight."

"Tell you, Señor Fed, some strange shit goin' on. You see I ain't talkin'. They gonna kill them kids, them *gringos*, the *gringa*. You hear about it, 'member I tell you firs'. Man got the evil eye. Evil eye."

Fed closed the door and went back to the street. Who's gonna kill what kids? he thought. Fed headed toward El Loco's to see what he could find out.

Over at the jail, Rip Ford sat in his office looking at the picture of Ava Gardner he kept in a plastic frame on his desk. It was a full-face photo taken in 1954 by a Frenchman, Philippe Halsman. Rip knew this because the photographer's name and the date were printed on the back of the picture. It was a postcard, really, but set into the frame like it was made it look proper, as if it were his wife or fiancée. In the picture, Ava Gardner's tousled black hair obscured her right eye, and her full, closed lips were pulled slightly to the right, resulting in something less than a smile. They looked as if they'd been smeared shut with red paint, though the photo was in black and white. It wasn't so much a fuck-me face as a I've-been-there-and-back look, the kind of expression you see only on the most expensive whores. This was Ava at her best, right after *Mogambo*, which Rip had seen as a boy from the balcony of the Joy Rio in El Paso. It was ten o'clock on Saturday night and he stared at Ava Gardner's immutable face, the face of a lifetime a lifetime ago. Rip let the telephone ring for thirty seconds before he picked it up.

As Romeo drove, Estelle Satisfy thought about her
mother, Glory Ann Blue Satisfy, and wondered whether
she'd ever see her again. Glory Ann had been born and

BAD ROAD

raised in Divine Water, Oklahoma, a place she dearly
loved and wished she'd never left. The house on Worth
Avenue in Dallas, where Estelle had grown up, never
pleased Glory Ann, nor did Dallas. Glory Ann never
stopped complaining about the city. "When I wake up
in the mornin'," she'd say to Estelle, "I like to know
who I'm goin' to see that day. There's too many surprises
here in the Big D."

Glory Ann weighed three hundred pounds now. Her
husband, Estelle's daddy, Ernest Tubb Satisfy, who'd
been named after the famous singer, stood five-feet four
and weighed one-hundred-ninety-five. He drove a 7-Up
delivery truck and smoked Larks but took only three puffs
of each one before putting it out. Ernest Tubb claimed
the Larks lost their taste after the first two drags. He took
the third one, he said, just to keep proving it to himself.

Estelle remembered her dog, Gopher, who died after
he ate an entire extra large anchovy and onion pizza
when she was in the seventh grade. Ernest Tubb buried
Gopher under the plum tree in the backyard and Estelle
still placed flowers on the grave every year on the an-
niversary of Gopher's death, April fifth. Estelle thought
about these and other things that had happened in her
life as the Cherokee bounced down a bad road to only
the devil knew where.

Romeo, if that really is his name, looks like the devil,
thought Estelle. And that Perdita woman looks weird and
dangerous, too. I just hope they're not going to kill us,

not before I've even got my cherry popped. That'd be a slap and a half, for sure, after all I've done to preserve my chastity. I should have left it to Stubby Marble. Grace Jane says the Marble boys, Eugene and Stubby, do it better than anyone, and I guess to hell she knows. Stubby kept after me the better part of a month before he gave up. Duane now, he acts like he don't care. I don't know, maybe he don't. I wish I knew what's goin' on here, really. I'm just a college girl with a lot of potential in the field of commercial art who ain't never even got laid yet. I know life ain't fair or even supposed to be, but this is somethin' different.

Duane pretended to be asleep. He kept his head down and tried hard not to think, but he couldn't help it, the thoughts just kept on coming. This wasn't the end of a good time, it was the beginning of a bad one. If Estelle hadn't insisted on goin' out for a beer, Duane thought, we'd be in our hotel room now and maybe she'd be lettin' me. Be a shame to die havin' been with only one girl, and her just Grace Jane Bobble, who the Marbles nicknamed "The Wide Missouri" not for no good reason. This gal Perdita is a picture, though. Reminds me of that poisonous snake from South America in the reptile and amphibian book we used in biology, one with the triangle-pointed, yellow-red face and orange ice eyes. She's the type'll bite and once the teeth are sunk you'd have to chop off the head with a hatchet to pry loose.

Duane opened his eyes and looked at Estelle. She had her eyes shut and was biting her lower lip and crying. Duane felt like crying, too, but he didn't. He wouldn't stop himself if he started, but no tears came. Maybe I can figure a way out of this, Duane thought. Estelle would be grateful, I bet, and let me do it. I wonder who done it to her other than the Marbles. They said she was some sweet meat. This life's sure got question marks scattered around like dogshit in a empty lot, the way Daddy says. I guess I ain't been steppin' careful enough.

"Tell you who my heroes are, Duane. That way you get a better idea of who I am."

Romeo and Duane were sitting in chairs on the porch

of the main house at Rancho Negrita Infante. Estrellita, as Romeo insisted Estelle be called, was asleep in a locked bedroom. It was almost midnight.

"I on purpose am leavin' your legs free, Duane. Sorry about your hands, though. You tell me if the wire's too tight."

"No, it ain't."

"*Bueno, bueno.* We got to keep the blood circulatin'. So here's my list: James Ruppert, George Banks, Howard Unruh, Pat Sherrill, Charles Whitman, R. Gene Simmons, Sr., James Oliver Huberty, and Joseph Wesbecker. Know every name by heart. Recognize any?"

"Don't think so."

"Not even Whitman?"

Duane shook his head no.

Romeo laughed. "Guess you don't do so good in history class."

"Got a B."

"Maybe they didn't cover this part yet. Here's what these men done. Ruppert killed eleven people, eight of 'em kids, at a Easter Sunday dinner in Ohio. Banks took out twelve, includin' five kids, in Pennsylvania. Unruh shot thirteen people in twelve minutes in Camden, New Jersey. He was somethin' else, too. Said, 'I'd've killed a thousand if I'd had enough bullets.'

"Sherrill murdered fourteen at a post office in Oklahoma. Simmons, Senior, got fourteen, too, all family members, in Arkansas. Buried a dozen under his house.

Huberty slaughtered twenty-one at a McDonald's in San Diego, I believe. Wesbecker shot seven and wounded a bunch in a printing plant in Kentucky. And Whitman, of course, cut down sixteen from the tower on the campus of the University of Texas in Austin. Surprised you ain't heard of him."

"When did he do it?"

"About 1966, around in there."

"Before my time."

"Hell, boy, so was Hitler, and you can't tell me you ain't heard of him!"

"I heard of him."

"How about Attila the Hun? You heard of him?"

"I guess so. He was some kind of Turk or somethin'."

"Well, I don't include those guys had armies or other people doin' their killin' for 'em. I just rate the ones take it into their own hands. Also, I don't count the serial murderers, the ones done it over a long, drawn out period of time. It's only the ones just all of a sudden know they can't take no shit no longer and just explode on the world! There's more than those I mentioned but those are right off the top of my head. This kind of thing is a particular study of mine."

Perdita came out on the porch and rubbed her left thigh against Duane's right arm. She put her left hand into his thick blond hair and rubbed it around.

"You been tellin' the boy a bedtime story, Romeo?" she said.

"Just fillin' in a few holes in Duane's education."

Perdita smiled. "I got one or two need fillin', too. You two intellectuals feel like helpin' a lady out?"

Romeo unlocked the door to the bedroom and entered. He stood still for a full minute, listening to Estrellita's breathing. There was a shrill, brief whistle each time she

exhaled. Romeo closed the door, bolted it, and put the key in his right front pants pocket. He walked to the bed and sat down on the edge. Estrellita had long, honey-brown hair, and Romeo stroked it slowly and softly with his left hand. She stirred slightly and he stopped, allowing her to roll over on her back, her head turned to the right. Her eyelids fluttered and she pursed her full lips, then relaxed again, whistling softly.

"Hey, Little Star," Romeo whispered. "Come, Estrellita, *niña*. Romeo *es aqui*."

She didn't move, and her breathing seemed to cease altogether. Romeo smiled. He knew she had to be awake.

"Little Star, don't pretend," Romeo said, in a normal voice. "You can open your eyes. All you'll see is me."

A rivulet of moonlight squeezed into the room through a crack in the second to the highest board covering the window. Estrellita did not move other than to barely open her left eye. She saw Romeo's face in purple shadow, then closed it again.

"You think I come to harm you, huh?" he said. "Why would you think so? Your friend, Duane, he's not bein' harmed. He's getting happy, probably, by now."

"Where is he?" asked Estrellita. "Is he dead?"

Romeo laughed. "No, of course not, señorita. He's assisting a damsel in distress. Another fair lady, such as yourself."

Estrellita turned her face to Romeo and opened both of her eyes. He looked like a giant bat.

"You mean Perdita's got him?" she said.

"Yeah, I suppose that's a good way of puttin' it."

"She reminds me of a kind of snake."

Romeo smiled. "A pretty snake, though."

"She looks cold."

Romeo moved closer over Estrellita's body and touched her left cheek with his right hand.

"Estrellita, *mi flora blanca de la noche. Tu es la luz de mi vida.*"

She moved her head and shoulders slightly to the right, away from Romeo's touch.

"Don't be afraid, Little Star. You're safe with me."

Estrellita started to laugh, then suddenly stopped and began to cry. Romeo watched the tears stream out of Estrellita's eyes and roll down the sides of her face into the pillow. Slowly he bent his head and with his tongue licked the tears from her cheeks. Estrellita couldn't move. It was as if Romeo's gesture paralyzed her and his saliva made her face numb. She'd never felt this way before.

"Close your eyes again, Estrellita, *bonita,*" Romeo said, and kissed her left ear, her honey-colored hair, her left eyebrow, the tip of her nose. "Romeo is going to take care of you."

"Well, which one is it gonna be?" asked Romeo. "You think maybe the boy?"

Perdita kicked at the dirt with one of her rattlesnake-

skin boots. A soft wind was blowing from the south and it flicked at the ends of her loose black hair.

"*No sé*, baby. This is a tough one."

"You sweet on him, huh?"

"Be more fun to keep him around for a while, anyway. How about your little *vaca*, Estrellita?"

Romeo took off his straw Stetson and wiped his thick red-black hair with his left hand. He was sitting on the top rail of the corral fence next to the ceremonial hut. The sun was very strong, as usual, but there was a threat of rain in the air. Perdita leaned against the fence, looking east at the scabrous brown hills.

"She was the real thing, chica, *una virgen*. Bled hot and plenty, like *crème de caramel*."

Perdita laughed. "Too bad we didn't know it before. To sacrifice a virgin would have made us some serious *mayombérias*."

"Maybe better to use a local, is what I'm thinkin' now," said Romeo. "Get a kid from Zopilote. Duane and Estrellita might come in handy down the line."

"Tell Adolfo to be sure to have enough garlic this time."

Romeo laughed. "You should have seen his face when I told him how when Satan walked out of the Garden of Eden, garlic sprouted from wherever his left foot hit the ground. Adolfo crossed himself and said, '*Madre de dios, es verdad?*' "

4

4

Perdita felt an itch between her legs, reached down with her right hand, balled it into a fist, and rubbed her clit hard.

"You know, Rome," she said, "the only two real pleasures left to man on this earth are fucking and killing. When those are gone, *guapito*, so are we."

Rip Ford was in bed with a prostitute named Lupita Luján when Federal Phillips called.

"Sheriff, I'm down here at El Loco's Round-Up. A

couple of the boys recognized Romeo Dolorosa, that snake-priest dope dealer from Zopilote, and his girlfriend, The Priestess. Apparently they had a beer or two and suddenly disappeared. Nobody noticed they were gone until they were."

"That it?"

"So far. Gonna check it out further, see if I can get a fix on if the bastard's runnin' anything through here. Be kinda surprised if he is, seein's how he didn't attempt no disguise or nothin'. And, oh yeah, that old drunk Ramon Montana's talkin' some shit about people killin' a couple Anglos. Might be somethin' to do with Dolorosa since Ramon was carryin' on about a dude with a evil eye. That's *santería* talk."

"Call me back you hear more."

"You got it."

Rip hung up and returned his attentions to Lupita.

"Oh, ho-ney," she said, "where you get this scar from on your shoulder?"

"Oil spilt from Psyche's lamp."

Lupita frowned. "How a lamp can do this to you?"

"Just teasin', sweetheart. Old bullet wound from Nam. Guess you never heard about how Psyche woke up Cupid the middle of one night when a drop of oil burned his shoulder, and how his mama, Venus, made the poor girl's life a misery."

Lupita shrugged, rolled over and pulled the sheet up over her short plump body.

"I don't hear about nothin' stuck in this pisshole. Who was this bitch?"

"Psyche?"

"Yeah."

"The most beautiful female mortal on earth. Stole away her mother-in-law's admirers."

Lupita snorted. "No wonder she hated the girl. You know her pretty well, huh?"

"We never exactly met."

"Then how come you so interested? You lookin' to nail her ass, hey?"

Rip got up and pulled on his pants.

"Time to separate reality from myth, Lupita. *Vamonos.*"

Lupita threw back the sheet and stretched. High on her right thigh was a tattoo of a black scorpion with a red stinger poised to strike, sitting on a purple rose. Written on a blue banner beneath it were the words MALA CHICA.

"She have any kids, this *perfecta?*" asked Lupita.

"Matter of fact, yeah," Rip said. "A daughter, named Pleasure."

Lupita laughed. "She ever hit the street, she don't need to change it, *es seguro!*"

Romeo listened to the train whistles in the distance. They sounded like wheezes from an organ with a mouse running across the keys. He sat in the driver's seat of the

IL AFFARE

Cherokee, smoking, the windows rolled down, waiting for his cousin, Reggie San Pedro Sula, and Marcello "Crazy Eyes" Santos. It was almost two o'clock in the morning. The crescent moon lit the desert landscape partially, giving it the feel of a bombsite, twenty years after, the only residents rodents, insects and reptiles.

The deal sounded strange, thought Romeo, but if Santos was involved it would, of necessity, be very profitable. Reggie had worked for Santos before, several times, usually as a shooter. He'd do the job, pick up his money and go back to the islands. The money lasted quite a while in Caribe, but sooner or later he'd need another jolt, and as long as Santos survived there would be work for Reginald San Pedro Sula. Romeo was agreeable to the meet, although this was a slightly unusual procedure in a couple of ways. First, Reggie rarely was involved at the top of a deal; and two, Santos seldom ventured out of his hometown of New Orleans. But Romeo was prepared to listen. He knew when and how to be patient.

Romeo heard the car coming. He tossed away his cigarette and waited, listening for half a minute as the engine noise grew louder. The long, black car pulled off the highway across from Romeo and came to a dusty stop. The motor idled and Reggie got out of the back seat, closed the door behind him, and walked over to Romeo.

"Hola, primo," Reggie said. "Que tal?"

"You tell me," said Romeo, as they shook hands.

Reggie was very tall, at least four or five inches over six feet, and heavyset. He was about fifty years old, his skin was the color of milk chocolate, and he wore a lavender leisure suit. His bald head reflected the moonlight. It was odd, Romeo thought, for Reggie not to be wearing a porkpie rain hat. In fact, Romeo could not recall a time he'd seen Reggie without a hat, other than when he went to sleep, since he'd lost most of his hair.

"I think I let the man, Señor Santos, tell you himself," said Reggie. "It's a good deal, a fair arrangement, you'll see."

Reggie smiled broadly, revealing his numerous gold teeth.

"There must be some danger in it, though," said Romeo, "for him to get you off the island."

Reggie gave a brief laugh. "There is usually some danger involved, is there not?" he said. "Though the man needs me for another matter, for where we are heading from here."

"I see. And how is everyone back home? Danny Mestiza wrote to me that Rocky James got a double sawbuck in the joint."

"Oh, yes, but he's out now again. I think for good. There was some irregularity but Señor Santos was able to clear it up for him. Halcyan an' Rigoberto is fine an' healthy. The money you sent helped out very good. I talk very strong about you to Señor Santos so he would consider you for this job."

"What is the job?"

"You come to the car an' he tell it himself. Remember you don't call him 'Crazy Eyes.' He don't like it when he see it in the newspaper, how they do just to annoy him."

Romeo climbed down, walked across the road and got into the back seat of the Mercedes-Benz limousine. Reggie closed the door and stood outside. A soft light was on inside the car. Marcello Santos had a drink in his right hand, three fingers of his favorite single malt Scotch whisky, Glenmorangie. He was wearing a dark gray suit with a blue shirt and a red tie; a pair of black Cole-Haan loafers, with tassels, and red, blue and yellow argyle socks; two-dollar drugstore sunglasses with bright yellow frames; and a large gold or diamond ring on each finger of both hands, excluding his thumbs, one of which was missing. He had a brownish-black, curly toupee glued to his head; some mucilage had trickled onto his forehead and dried there. Santos was sixty-eight years old and had ruled organized crime in the southern and southwestern United States for a quarter-century without ever having been convicted of either a felony or a misdemeanor.

"*Buona notte*, Mr. Dolorosa. Romeo," said Santos, extending his left hand, the one minus a thumb, as would the Pope or a princess. "Good to see you again."

Romeo squeezed the fingers.

"It is always my pleasure," he said.

"This is somewhat of an unusual place to meet, I know, Romeo, but as we are on our way to another meeting, and I hate to fly, I thought it would be the most expedient. I'm glad you could come."

"It's no problem, Marcello, in any case."

"*Bene*. Your cousin, Reginald, speaks well of you, you know. He tells me you take care of your family and friends back on the island. It's commendable of you."

"I do what I can."

Santos nodded and sipped his Scotch whisky.

"Would you like a drink, Romeo?"

"No, thank you. I am driving, and it's very late."

"Yes, all right. Here is my proposal. It is very simple. There will be a truck here at this spot forty-eight hours from now, a refrigerated truck, accompanied by a car. The truck will be loaded with human placentas to be used in the cosmetics industry. They are blended in skin creams that some people think can keep them looking young. Maybe it does, maybe not. I don't know. This load must be delivered as soon as possible to a private laboratory in Los Angeles. I would like you to drive the truck there for me. That way I know the shipment will be in good hands. The driver of the truck will turn it over to you, should you decide to do this, and leave in the accompanying automobile. All you have to do is deliver it to the address in Los Angeles that this man will give you. I have ten thousand dollars for you now, in old bills, fifties and hundreds. When you arrive safely in L.A., your cousin, Reggie, will be there to give you another ten thousand dollars, also in old bills, and in similar denominations."

"Why don't you just have Reggie drive the truck?"

"I need him with me for a situation between now and when the delivery must be made. He'll fly to California as soon as this other business is finished. Can you do this?"

Romeo nodded. "Certainly, Marcello. I am glad to help you however I can."

Santos took off the cheap yellow sunglasses and looked at Romeo. His eyes were grayish-green with large red pupils that jumped and shimmied like flames. Crazy eyes. Despite himself, Romeo shivered.

"*Bene! Molto bene!*" said Santos, patting Romeo on the knee with the four fingers on his left hand. He put the sunglasses back on and drank the remainder of his whisky.

Santos flipped open a panel in the floor and took out a package and held it out to Romeo.

"*Buona fortuna, amico mio,*" said Santos. "Remember always that God and I, we both are with you."

Romeo accepted the package.

"I won't forget," he said.

When Adolfo unlocked the shed door, the boy, even though he was blindfolded, looked up, his head cocked toward the noise. His mouth was gagged with a black

THE HOUSE

OF DREAMS

rag, his hands tied behind his back and his feet bound together with heavy clothesline. He made no sound.

"*Tiene años?*" asked Romeo.

"*Diez,*" said Adolfo. "Perdita made the choice."

"What do you know of his family?"

Adolfo shrugged. "A poor one, like most of those in Zopilote. He is one of four brothers, I think. Maybe two or three sisters. Perdita said it must be a boy. Maybe they don't even miss him."

"Is Perdita here?"

Adolfo nodded. "Preparing for the ceremony."

"Have you notified the others?"

"Everyone will assemble at ten o'clock. Carlos and Teresa are coming from Mexico City."

"What about the DeLeon family? And the Acostas?"

"No word from Jorgé Acosta, but all of them are notified."

Romeo turned to go, then looked back at the boy.

"Do you know his name?" he asked.

"He is nothing special. His name is Juan."

"*Oiga, Juanito,*" said Romeo. "At ten o'clock tonight you will become immortal. Do you know what that means?"

The boy did not move. Romeo noticed the dark stain that ran all the way down the boy's left pantsleg. In the dirt next to his bare left foot was a wet spot the size of a dinner plate.

"It is no matter," Romeo said.

"This is something an ordinary man can never know. You will enter the House of Dreams, Juanito, where you will live forever. Your mother and father and sisters and brothers, your grandparents, aunts, uncles, cousins, all you will greet in their dreams. And only you, among them, will be safe."

Romeo went out and Adolfo followed, closed the door and locked it.

THE

HOUSE

OF

DREAMS

o

"So, it's agreed, then. After this we drive to L.A. for Santos."

"I always wanted to see California," said Perdita.

QUIET TIME AT

THE RANCHO

NEGRITA INFANTE

"Duane and I can take turns drivin' the truck, and you and Estrellita can handle the Cherokee."

"How soon does Santos want it there?"

"Fast as possible. He's not paying me twenty thousand dollars to stop and take a donkey ride through the Grand Canyon. Get what things you want to take together now and put 'em in the Jeep. I want to be ready to go."

Perdita was painting her toenails shocking pink. Her cunt itched but she knew Romeo wouldn't fuck her, never before a big show. That's how she thought of it, as a performance, like in the circus. She'd only seen a circus once, when she was six years old in Corpus. It was a small troupe, about a half-dozen wagons; one tent, one ring. They'd had an unusual attraction: an albino tiger. Perdita and her older sister, Juana, had stood in front of the cage and watched the beautiful white beast pace back and forth without stopping. Every thirty seconds or so, the tiger would utter a low growl, a lugubrious, slow rumble that seemed to unravel as it hit the air. This noise, Perdita felt, came from extremely deep within the animal, that he was just waiting for the proper moment to release his real feelings, his frustration and wounded pride. At that time his roar would be so deafening, so powerful that the people within aural reach would be paralyzed by fear, and the giant white cat would pounce on them and eat them up.

For weeks after the circus left town, Perdita had dreamed about the tiger. He would stand over her, straddling her lithe girl's body, then pin her to the ground with his paws, his saliva dripping down on her face, before slowly, carefully taking her head into his huge mouth and crushing it with one big bite. This dream did not frighten Perdita. It gave her a warm feeling. The tiger's mouth, she imagined, would be hot and wet, the enormous teeth, gleaming like polished swords, piercing her skin and bones cleanly, painlessly. And then the tiger would chew her, separating Perdita into smaller and smaller parts, until finally, when the beast had swallowed everything, she would wake up.

Perdita had told this dream to only one person in her life, an old man named Pea Ridge Day, who pumped gas in the Green Ace filling station in Corpus. Perdita and Juana would go there to buy grape NeHi sodas from the machine, and Pea Ridge, who was usually just sitting in his red flamingo chair, would talk to them. He told the girls that people called him Pea Ridge because he'd been born in Pea Ridge, Arkansas, but that his Christian names were Clyde and Henry. He said that when he'd been a younger man he'd pitched in the National League for St. Louis, Cincinnati, and Brooklyn, wherever they were. Pea Ridge claimed he'd left a note to his wife and kids thirty years before, saying that he was going off into the Ozarks to commit suicide, but instead he hitchhiked down to Texas, where, as Perdita and Juana could plainly see, he was still very much alive. After Perdita told Pea Ridge Day her dream, he stopped talking to her as much, and one morning, when she and Juana went to the Green Ace station for a grape Nehi, he was gone. Perdita decided that Pea Ridge had probably gone back to Arkansas to see his family before he really died. She never absolutely believed that his disappearance was connected in any way to her having told him her dream, but Perdita decided then and there not to tell anyone else about it just the same.

"That sound all right to you, honey?" Romeo asked.

Perdita blew on her toes.

"You know me, baby. I travel light."

"We live on one side of the river, the side of the Great Light. On the other side of the river, the side of the Great Night, is where we must go. We must cross over the river into the Great Night so that we may gain power to live. We must cross over and cross back. We must replenish our power over others, over our enemies, over the ones who would keep us in pain, in sorrow, in misery. This is the Truth, the one Known Truth, and it will keep us alive, keep us strong, enable us to devour our enemy before he devours us."

THE OTHER SIDE

OF THE RIVER

Romeo stood alone in the middle of the room, his eyes closed, his head tilted back. In front of him was an altar surrounded by flickering candles, the only light in the room. On the floor around the circle of light were strewn dozens of crosses, costume jewelry, framed pictures of the saints, dog, cat, cattle and chicken bones, bird feathers, strips of black material, balls of hair, safety pins, saucers filled with milk, silver and gold coins, and pieces of paper with names written on them.

There were approximately sixty people crowded into the room, staring at Romeo or sitting still with their eyes closed, concentrating, listening. Closest to the altar, seated on the floor, were Perdita, Estrellita and Duane. Perdita embraced herself and swayed gently, slowly. Estrellita and Duane held hands level with their waists, their upper arms bound tight to their bodies by clothesline, their eyelids taped open so that they were unable even to blink.

Adolfo sat to the left and slightly to the rear of Romeo, keeping a steady beat with his hands on both sides of an hourglass drum. Romeo shuddered, his body quivering, then undulating, twisting and turning snakelike, and he began to moan. As he moaned louder and his movements became more spasmodic, others in the room moaned and moved their bodies, gyrating and jerking uncontrollably. The temperature in the already close room became hellish. Sweat poured off the faces of the witnesses, as it did down the forehead and cheeks and bare arms of Romeo Dolorosa, the *nanigo*, the *santero*, the magician, the High Priest of the Goat Without Horns Ceremony.

Romeo opened his eyes and looked around the room. His eyes grew large, then very large, the pupils dilating so that they filled the iris. He began to tremble, to shake more violently now, his eyes bugging out, swelling hideously, seemingly about to burst from his head. His body puffed up like a gigantic mosquito sucking blood from a baby. Adolfo beat harder on the drum, humming and moaning tunelessly, as did most of the witnesses.

The door to the outside opened and two men, wearing white shirts, black pants and black hoods over their heads, entered, carrying the boy, Juan, on a litter, which they placed on the altar. Juan lay perfectly still as the men withdrew into the audience, his eyes closed. He was completely naked and his body had been painted white and covered with sweet-smelling oil and garlic. Romeo bent over the boy and vomited on his chest. Juan's eyes remained closed. Romeo picked up a large knife from the altar and held it over Juan's neck.

"Shango!" Romeo shouted, and suddenly slit the boy's throat.

Blood spurted straight up from the wound like black oil from an uncapped well. It poured out over Romeo, and as he shook himself the blood spattered those closest to him. Juan's legs and arms kicked and flailed and Romeo jumped and danced, groaning and shouting, "Shango! Shango!" Everyone in the room watched now as Romeo returned to the body and plunged the knife deep into little Juan's chest, sawing and hacking until he had pried loose the boy's heart. Romeo dropped the knife and lifted the bloody, pulsating heart and drank from it, his face, hands, arms and chest shimmering red in the puce light.

Romeo went to the body once more, reached in with both hands, the heart having been discarded on the altar, and pulled out the dripping viscera. He stepped out of the circle, Juan's innards dangling from Romeo's fists, and passed among the observers, many of whom made shrill, shrieking sounds as the possessed *babalao* wiped his soiled hands on their lips and foreheads, smearing them with the sacrificial flesh and blood. Romeo returned to the circle and collapsed. Adolfo ceased his drumming. The people rose and left the room as quickly as possible, pushing together into the night, avoiding each other's eyes.

Only Perdita, Estrellita, Duane and Adolfo remained with Romeo and Juan's mutilated corpse. Perdita and Adolfo both lay down on the floor and fell into a heavy sleep. Estrellita and Duane, their eyes taped open, sat motionlessly, fingers locked, minds frozen. A small calico cat with green eyes came in the open door, walked slowly over to one of the saucers filled with milk, and drank.

"You talk to the girl's parents, too," Rip asked, "or just the boy's?"

"I only could get hold of Mrs. Satisfy," said Fed.

"Glory Ann. She says the FBI's already on the job. They got some kind of deal with the Drug Enforcement agents who been after this Romeo Dolorosa for a time now. Apparently the DEA had him set up at Del Rio, but he got away. Now that there's a probable double kidnap across the border, the FBI's buttin' in."

Rip got up from his desk and walked over to the window. Because of the heat, Calle Brazo was practically deserted at three P.M.

"Don't underrate those boys, Fed. Them and us always has got along good."

"You gonna follow up on Ramon's tip about a dropoff at Junction?"

"Have to. Figure to camp out on the highway there tonight."

"Want company?"

"Come if you want, Fed, though I doubt there'll be anything movin' but the usual, wetbacks and coyotes."

"There is, we'll be on 'em like a king snake on a peg-leg rat."

Rip and Fed headed toward Junction, which was at the extreme southern end of Larry Lee County, fifty miles south of Susie, at nine o'clock that night. Before he'd become a drunk, Ramon Montana had been a lawyer, a successful one, and as such had kept up on most of the significant doings in South Texas. The bottle claimed him now, but Ramon still listened carefully to what people said and how they said it, and he managed to remember about half of what he heard. When he eavesdropped on the Castillo brothers, Eddie and Lou, at the bar in El Loco's, and caught the name Marcello Santos, Ramon, even though he was half in the bag, paid particular attention. One of the Castillos' cousins, Pete Armendariz, was a soldier in the Santos family. Armendariz had recently called the Castillos and talked about having to deliver a truckload of goods down at the Junction highway, after which he intended to drop in on Eddie and Lou. The Castillos were looking forward to Pete's visit.

"With soldiers like Armendariz," Fed Phillips told Rip, "ain't no call for Santos to hire a publicity agent."

Rip laughed. "Pete ain't exactly the genius in the group," he said, as they tooled along in the unmarked white Ford Crown Victoria.

At Junction, which was nothing more than a crossroads leading north to McAllen, south to Reynosa, northwest to Laredo, and east to Brownsville and Matamoros, Rip pulled off the road and drove a few hundred yards into the scrub. When he was far enough from the highway not to be spotted, Rip cut the engine and he and Fed got out.

"We'll hike back over and find us some cover," Rip said. "Grab that thermos from the back seat. I made fresh coffee. Be interestin' to see if this is gonna turn out to be anything. Just hope it ain't somethin' Ramon overheard in Wild Turkey town. What else you know about this black magic dope-runnin' cult operatin' out of Cándido Aguilar or Zopilote, or wherever it is?"

"Just that the dude runnin' the show, Dolorosa, is supposed to be some kinda supernatural freak can change into a snake or a jaguar. Least that's what the Mexicans say."

"Nagual."

"What's that?"

"Nagual's got the body of a jaguar and head of a man. Indians believe only a *brujo* can transform himself like that."

"Well, whatever he is, he's sure got all the peons between Corpus and Tampico spooked proper. Whole state of Tamaulipas is afraid of this cat and his bunch. Keeps the power over 'em, that's for certain."

"Religion's about the most powerful force there is, Fed. It's just sex by another name. Think about all the damage been done throughout history in the name of some religion or other. Every blamed war been a so-called holy war. Not much you can do to persuade a person's dead convinced they got God on their side other than get 'em down and make sure they can't get up again."

"My daddy, Federal Lee Phillips, before he died, used to say, 'If God had any mercy in Him, he'd keep me clean.' "

"Man had a conscience, Fed. That's somethin' to take refuge in."

"Just couldn't abide bein' a sinner and not bein' able to do nothin' to prevent it. Finally, he stuck a forty-four in his right ear, the deaf one. You know that Blackhawk I got at the office in the left side bottom desk drawer with the *Hustlers*? That's the weapon he done it with."

Rip stopped walking.

"This here's prob'ly the best brush for us to hide behind," he said. "Got a good view of the crossroads."

"Rip?"

"Yes, Fed?"

"You reckon there really is a man can change into a jaguar?"

"Doubt it, but I suppose in these times anything's possible."

"Dolorosa would have to be the devil himself then, Rip, loosed upon the land, not no ordinary human."

Rip took out his Smith & Wesson .357 revolver, checked to see that it was fully loaded, and replaced it in the holster.

"Like I say, Fed, it wouldn't take more than a little to surprise me. Meantime, all we can do is keep our good eye on the road."

Perdita did not like the idea of having to drive all the way to Los Angeles with Estrellita.

"Why can't I drive Duane and you take Estrellita in

the truck?" she said.

"What if he overpowers you and steals the Cherokee?" asked Romeo.

"We'll tie him up."

"Bad idea, *mi amor*. Someone sees the kid, it's trouble. I figure you can handle Estrellita better. She's scared shitless of you, anyway. She won't try anything. And Duane will be under my control. Trust me, *chica*."

"You know," said Perdita, as she lit a Marlboro, "I never like it when you call me '*chica*.' Maybe because that guy I used to know I told you about, Bobby Peru, he called me that. He's dead now, of course, and it don't really matter, but I'd just same rather you didn't."

Romeo closed the back of the Jeep, took out a red and white kerchief from his back pocket and wiped the dust from the tops and toes of his steel-tipped purple and black lizard-skin boots. He replaced the kerchief in his pocket and smiled his movie actor smile at Perdita. Romeo's large white teeth shone in the moonlight. Perdita looked at him. Romeo's teeth were a lot nicer than Bobby's, she thought.

"Didn't realize you were so sensitive, sweetheart," Romeo said. "Still got that tough boy in your mind, huh?"

Perdita took a deep drag on her Marlboro, blew out the smoke in a fast, thin pink stream, and flicked the butt off a cactus.

"I ever tell you how he was killed?"

"Not that I remember."

"He was attemptin' to rob a feed store in West Texas and a patrolman shot him."

"You saw this happen?"

"No. I heard about it later, on the radio."

Romeo shrugged his shoulders and dropped his smile.

"Life goes bad that way sometimes," he said. "And you move with it from there. You felt something sincere, then, for this Peru."

"He wasn't no real friendly person. It's not easy to say just what there was between us. I ain't particularly upset he's dead, if that's what you mean."

"What if I were killed, Perdita, would you mourn?"

Perdita studied Romeo's face hard for a moment, then looked away. She thought about Tony, Juana's husband, and how he'd once tried to force her to suck his cock while Juana was taking a shower. Perdita would have bit it hard if Tony had been able to pry open her mouth but he hadn't. She'd told Juana about it as soon as she came out of the bathroom, and Juana had grabbed a kitchen knife and stuck it into the thigh of Tony's left leg. Perdita could still remember the way Tony's face twisted up with pain and how he staggered out the front door to his Eldorado and drove off to the hospital with the black knife handle sticking up out of his leg. She and Juana had laughed a lot over that one, both then and at later times when one of them would mention it. The thought of Tony hopping to the car made Perdita laugh now. Juana and Tony were dead so there was nobody left but herself to remember what happened and laugh about it.

"Ain't it time we got goin'?" she said.

BON VOYAGE

Pete Armendariz was a pill lover. He didn't care what kind of drug or vitamin he ingested, he just enjoyed the act itself, feeling the tablets, big or small, on his tongue, and then the exquisite infusion of water or whisky that washed the round or oblong things down his throat. Tonight Pete had taken six bumblebees, enough speed to keep even a big man like him—six-four, two-seventy—going for up to forty-eight hours, along with his usual evening complement of twelve thousand milligrams of vitamin C; two dozen Stresstabs with zinc, calcium and magnesium; twenty-two Super Hy-Vite time-release multivitamins with twenty-eight nutrients coated with natural alfalfa juice concentrate; and sixteen Giant E-ze with 3-rivers oyster extract to keep his libido bopping. Pete prided himself on his enormous capacity for fucking, fighting and eating. He credited the vitamins with keeping him fit and looking younger than his twenty-nine years.

As he guided the truck closer to Junction, Pete grew more and more excited by the thought of partying with his cousins, Eddie and Lou. It had been no little while since the three of them had done some serious shitkicking together. Pete enjoyed his size, his muscle, his overwhelming appetites. He'd played offensive tackle at Baylor University in Waco for a year, but got kicked off the team for beating up an assistant coach who suggested too strenuously that Pete quit calling the quarterback "Cunt Lips." Pete hated quarterbacks, believing they got all the glory while the linemen, such as himself, did all the real work. He played part of another year for the Red Raiders of Texas Tech at Lubbock, but got expelled

6
4

for sexually assaulting a student nurse who was attempting to prevent Pete from stealing a vial of Darvocet at the university medical center. After college, Pete went to New Orleans, where he tended bar in three or four places until he went to work for the Santos family.

Pete pulled the truck over on the northwest side of the highway, turned off the ignition and jumped down from the cab. Dede Peralta came up right behind the truck in the Lincoln Town Car. Pete walked over to the driver's side of the Lincoln and Dede rolled down his window.

"We're a little early," said Dede. "You were really barrelin' that baby."

Pete grinned, causing his *bandido* mustache to curl up slightly at the ends.

"Got some people to see," he said. "Hopin' you could drive me up to Susie, about forty-five minutes from here. I'll get back to N.O. on my own."

Dede nodded. "Don't see why not."

Romeo and Perdita, accompanied by Duane and Estrellita in the back seat, drove up in the Cherokee and stopped behind the Lincoln. Romeo got out and walked up to Pete.

"I am Romeo Dolorosa."

"You're right bang on time, Mr. Dolorosa," said Pete. "Mr. Santos appreciates it. Mr. Peralta, in the car here, has got your instructions."

Dede handed a nine-by-twelve-inch manila envelope to Romeo.

"The directions to the delivery location in Los Angeles are very clear," Dede said. "If you encounter any difficulties along the way, or once you are in L.A., that you are unable to take care of yourself, there is a number to call. Mr. San Pedro Sula will meet you at your destination, as you know. Mr. Santos says he has great confidence in you, Mr. Dolorosa. I know you will justify his faith."

Romeo saw Rip Ford and Federal Ray Phillips jump out from the dark, guns drawn, just before the sheriff shouted, "Hands up, *amigos!* Hang 'em on your ears!"

Pete dived to his left and rolled behind the truck before Rip or Fed could squeeze off a shot. Romeo hit the deck and Dede pulled a nine-millimeter Heckler & Koch semi-auto loaded with hot Israeli ammo from his crotch, turned toward the cops and got a bullet between his eyes. The index finger of his right hand locked on the trigger and fired seven rounds through the roof of the Town Car after he was already dead.

Pete crawled under the truck, took out his .45 Browning automatic and blasted away. Romeo heard one of the cops cry out, followed by several more shots, then nothing. He lay on the ground behind the Lincoln, waiting for a voice, a noise. From where he lay, Romeo could not see inside the Cherokee. He shifted his position and looked under the

BON VOYAGE

o

65

truck, but Pete wasn't there. Romeo waited for thirty seconds before he crawled around the rear of the Town Car. He looked up at the front window of the Cherokee but no faces were visible. He figured that Perdita and the others were on the floor, keeping their mouths shut.

He peered around the end of the car and saw both cops lying perfectly still on the ground. Romeo crawled toward Rip and Fed on his hands and knees, made sure that they were dead, then looked over by the side of the truck for Pete. He was lying on his back, his head toward Romeo, the .45 still in his right hand. Romeo stood up and walked over to him. There was a hole in Pete's chest the size of a silver dollar. He was dead, too. Romeo took the gun out of Pete's hand, then went back over to the cops and took their guns and ammunition belts. He carried the guns and belts to the Cherokee and tapped on the window of the passenger side. Perdita raised her head from the seat.

"Take these and stick them in the lock box," Romeo said. "Everyone else is dead. Duane, you come with me in the truck. We'd better get started. It's a long way to go and no tellin' what other fun and games the gods got in store for us."

Perdita lit a Marlboro. Estrellita was curled up on the back seat, shaking and crying.

"I tell you, Romeo," said Perdita, "this bitch of yours don't straighten up, she ain't gonna make it to no California."

Estrellita watched Perdita smoke. Perdita kept both hands on the steering wheel of the Cherokee and controlled the cigarette with her lips and teeth. She puffed

GHOULS

on the Marlboro while it was between her lips and held it in her teeth when she exhaled. Perdita's long, loose black hair rested on the shoulders of her magenta tee shirt. She was wearing black cotton trousers and huaraches. Hidden by her hair were large silver hoop earrings, to each of which was attached a thin strip of red ribbon. Romeo had told her that a piece of red or brown material worn on the body neutralized the power of one's enemies, drained it from them like a grounding wire pulling electricity into the earth.

"How long you been smoking?" Estrellita asked.

Perdita did not respond. She did not really dislike Estrellita; she cared nothing about her.

"I only tried it twice," said Estrellita. "The first was in the summer before high school. I was with Thelma Acker at her house when her parents were gone. Her mother had an opened pack of Pall Malls in a kitchen drawer, so we smoked one. Only about half of one, really. I took about three puffs and coughed like crazy every time. Then around a month ago at a Sig Chi party I tried a Sherman. You ever have one of those? They're black. Kind of sweet tastin', too. Didn't care for it, either, though I didn't cough so much as with the Pall Mall."

Perdita took a final drag on her Marlboro and put it out in the ashtray.

"I know I'm just talkin' about nothin', and that you hate me," said Estrellita, "but I'm so scared I don't know what to do. I always talk a lot when I'm nervous. Do you talk a lot when you're nervous? Are you ever nervous? Are you ever gonna talk to me?"

Perdita looked quickly at Estrellita, then back at the road.

"You're gonna murder us, too, eventually," Estrellita said. "Isn't that right? Duane isn't very smart, really. I hope you know that. I mean, he's okay so far as pullin' on his pants one leg at a time, but he can't understand you people."

Perdita grinned slightly. "Do you?" she asked.

"I think you and Romeo are incredibly deranged individuals with no morals. You're the most evil creatures on the planet. I know you'll kill me soon so I'm sayin' it. My only hope is in the next life, which is what my Aunt Crystal Rae Satisfy always says. Now I know she's been absolutely correct all this time, that it's literal truth. There's too much ugliness on this earth, seein' how it's crawlin' with soulless ghouls."

"What's a ghoul?" said Perdita.

"What you and Romeo are. The worst kind of evil person. A person who'd violate a corpse."

Estrellita bit her lower lip but didn't cry.

"Whoever gave you the notion you was God's perfect child?" Perdita said. "Does Romeo call you *Santa* Estrellita when you go down on him? He always likes the religious angle. Tell you straight, Miss Satisfy, honey, you're right. It was up to just me, you'd be buried by now out in that desert along with them others. Your blond pussy's what's keepin' you alive, so you'd best make use of it for all it's worth. Girls like you got a kind of sickness, the only way to cure it is to kill it. Always talkin' about love and what's good, that shit, when you're same as me, just no particular piece of trash."

"You really think that? That we're the same kind of person?"

"Ain't seen no evidence to doubt it."

"Well, you're plenty wrong, I don't mind tellin' you. God may create people equal, but after that they're on their own."

Perdita laughed. She shook another Marlboro from the pack on the dash, stuck it between her lips and punched in the lighter. She kept her eyes on the jittery red taillights of the truck.

"A person don't never know who they are till someone knows better tells 'em," said Perdita. "A person won't listen might never know, they never stop to hear. Romeo's good at figurin' out people."

The lighter popped out and Perdita took it and lit her cigarette.

"He's a kind of fake, 'course," she said, "but he's got a unlimited way of seein' things. He's got the power to make people believe him."

"He's horrible," said Estrellita. "You're both so horrible I bet God don't even believe it."

Perdita laughed as she spit out the smoke.

"God don't take everything so serious, *gringa*. You see pretty soon how much He cares about you."

Romeo turned up the radio. Ernest Tubb was singing "When a Soldier Knocks and Finds Nobody Home."

"This is one of my daddy's favorites," said Duane.

LIVES OF

THE SAINTS

"It's real sad. He used to sing it to us when my brother Herschel Roy and I were small. It and Jimmie Rodgers tunes like 'Why Should I Be Lonely' and 'Somewhere Down Below the Dixon Line.' "

Romeo kept the truck headed west at a safe speed.

"One I always enjoyed was 'My Darlin' Clementine,' " Romeo said. "I seen that old movie, too, where the sheriff, Wyatt Earp, says, 'Sure is a hard town for a fella to have a quiet game of poker in,' after Doc Holliday runs off a cheater in the Tombstone saloon. The best line, though, is from Walter Brennan, who plays Pa Clanton, father of the meanest boys in the territory. After Earp busts up the sons' tormentin' of a travelin' actor, Brennan comes in and horsewhips 'em, then says, 'When you *pull* a gun, kill a man.' That's beautiful, Duane.

"Also, when Saint Henry Fonda, who's Wyatt Earp, walks out of the hotel into pourin' rain at three in the mornin' on the night his youngest brother's been killed, he walks alone away from the camera along the plank-covered street, and everything's gray and black streaks, like real life."

Duane was silent, watching the shadows jump past as the refrigerated truck, carrying two thousand-plus pounds of female detritus, stuck East Texas in its back pocket.

"Man, I remember when I was in Tampa, Florida," said Romeo, "seventeen years old, at my grandmother's house, and I saw the movie *Vera Cruz* on television. It changed my life, the way Saint Burt Lancaster looked and talked. He had about 108 giant gleaming teeth, and wore a dusty black outfit and black drawstring hat, a black leather wristband and a silver-studded black gunbelt with a pearl-handled revolver strapped to his right thigh. You ever see that one, Duane?''

Duane shook his head no and stared out the window. The desert at night looked like a tigerskin rug.

"Saint Burt is an outlaw,'' Romeo continued, "operating in Maximilian's Mexico, who hooks up with Saint Gary Cooper, playing a former Confederate colonel from Louisiana who has no desire to live under Yankee rule. Saint Coop's idea is to score enough loot to refinance the Rebel cause. Saint Burt is the greatest gunslinger alive. He can shoot equally well with either hand, and even backhanded! He and Saint Coop and their gang join up with Maximilian rather than Juarez because the Emperor pays better. They agree to help escort a French countess and her carriage to Vera Cruz. The trick, of course, is that a load of gold is hidden in the carriage, and everybody wants it. One of Juarez's generals, Ramirez, pulls a superb stunt when he surrounds Saint Burt and his men on the walls of a town square. Burt rotates his lion's head as dozen after dozen of Ramirez's peasant army appear, and when our Black Saint sees he's trapped, he unleashes his magnificent grin and the world stops, blinded by the glare. The scene resembles a painting by Velasquez.

"Saint Burt's name is Joe Erin; Saint Coop is Ben Train. Joe is slick, crude, flashy, schooled by old Ace Hannah, the man who gunned down Joe's father. And Joe makes a point of telling Ben how and when Joe paid Ace back. Ben Train is elegant, older, gentler. It's sincerely wonderful when Joe says of Ben, 'I don't trust him. He likes people; you can never count on a man like that.' Joe spills wine on himself when he drinks from a glass. Ben speaks French and charms the countess, much to Joe's dismay. They make a great pair.

"Joe Erin is the kind of man I wanted to be: fierce, daring and dangerous, combined with the elegance of Ben Train. The Great Burt approaches that at the end of *Vera Cruz*, when he and Saint Coop have their showdown. Saint Burt twirls his pistol one last time into his holster before collapsing, grinning more brilliantly than ever as the reluctant but superior shooter Ben Train's bullet takes his life. It is a dramatic ending, Duane, the most perfect ending for a man. It's the path to sainthood.''

"You gonna shoot us, Mr. Dolorosa,'' said Duane, turning toward Romeo, "after we get to the West Coast, maybe. Ain't that right?''

Romeo whistled softly, gritted his teeth and grinned.

"We ain't got to that part yet," he said. "There's no script, like for a movie. Be best to work things out as we go along, *amigo*, don't you think?"

"I'd appreciate it."

"Thought you would."

"When I was twelve years old," said Estrellita, "my mama and I and my friend Daisy Samples and her cousin Cutie Lewis were sitting on our front porch one summer

COMMUNION

evenin' talkin', when here come the preacher and his wife, and couple or three children and a pair or more other poor relations, to find out why it was our family hadn't been to church lately.

" 'Evenin', Mrs. Satisfy,' the preacher said. 'Evenin', Estelle. Evenin' all of you.' We're Baptists, sort of. What I mean by that is none of us is really much on churchgoin' anymore. When I was real small we went more, maybe two or three times a month. But it was around the time I'm talkin' about, I guess, that we began to really slack off.

"Anyway, the preacher's talkin' about how terrible wet the air is, and how that brings out the mosquitoes, and so on, and his dumb kids are scratchin' and kickin' at each other, fightin', bored out of their skulls, the mother's shushin' 'em, and the couple of dumb souls are startin' to wander off in different directions. So the preacher asks mama why we ain't been around in church lately, and she tells him things has been shaky with her and Ernest Tubb, but we'll be back in by and by, the next Sunday, prob'ly.

"Then he asks Daisy Samples if she'd be interested in comin' on Sunday, too, and Daisy says, 'Not me, preacher, I'm a Catholic.' Well, this takes the preacher back, 'cause you know how bad the Baptists hate the Catholics. He keeps up his smile, though, and turns to Daisy's cousin, Cutie, but before he can ask her, my mama, Glory Ann, says, 'Don't think you'll be wantin' her, either, seein' how Cutie's half a Catholic and half a Jew.'

"Whew! Hearin' that word, *Jew*, just stunned the man, and he begun herdin' his people back to the car, tippin' his beat-up gray slouch hat with the sweat stripe around the middle, and tellin' mama and me he'd see us in church. I don't recall whether we went that week or not."

Perdita kept her eyes on the road.

"We were Catholics," she said.

"Did you go to church a lot?"

"When I was young, I did. Didn't impress me much, though, not like it did my sister, Juana. She was sold on it for a bit, until our neighbor, Cruz Fierro, told her about how the nuns ate their own babies."

Estrellita looked at Perdita, then out the passenger side window. Blue shark's teeth nibbled at the black curtain.

"What do you mean, ate their babies?"

"To get rid of the evidence, so nobody'd find 'em. Better than buryin' bodies could be dug up. Cruz was a hustler up in Houston, and a junkie, but he wasn't a liar. The dope killed him. He made it with a priest, who told him that a nun who had a baby was made to eat it herself, as a punishment. That turned Juana off from wantin' to be a bride of God. She married that fucker Tony instead."

Perdita laughed. "Juana woulda done better," she said, "even if she'd had to eat her own kid. Might be she'd still be alive."

Woody Dumas, special agent in charge of the United States Drug Enforcement Administration's regional office in Dallas, leaned back in his chair and put his feet up

THE WORLD AND

EVERYTHING IN IT

on his desk. He tore open a jumbo bag of salted peanuts and cracked and ate them as he spoke.

"I'm hearin' you, Doyle, loud and clear," Woody said into the telephone cradled between his left cheek and shoulder, "no need to shout. Don't take no whiz kid to figure out Santos is involved at the top of the deck, either. This the first you FBI geniuses heard of him? Okay, okay, Mr. Cathcart, sir! Soon as I got a bead on these tree squirrels, you'll know about it. My guess is they got some *maquila* around El Paso, but could be they're movin' the goods all the way to the West Coast. I got my best bird dogs on hunt, so don't take a header. You bet, Doyle, good buddy. *Adios* for now, huh?"

Woody hung up, cracked open another peanut and popped it into his mouth. He'd turned fifty the day before but looked ten years younger. He still had a full head of thick, sandy brown hair and a mostly unwrinkled face. Woody Dumas had never married and never been tempted to. At six-two and one-eighty-five, he moved at a leisurely pace, took a multivitamin pill daily with his orange juice, didn't eat sweets or drink coffee, worked out three times a week on a LifeCycle and with weights at the Downtown Health Club, and got at least six hours of sleep each night. His favorite reading material was the sports section of the newspaper. Woody did not believe in cluttering up his mind with a lot of unnecessary information. Life was complicated enough, he felt, without mixing in a bunch of half-baked ideas.

Woody knew that Crazy Eyes Santos was behind the skin business, just as he was behind virtually every other major illegal enterprise across the South and Southwest. The Mexicans had tied him to most of the cocaine and marijuana being smuggled across the border, and Doyle Cathcart, the special agent in charge of the Federal Bureau of Investigation office in Houston, was certain that Santos was using his dope network to transport experimental cosmetic materials. There was some ugly shit going on down around the border, too, that Woody had been hearing about, all kinds of so-called religious garbage, including animal and even human sacrifice.

At precisely four-thirty P.M., Woody Dumas swung his maroon and white Tony Lama boots to the floor, tossed the bag of peanuts on the desk and stood up. He brushed himself off, picked his white Stetson from the hatrack and placed it firmly on his head. There was more sickness in the world today, Woody believed, than at any time in history. Walking out of the Federal Building he thought of an incident he'd read about in the *Morning News*, something that had taken place in San Francisco shortly after the recent earthquake there. A man named DeSota Barker had been directing traffic at a busy intersection after the city-wide power failure knocked out the stoplights, and an impatient, probably cracked-out motorist had shot and killed him. Barker was subsequently listed among the victims of the earthquake.

"The more things there are to figure," Woody thought, "the more things there are get figured wrong."

He climbed behind the wheel of his brown 1978 Malibu Classic and cranked it up. Woody sat in the car, letting the engine idle, thinking about Salty Dog, the Airedale he'd had when he was a boy. When Woody was fourteen and the dog was four, Salty had bitten two old ladies—one while she was watering her lawn, the other as she was walking up the steps to her house—within a week. He'd never bitten anyone before that, but the county took Salty away and put him to sleep. Woody didn't understand why he thought about Salty Dog almost every day at this time. It had been thirty-six years since they'd gassed Salty, Woody realized, and the world just hadn't been right since.

"Didn't you tell me you used to live out here?" Romeo asked Perdita.

They were at the Rim City Truck-o-Rama, fueling up.

THE BIG DAY

It was not quite six o'clock of a new day. Perdita looked around. A sharp wind came up and blew sand into her face. She put on her sunglasses.

"Not too far," Perdita said.

She pulled a Marlboro out of the pack she'd stuck in the front of her Wranglers and put it between her lips but did not try to light it. Perdita walked over to where a dozen Macks and Peterbilts dozed, night sweat sparkling on their metallic hides. She kicked at a wad of red mud caked on one of the giant tires.

"How you doin'?"

Perdita turned around. It was Duane. She still had the unlit cigarette in her mouth, so Duane took a book of matches from his pocket and fired it. He watched Perdita's straight black hair fly back from her Chiricahua cheekbones like a quarter horse's tail in deep stretch at Ruidoso Downs. The weak sun brushed red streaks on it.

"We gonna drive straight through, you think," Duane asked, "or what?"

"Romeo'll likely want to sleep during the day and drive at night. You figure you and Little Miss Poison maybe could slip out on us?"

Duane half-laughed. "I don't guess," he said.

Perdita leaned back against the tire she'd kicked.

"You ever think that someone might be watchin' us?" she asked.

"Who someone?"

Perdita took a hard drag on her Marlboro, then flicked it away.

"I mean some kind of super intelligent bein'. Somethin' invisible, like a ghost. Someone who knows everything's goin' on."

"Guess it's possible. Sounds like you're talkin' about God, though."

Perdita shook her head. "This ain't no god."

"Why can't we see him then?"

"He'll step in on his own sweet time. When the big day comes, and it's comin' quick."

"What'll happen on the big day?"

"Snakes and spiders, rainin' on the people."

"Heard that after the hurricane in South Carolina last month, snakes was everywhere. Moccasins, copperheads, all kinds, blown out of the swamps."

"This'll be worse. He knows what we're doin', all of us. There ain't nobody innocent, not you, not me, not Estrellita."

"Or Romeo."

Perdita nodded. "Sky'll fall on him, too. Maybe especially on him."

The sun stood up and chopped the chill in two.

"Hey, you two lovebirds!" Romeo shouted from where he was pumping gas. "Let's go inside the cafe here and get some breakfast."

The four of them sat in a booth. Bill Monroe was singing "A Fallen Star" on the jukebox. After they'd ordered, Romeo went over to the cashier's stand, bought a *San Antonio Light*, came back and sat down.

"Now here's a good one," he announced, "about a guy named Bubba Ray Billy, a con in Angola, Louisiana, who got fried yesterday. Seems this Billy, who was twenty-six, raped and murdered by stabbing seventeen times an eighteen-year-old girl named Lucy Fay Feydaux. Bubba Ray had picked up Lucy Fay, it says, in his 1954 blue and white Oldsmobile Holiday on a country road outside Opelousas one night four years ago. 'He must of took her against her will,' said the girl's mother, Irma. Mr. Archie Bob Feydaux, Lucy Fay's father, attended the execution and told reporters that he and his wife supported the death penalty and had been waiting four years for Billy to die."

Their food had begun to arrive while Romeo was reading, and he gulped down his orange juice and half a cup of coffee before continuing to paraphrase and quote from the paper. Perdita kept her dark glasses on and smoked her way through the meal while Duane and Estrellita kept their heads down as they ate their eggs, toast, sausages and grits.

"So the good old boys over to Angola strapped Bubba Ray Billy into Gruesome Gertie," Romeo said, "the big oak electric chair, and ended Archie Bob and Irma Feydaux's vigil. Billy was one mean cat, according to this. He'd had a Grim Reaper tattooed on his chest while in the Death

House and confessed to at least two other killings in addition to the kidnapping and attempted murder of a Poplarville, Louisiana, teenager and the rape of the boy's girlfriend.

" 'I don't run from nothing,' Billy said. 'People say I'm an animal, but they wouldn't say it to my face. I wouldn't say I'm an animal,' he told reporters, 'but I am a cold person.' Boy was a regular case, wouldn't you say, Perdita, honey? Get this: his daddy, Guinn 'Boss' Billy, spent twenty-eight of his fifty-five years in the slam for cattle theft, aggravated battery and manslaughter. When queried by the press as to his reaction to Bubba Ray's impending execution, Boss Billy just told them that he would sleep through it and said his son deserved to die."

Romeo whistled long and softly through his teeth.

"Man, the boy's daddy's an even harder case. This last part's the best. Bubba Ray apparently didn't talk much during the big day. He ate a last supper of fried oysters and shrimp, even though, as he said, he didn't feel much like eating. When a reporter commented to him that he'd nevertheless cleaned his plate, Billy smiled a little and said, 'I guess some old habits is just tough to break.' "

Romeo put down the newspaper, stabbed a pat of butter with his knife and stuck it in his bowl of oatmeal, poured half a glass of milk over it, and signaled for the waitress, who was an elderly, lame Mexican woman with one half-shut eye.

"Señora," he said, when she limped over, "I sure would appreciate it if you could scare up some molasses for me to sweeten up this cereal. Oatmeal just don't taste the same without it."

"You want the usual, Mr. Dumas?"

"Maybe a little extra ice, Sherry Louise, if you don't mind. It's a warm one."

A VISIT TO

SPARKY & BUDDY'S

Woody loosened his tie and arched his back. He didn't like sitting on stools but tonight, for some reason, he felt unusually tired. Ordinarily, he stood at the bar. It was a slow evening at Sparky & Buddy's; there were only two other customers in the place.

"There you go, Mr. Dumas, cranberry juice and soda with a slice of orange, two maraschino cherries and extra ice, in a chimney."

"Sherry Louise, you take good care of me and I want you to know that I appreciate it."

Woody slid a five dollar bill to her across the black mahogany.

"This is yours," he said.

"It's my pleasure, Mr. Dumas. Always is."

Woody watched Sherry Louise walk back to the other end of the bar. She undulated, like a giraffe. She must be a half-inch or so over six feet tall, Woody figured, in the green and white New Balance running shoes she wore while she was on duty. Her bright red hair was piled up on her head, adding a good three or four inches of height. Tall and *mucho* skinny, too skinny for his taste, Woody decided. Sherry Louise looked like a section of two-inch pipe stood on end with a bird's nest set on top. She was extra sweet, though, and Sparky said she was the most dependable and honest bartender they'd ever had. Her husband, Eddie Dean Zernial, a former stock car driver, was a carpet layer. Sherry Louise was always going on about how messed up Eddie Dean's back and knees were, both from collisions and rug tacking, but one night she'd told Woody that didn't interfere with their sex life any, since she preferred riding high to lying low. Woody had a difficult time imagining what it would be like to make love to Sherry Louise. It was better that way, he thought; one less thing to have to think about.

A short, stout man of about forty came in and sat down two stools to Woody's left. He was perspiring heavily and used a bar napkin to wipe the sweat from his mostly bald head. Sherry Louise smiled at Woody as she passed him.

"What can I do you for, handsome?" she asked the man.

He held up his right hand and horizontally extended three fingers.

"Wild Turkey," the man said, "straight. Water chaser, with plenty of ice."

"Appears all you gentlemen need coolin' down this evenin'," said Sherry Louise. "Ain't all that hot, I don't think."

She poured the whisky into a double shot glass, filled another with ice and tap water and set them both in front of the customer. He put his money on the bar, Sherry Louise took it, walked to the cash register, made change and brought it back.

"Just shout, you need me," she told him, and smiled again at Woody. "You all right for now, Mr. Dumas?"

Woody smiled at her. "Just fine, Sherry Louise."

"Sons of bitches ain't never gonna find her," said the short, bald man.

Woody turned toward him.

"Come again?"

"Go over that border don't expect no favors, what I always say."

"Woody Dumas," said Woody, offering his right hand to the man.

"Ernest Tubb Satisfy," he said, giving Woody's hand a quick, wet shake, after which Ernest Tubb picked up the shot glass and sipped noisily.

"What border you mean?" Woody asked.

"Messican, 'course. Chink counterfeiters makin' Rolexes, computer innards, that shit, government'll go after like cockstarved banshees. Let it be some poor little Texas gal gets grabbed off the street and they can't figure their asshole wipes north or south. Yesterday on the Blaupunkt in my Mark IV, I heard about G-men bustin' a Hong Kong ring of fake soy sauce manufacturers. Seized more than one hundred thousand bottles of bogus soy along with the perpetrators. Economics is what it is, pure smilin' simple. That's what I say."

Ernest Tubb swallowed the rest of his three fingers, gave it a fast chase and cracked an ice cube with his back teeth.

"Goin' after 'em myself," he said. "Glory Ann, she thinks I'll get myself killed, but a man's gotta do what he feels deepest in his heart is the right thing. That's what I say. So I'm goin' after Estelle. She's my baby."

Ernest Tubb hopped down from his stool.

"Good talkin' to ya," he said to Woody, and walked out.

Sherry Louise came over.

"What was Elmer Fudd there so fired up about?" she asked.

"Man's on a mission of some kind," said Woody. "No doubt about it."

"Ain't much left in this lonesome world got no doubt in it," Sherry Louise said.

Woody laughed. "No real comfort in knowin' that, either, I suppose."

Sherry Louise cleared away Ernest Tubb Satisfy's glasses and wiped the bar clean.

"Seems like sometimes bein' even a little intelligent just don't pay, Mr. Dumas. You know what I mean?"

"Thought it'd be a good idea to see a movie," said Romeo. "Might relax everybody a little bit."

Romeo, Perdita, Duane and Estrellita were in a room

CRITICS

at the Orbit Motel in Buck's Bend, New Mexico, halfway between El Paso and Las Cruces. It was four o'clock in the afternoon; they'd slept eight hours.

"We can get back on the highway right after it's over, when it's dark. Noticed on the way into town one of them multi-theater complexes out at the shopping center. What kind of pictures you like, Estrellita, honey?"

Estrellita sneezed and coughed.

"You catchin' cold?" asked Romeo.

"I'm okay," said Estrellita. "I don't care much what show we see."

"What about you, Duane?"

"Don't care."

"Hey, c'mon everybody! Cheer up!" said Romeo. "After all, I'm buyin'."

Perdita did not comment.

Romeo herded everyone into the Cherokee, leaving the truck parked under the Orbit sign, which was an orange neon planet with a purple spaceship, connected on one side by a metal spoke. Several yellow-white stars twinkled on and off around the planet, and a few that didn't work buzzed and hissed.

At the movie complex, Romeo said, "This *Shocker* sounds like fun. Accordin' to the poster here, a mass murderer gets sentenced to the electric chair, only instead of it killin' him, he feeds on the juice and becomes crazier and more powerful. Let's go."

Romeo bought the tickets and they went inside. The

movie turned out to be even more bizarre than the advertising promised. An insane, sadistic killer, who'd worked as a television repairman and with other electronic devices, is scheduled to die, and his last request in the prison is for a TV set. He hooks his hands up to the television tubes with jumper cables and transfuses himself with electrical current. The guards rush in and disconnect him, and in the ensuing struggle he practically bites off one's lower lip and breaks another's fingers. When they finally give him the big jolt, the chair and the entire penitentiary power system shorts out, and the killer's electrified self, in the form of phantom particles, escapes and wreaks havoc all over again. The film moves back and forth between dreams and reality, and the monster manages to plug himself into a satellite and transmit his ens through television all across the country. He runs rampant among cable and network landscapes until he's programmed into oblivion by the hero, who's been chasing him over the airwaves.

"Man, I'll bet that con in Louisiana," Romeo said when they were all back outside after the movie, "Bubba Somethin', who got singed the other day, woulda asked for a TV set, too, instead of shrimp and oysters, if he'd seen this picture first."

"It was kinda interestin'," said Duane.

"I enjoyed the hell out of it," said Romeo. "Just shows how capital punishment don't really make much of a difference, after all. What'd you girls think?"

"It was disgusting," Estrellita said. "These kinds of movies are for morons."

"Hear that, Duane?" laughed Romeo. "Your sweetheart here's callin' you a moron."

"Least he's got company," said Perdita, lighting up a Marlboro.

"Well, Duane, *amigo*, there you go," Romeo said. "Everyone's a critic. No wonder now, is it, why the world's in such a mess. Can't nobody agree on nothin'."

Marcello Santos was unhappy. Dede Peralta had been a long-time associate of his, a friend in a business where few men could truly consider themselves friends. Dede

THE CHOICE

was dead, as was his soldier Pete Armendariz, and Crazy Eyes was upset. He had called a meeting to be held in the farmhouse of his six thousand acre property west of New Orleans. Set in the middle of a swamp, with only one heavily guarded road leading in and out, it was the only place Santos felt totally safe. He had named this haven "*Il Giardino d'Infanzia*," the nursery. It was as The Nursery that Santos and others, including federal and local police agencies, referred to it in conversation. A small handpainted sign hanging over the entrance to the house read, "Three can keep a secret if two are dead."

Present at the meeting, called for eight o'clock on a Tuesday night, were Santos; Alfonse "Tiger Johnny" Ragusa, the crime boss of Houston and El Paso; Beniamino "Jimmie Hunchback" Calabrese, a capo in the Gambino family, from New York; Nicky "Bigfoot" DeAngelis, the Alabama and West Florida drug king; Reggie San Pedro Sula, who stood by Marcello; and the bodyguards for each of the others: "Papaya Phil" Romo, with Ragusa; Provino "The Fist" Momo, with Calabrese; and Vincent "Pit Bull" Deserio, with DeAngelis.

The air conditioning was fighting a losing battle against the ninety-five-degree heat and ninety-nine-percent humidity of the Southern Louisiana night. Santos took off his jacket and mopped his forehead with a black silk handkerchief.

"Thank you, gentlemen," he said, "for coming to The

Nursery. You all know how this tragedy of Dede has hit me so hard. I have been in mourning since the news reached me. The reason for calling you together is that we have a problem, a most serious problem, that, if we are going to be able to continue what has been so far a profitable participation in the cosmetics trade, we must solve.

"The problem is this Dumas, who is, of course, the special agent of the Drug Enforcement Agency in Dallas. Our friend from Dallas, Joseph Poca, whom you all know as 'Joe Polkadots,' is, unfortunately, at the present time in prison. Therefore, we are empowered, with the permission of Joe Polkadots, that I have very recently obtained, to act on our own behalf concerning special agent Dumas. I call for suggestions."

"Marcello," said Tiger Johnny, "I'll be happy to take care of this creep. He is, after all, in Texas, which is my state. I can arrange for a pipe bomb to be placed in the man's car, and it will be done. Allow me this privilege."

"A thought," said Jimmie Hunchback. "It might be wiser to have an outside representative handle the job. Why not I leave The Fist here go up to Dallas to take care of it himself? Killing a federal agent is a thing the government won't forget, but in this case I don't think they'd suspect someone from my part of the country."

"Nicky Bigfoot," said Santos, "what do you feel is the correct thing?"

At seventy-nine, Nicky DeAngelis was the oldest of the group. He had ruled the Florida Gulf Coast area for forty years, and Marcello sincerely respected his opinion. Like Santos, Nicky Bigfoot, who earned his nickname because he'd made a large and lasting impression in the course of his career, wore dark glasses most of the time. Unlike Santos, who wore them to cover up his strange eyes, Nicky used them so that he could catnap without anyone knowing he was dozing off. His bodyguard, Pit Bull Deserio, was fiercely protective of his boss, and listened closely to everything that was said in his presence in case Nicky needed him to whisper into his ear any information the old man had missed. Deserio did this now, and it took several moments before Nicky responded to Santos's question.

"I go with Jimmie the Hunch," said Bigfoot. "You understand that's how come he's called Jimmie Hunchback. Not because he's got a crippled back, which, as you can see, he don't. If he says his man will do the job right, we should honor his judgment. With all respect to you, Johnny Ragusa, it should be a hitter from someplace out of Texas."

Santos held up his left hand, the one minus a thumb.

"It's settled, then," he said. "Jimmie's man, Provino Momo, will take care of the agent Dumas. Now we can relax and play some serious pinochle! Reggie, give Signore DeAngelis another cup espresso so he can't say he's asleep when I beat him with the cards. Everyone, have more wine, whisky, whatever you want. There is plenty food, also, spaghetti and oysters. You know we like to eat in Louisiana!"

Santos held up a glass filled with wine in his right hand.

"To you, *Il Pugno*, our blessing. And to us all, *salute!*"

"Thanks, especially, for sending up the files on Dolorosa and Durango, Doyle. They're quite a pair."

Woody Dumas had been reading the FBI reports on

the skin-business smugglers that Doyle Cathcart had faxed to him overnight, and Doyle had just telephoned to make sure the information had arrived.

"Didn't recall who she was right away," Woody said, "but that name, Perdita Durango, was stuck in my head from someplace."

"She was hooked up with that feed store holdup awhile back in Iraaq," said Doyle. "Remember? One of the stickup men got his head blown off and the other one was captured and sent to Huntsville. The Durango gal was the getaway driver, and danged if she didn't get clean away."

"So now you figure she's mixed up with this bare-footin' dope dealer."

"Right. He's also some kind of *santería* priest. They apparently murdered a boy in a ceremony, and the Mexicans want 'em."

"Well, I'm about to saddle up, buddy, and get on the trail. Word is the target is in Los Angeles, so I'm headin' west."

"Just watch your tail, fella. They shoot horses, don't they? They'll sure as shit shoot you, too."

Woody laughed. " 'Preciate your concern, son. You take care, too, now. Hear?" he said, and hung up.

Jimmie Hunchback's best boy, Provino Momo, sat in a rented dark gray Ford Thunderbird across the street from the Federal Building. The Fist was an expert at sitting and waiting. As a child, he'd had tuberculosis and had to spend nearly two years resting. During those two years, from the age of eleven until he was thirteen, The Fist mostly slept and read comic books. An only son, he was not allowed to play at all with other children during his illness, and was kept on a strict low-fat, salt-free diet. He didn't realize how angry he had become during this hiatus until five years later when, during a disagreement in a poolhall in the Red Hook section of Brooklyn, the now fully-grown Provino Momo beat a forty-year-old man to death with his hands. It was from this incident that his nickname derived. Word got around about this big, tough, quiet kid with the grip of steel—he was six-four, two-fifty at eighteen—and The Fist went to work as a soldier for the Gambinos, New York's largest organized crime family. Eventually, he earned the confidence of Jimmie Hunchback, and became the capo's right-hand man.

Now, as The Fist sat in the rented T-bird, watching for the Drug Enforcement agent whose photograph he had next to him on the front seat, he thought about the various men and women he had personally whacked on behalf of the business. Usually, The Fist avoided this kind of rumination, but for some reason, perhaps because he would turn forty years old tomorrow, the same age as his first victim had been, he allowed himself to review this side of his life. Altogether, The Fist figured, he had murdered at least twenty people, most of them without any weapons other than his own hands. That wasn't so many, he thought, not in twenty-two years. He didn't know whether to be pleased or not by this, but his reverie ended a moment later, as soon as he spotted Woody Dumas walking out of the building.

Woody's Malibu was parked directly across from The Fist's T-bird. The agent unlocked his car, got in, started it up and drove away. Didn't even check for a bomb, The Fist thought, as he followed him, wondering why anyone who made a halfway decent living would drive such a crummy-looking car. Maybe these federal guys didn't get paid so well. In any case, he figured, Dumas could drive a better short than this turd-colored piece of junk. It looked too much like a cop car to even be a cop car. The Fist owned an identical pair of white '88 Cadillac Sedan de Villes. He drove them on alternate days, and when one of them was in the repair shop he always had the twin to use. Even though it was too small for a man his size, he didn't mind driving this T-bird. It had pretty good pickup and held the road okay. He wouldn't hesitate to rent another one.

Woody drove slowly through the downtown traffic headed toward his athletic club, which was in the newly gentrified warehouse district. He wanted to get in a good workout before the trip to L.A. After parking his car in the alley behind the club, Woody opened the trunk to get his gear. As he bent over to take out his gym bag, the trunk lid came down hard

RUBOUT

89

on his back, causing his legs to collapse. Woody fell to the ground. All he could see were two large, brightly polished brown Cordovans. Woody reached his right hand down to his left ankle and pulled from its holster his Charter Arms Bulldog Pug .44 long snub-nose revolver. He felt himself being lifted and squeezed at the same time. Suddenly, he found it very difficult to breathe and realized he was being crushed to death by an enormously powerful person. Woody brought his backup gun as close to his own head as he could and just as he was about to lose consciousness glimpsed the face of his attacker. He squeezed the trigger, hoping the business end was pointed in the right direction.

The Fist fell backward, his gigantic fingers still gripping the agent's arms, so that when Woody again opened his eyes he saw that he was lying on top of a huge man without a nose. The gun had discharged point blank into The Fist's face and the Glazer safety slug had ripped apart his nostrils, leaving an ugly, large red hole above his upper lip and between his two bloodshot eyes, both of which were wide open and staring up emptily at Woody.

A vision of Salty Dog came immediately to Woody's mind, and he closed his eyes and rolled off The Fist onto his back. Salty was chasing an old woman who was wearing a black raincoat, the tail of which the bounding Airedale held tightly in his teeth.

"Get her, Salty," Woody said. "Get her, boy!"

Mona came up for air and Santos barked at her, "No, no, *cara mia*, don't stop! I'm almost there!"

"I need a break, Marcello, please. My mouth gets tired, and besides, look, it's *fiacco*."

OUT OF

THE PAST

Santos groaned heavily. "Everything is difficult these days. Life is *una pioggia continua*."

Mona got up off her knees and went over to the bar, put a teaspoonful of sugar in a glass, half-filled it with Bombay Sapphire, stirred it with a red swizzle stick that had the words RIZZO'S SOCIAL CLUB • NEW ORLEANS lettered on it in gold, and took a healthy swallow.

"Relax, Marcello," she said. "I'm gonna take a bath."

Crazy Eyes Santos watched his mistress of ten years, Mona Costatroppo, walk out of the room. He listened to the water run into the bathtub. Mona was thirty-one years old, still beautiful, Santos thought, but no longer slim-figured. When he'd first seen her, working as a teller in Grimaldi's bank in Gretna, she looked like Claudia Cardinale, only skinnier. The big dark-brown eyes, long mouth with thick red lips, perfect uptilted breasts. Mona ate too many syrup-filled chocolates now, and drank too much of that fancy gin. Two more years of this, Santos figured, and she'd look exactly like his wife, Lina. At least Lina had provided him with four children.

"Marcello," Mona called from the bathroom. "Be a *costata di agnello* and bring me another drink, would you?"

Santos stood, stuffed his penis inside his pants, and zipped them up. He walked out of the apartment and closed the door softly behind him.

"Marcello!" Mona shouted. "Marcello, are you coming? And don't forget the sugar!"

A few miles east of Tucson, Romeo turned south off the interstate. He checked his sideview to make sure that Perdita had made the unexpected turnoff in the twilight.

"One thing about our little Apache princess there, Duane boy," Romeo said, "she can handle a vehicle good as any man, better than most."

"Why we takin' this two-lane all of a sudden?"

"There's an *hombre* I'd like to see in Nogales, on the Mexico side, long as we're so close by. Man owes me. Name's Amaury 'Big Chief' Catalina. Calls himself Big Chief because he claims he's a direct descendant of some Aztec king. Hell, we're all descendants of one kind of king or other. Runs a restaurant called La Florida. Pretty sure he'll be there, unless he's dead, which he should be. Man shouldn't get used to owin', Duane. It's unhealthy."

In the Cherokee, Perdita pulled on the lights.

"What's our hero up to now?" she asked herself, following the large white refrigeration truck down Arizona State Highway 82.

"What did you say?" said Estrellita, who was about half awake.

Perdita looked quickly at her, then fastened her eyes back on the narrow, darkening road. She hated the girl's bright blond hair.

"Sonoita? Patagonia? Where are we?" Estrellita asked, reading a distance sign.

Perdita punched in the dash lighter, put a cigarette between her teeth, and as soon as the lighter popped back pulled it out and lit up.

"You sure smoke a hell of a lot," Estrellita said.

"Won't be botherin' you too much longer, I got anything to say about it. Don't you worry."

They rode in silence until Romeo rolled through the crossroads that was Sonoita and headed for Patagonia. Perdita had no choice but to follow the white truck.

"Must be he's goin' to see someone owes him money," she said. "Just another detour on our way to nowhere."

At Patagonia, a one-street town about twenty miles north of the border, Romeo pulled the truck over and stopped. Perdita slid the Cherokee to a halt right behind him. Romeo hopped down and came over to Perdita's window, which she lowered all the way.

"Bet you're wonderin' what I'm up to, huh, ladies? Well, there's a kind of spooky gentleman in Nogales, on the Mex side, I mean to pay a quick call on, see if I can shake some of what he owes me out of his jeans. We'll be on our way to L.A. again in no time. Perdita, sweet thing, in Nogales I'll park this rig on the U.S. side, in the Safeway foodstore lot. We'll leave both vehicles there and walk across the border. I think Estrellita, here, and our good buddy Duane will behave proper, don't you? Now I'm just gonna make a phone call from the booth over there next to the old railway depot. Shouldn't take long."

In the telephone booth Romeo opened the manila envelope Dede Peralta had given him. He found the sheet of paper he was looking for and held it up to read the number as he dialed. Romeo dropped in the necessary coins, and after the third ring someone answered.

A man's voice said, very softly, "Bayou Enterprises."

"This is Romeo Dolorosa. I'd like to speak with Mr. Santos, please."

"Mr. Santos is out of town. What's this about?"

"I just wanted to tell him that I'll be a little late to the party. I'm having car trouble, but it's being fixed. Can you please convey this information to Mr. Santos when you speak to him?"

"Sure, he keeps in touch. That it?"

"Yes, that's all. Tell him I'll be there as soon as I can."

"I'm sure you will," the man said, and hung up.

Romeo hung up on his end and walked back over to Perdita. He smiled at her and leaned forward with one hand on either side of the door.

"Santos isn't a man to fuck with, Romeo," she said. "I hope you're not fucking with him."

"I can handle it, Perdita, darlin'. You know me."

Her eyebrows twitched, the snakes coiling, but Perdita said nothing as she watched Romeo walk to the truck and climb back in.

"Bet you wish sometimes you didn't," said Estrellita.

Perdita started up the Cherokee and followed along. A half hour later she parked behind Romeo in the Safeway lot in Nogales. All of them got out.

"You kids do what I say and you'll be all right," Romeo told Duane and Estrellita. "If either of you say anything to the customs, I'll shoot you both on the spot, and the customs officer, too. Okay, *vamonos*."

The four of them filed through the turnstile into Mexico. Romeo led them past rows of beggars and through a maze of hustlers and shills, down a comparatively deserted sidestreet and into a courtyard. A white neon sign that said BILLARES blinked and sputtered over one of two doors. Over the other was a dull yellow globe with *LA FLORIDA* painted on it in black script.

"My memory's not so bad," laughed Romeo. "It's been four or five years since I've been here. Come on, let's go in."

There was a long bar to the right of the entrance, and perhaps a dozen tables to the left in front of a small stage. Several men sat at the bar; none of them were well-dressed. Only two of the tables were occupied. A man in a shabby black tuxedo with a red cummerbund came up to Romeo and asked if the four of them were there for dinner.

"Possibly," said Romeo. "We'll see."

The host smiled and showed them to a table.

"*Señor Catalina esta aqui?*" asked Romeo, as they were seated.

"He will arrive in perhaps ten minutes," said the host, who gave each of them a menu. "Are you a friend of his?"

"Oh yes," said Romeo, "a very old one."

"I will tell him you are here when he comes in. What is your name?"

"Dolorosa. Just say Dolorosa."

The host kept his smile and said, "As you wish. Your waiter will be with you in a moment."

When the waiter came, Romeo ordered margaritas all around. He'd drunk half of his when he saw Amaury Catalina approaching, weaving sharklike through the other tables. The Big Chief was not smiling.

"Romeo, *amigo! Que tal?* What a marvelous surprise to see you!" Catalina exclaimed, smiling now with every part of his round brown face except the eyes, which were hard and dull, motionless black pellets.

Romeo rose and embraced him.

"I thought it might be," Romeo said, also smiling a smile without mirth.

Big Chief Catalina was topheavy, carrying well over two hundred pounds on his medium-large five-foot ten-inch frame. With his caterpillar mustache and thinning black hair greased straight back on his wide, flat head, Catalina looked ten years older than his thirty-four.

"Say, Chief, why don't we go someplace and talk?"

"Of course, of course. We can use my office."

"Be back shortly, Perdita," said Romeo. "You keep an eye on the kids. Make sure they eat their vegetables."

Catalina signaled to the waiter, who came over immediately.

"See that these people have anything they want," said the Big Chief, "without charge."

Catalina's office was an eight-by-eight windowless box, with a desk, two chairs, and a filing cabinet. On the wall to one side of the desk was a postcard photo of Pancho Villa on his horse in front of his army in 1914. Catalina took a bottle of Gusano Rojo mezcal and two glasses from a drawer and put them on top of the desk, then poured double doses for Romeo and himself.

"Before you ask me about the money, *amigo*, we have a drink, yes? This is good mezcal, from Oaxaca."

"*Cómo no?*"

"To your health!"

They swallowed the shots of mezcal and set the glasses back on the desk.

"Now, Señor Pain, you can ask me about the money."

"Do you have it?"

"No. I have money, but not for you, unfortunately."

"Do you mean that you do not have it for me now, or that you will never have it for me?"

Catalina laughed abruptly but did not smile.

"This is a choice you are welcome to make. Choose the answer that makes you most comfortable."

"May I have another drink?"

"Of course, help yourself."

Romeo stood, picked up the bottle of Gusano Rojo and pushed it with all of his strength into the Big Chief's face. The glass shattered and cut into Catalina's nose, cheeks, and chin. Romeo picked up the largest piece and stabbed both of the man's eyes, then jammed the jagged edge into his throat and tore it open. Blood gushed out of the Big Chief's face and neck, but he made no noise other than a slight gurgle before collapsing to the floor behind his desk. Romeo leaned over him and saw the mezcal worm lying on the floor. He picked up the worm and dropped it into Catalina's mouth.

"There you go, *macho*," Romeo said. "You've proved your manhood now."

"We're not staying for dinner," Romeo said as he took Estrellita's arm and lifted her to her feet. "Come on, Perdita, Duane. I just heard the food here's not so good."

FLIGHT

Due to the powder burns, Woody Dumas had most of the left side of his head covered with a gauze bandage. Firing the gun so close to his face had left him at least temporarily deaf in his left ear. Woody was on a plane to Los Angeles, slumped in a window seat sipping orange juice, thinking about his life, which had almost been squeezed out of him by Provino "The Fist" Momo in a Dallas alley.

It wasn't really so terrible, he figured. Look at the situation in Eastern Europe, where so many people are desperate to escape to the West, leaving behind them possessions, parents, even children in their feverish rush to freedom. Or in China, with the soldiers shooting students down like dogs in Tiananmen Square. The government here had done that, too, of course, back in the sixties, and the Mexicans murdered dozens in '68 before the Olympics. Person-to-person violence is never as horrifying as faceless, wholesale slaughter, Woody decided, not ultimately. As gruesome and senseless as some individual murders are, he thought, the impersonality of mass maiming and killing is sordid and perverse beyond belief.

Woody remembered an old guy named Buzzard who used to hang around the neighborhood when Woody was a kid. Buzzard was almost a bum, but not quite. He fixed zippers and did some sewing for people, so Woody figured he must have been a tailor at one time in his life. Buzzard always had about ten days' growth of whiskers sticking out of his long, mule-like face, and he walked around flapping his arms as if they were wings, which was why everyone called him Buzzard.

He wore a red-and-black-checkered lumberjack coat that obviously had never been cleaned, and a blue peaked cap with earmuff flaps tied together on top. His eyes, Woody recalled, were clear green with black specks in them. Nobody knew where Buzzard slept until he was found poisoned to death in an unused trash bin behind the public library. He'd been drinking black liquid Shinola shoe polish, using a slice of Wonder bread as a filter, pouring the Shinola through the bread into a coffee can. The only other thing in the trash bin with Buzzard's body was a dog-eared hardcover copy of the 1914 A. L. Burt Company edition of *Tarzan of the Apes* by Edgar Rice Burroughs, which was tucked like a pillow under Buzzard's head.

A stewardess came by with a cart and said something to Woody. He turned his head so that he could listen with the good ear and asked her what she'd said.

"May I bring you another orange juice?" she asked.

"Sure, sure, I'd like that," Woody said, handing her his plastic cup. Then he had another thought. "Oh, miss? Could you please make this one a screwdriver?"

She nodded, refilled the cup with juice, and gave it back to Woody along with a miniature bottle of Wolfschmidt. He paid her, unscrewed the cap and poured the contents into the orange juice, mixing it around with the index finger of his right hand. Woody had not drunk an alcoholic beverage in nearly a decade and he wasn't certain why he'd decided to do so now; it just seemed like the right thing to do. Woody lifted the cup.

"For Buzzard," he said.

Perdita didn't like what was happening. She was pleased to be going to Los Angeles, but she knew already that it was over between her and Romeo. She wouldn't say

anything yet, just let the deal go down and pick her spot to split. Maybe take care of this Estrellita bitch before then.

"What's on your indecent little mind tonight, honey?" asked Romeo. "You been awful quiet lately."

Romeo and Perdita were at the Round-up Drive-in in Yuma, waiting at the take-away counter for their order. They'd left Duane and Estrellita tied up together back in the motel room.

"Nothin' much, tell the truth. Just appreciatin' the beautiful evenin'."

Cars and trucks zoomed by on the street in front of the drive-in. The air was sickly warm and sticky and stank of burnt oil. A grayish haze hung like a soiled sheet across the sky. The breeze kicked at a corner of it now and again, wrinkling the gray just long enough to permit a peek at the twinkling platinum dots decorating the furious fuchsia. A tall, lean, cowboy-looking guy in his late twenties walked up to the take-out window.

"How you people doin' tonight?" he said.

"Not bad," said Romeo. "Yourself?"

The cowboy took off his black Stetson, reached into it and took out a half-empty pack of unfiltered Luckies. He offered it to Romeo and Perdita, both of whom declined, then shook one between his lips, flipped the pack back in and replaced the hat over his thick, tangled dark-brown hair.

"Can't complain," he said, and pulled a book of matches from the left breast pocket of his maroon pearl-buttoned shirt and lit the cigarette. He bent down a little and looked in the window.

"Hey, Betsy!" he called. "How about a couple double-cheeseburgers and a side of chili and slaw."

"Be a few minutes, Cal," a woman shouted from within. "You want any fries with that?"

"Why not?" said Cal. "I'll take whatever you got to give, Betsy."

The woman laughed and yelled back, "Oh, hush! You know that bar talk don't cut it with me."

Cal smiled and straightened up. He stood off to the side of the window away from Romeo and Perdita and puffed on the Lucky Strike.

"So what's doin' in Yuma these days?" asked Romeo.

Cal looked at him and said, "That your Cherokee there, with the Texas plates?"

"That's right."

"You all from Texas, then?"

"Right again."

"Passin' through, I suppose."

"You got it."

"Headed for California, I bet. L.A."

"You're on the money tonight, cowboy."

Cal laughed, took a last drag, and tossed away the butt.

"Not a whole lot to keep people here, I don't guess," he said. "It ain't the most excitin' city in the world."

"Nothin' wrong with peace and quiet, that's what you want."

"Ain't much of that here, either. Heat gets people mean, fries their brains and makes 'em dangerous. Tough on every livin' thing except salamanders."

"Salamanders?" said Perdita.

"Yeah," said Cal, "you know, them lizards can withstand fire."

An eighteen-wheeler downshifted and belched as it passed by, spewing a brown cloud of diesel smoke over the drive-in. Perdita coughed and turned away.

"Here's your order, sir," Betsy said to Romeo from the window, shoving it through. "Be $17.25."

Betsy was a middle-aged Asian woman with badly bleached blond hair.

Romeo put a twenty down on the counter, picked up the bag, and said, "Change is yours."

" 'Preciate it and come back now. Yours is comin' up, handsome," she said to Cal.

"I ain't goin' nowhere."

"No kiddin'," she said, and laughed.

"You folks take care now," Cal said to Romeo and Perdita.

"Do our best," said Romeo. "You, too."

Driving back to the motel, Perdita said, "You get a good look at that gal back there?"

"You mean Betsy?"

"Woman had the worst hair, Jesus. Never saw no Oriental person with blond hair before."

"Plenty more surprises where we're headed, Perdita. Just you wait. I got big plans for us."

She turned and stared at Romeo. He was grinning, confident, full of himself.

"Don't make me no promises you can't keep," Perdita said. "There ain't nothin' worse for a woman than a man punks out on her. That happens, no tellin' what she'll do."

"I'll keep this in mind, sweet thing," said Romeo, nodding and grinning, "I surely will."

"E. T. Satisfy, is it? Hometown, Dallas."

"Right the first time."

The clerk looked up from the registration card across

the desk and down at Ernest Tubb.

"How you mean to pay for this?"

"Cash," said Ernest Tubb, handing the clerk a hundred dollar bill.

The clerk took it, examined both sides, went into another room for a minute, then came back and gave Ernest Tubb his change plus a receipt and a room key.

"You got 237. Upstairs and around to the right. Ice and soda pop machines by the staircase. Need more you holler."

"I'm obliged."

In the room the first thing he did was phone home.

"Glory Ann? It's me, Ernest Tubb."

"Just where in Judas's country are you?" she asked. "I been worried crazy!"

"Easy, woman. I'm at the Holiday on Madre Island. Got a lead in Larry Lee County that Estelle and Duane Orel mighta come down here. College kids on break partyin' both sides of the border. Heard about two were kidnapped a week ago. Might be them. I'm headed for Mextown soon's I hang up."

"Kidnapped! Save Jesus! Rita Louise Samples is here with me now, and Marfa Acker's comin' back later. They been my cross and crutch since you disappeared on me."

"I ain't disappeared. I told you, I'm huntin' for Estelle."

"If I lose you, too, don't know what I'll do."

"You ain't lost nothin', Glory, includin' weight. You stickin' to that lima bean diet Dr. Breaux put you on?"

"Ernest Tubb, be serious! Who can think about dietin' at a time like this?"

"I am serious, Glory Ann. You keep eatin' like a herd of javelinas cut loose in a Arby's and you'll flat explode! Rita Louise and Marfa be scrapin' your guts off the kitchen walls and collectin' 'em in a box to bury. You keep clear of them coffeecakes, hear?"

Glory Ann began to cry.

"Oh, Ernest Tubb, you're just a mean tiny man."

"Lima beans, Glory Ann, Lima beans," he said, and hung up.

Ernest Tubb backed his Continental out of the parking space, drove to the motel lot exit and turned right. He was thinking about the last time he and Glory Ann had made love. She'd insisted on being on top and just about squashed him. He'd felt like he imagined those people in their cars felt when that freeway fell on them during the big quake in California.

It was several seconds before Ernest Tubb realized that he'd turned his Mark IV in the wrong direction on a one-way thoroughfare. By the time he saw the nose of the White Freightliner and heard the horn blast it was too late for him to do anything about it.

"Oh, Glory!" Ernest Tubb said, and then he was history.

"You understand what has to be done?"

"I do."

"You have no problem about it?"

BACK AT

THE NURSERY

Reggie hesitated, then shook his head no.

"Good."

Santos poured more Glenmorangie into his glass, swirled the brown liquid around and stared down into it.

"You and your cousin have been close friends, have you not?"

"We were raised together as boys, but then Romeo and his mother left Caribe. Since then we are in touch."

Santos took off his yellow-framed sunglasses and set them on the table. He rubbed his eyes with his abbreviated left hand, then smoothed back his hair. He looked at Reginald San Pedro Sula, who wanted to turn away from the two small darting animals imprisoned in Marcello's face, but Reggie steeled himself and did not flinch. Santos's eyes were the color of Christmas trees on fire.

"It's not that there is anything personal in this," Santos said, "but Romeo has done some terrible things, things so terrible that not even the Mexican authorities can allow him to operate there any longer. I have sent some people in to take care of the situation in Zopilote. From now on we will handle the business. It was necessary to remove your cousin from the area in order to effect the change. In the meantime, he does us the favor of transporting other goods for us, for which he is fairly compensated. After the delivery is secured, you will pay him the remainder of what we have agreed, and then you will kill him."

Santos lifted his glass with the fingers and opposing digit of his right hand and drank most of the Scotch in it.

"After Romeo is dead, of course," he said, "the money is no good to him, so you will take it as payment for doing me this favor."

"That is most generous of you," said Reggie.

Santos closed his eyes and shook his head.

"Not generous, Reggie—just. There is a difference."

He reopened his eyes and put his sunglasses back on. Reggie relaxed, taking off his powder-blue porkpie hat and wiping the sweat from his bald head with a lime-green handkerchief.

"Deception is merely a tool of resourcefulness," said Santos. "Have you ever heard of Captain Philippe Legorjus?"

"I don't believe so, sir."

"Well, he is the commander of France's elite anti-terrorist forces. Not long ago he was sent by his government to New Caledonia, which is in the South Pacific, to quell an uprising by the Kanak rebels on the island of Ouvea. New Caledonia is part of the French Overseas Territories, and so it was necessary to protect the French citizens who live there. It is also the place from which the French conduct their nuclear tests.

"In any case, Captain Legorjus was kidnapped by the rebels, along with twenty-two others. The leader of the Kanak Socialist National Liberation Front, I believe it was called, was something of a religious fanatic, and had been trained for guerilla warfare in Libya by Khadafy. This man vowed to maintain a state of permanent insecurity in the French South Pacific Territory if the separatists' demands for independence were not met. A familiar story. I remember a newspaper photograph of him, wearing a hood and holding a rifle, the pockets of his field jacket stuffed with cartridges. He threatened to kill a white person a day so long as the French government occupied Noumea, the capital of New Caledonia.

"While the Kanak leader carried on making speeches to the press, Legorjus organized the hostages and not only led them to freedom but took control of the separatist stronghold, disarmed the rebel soldiers, and captured their leader, enabling several hundred French naval infantrymen to swarm in and restore order. Upon his return to Paris, Legorjus was accorded a parade down the Champs d'Elysées and declared a national hero."

Santos paused and looked at Reggie, who smiled and said, "He must be a brave man, this captain."

Santos nodded. "Brave and cunning, Reggie. I make a point of studying these kinds of extraordinary men. There is much to be learned from their behavior. My firm belief is that life must be lived according to a man's own terms, or else it is probably not worth living."

"I am sure you are right, Mr. Santos."

Marcello licked the stub on his left hand where his thumb had been.

"I know you will do a good job for me," he said, walking over to the window and looking out at the sky.

"Ah, *si sta facendo scuro*," Santos said. "It's getting dark. You know, Reggie, I am almost seventy years old, and despite all I know, there is still nothing I can do about that."

Woody looked out at the swimming pool. There were three kids and a dog in it, a golden retriever. Apparently the motel people didn't mind that the dog was swim-

ming. He'd been in there for at least fifteen minutes and nobody had said anything about it. California was a different world, anyway, Woody thought. Maybe the animal rights group had successfully lobbied for legislation allowing dogs to use motel pools.

The Wild Palms Motel, where Woody Dumas was staying, was in the middle of Hollywood, one block south of Sunset. It was not the kind of place Woody thought he could ever get used to, let alone like. The weather was good enough, he supposed, but the people in L.A. had a way of talking that put him off. It was as if they were convinced everything they said either had a deeper meaning or meant something other than what Woody thought they were saying. Maybe it was the spectre of the film industry that made everyone want to feel as if they belonged in it, like a club, and were therefore integral to the machinery of the place. He couldn't quite put his finger on it, but whatever it was, Woody didn't get it.

Not that it mattered, anyway. Woody was in town to do a job, and tonight he would be staked out across the street from a warehouse on Ivar just off Hollywood Boulevard, a few blocks from the Wild Palms, awaiting the arrival of a shipment of illicit skin. According to the best information available to the various authorities, Crazy Eyes Santos was operating cosmetics factories on the West Coast, using wetbacks to do most of the work.

Seizing a delivery of the proportion expected tonight or tomorrow would be a major step in cracking the operation.

Woody decided to have lunch and then come back to the motel and take a nap. He walked past the swimming pool on the way to his car and noticed a beautiful young woman sitting in a lounge chair dedicatedly applying suntan lotion to herself. She had long blond hair, a slender figure and very long legs. She wore an orange, tiger-striped bikini and oversized blue sunglasses, the frames of which were shaped like butterfly wings. The golden retriever had his paws up on the side of the pool in front of the young woman and was barking excitedly in her direction. A terrifically fat man wearing a pair of lavender Bermuda shorts and nothing else to cover his vast, very pale expanse of skin, came out and jumped into the pool, displacing no small amount of water, most of which splashed on the young woman, disturbing her ministrations.

"Marv, you fat piece of pigshit!" she screamed, jumping up. "Did you have to do that?!"

The golden retriever clambered out of the pool and shook himself furiously right next to her.

"Goddammit!" she said, throwing her plastic bottle of lotion at the dog, somehow missing him by a good six feet. "This is going to be a great fucking time!"

Woody continued to the parking lot, unlocked the government K-car, got in and started it. He decided to drive out to Santa Monica, to the ocean. It might be nice, Woody thought, to buy a sandwich and sit and look at the water for a while.

He'd eaten half of a BLT and was sipping from a can of Canada Dry ginger ale through a straw, when a tall, gaunt-faced man who looked to be in his mid-forties, sat down on the bench next to Woody. The tall man, Woody thought, resembled the actor John Carradine, but a beaten-down, hard-luck version; more the way Carradine looked as the ex-preacher in the movie of *The Grapes of Wrath*. The man's clothes were shabby, worn-out, and he needed a shave, but he held himself erect and gave the appearance of being at ease.

"Do you mind if I speak to you?" the man said.

"No," said Woody.

The man stared at Woody and examined the gauze bandages. His eyes were black, without light. When he spoke, Woody noticed that several of his teeth were missing.

"You've been injured."

"Burned," Woody said.

"I hope you're not too uncomfortable."

"I'm doing fine, thanks."

W
A
V
E
S

o

1

0

7

The man turned his face back toward the ocean.

"Waves are the heartbeat of the earth," he said.

"That's not bad," said Woody. "I like that."

"I used to be a poet. A singer, too, in nightclubs. I sang the songs I wrote. But no longer."

"Why'd you stop?"

"You probably think I'm an alcoholic, or a drug addict, but I'm not. I like to have a martini now and then, of course, and I've sampled drugs, but they're not to blame for my condition, which, as you can see, is less than glamorous. I just lost interest in life, that's what happened. There's nobody to blame, not even myself. I'm not crazy, either. At least I don't think I am. One day the carriage stopped for me and I waved it on."

"Are you hungry?" Woody asked. "You can have this half of my sandwich, if you like."

The man took the sandwich from Woody and held it in his lap.

"You're very gracious," he said. "Are you a religious person?"

"Not really, no."

"Neither am I, never have been. Organized religion is unseemly."

"Here, you can have the rest of this, too," said Woody, handing the man the can of ginger ale.

Woody stood up. "I've got to go."

"I know, your carriage is here."

Woody laughed. "I suppose it is."

"You understand," said the man, "it's not as if I had no choice."

"I believe you," Woody said, watching the man bite into the sandwich.

"Hey, buddy, it's been a long time!"

"Too long, I guess."

Doug Fakaofo and Romeo hugged each other and smiled.

"I was glad to hear you were comin' out," said Doug. "What brings you?"

"Business, what else these days, huh? Not that we can't put in some good party time, too, of course," laughed Romeo.

"That's great, man!"

"But I got a favor to ask you, Doug. I got some people with me and I want to leave 'em here while I take care of something. It shouldn't take long, maybe only a couple of hours. We're just in off the road and they'll prob'ly sleep for a while anyway."

"Hey, you know it's no problem. They'll be safe here. Bring 'em into the house."

"Thanks, man. I knew I could count on you."

"Any time."

Romeo had spoken to Lily Fakaofo, Doug's wife, from a pay phone in El Centro. Doug was out at the time, but Lily had told Romeo they'd be happy to see him. The Fakaofos lived in Hacienda Heights, a largely Samoan-American section of Los Angeles. The Samoan community was a tight one, distrustful of mainstream America; they kept mostly to themselves. Not even the police knew much about the people there, and Romeo figured it would be a perfect place to stash Estrellita and Duane while he and Perdita delivered the shipment to Reggie in Hollywood.

Doug "Big Brown" Fakaofo had been in the Marines with Romeo, and they'd kept in touch. The Fakaofos were heavy reefer users and they greatly appreciated the kilos Romeo sent them via UPS from Texas on their birthdays and at Christmastime. Both Doug and Lily were large individuals, Doug going about two-eighty and Lily a nifty two-ten or so. Lily's brother, Tutu Nukuono, whom Romeo had met only once, weighed well over three hundred pounds. Tutu had worked as a plumber with Doug until a few months before, when he beat a cop to death with a chain during a brawl in the parking lot of the Moonlight Lagoon, a local bar that catered mainly to Pacific islanders. Tutu was now serving a life sentence without possibility of parole at Folsom.

"I sure was sorry to hear about your brother, Lily," Romeo said. "He's a good kid."

Lily shrugged. "He shoulda known better than to stomp a uniform. Him and a bunch of his biker buddies got carried away wailin' on some Devil's Dragons, I guess it was, who'd strayed into the neighborhood."

"White boys lookin' for strange-colored pussy," said Doug. "They got into it with Tutu's gang, the cops come, one of the blues tangled with Tutu, and that was it. Only reason he didn't get the gas was there weren't no way they could prove premeditation."

"Well, I know Folsom ain't no picnic," said Romeo.

Doug nodded. "Yeah, but Tutu already got himself some friends inside. Anybody can handle it, he will. Let's go get your people."

Lily told Romeo she'd feed Duane and Estrellita, then lock them in the back bedroom, the one Tutu had used. Doug volunteered to ride shotgun for Romeo in the truck; Perdita would follow them in the Cherokee and they'd all drive back together to Hacienda Heights.

"She's some tough, sexy-lookin' lady, that Perdita," Doug said to Romeo as they headed off to deliver the goods.

Romeo grinned. "Think she's a keeper, do ya?"

Doug laughed. "Guess I could keep her occupied for a hour or few, I concentrated hard enough," he said.

"Never doubted you for a minute, Big Brown. Perdita Durango's somethin' all right. Picked her up at a fruitshake stand in New Orleans. The creature's got a mind of her own, though, you know?"

"Just have to be sure she don't stay awake longer'n you do, she's angry about somethin'. Some women you need to watch like that. Lily's on my side all the way, always has been."

"You're a lucky fellow, Doug. Stay that way."

"Tryin' to. What you plan to do with those kids?"

"It's a good question. Think we've squeezed just about all the use out of 'em. They've seen too much to cut loose. I'll deal with that pretty quick, soon as this is finished."

Romeo kept checking in the sideview for Perdita. She stayed right behind them all the way. When Romeo brought the truck to a stop in front of the warehouse on Ivar, Perdita drove the Cherokee past it and parked a half-block up the street. Doug and Romeo got out and Romeo walked over and knocked on the side door of the building.

"*Hola, primo!* You made it okay, I see," said Reggie, after opening the door. "Come on in."

"I have a friend with me. This is Doug Fakaofo. You remember I told you about him, Reggie. 'Big Brown.' He was with me in Beirut."

"Of course," Reggie said, shaking hands with Doug. "Come in."

As soon as the door closed, Woody Dumas got out of the K-car and motioned with his right arm to the men on the roof of the building next to the warehouse. At that moment, a dozen vehicles, carrying both federal and local law enforcement personnel, converged on the street, entering from either end. Two men used a battering ram on the door, which easily gave way, and most of the rest of them, led by Woody Dumas, ran in single file.

Woody saw Reginald San Pedro Sula, dressed in a blue denim leisure suit and wearing a Los Angeles Dodgers baseball cap, fire two rounds from a .45 automatic; the first into the forehead of Romeo Dolorosa, the second into the left temple of Doug Fakaofo, killing each of them instantly.

"Federal agents!" Woody shouted, as the men surrounded the shooter.

Reggie dropped the gun and raised his hands. He started to smile, but before he could complete it several men grabbed him and threw him to the ground, causing his head to bang against the concrete floor. Woody knelt by the men who had been shot, verifying that they were dead. The forehead wound in the smaller of the two looked large enough for a decent-sized sewer rat to crawl through. The man's mouth was open and Woody could not help but be impressed by his extraordinarily large, perfectly formed teeth that even in death radiated a powerful white light.

Lily Fakaofo was up late, sitting at the kitchen table reading the newspaper, listening to the 24-hour news station on the radio, smoking a cigarette and working

AFTER HOURS

her way through the second box of Nilla Wafers she'd eaten since Doug, Romeo, and Perdita had left two and a half hours before. Estrellita and Duane were asleep in Tutu's room.

"From Harare, Zimbabwe, comes this story," said the radio. "The Zimbabwe Football Association banned four players for life yesterday for publicly urinating on the field at a Harare soccer stadium. Association chairman Nelson Chirwa said the organization was appalled by the behavior last Sunday of the four players of the southern Tongogara team. 'It is a public indecency for a player to openly urinate on the football pitch,' Chirwa said. 'We all know that it is all superstition and that the belief in juju that almost all the clubs have taken to believe in is strongly deplored by the association.' He said the four were advised to urinate on the field by witch doctors, who said it would ensure a victory. It didn't. Tongogara lost, two to nothing."

Lily laughed and took a puff on her Bel-Air Menthol Slim. Doug had told her that he thought Romeo Dolorosa was mixed up with some kind of voodoo cult down in Mexico or Texas, but she didn't want to know about it. There was enough real mysterious shit going down in the world, Lily thought, without getting sucked into that phony black magic crap. Take this strange business in Russia she was reading about.

A forty-two-year-old French-Armenian multimillionaire art dealer, who was also a well-known poet, had disappeared in Moscow five months ago. He'd been having a meeting with three Soviet business associates in his hotel room near Red Square when he received a telephone call. He spoke briefly to the caller, hung up, and told his associates to wait there, that he had to go out but would return within the hour. They saw him get into a black Zhiguli limousine and speed away, and that's the last anyone had seen or heard of him, including his family in Paris.

Police, KGB agents, and the Soviet government, specifically the Visual Arts Department of the Cultural Affairs Ministry, with whom he'd had dealings for several years, were pursuing the case. Speculation was that with the restructuring of the Soviet society and increasing entrepreneurial climate, the art dealer had engaged in unlawful export of Russian Ortho-dox icons and other art items in league with the various crime organi-zations operating throughout the Soviet Union. Authorities in Moscow were paying particularly close attention to the case because of their feeling that it could lead to the exposure of a homegrown Mafia.

According to an official in the Department of Cultural Affairs, this art dealer was a clever man who spoke several languages fluently, had a wide variety of friends in many countries, was very confident and thought there was nothing he couldn't handle. He had made his millions in a very short period of time, a decade or so, having started out with next to nothing in a small Paris gallery. His family were convinced that he had no dealings with gangsters.

Those involved in the investigation theorized that the art dealer had become enmeshed in a power struggle among the seven major Moscow Mafia families, and found himself in a situation he could not handle; or, that he had simply been double-crossed and disposed of. Another rumor circulating in Armenia and Paris held that he had been selling artworks to the Soviet government itself, that a number of the items were revealed to be forgeries, and he had been killed by the KGB, who dumped his body in a forest outside Moscow. This version maintained that the body had been discovered five days after his disappearance, and the family was fostering the pretense that they had heard nothing from or about him in an effort not to discredit the gallery or his reputation. It was, therefore, a mystery that might never be solved.

"Ha!" said Lily, turning the page. "Another hotshot too smart for his own good."

Lily wolfed down another Nilla Wafer and stretched her back. She figured Doug might stay out partying with Romeo and Perdita after they'd delivered whatever it was they had, and she was thinking that she might just as well go to bed, when the radio brought her up short.

"In Hollywood tonight, a gun battle left two men dead and resulted in the capture of another by federal drug agents, the FBI and the Los Angeles County Sheriff's Department. An illegal cosmetics factory, specializing in the use of unauthorized products and operated in central Hollywood by organized crime, was raided at midnight during a delivery of approximately one solid ton of human placentas. Authorities identified the dead men as Romeo Dolorosa, of Tampa, Florida, and Douglas Fakaofo, of Los Angeles. The man taken into custody was identified as Reginald San Pedro Sula, a citizen of the Central American republic of Caribe. All of the men are suspected members of the crime family headed by Marcello 'Crazy Eyes' Santos, which is based in New Orleans, Louisiana, and Dallas, Texas. According to Drug Enforcement Special Agent Woodrow W. Dumas, who led the raid, seizure of the two thousand pound shipment of placentas, used in the manufacture of anti-aging skin creams, and discovery of the illegal plant is a major breakthrough. More arrests are expected. Well, folks, that's another kind of Hollywood skin factory, isn't it?"

Lily dropped both her cigarette and the cookie she'd just taken from the box and stood up, knocking over her chair. She rushed to the rear bedroom, unlocked the door and flipped on the light.

"Get up! Get up now!" she screamed at Estrellita and Duane, who were huddled together on the bed. "Get up and get out! Get out of the house! Go, go!"

Estrellita and Duane ran out into the night, taking off down the street as fast as they could. Lily collapsed on the floor of Tutu's room.

"Doug!" she cried. "Doug, you big brown dummy! You poor, big, beautiful, dead dummy! What's your ugly old Samoan mama Lily gonna do now?"

As soon as Frankie Toro spotted the woman he pulled his metallic cherry Lexus to the curb, leaned over and lowered the window on the passenger side. She was

LATE DATE

leaning against a mud-encrusted black Jeep parked in the space closest to the street in the lot of an Oki-Dog on Santa Monica Boulevard, holding a soft drink cup and smoking a cigarette.

This was easily the hottest-looking chick Frankie Toro had seen that night. Twenty-two or three, he figured, about five-six, a hundred and ten, hard body, shiny black hair almost to her ass, skin like *café con leche*. A genuine *chicana* doll. She reminded Frankie of Tura Sultana, that steel-cheekboned, *nagual*-eyed, Japanese-Cherokee leather bitch he'd seen in Russ Meyer's desert chase tit movie, *Faster Pussycat, Kill! Kill!*

"Hey, *guapita*," Frankie yelled to her, "you want a date?"

Perdita picked up her bag and slung it over her left shoulder, then walked slowly to the Lexus and looked at the grinning, eager idiot. She smiled at him, stretching the cobras. Frankie pushed open the door.

"Been dyin' for you to ask," she said, and slid in.

"Mama?"

"Estelle? Is that you? This is Rita Louise."

"Oh, Mrs. Samples. Is my mama there?"

LIGHT IN

THE FOREST

"No, honey, no, she's down at the funeral home, makin' the arrangements. She's been out of her mind worried about you. Where've you been? Are you all right?"

"What arrangements, Mrs. Samples? Why's she at a funeral home?"

"Oh, my word, Estelle. Of course, you wouldn't know."

"Know what? What wouldn't I know?"

"Your daddy, Estelle, honey. Ernest Tubb. He got kilt in a car crash on Madre Island. The body just arrived today."

"Car crash? Daddy's gone?"

Estelle dropped the phone, fell to the floor of the booth and fainted dead away.

"Estelle? Estelle, are you there?" Rita Louise's voice jumped out of the dangling receiver.

Duane half-lifted Estelle with his right arm and put the telephone to his left ear.

"Mrs. Samples? It's Duane Orel. Estelle's sorta passed out here. Just tell Glory Ann we're safe now, we got away, and if she could to please wire us the airfare to come home."

"I will, Duane, of course, but where are you?"

"Los Angeles, California, ma'am. Western Union downtown'll do. We'll head there soon as Estelle comes to. We been hidin' in the bushes all night."

"Goodness, Duane, isn't life a mess sometimes."

"Yes, ma'am. You'll pardon me sayin' this, but shit happens."

Santos hung up but kept his right hand on the telephone. He groaned and pressed his lips tightly together.

"Bad news, huh, Marcello?"

THE OLD

TESTAMENT

He sat back in a leather armchair and looked through his dark glasses across the room at Mona Costatroppo, who was perched on a white satin loveseat, her freshly shaved and lotioned legs tucked back under her spreading rump. She had on a low-cut black dress and a single strand of pearls that Santos had bought for her at Cartier in New York. They had cost him nine thousand dollars, Marcello recalled. Mona had a drink in one hand, an unlit black cigarette in the other. She always had a drink in her hand, Santos thought.

"*Una pioggia continua*," he said.

"What now?"

"What now? Now is as before. All fucked up. First, it was Dede. Then *Il Pugno*, The Fist, who we send to hit and who himself gets hit. Now, Reggie, along with the West Coast factory."

"Who Reggie? You mean the *tutsun* from Puerto Rico?"

"Caribe, not Puerto Rico. Caribe."

Mona swallowed a mouthful of gin.

"You drink too much," said Santos. "You're getting fat, too."

"Like Lina, you mean," Mona said. "You got a fat wife, you don't want a fat girlfriend, too, huh? You gonna dump me, Marcello? Is that what you want to do?"

Santos removed his hand from the phone, formed it like a gun, with the third finger and pinkie folded back, the thumb up, and the index and second fingers pointed at Mona. She froze.

"Bang," he said.

"Hear you had a good trip."

"Don't know about good, Doyle. Successful, anyway. We got what we went for. That L.A. is a whole other state of mind, though."

"Didn't lose anyone, either, they tell me."

BACK FROM

ETERNITY

"No white hats, but I woulda preferred to've brought in the delivery boys. Santos's trigger man took 'em both out before we got there."

"Why you suppose they whacked Dolorosa?"

"Santos set him up. Crazy Eyes controls the border and Dolorosa got the area freaked out with his *santería* routine. Killing the boy was the last straw far as Santos was concerned."

"Kidnapped two college kids, too. They turned up in L.A., you know that?"

"Only heard about it after I got back to Dallas. What'd they have to say about Perdita Durango?"

"Didn't want to talk about her much, just said she's plenty weird and dangerous. They're pretty shook. The girl's father was killed in a car wreck while she was gone, which doesn't help. Happened while he was out huntin' for her, apparently."

"That's rough, all right. What's her name?"

"Satisfy. Estelle Kenedy Satisfy. His is Duane Orel King."

"That Satisfy sounds familiar, but I can't place it just now."

"Well, Woodrow, I got to run. Hell of a job, bud."

"*Gracias*, señor."

"Oh, by the way, how's your hearing?"

"Back in stereo."

"*Bueno*. Be talkin' to ya."

Tattooed on the bicep of Shorty's left arm were the words ONE LIFE ONE WIFE and tattooed on his right bicep was the name CHERRY ANN.

59° AND RAINING

IN TUPELO

"That her?" Perdita asked him.

"Who?" said Shorty.

"Cherry Ann your wife's name?"

"Was."

"She change it?"

Shorty laughed and shook his head no.

"Changed wives," he said.

"Kinda puts the lie to your other arm, don't it?"

Shorty yawned and closed his eyes. He opened them and picked up his glass and took a long swallow of Pearl.

"Ain't nothin' stays similar, sweetheart, let alone the same. Or ain't you figured that out yet?"

Perdita Durango and Shorty Dee were sitting on adjacent stools at the bar of Dottie's Tupelo Lounge. It was eight-thirty on Friday night, December thirtieth. Oklahoma State was playing Wyoming in the Sea World Holiday Bowl football game on the television set above the bar.

"Know what I like to watch more than anything else?" Shorty said.

"Not knowin' you any better than I do, which is not at all practically," said Perdita, "I'd be afraid to ask."

"Punt returns."

"That so."

"Yeah. Some people it's triples. Me it's punt returns. I like any kind of runbacks: kickoffs, interceptions, fumbles. But there's somethin' special about a little jackrabbit of a guy takin' a tall ball and turnin' on his jets."

Shorty took another sip of beer.

"You been in town long?" he asked.

"Few days."

"How's it goin' so far?"

"Been rainin' since I got here. Weather always like this?"

"Time of year it is. Fifty-nine and rainin' sounds about right for Christmas."

"What else Tupelo got to offer?"

"Other than bein' the birthplace of Elvis Presley, you mean?"

Perdita laughed. She swept back her long, straight black hair with one hand and picked up her glass with the other.

"Didn't know about Elvis bein' born in Miss'ippi," she said, and took a sip of beer.

"Where you from?" asked Shorty.

"Here and there. Texas, mostly."

"Brings you this way?"

"Lookin' for somethin', I guess."

Shorty offered his right hand.

"Shorty Dee. Glad to be of service if I can."

She squeezed his fingers.

"Perdita Durango. Pleased to meet you, Shorty. You still married?"

Shorty laughed. "Thought we was beginnin' a conversation here."

Perdita smiled. "How about buyin' me a new beer?"

"Now you're talkin', honey," he said, signaling for another round. "Got any more potentially embarrassin' questions you want to get out of the way?"

"You rich?"

The bartender set two more bottles on the bar in front of them.

Shorty laughed again. "Nigger rich, maybe," he said.

"Bein' nigger rich is all right, I guess," said Perdita, "long as a body got enough friends is rich for damn sure."

They picked up the fresh bottles of beer and tapped them together.

"There you go," said Shorty.

Perdita smiled. "Here I go," she said.

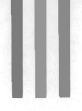

SAILOR'S
HOLIDAY

A woman in a red dress came in the door unsteadily. "Whoopee," she said, "so long, Red. He'll be in hell before I could even reach Little Rock."

WILLIAM FAULKNER, SANCTUARY

III

"Mama, I do appreciate all you been doin' for me, you know that."

"Listen, Lula, you can't go on workin' in a 7-Eleven

LULA CALLS

like this. You're too smart to be wastin' your time sellin' Slurpees to high school kids and cans of King Cobra to drunks. I don't mind supplementin' your income, 'specially where Pace is concerned, long as I got it to give. But you can do somethin' better with your life."

Marietta Fortune took a big sip of Martini & Rossi sweet vermouth and raised her eyebrows as she looked at her friend Dalceda Delahoussaye, who sat across from her at the patio table sipping the same. Marietta wanted Dal to know how exasperated she was by her daughter's seeming dearth of ambition.

"Well, Pace'll be out of school next week," said Lula, "and I gotta figure out what to do with him for the summer. I can't very well start on a new career with a ten year old trailin' after me."

"*New?* You ain't never had one career yet, Lula, and here you are thirty years old."

"Twenty-nine and a half, Mama. Keep it accurate."

Marietta took another sip. "You could get married."

Dal frowned at Marietta and shook her head side to side in disapproval.

"Okay, Mama, I can see where this conversation's headin', and I ain't goin' along with it. Far as that's concerned, you might be considerin' it yourself. Johnnie's still willin'."

"Lula, we're not discussin' me. It's your life got to be lived."

Lula laughed. "Mama, you ain't fifty till tomorrow and

127

you talk like you got one foot and four toes in the grave. Look, I gotta go pick up Pace. We'll be over around noon for your birthday. Say hi to Dal if she's still there. Bye."

Marietta hung up and sighed.

"You and that girl don't never give each other a smidge of space," said Dal. "Why don't you just pretend to be the mature one and back off a spell, let Lula work her life out her own way."

"Oh, she's done great this far, Dal, ain't she? Lula's approachin' middle-age and all she's got's an illegitimate child can't sit still for more'n two minutes 'cause he ain't never had no man around, and no prospects of any kind I can tell. I'm supposed to be comfortable with that?"

"Marietta, you're in a state for nothin'."

The telephone rang and Marietta picked up the receiver.

"Yes?"

As soon as Marietta heard who it was she sat up straighter in her chair and her face lost most of its wrinkles.

"Why, Marcello, what a surprise. Uh huh, I think so. I certainly don't see why not. Around twelve-thirty would be fine. I'm already lookin' forward to it. Thank you for thinkin' of me. Oh, you're awful sweet. Bye, now."

Marietta hung up.

"Don't tell me that old gangster Crazy Eyes Santos is comin' here?" said Dalceda.

Marietta nodded. "Tomorrow afternoon, for my birthday. He remembered."

"I just don't plain believe this!" Dal said, setting down her glass on the table. "I thought he'd done a fade after Clyde died."

"He did. I guess he's just sentimental now we're gettin' older."

"Man's a killer, Marietta. He's been runnin' the rackets down here since we was girls together at Miss Cook's in Beaufort. He's married, too, of course. And besides, Johnnie Farragut's comin' tomorrow, ain't he?"

Marietta relaxed, sinking down in her chair and closing her eyes.

"Won't matter."

"The hell it won't. I wouldn't miss this party for the world."

"One thing about the rest of the world, Dal, they don't give a fig about us and they never have. That's why we got to stick together."

Saturday morning it rained. By noon the rain had mostly stopped but the sky stayed grainy and the air was unseasonably cold. Marietta hated birthdays, especially her

own. She'd learned, however, that there was no use denying them, so now she accepted the attention at these little gatherings if only for her grandson's sake. Like most children, Pace just loved birthday parties, and since Lula kept him and events under control, Marietta more or less sat back and endured the goings-on in relatively good humor.

As expected, Pace and Lula were the first to arrive.

"Happy birthday, Marietta!" Pace shouted, as soon as the door opened.

He gave her a hug and Marietta offered him her right cheek to kiss, which he did, and not ungladly, as he sincerely liked his grandmother, the only one he had.

"That's one of the nicest improvements about this boy, Lula, that he don't call me 'Grandmama' any more."

"Why's that, Mama? I thought you liked bein' considered old and put to pasture."

Lula kissed Marietta on the other cheek and handed her a small package wrapped in red and green Christmas paper.

"Sorry about the inappropriate wrappin's," she said, "but it's all I had. Got ten rolls of it for a dollar at the 7-11, left over from last year. Tell me, you want any."

"Open it now, Marietta!" Pace said. "Before anybody else gets here."

"All right, Pace, I'll just do that."

Marietta carefully unwrapped the gift, handing Lula the ribbon and paper to discard.

1
2
9

"Well, my goodness," Marietta said, holding up a matching teacup and saucer. "This is a lovely surprise."

"It's real old, Grandmama—Marietta, I mean. Mama found it in a junk shop."

"Lady said it's two hundred years old, Mama, but it's real pretty, I think."

"Certainly it is. Just look at the gold edges. It's fine China, I can tell. I hope you didn't spend too much on this, Lula. I hear 7-11 wages ain't all that generous."

"Enjoy it, Mama. I'll go see about the cake."

The doorbell rang and Pace said, "I'll get it!"

"Why, hello, honey," Dal said, coming in. "Don't you look handsome today."

"Mama scrubbed me brand clean, Auntie Dal. She says it makes a difference."

Dal laughed. "It can indeed. Hello, Marietta," she said, giving her a hug. "I won't say happy birthday because of your complex."

"What's a complex?" asked Pace.

"A foolishness that's recognized for what it is," said Dal.

"Mama says I'm foolish lots of times."

"That's different, dear," Dal said, "everyone is. You ain't old enough for the other thing yet."

"I ain't old enough for much. When'll I be old enough for a complex?"

"For some it's all too soon and never too late."

"Dal, hush," said Marietta. "Leave the boy be. Pace, you go on in the back, see you can help your mama with things."

Pace walked toward the kitchen and the doorbell rang again. Dal opened the door.

"Afternoon, Dalceda. Am I early or late?"

It was Johnnie Farragut, the private investigator from Charlotte who'd been sweet on Marietta for thirty years.

"You're plumb on time, Johnnie," said Dal. "Marietta's right here."

Johnnie gave Marietta a kiss on the cheek and handed her an envelope.

"Marietta, I ain't much of a shopper, as you know," he said, "but this is a certificate for a subscription to a ladies' magazine I thought you might like to look at while your hair's dryin' or somethin'."

Marietta opened the envelope, took out the certificate and read it.

"*Spiffy*, 'The Magazine for the New Woman.'"

Dal giggled. "See, Marietta, it ain't for *old* women."

"Sounds like the name of a peanut butter," said Lula, coming up to Johnnie and kissing him. "That's so sweet of you, Johnnie. I'm sure Mama'll love readin' it."

"Sure I will," said Marietta, taking one of Johnnie's hands. "It's real thoughtful."

"Prob'ly be a few weeks before the first issue arrives," Johnnie said.

"That won't bother Mama. You're familiar with her gift for patience."

There was a knock on the door and Lula opened it. A short, wide, impeccably dressed man who looked to be about sixty, wearing a black toupee and yellow-framed sunglasses, stood in the doorway holding a large box with both hands. Lula noticed that his left thumb was missing.

"This is the home of Marietta Pace Fortune," he said. It was not a question.

"Yes," said Lula. "Won't you come in?"

The man entered, saw Marietta and went to her.

"Marietta," he said, balancing the box on one knee and bending forward to take in his own and kiss the hand she'd just held Johnnie's in, "you're still a gorgeous woman. Your Clyde, *era nato colla camicia.* He was born lucky to have had you for a wife. But now, of course, he is dead and we are living."

"Clyde been gone a whole lotta years, Marcello," said Marietta. "Why don't you set down that box?"

"Thank you," he said, putting the box on the floor.

Pace came running up.

"Can I open it, Grand—Marietta?"

"In a moment, perhaps," said Marietta. "Marcello, this is my daughter's boy, Pace Roscoe Ripley. And this here's his mama, my precious Lula. This is my oldest and dearest friend, Dalceda Delahoussaye, whom you might remember. And here's Johnnie Farragut, who's in law enforcement over in Charlotte, an old pal of Clyde's. Everyone, this is Mr. Santos."

Santos nodded and smiled at all of them without removing his dark glasses.

"Mr. Santos?" said Pace.

Santos turned to him, smiling.

"Yes, boy?"

"What happened to your thumb?"

Lula almost said something but held her tongue. She wanted to know what had happened to it, too. Marietta, she figured, already knew.

"You really want to know, hey, boy?" said Santos.

Pace looked up at Santos's large, flat red nose and blue lips and nodded.

"Marcello, you don't have to," Marietta said.

He held up the four digits remaining on his left hand.

"When I was only a few years older than you are now," Santos said to Pace, "I worked in a slaughterhouse, where animals are killed and carved up and their body parts packaged to be sold in stores to be eaten.

An older man attacked me because he did not like some things I had said about his work. I had said that he was lazy and a bad worker because he was drunk much of the time, and because of this the rest of us in the slaughterhouse had to work even harder at what already was hard work. The man became enraged and with a hatchet crusted with blood from the animals tried to chop off my left hand. Before he could do it I pulled my hand back and all he got was the thumb."

"I bet you were real angry at him," said Pace.

Santos nodded. "Yes, I was. I was so angry, that even though this man was older and bigger and stronger than I was, I took the hatchet away from him with my other hand and hit him with it between his eyes."

"With the blade part?" asked Pace.

"Yes, boy, with the blade."

"Did you kill him?"

"He died," said Santos. "It was his own foolishness that killed him."

"Oh, I know about that," Pace said. "He musta had a complex."

Dal laughed and then quickly covered her mouth with her hands.

"Marietta," Santos said, "I regret that I am unable to stay longer, but there are people waiting for me. I will call you soon, if I may."

"Please do, Marcello," she said. "And thanks so much for my present."

Santos smiled. "The present, yes. Well, it's a little something."

He turned to the others.

"It's been a pleasure," he said, and went out.

All of the adults gathered in the doorway and watched Santos climb into the backseat of a black Mercedes-Benz limousine and be driven off.

"Look, Marietta, look!" Pace shouted.

Everyone turned from the door and looked at Pace. He had opened the box Santos had brought and was holding up a huge purple silk robe with black velvet lapels.

"There's writin' on it," said Pace, showing them.

Across the back of the robe in bright gold capital letters were the words SANTOS BOXING CLUB, and underneath, in slightly smaller, silver letters, it said, BILOXI & N.O.

"Can I put it on, Marietta? Can I?" Pace asked.

"Yes, child, put it on."

"What a strange man," said Lula.

"Everybody got their way," said Marietta.

"Santos is someone used to gettin' *his* way most all the time, is my guess," said Dal.

"So that was Crazy Eyes Santos himself," said Johnnie.

"Well, come on now, Lula," said Marietta, "this is my birthday party. Let's get these folks some cake!"

All of the urinals were occupied, so Sailor Ripley used one of the stall toilets to relieve himself. As he did, he read the graffito someone had scrawled with a black felt-

THE THEORY OF

RELATIVITY

REVISITED

tipped pen on the wall container of Protecto toilet seat covers: *IRANIAN DINNER JACKETS*. Sailor snickered, zipped his jeans, picked up his suitcase and went back out into the Greyhound terminal. His bus to New Orleans was not scheduled to depart for another hour, so he bought a Jackson *Clarion-Ledger* from a vending box and sat down to read it on one of the hardwood benches.

ATLANTA'S BLACK MAYOR VISITS 'REDNECK BAR' caught his eye right away. The mayor of Atlanta, seeking white votes in his effort to become Georgia's first black governor, had gone to a Cobb County bar and defended the owner's right to put racist records on the jukebox. The candidate said, "I'll go anywhere to talk to anybody about the future of Georgia," and had brought with him a couple of records to give the owner, one by Ray Charles and one by Hank Williams, Jr. The bar owner told reporters that to avoid embarrassing the mayor he had removed two records from the jukebox: "Alabama Nigger" and "She Ran Off With A Nigger." He intended to put them back, he said, after the visit.

"Life don't get no less stupefyin', that's certain," Sailor whispered to himself, and turned the page.

Sailor had been working as a truck loader in a lumberyard out toward Petal, Mississippi, "The Checkers Capital of America," for six months, living alone in a crummy transient hotel in Hattiesburg, drinking too much, and thinking hard about Lula and their son, Pace. He hadn't known how awful it would be not to see them at all, especially Pace. During the almost ten years he'd spent in prison on the armed robbery conviction he'd kept alive the idea that when he got out they'd all be together and life could continue from there. Once he'd seen Pace and Lula, however, he'd panicked and run. The time since then had been hell for him. Sailor hated his life in Hattiesburg, where he'd gone for no reason other than he'd once heard a fellow inmate talk about how beautiful Hattiesburg was in the spring when the magnolias blossomed. The magnolias blossomed all right, but their beauty did not improve Sailor's mood. He needed a change, and New Orleans, where he and Lula had been happy for a few days a decade ago, was an easy target.

Sailor was thirty-two and a half years old, but he felt a lot older. The hard time in Huntsville had changed him, he knew that. Very little that he observed about the workings of the world made sense. Without the hope of ever again seeing the only two people he cared anything about, there didn't seem much point to life. *His* life, anyway. The hour passed and Sailor rose when he heard the passenger page for the bus to New Orleans.

He stowed his suitcase in the overhead rack and took a seat next to a window. Just as the bus turned down the street toward Interstate 59, Sailor saw a woman get out of a new blue BMW convertible, a cigarette stuck between her teeth, and toss her long black hair back over the collar of her suede jacket. Perdita Durango looked the same as she had ten years earlier, Sailor thought, when she'd dropped off him and her boyfriend Bobby Peru in front of the Ramos Feed Store in Iraaq, Texas. Five minutes later Bobby was dead, Sailor was caught red-handed and Perdita was to hell and gone in the getaway car. Suddenly life seemed a whole lot shorter to Sailor than it had the moment before.

"You're goin' where?"

"New Orleans, Mama, to visit Beany. You remember, Beany Thorn? She wrote invitin' me and Pace, soon as school's out."

PLAN A

"How could I ever forget that wild-ass child? She give away two, or was it three fatherless babies before she was seventeen?"

"One, Mama, and the boy woulda married her only Beany wouldn't. He was gonna be a dogcatcher like his daddy. Other two she had done away with early."

"Cracked up Lord knows how many automobiles, too. And it was her lawyer daddy, Tapping Reeve Thorn, bribed a federal judge and got caught and both he and the judge did three years at some country club in Alabama. Then her mother, Darlette, drank herself brainless and had to be shipped out to a zombie camp up in the Smoky Mountains. After servin' his time, Tap threw himself away on a topless dancer in Charlotte and bought her a condominium. Last I heard he was racin' stock cars at the speedway and there was talk of him bein' indicted again for some junk bond scam. Them Thorns ain't exactly simple to forget, Lula. What's the trashy daughter up to in New Orleans? Hookin'?"

"She's married now, to a good man named Bob Lee Boyle, owns a alligator repellent manufacturin' company. They got a son, Lance, who's six years old; and a new baby girl, Madonna Kim. They live in a fabulous big house in Metairie, over in Jefferson Parish, and Beany says there's plenty of room for Pace and me to stay as long as we want. Plan A is to give my notice at the 7-Eleven."

"Well, that's somethin'."

1

3

5

"Mama, be honest. You got more than a little to be thankful for."

"I'm late for the Daughters, Lula. Let's talk later."

"I'm sure the memory of the Confederacy'd live on without you, Mama, but okay."

"Bye, precious. Love you."

"Love you, too."

"Most gators go for gars. Not often one tackles somethin' much larger, like a human."

"Bob Lee knows more about alligators than anyone, almost," said Beany. "Least more about 'em than anyone I ever knew, not that I ever knew anybody before *cared*."

Lula, Beany, and Bob Lee were sitting at the dining room table in the Boyle house in Metairie. Lula and Pace had flown in late in the afternoon, and they had just finished dinner. Pace and Lance were upstairs in Lance's room watching TV, and Madonna Kim, the baby, was asleep.

"It sounds fascinatin', Bob Lee," Lula said, fiddling with the spoon next to her coffee cup. "How'd you get started on gators?"

"Grew up around 'em in Chacahoula, where my daddy's folks're from. I spent considerable time there as a boy. We lived in Raceland, and my mama's people come from Crozier and Bayou Cane, near Houma. Later I worked for Wildlife Management at Barataria. Started workin' on my own mix after a biology professor from Texas A&M came by askin' questions. Told me a man could make a fortune if he figured out how to keep crocs from devourin' folks live on the Nile River in Africa, for instance, and in India and Malaysia. Crocs and gators react about the same to stimuli. Secret to it's in their secretions, called pheromones. They got glands near the tail, emit scents for matin' purposes. Other ones around their throat mark territory. Beasts use the sense of smell to communicate."

"Lula and I've known a few pussy-sniffin' beasts ourselves," said Beany, making them all laugh.

"If that's true, Lula," said Bob Lee, "then you know what I'm talkin' about. Same thing goes for these reptiles."

"What do y'all call your product?"

" 'Gator Gone.' Got it trademarked for worldwide distribution now. Warehouse is in Algiers and the office is on Gentilly, near the Fair Grounds. Come around some time. Right now, though, I gotta go make some phone calls, you ladies don't mind."

"We got lots to talk about," Beany said. "You go on."

Bob Lee got up and went out of the room.

"He's a swell man, Beany. You're fortunate to have him."

"Only man I ever met didn't mind my bony ass!"

They laughed.

"And he don't beg me to give him head all the time, neither. Not that I ever cared particularly one way or the other about it, but it's a change. Only thing is the name, Beany Boyle. Sounds like a hobo stew."

"You look like you-all're doin' just fine."

"Pace sure is a sharpie. Image of his daddy."

"Ain't he? Breaks my heart, too."

"You and Sailor ain't in touch, I take it."

Lula shook her short black hair like a nervous filly in the starting gate.

"Haven't heard from him since he got out of prison over six months ago. We met that one time for about fifteen minutes at the Trailways, and then he just walked off in the night. Guess it was too much to expect we could work anything out. And I think seein' Pace scared Sailor, made those ten years I never went to visit him jump up in his face. I don't know, Beany, it's hard to figure out how I feel for real. And Mama don't make thinkin' for myself any easier."

"Marietta's a vicious cunt, Lula, face it. She ain't got a life and she's afraid you'll get one. That's why she freaked when you and Sailor run off. I'm surprised she let you come here, knowin' how she hates me."

"She don't hate you, Beany, and she ain't really vicious. Also I'm twenty-nine and a half years old now. She can't exactly tell me what I can or can't do."

"Don't stop her from manipulatin' you every chance. So what's the plan?"

"Thought maybe you could work on one with me. I need help and I know it."

Beany reached across the table and held Lula's hand.

"I'm with you, Lula, same as always. We'll figure out somethin'."

The baby began to cry. Beany smiled, squeezed Lula's hand and stood up.

"There's my Madonna Kim," she said. "Another complainin' female. Let's go get her in on this."

Carmine "Poppy" Papavero put his lime green seer-sucker-jacketed right arm around Juju Taylor's D.J. Jazzy Jeff and the Fresh Prince tee-shirted shoulders and smiled.

POPPY AND

PERDITA

"You know, Juju, you keep doin' good like this, I'm gonna have to say somethin' nice about you to Mr. Santos."

"It definitely be a pleasure workin' for you, Mr. Papavero. Tell Mr. Santos can't nobody cover like Juju's Jungle Lovers. We handle however much shit you want. Got Lovers be in Alabama, too, you want to spread it out."

"I'll keep it in mind. Meanwhile, you take care of Mississippi north of the Gulf and we'll see how it goes. What's this I hear about an L.A. gang moving in?"

"They show up here we be all over 'em like smoke on links."

Poppy patted Juju on the back, then squeezed his thick neck.

"Be seeing you soon, Juju."

Poppy walked out of the gang's safehouse and saw Perdita Durango leaning against the blue Beamer. He went over and kissed her forehead, which was on a level with his chin. Poppy went six-three and a hard two-forty. Perdita had never had a steady his size before. Poppy punished her during their lovemaking but never to the point where it became painful. She'd learned to enjoy the weight.

Perdita had met Poppy at Johnny Black's Black & Blue Club in Gulfport, where she'd gone with an acquaintance named Dio Bolivar, a local liquor salesman and small-time hoodlum with a pencil-thin mustache and flashy clothes. Poppy had come over to their table and asked what a beautiful lady like her was doing in a low-rent joint with an unsuccessful pimp. Dio heard this and jumped up like a jack-in-the-box, ready to duke until he saw who'd said it.

"Oh, good evenin', Mr. Papavero," Bolivar said, having recognized Crazy Eyes Santos's chief enforcer on the Gulf Coast. Poppy led her away, and that was the last Perdita ever saw of Dio Bolivar.

She had told Poppy about her childhood in Corpus Christi; how her sister, Juana, had been murdered by her husband, Tony, who had also murdered both of his and Juana's daughters before shooting himself, but not much else. She didn't want him to know about the jams she'd been in in Texas and Mexico and California. It was a good idea, Perdita thought, to start fresh, keep her mouth shut and let this big man pay the bills. He didn't seem to mind so long as she kept herself pretty and available. It wasn't hard work and Papavero wasn't nearly as moody as most of the other guys she'd known. Besides, Perdita felt grown up with Poppy, respectable, like a regular woman rather than a piece of Tex-Mex trash. She decided that this was a gig worth holding on to.

"These Jungle guys are turning out better than I thought," Poppy said to Perdita as he drove them away. "They force people to buy shit even if they're not users, just to stay healthy. Not even Santos thought of that!"

Perdita sat in the passenger seat with her body turned toward Poppy, making sure that her tight black skirt rode halfway up her thighs. Poppy looked over at her and stroked her legs with his hairy right hand.

"You really do please me, Perdita," he said. "I never told you, but I was married once. It didn't last too long, about five years. It ended, let's see now, when I was thirty, fifteen years ago. Her name was Dolores, but everybody called her Dolly. She worked in the Maison Blanche on Canal Street when I met her, in the women's apparel department. I went there to buy a birthday present for another girl. I saw Dolly and forgot all about the girl. She had big tits, a big nose and a flat ass. There was something about her, though, that got me, aside from her tits. Dolly had a way of looking at you that made you think she knew all about you, who you really were deep inside. It sounds dumb, I know, but if you'd met her you'd understand."

"It don't sound dumb. I've known people like that. One guy, especially, who was a kind of strange, religious person. He's dead now."

"Yeah? You have? Well, Dolly's the only one I've ever known had that look, like she knew every rotten or good thing you'd ever done in your entire life. It was spooky."

"So what happened to her and you?"

"I married her, like I said. It was going along good enough, I guess, but she didn't like not knowing what I did every day, where I went, and that sometimes I was out until five or six in the morning or took off without telling her for a few days."

Poppy shook his head, remembering.

"No, she didn't like what I was doing. Dolly knew I was moving up in the organization, bringing home more money, which was okay because I'd made her quit her job at the Maison Blanche. But then she wanted a child and no matter what we did, she couldn't get pregnant. We went to a couple of doctors and they both said it was because of some defect she had in her system, and there was no way to correct it. They suggested we adopt, which Dolly didn't want to do. I wouldn't have minded. There's plenty of orphans need homes and that way she could have a kid, but for some reason she didn't want one unless it was her own. Her parents and grandparents were all dead, she didn't have any family but me."

"What color hair did she have?" asked Perdita, lighting up a Marlboro.

"Kind of reddish-blond. Her mother was Polish, she told me, and her father was Czech. She kept pictures of them on the bedroom dresser. I came home one night late, about four A.M., from the Egyptian Sho-Bar on Napoleon Avenue that I was running then, and Dolly wasn't there. At first I thought maybe she'd gone down to the all-night pharmacy on Esplanade for something, but when she wasn't back by five I knew that wasn't it. I looked at the dresser, and the pictures of her parents were gone. Dolly walked out on me. No note, no phone call, nothing. I was upset at first, of course, but after a week I didn't care. I just hoped she was happier wherever she was, and I went on with my life."

Perdita didn't say anything as Poppy sped them south on 59 toward New Orleans. They passed a Greyhound and Perdita thought how much better it was to be traveling in a new BMW than on a bus. She lowered the tinted window a crack and tossed out her cigarette butt. Sailor Ripley saw the blue car zoom by and a cigarette fly out and bounce off the side of the bus just below where he was sitting.

"What do you think, Perdita?" asked Poppy. "Is that a sad story or not?"

"Heard lots sadder," she said.

Poppy Papavero laughed and grabbed her left thigh.

"So have I, pussycat. So have I."

"She left when?"

"Yesterday. I tell you, Dal, this is just another way for Lula to avoid facin' the future, if she's ever gonna have one's worth a thing."

"Marietta, it don't matter how much or how little you fuss. Lula's gonna find herself or not and you can't do nothin' about it."

"Okay, Dal, I believe you, but that still don't make me feel any better. And why is it in the back of my mind I got this sneakin' notion Sailor Ripley ain't out of the picture?"

"He is the boy's father, after all. And it's plain Lula ain't yet resolved her feelin's about him."

"But, Dal, it's been more'n ten years she's had to figure it out."

"That ain't nothin' where love's concerned, Marietta, you know that. And Lula feels guilty as get-out over not havin' gone to see Sailor all that time he was shut away from society. You didn't have no little to do with that, either."

"Dal, I swear on my grandmama Eudora Pace's grave I never told Lula not to visit Sailor. She was just busy bringin' up her son by herself and couldn't never get away."

"This ain't worth our arguin' now, is it? You and I know well enough how much influence you keep over that girl."

"I got to. Look at the fix Lula got herself in the last time she ran off. Mixed up with a bunch of deranged criminals in a West Texas desert, people gettin' shot and killed all around, and her pregnant besides. If Johnnie and I hadn't tracked Lula down in that Big Tuna hellhole who knows where she'd be today? Prob'ly'd have two or three more illegitimate children and be lost out in some godforsaken place like California, surrounded by a hundred kinds of drug-crazed devil worshipers."

"Marietta, how you can carry on. Lula's just in New Orleans visitin' an old friend. It'll be good for her, gettin' away for a bit. By the way, you heard any more from Santos?"

"Two dozen red roses arrived this mornin', with a card."

"I'll be. What'd it say?"

"Oh, somethin' like, 'To Marietta, who always deserves the best, from Marcello.' "

"Natalie Suarez knows someone in N.O. knows Mona Costatroppo, the woman your playmate Crazy Eyes been keepin' down there the last few years."

"So?"

"Natalie says this friend of hers heard from Mona Costatroppo that Santos cut her off flat about a month back, threatened to kill her if she made a fuss."

"Now, Dal, do you believe that? People're always tryin' to find somethin' ugly to talk about. Here you are, always settin' yourself up as the voice of reason far as me and Lula's concerned, and you fall for this silly third-hand gossip out the mouth of a woman we both know don't have the brain of a peacock on mood pills."

"I ain't fell for nothin'. I'm just tellin' you what I hear concerns Santos, is all. It may or may not be true, but it's out there in the air and I thought you deserved to know. Apparently the Costatroppo woman sold some of the jewelry and furniture Santos had given her and moved to New York or Chicago, afraid for her life."

"I'd be more afraid for my life in one of those places than I would down here anywhere. And anyway, how do we know what this Troppo person done to Marcello riled him in the first place, if in fact there's any truth to the story at all?"

"Natalie Suarez claims he just got tired of her after she got a little fat and sloppy. Her friend said she'd developed a drinkin' problem."

"There you are, then! Who wants to be around a drunk?"

"And of course there's his wife, Lina, who pretends ain't a thing wrong."

"Maybe there ain't, Dal, you ever consider that? Marcello's a man knows his own mind, always has. Clyde didn't never have a bad word to say about him when he was alive, and I don't either. I vote we end this part of the conversation right now."

"Fine with me, Marietta. Sorry I couldn't get to Tuesday's meetin' of the Daughters. Louis made me go with him to visit his mama in the nursin' home in Asheville. Don't make no sense draggin' me, I told him, she's so gaga. But I guess it helps him, me bein' there. What'd I miss?"

"Oh, Dal, you won't believe what Esther Pickens heard about Ruby Werlhi and Denise Sue Hilton's son-in-law. You know, Walker French-Jones, the tennis pro?"

As soon as Sailor got off the bus he headed toward the Hotel Brazil. He didn't know if it was still there but he didn't bother to check a city directory, figuring he'd

BRIGHT LIGHTS,

BIG CITY

find something similar in the neighborhood if necessary. From Elysian Fields he cut across the park, surprised to see so many homeless people camped out and sleeping on benches. He turned left on Frenchmen Street and there it was, the Brazil, looking as dilapidated as it had ten or more years before, but still standing. He entered, asked the elderly white male desk clerk for a room over-looking the street, paid thirty dollars for two days in advance, took his key and hiked up the stairs to the third floor. Sailor could not remember which room he and Lula had stayed in, but this one was pretty close. He opened the window, leaned out and looked east. There was the river, huge and green, with a gray Yugoslav freighter, flanked by black tugs, pushing past the Bien-ville Wharf.

He lay down on the bed and lit up an unfiltered Camel. The hint of a breeze blew into the room, startling Sailor for a moment. It was unexpected and caused him to shiver, despite the intense heat and high humidity. The Hotel Brazil did not provide room-cooling except during winter, when there was no heat. A strange sensation came over him, as if an invisible, gauzy-feeling sub-stance had intruded on the finger of fresh air and draped itself around his body. Sailor's cigarette burned down steadily between the index and second fingers of his right hand, its ash building but remaining attached due to his immobility.

"Lula's here," Sailor said. He trembled and the ash fell off the cigarette onto the floor.

Sailor swung his legs off the bed, stood up and went back over to the window. He took a swift drag on the Camel and flicked it out into the street. Directly below, two old men, one black the other white, were struggling over a half-pint bottle of Old Crow.

"That's mine!" the black man shouted.

"Hell it is!" said the white man.

"I bought it, I'mo drink it!"

"Bullshit! Half's my money! Give it!"

"I knock yo teef out, ugly mufuck, you had 'ny."

The white man lurched toward the black man, fell to his knees and wrapped his arms around the black man's legs.

"Let go, fo I smack yo bleach head!"

"Mine, mine!" screeched the white man, who was crying now.

The black man raised the bottle to his mouth and took a long swig. People walking along the sidewalk avoided them. The black man staggered to the curb, dragging the white man, who clung stubbornly to his legs. The black man stopped and took another long drink, killing the bottle.

"Here go, mufuck," he said, bringing the dark brown bottle down hard on the white man's head.

The glass shattered, cutting into the bald, freckled skull of the genuflecting man, the pieces scattering over the sidewalk. The white man did not release his hold on the black man's legs. He remained attached, sobbing loudly, his body heaving, the top of his head a puddle of blood and broken glass. The black man balanced himself with his hands on the hood of a dirty beige '81 Cutlass parked by the curb and kicked loose his legs, leaving the white man slumped on the ground as he stumbled away.

Sailor looked down at the crying, bleeding man whom passersby continued to ignore. A New Orleans police car pulled up in front of the hotel and two cops got out. They lifted the injured man, holding him under each arm, deposited him in the backseat and drove off. The black man, Sailor noticed, was sitting on the ground, leaning against a shabby white building on the opposite side of the street. Above the man's head, in faded black paint, were the words JESUS DIED FOR THE UNGODLY. The man's eyes were closed and there were splotches of bright red, undoubtedly the other man's blood, on the front of his short-sleeved white shirt.

Sailor went back to the bed and lay down on his back. He had no idea where to begin looking for Lula, and he did not want to contact Marietta. A picture of Perdita Durango standing on the street in Hattiesburg flashed in his brain. Lula used to say the world was weird on top, he thought. She sure was right there. Sailor rolled over into a fetal position and closed his eyes.

Elmer Désespéré put his railroad engineer's cap over his stringy yellow-white hair and went out. At the foot of the stairs of his rooming house he stopped and took a

SAVING GRACE

packet of Red Man chewing tobacco from the back pocket of his Ben Davis overalls, scooped a wad with the thumb and index finger of his right hand and planted it between his teeth and cheek in the left side of his mouth. Elmer replaced the packet in his pocket and strolled down Claiborne toward Canal Street. The night air felt thick and greasy, and the sidewalk was crawling with people sweating, laughing, fighting, drinking. Police cars, their revolving red and blue lights flashing, prowled up and down both sides of the road. Trucks rumbled like stampeding dinosaurs on the overhead highway, expelling a nauseating stream of diesel mist.

Elmer loved it all. He loved being in the city of New Orleans, away from the farm forever, away from his daddy, Hershel Burt, and his older brother, Emile; though they'd never bother a soul again, since Elmer had destroyed the both of them as surely as they had destroyed his mama, Alma Ann. He had chopped his daddy and brother into a total of exactly one hundred pieces and buried one piece per acre on the land Hershel Burt owned in Evangeline Parish by the Bayou Nezpique. After doing what he had to, Elmer had walked clear to Mamou and visited Alma Ann's grave, told her she could rest easy, then hitchhiked into N.O.

Alma Ann had died ten years ago, when Elmer was nine, on November 22d, the birthday of her favorite singer, Hoagy Carmichael. Alma Ann's greatest pleasure in life, she had told Elmer, was listening to the collection of Hoagy Carmichael 78s her daddy, Bugle Lugubre, had left her. Her favorite tunes had been "Old Man Harlem," "Ole Buttermilk Sky," and Bugle's own favorite, "Memphis in June." But after Alma Ann was worked to death by Hershel Burt and Emile, Hershel Burt had busted up all the records and dumped the pieces in the Crooked Creek Reservoir. Now Elmer had buried Hershel Burt just like he'd buried Bugle Lugubre's Hoagy Carmichael records. It made Elmer happy to think that the records could be replaced and that Hoagy Carmichael would live on forever through them. Alma Ann would live on as well, by virtue of Hoagy's music and Elmer's memory, but Hershel Burt and Emile were wiped away clean as bugs off a windshield in a downpour.

The only thing Elmer needed now was a friend. He'd taken the two-thousand-four-hundred-eighty-eight dollars his daddy had kept in Alma Ann's cloisonné button box, so Elmer figured he had enough money for quite a little while to come. Walking along Claiborne, watching the people carry on, Elmer felt as if he were a visitor to an insane asylum, the only one with a pass to the outside. When he reached Canal, Elmer turned down toward the river. He was looking for a tattoo parlor to have his mama's name written over his heart. A friend would know immediately what kind of person Elmer was, he thought, as soon as he saw ALMA ANN burned into Elmer's left breast. The friend would understand the depth of Elmer's loyalty and sincerity and never betray or leave him, this Elmer knew.

The pain was gone, too. The constant headache Elmer had suffered for so many years had vanished as he'd knelt next to Alma Ann's grave in Mamou. She soothed her truest son in death as she had in life. Jesus was bunk, Elmer had decided. He'd prayed to Jesus after Alma Ann had gone, but he had not been delivered. There had been no saving grace for Elmer until he'd destroyed the two marauding angels and pacified himself in the name of Alma Ann. It was he who shone, not Jesus. Jesus was dead and he, Elmer, was alive. He would carry Alma Ann's name on his body and his friend would understand and love him for it.

"Say, ma'am," Elmer said to a middle-aged woman headed in the opposite direction, "there a place near here a sober man can buy himself a expert tattoo?"

"I suppose there must be," she said, "farther along closer to the port."

"Alma Ann blesses you, ma'am," said Elmer, walking on, spitting tobacco juice on the sidewalk.

The woman stared after him and was surprised to see that he was barefoot.

"Speakin' of abuse?" said Beany, as she fed Madonna Kim her bottle of formula. "I didn't know that's what Elmo was doin' until I saw them women on Oprah's

HEART TALK

show talkin' about how their husbands, mostly ex now, 'course, like Elmo and me, used to take all kinds of advantages. Worst is the ones beat 'em up, which Elmo only done once to me, when he was stewed and I threw a pet rock at him after I'd found out from Mimsy Bavard the baby Etta Foy was havin' was his."

It was nine A.M. and Beany and Lula were sitting on the front porch swing of the house in Metairie, discussing men. Pace and Lance were on the lawn shooting rubber-tipped arrows at a target, trading off turns with the only bow.

"Bob Lee wouldn't never hit me, even if he thought he had a reason to. He takes off, he's angry enough. Comes back about two hours later and raids the refrigerator."

"Where's he go?"

"Oh, mostly he'll drive around, or maybe go to a movie at the mall. One time he come home with this really strange look on his face. I asked him, 'You still mad at me, Bob Lee?' I don't recall now what it was set him off in the first place. I think somethin' to do with my lettin' Lance cry too long. Bob Lee's a real softie it comes to babies cryin', he'll just run and pick 'em up. I told him you got to let 'em settle down on their own or they just get so damned spoiled they're always fussin'. Anyway, he come in lookin' like a wild dog just bit the head off his favorite cat. And Lord knows, Bob Lee loves cats."

"How come you ain't got any then?"

"'Lergic. Me and Lance both. Bugs Bob Lee, but nothin' we can do about it. I tell him he's got his gators to pet."

"So what weirded him out?"

"I'm tellin' you, this movie he seen, called *Blue Velvet*. You seen it?"

"No. Ain't heard of it."

"After he seen it, Bob Lee couldn't even eat. He wouldn't let me go see it, though I wanted to. I woulda gone anyway, of course, but with Lance bein' a baby then I didn't get a chance. Bob Lee told me he coulda never imagined the awful behavior went on in that movie. He did say there was a couple pretty women in it."

"Was it a porno?"

"Don't think so. Bob Lee don't care for 'em, though I don't mind 'em once in awhile if there's some laughs in it. Sorta horrifies Bob Lee I can take sex less than serious sometimes. This *Blue Velvet*, though, must be somethin' else entirely. He said it made his brain shut down, like all the fuses blew."

"We oughta rent it for the VCR."

"Good idea. Watch it while Bob Lee's at work."

Pace came up on the porch and sat on the top step. Lance was still busy shooting arrows.

"What we gonna do today, Mama?" Pace asked.

"Thought maybe we'd go swimmin'. You like that idea?"

"I suppose."

"C'mon, Pace!" Lance shouted. "It's your turn!"

"Comin'!" Pace shouted back. He looked at Beany and said, "Lance ain't a bad kid, but he goes bugshit you leave him alone a minute. You notice that, Aunt Beany?"

Pace got up and resumed playing with Lance.

"That boy is a natural, Lula," said Beany. "Don't know where you got him."

"Got him from Sailor is where."

"He ever hit you?"

"Sail? You jokin'? Sailor Ripley wouldn't raise a hand to me or nobody."

"Hold it, Lula. He killed a man. Bob Ray Lemon. Remember?"

"That was different. He thought Bob Ray was tryin' to harm me. Imagine it still's eatin' at him, what he done."

"Bet he misses seein' his boy."

Lula watched Pace pull back the bowstring and send an arrow into the very heart of the target. Tears burst from her eyes and Beany handed her one of Madonna Kim's spit-up towels.

"He's just so beautiful and precious to me, Beany," Lula said, wiping her face, "just like Lance and Madonna Kim are to you. But he's really all I got in the world. If anything bad happened to Pace, I don't know what I'd do. Shoot myself, prob'ly."

Madonna Kim coughed and knocked the bottle away. Beany put her over her shoulder and patted the baby's back.

"Stop talkin' foolish, Lula. Ain't nothin' but good gonna ride that boy."

Madonna Kim let out a burp so loud that it startled Beany and Lula, and they laughed.

"Oh, Beany, I'm so glad I come to see you. It really means a lot to me, your takin' us in this way."

"Hush. Means a lot to me, too."

They looked at their boys playing on the grass in the morning sun, wrestling now, rolling around and laughing, Pace allowing the weaker, smaller Lance to pin him. They jumped up and ran over to the porch.

"Mama?" said Lance. "Pace says we're goin' swimmin'. Is it time yet?"

"Carmine, *come va?*"

"I am fine, Marcello. I know you are, too."

"And how is that?"

"The other night I ran into the Calabrese, Jimmie Hunchback, at Broussard's. I asked him about you, and he said, '*Il vecchio porta bene gli anni.*' "

Papavero heard Santos chuckle at the other end of the line.

"Old man, he calls me," said Santos. "I should call him up and tell him this old man still knows how *tenere il coltello dalla parte del manico.*"

Poppy laughed. "Nobody will ever doubt that you know how to hold the knife, Marcello, or that you would use it if you had to. *Non ho notizie di te da molto tempo.* What can I do for you?"

"I wanted you to know that I'm coming in two days. The thing with Mona has caused some trouble there I must take care of myself."

"*La Signora Costatroppo ha fatto parlare di sé.* The lady has caused much talk."

Santos sighed. "She knows too much, Carmine. *Il passato non si distrugge.* The past cannot be undone, but *non si sa mai quando può succedere una disgrazia.* One never knows when an accident might happen."

"One would think that after all you've done for her, given her, she would be more respectful."

"My friend, *a chi tutto, a chi niente.* Who can say what is enough or not enough for anyone? *Non fa niente,* it doesn't matter. I know where she hides and soon I can tell you, *mi sono liberato di un incomodo.*"

"Your life is long, Marcello. There is much to look forward to."

"Mona was once a morsel to be savored, Carmine, but *un pranzo comprende molte pietanze*. A meal consists of many dishes. Already *la ferita si sta cicatrizzando*. The wound heals as we speak. I have sent *un colpo di vento*, a gust of wind, to blow away the problem."

"I will be glad to see you, Marcello. I'll be here."

"*Bene*. I may need your help on a couple of matters. The business goes well with the *tutsuns?*"

"*Molto bene*, better than I expected."

"You are a smart man, Carmine. You earn my respect. *Ciao*."

"*Ciao*, Marcello. *Buon viaggio*."

The air seemed cooler in Audubon Park. Lula and Beany, who was carrying Madonna Kim in a pouch strapped to her chest, strolled slowly beneath the magnolia trees as

A WALK IN

THE PARK

Pace and Lance ran ahead, playing tag. Lula and the boys had swum most of the morning, and then they had all gone to the Camellia Grill and eaten a large, wonderful lunch which they were now walking—in the boys' case, running—off.

"I can't believe how safe and fine I feel," said Lula, "just bein' here. It ain't nearly so hot as I thought it'd be."

"Wish you lived nearby, Lula. It'd be great to be able to hang out together like this whenever we wanted to. And the kids are gettin' along so good."

Lula watched the boys circle a tree and take off at breakneck speed toward the lake, Lance chasing the fleeter Pace.

"Pace!" she shouted. "You take care Lance don't fall in!"

"I will, Mama!" Pace yelled, just before he and his pursuer disappeared behind a boathouse.

"I gotta admit, Beany, Sailor been on my mind a whole lot lately, more than I'm comfortable about. I mean, he ain't never been off it entire since we met when I was sixteen. It's amazin', but that's almost half my life."

"No point in fightin' it either, sweetie. Some things just meant to be. Guess it was destiny you and him'd be matched. But you don't even know where he might be, huh?"

Lula shook her head no, reached back with her right hand and wiped the sweat off the back of her neck.

"Don't know that I even want to see Sailor, really," she said. "Truth is, though, no guy I been out with before or since ever thrilled me like Sailor. I mean, really *thrilled* me, Beany, you know?"

"Not sure I do, Lula."

"Like I would always, *always*, get excited that Sailor was comin' to get me, or I was goin' to meet him. Even when things between us wasn't so smooth. Didn't ever seem to matter what kinda problems we were havin', or what else was goin' on, I'd get a actual *thrill* thinkin' about him. That never's happened with another man, Beany, not like that. There's been moments I been happy, of course, and thought I was doin' all right. But I made love enough with other boys to know there can't never be anyone but him makes a difference in my soul."

Lula stopped walking and Beany stopped, too. Lula put her forehead against the back of Beany's right shoulder and let the tears come. She was shaking, and Beany started to turn around, but Lula held her still.

"Wait, Beany, just let me rest my head on you like this. I'll be fine in a minute and I don't want you to look at me until I am."

Beany didn't move.

"There," Lula said, raising her head and smiling, giving her hair a shake, wiping her eyes with the backs of her hands, "I'm better. Guess that's what they mean, havin' a shoulder to cry on," she laughed. "Never took it for real quite the same way before."

Beany looked into her friend's red, watery, large gray eyes.

"You always got me to cry on, Lula," she said, "just like I hope I always got you."

Lula hugged Beany, being careful not to squeeze too tightly and crush Madonna Kim between them.

"You got me, Miss Beany, forever."

They disengaged and began walking again. Madonna Kim snoozed peacefully.

"Hey, where'd them boys go?" said Lula.

"Prob'ly runnin' around the lake. We'll find 'em. Lance been here lots of times. They won't get lost."

Just then Lance appeared from behind the opposite side of the boat-house and ran over to Beany and Lula.

"I can't find Pace," he said. "He must be hidin' on me."

Lula shivered. "Where'd you see him last?" she asked.

"I tagged him and run on ahead, and when he didn't catch up I turned around and Pace wasn't nowhere. Mama, can I get a ice cream?"

Lula took off running toward the lake. She followed the path around the water but did not see Pace. She stopped to rest and think, and Lance came running up behind her.

"Aunt Lula, Mama says come quick. A lady saw Pace go off with some man."

"Oh, shit. Oh, shit," Lula kept saying, as she and Lance ran back toward Beany.

Beany and a thin, gray-haired woman of about fifty, wearing yellow shorts, a red tank top and green Nike running shoes, with a Sony Walkman headset radio hanging around her neck, were standing next to the boathouse.

"Lula, listen," said Beany. "This woman says she saw a boy looked like Pace walk away with a man."

"The boy was about ten or eleven, with black hair," the woman said. "He was wearin' blue jeans and a blue tee shirt said 'Tarheels' on it in white block letters."

"Oh, shit," said Lula. "That's him, that's Pace!"

"Well, when I saw him I was joggin' into the park on the north path there, and this boy was holdin' hands with a young man not much more than a boy himself, maybe eighteen, nineteen. Was an odd-lookin' young man, too. Real slight build, wearin' overalls and a kind of railroad engineer's cap, with long, dirty-blond-lookin' curly hair hangin' down under it."

"Pace wouldn't just go off with some stranger!" Lula said.

"Are you sure this guy in the overalls wasn't pullin' Pace along with him?" Beany asked the woman.

"He mighta been, I don't know. I just ran past 'em, goin' kinda slow, of course, so I got a good look at 'em both."

Lula ran to the north path and followed it out of the park to the street. She stood there, breathing hard, looking each way, but there was nobody else around. Lula ran down the street to where it intersected a main thoroughfare. Cars whizzed by in both directions.

Lula grabbed a young black woman who was walking by and yelled at her, "Did you see my son? He's ten years old and has black hair and he's wearin' a Carolina Tarheels tee shirt. A white man wearin' overalls just kidnapped him!"

"No, lady," said the young woman, "I ain't seen him."

Lula let go and fell to her knees.

"Oh, shit! Oh, shit! Oh, shit!" she cried. "Sailor, Sailor, I need you now!"

Mona Costatroppo looked out the window of her room in the Drake Hotel in Chicago. Lake Michigan, she thought, staring at it, was as big as an ocean.

ONE NEVER
KNOWS

"What's the name again, this beach here?" she asked Federal Agents Sandy Sandusky and Morton Martin, both of whom were seated on the couch under a hideous oil painting of a tropical sunset.

"Oak Street," Sandusky said. "That's Oak Street beach."

"About a billion bodies on it," said Mona, "look like flies on dogshit."

She turned away from the window.

"So, you'll guarantee if I tell you all I know about Santos's organization you'll set me up someplace with a new identity?"

"Federal Witness Protection Program," said Martin. "Even Europe, you want to go there."

Mona nodded. "Okay, you bums get outta here now, let me think this over."

The agents rose together and Sandusky said, "We'll be here tomorrow morning at ten o'clock, Ms. Costatroppo."

"Never figured anybody'd be callin' me Miz, 'less slavery got legal again. You be here what time you want. But now, get out."

The agents left and Mona poured a healthy dose of Bombay Sapphire into a glass and drank it fast. She poured some more into the glass, emptying the fifth she'd bought that morning, and was about to swallow it when there was a knock at the door.

"Who's there?" she asked.

"Valet. I have your laundry."

Mona walked over, the glass in her left hand, and turned the doorknob with her right.

"Put it on the bed," she said, walking toward the window, not bothering to see who it was coming through the door.

As Mona lifted the glass to her lips and opened her mouth, she heard a loud pop. She dropped the glass and started to turn around, but before she could there was another loud pop, which she did not hear. Mona sat down suddenly on the floor, her head banging hard against the window that overlooked Oak Street beach and Lake Michigan, but she didn't feel a thing.

NIGHT AND FOG

Sailor was awakened in his room at the Hotel Brazil by a series of shrieks coming from the hallway. He jumped out of bed and stubbed the big toe on his left foot on the leg of the table next to the door, opened the door and limped into the hall. Two women of indeterminate age, one blond, one red-haired, were rolling on the carpet in front of the staircase attempting to mutilate each other in any way possible. They were screaming and cursing at the top of their voices. Sailor stood by the door to his room rubbing his sore toe and watching the women wrestle. He looked at his watch: it was a couple of ticks shy of six A.M. The more heavyset of the women, the blonde, stood and grabbed the redhead and dragged her to her feet, then ran her into the wall, knocking the red-haired wrestler stupid and busting her nose. Blood spurted on the wall, the floor and the blond bruiser, further infuriating her. She yelled, "You cunt!" and practically picked up the bleeder and threw her down the stairs. The blonde stood in the hallway panting hard, wiped her face with her meaty right forearm, and spotted Sailor standing there in his underwear with his left leg resting on his right knee, holding his toe.

"What the fuck you lookin' at, buster?" she said.

Sailor lowered his leg and looked behind him. He was the only spectator. He turned back to the woman.

"Thanks for the wake-up," he said, and went back inside his room.

The screaming ceased and Sailor limped over to the washbasin, where he rinsed his face, brushed his teeth and combed his hair. He pulled on his clothes and went out. There was no sign of the battling women, only a neck-high smear of blood on the wall.

The morning air was warm and foggy. Sailor headed for Rod's, a 24-hour cafe on Ursulines Street just off Decatur in the Quarter. He bought an early edition of the *Times-Picayune* from a machine, thinking he'd check out the job opportunities. Sitting at the counter in Rod's, Sailor ordered chicory coffee and a Spanish omelette. He lit up his first Camel of the day and opened the paper. There on the lower right of the front page was the heading, BOY VISITING CITY IS KIDNAPPED. Sailor read the article that followed.

> A ten-year-old boy, Pace Roscoe Ripley, visiting the city with his mother, Lula Pace Fortune, of Bay St. Clement, N.C., was kidnapped in broad daylight yesterday afternoon while on an outing with friends in Audubon Park. A woman who apparently witnessed the abduction while she was jogging in the park described the kidnapper as being approximately eighteen or nineteen years old, with long blond hair, wearing striped overalls and a railroad engineer's cap. Pace Ripley was described by his mother's friend, Mrs. Beany Thorn Boyle, of Metairie, as under five feet tall, black hair, wearing blue jeans, a blue and white tee shirt with the word "Tarheels" on it, and white sneakers. Anyone with relevant information should contact the New Orleans Police Department. Tel. 555-0099.

"You got a directory here?" Sailor asked the fry cook.

"On the floor behind you," he said, without turning around. "Under the phone."

Sailor flipped to the section listing residents of Metairie, and found BOYLE BOB LEE AND BEANY . . . 833 CHARITY . . . 555-4956. He put in a coin and dialed.

"Hello?" said Bob Lee.

"This is Sailor Ripley, Pace's daddy. Is Lula there?"

"Hold the phone."

Sailor dropped his cigarette and stepped on it.

"Sailor?! Is it really you?"

"Oh, peanut, yes! It's me! I'm in N.O. I just read about Pace in the paper."

"Please come here now, Sail. I don't know what to do."

"Don't do nothin', honey. I'm comin', your Sailor's comin'!"

Sailor hung up and ran out of the cafe. The fry cook heard the screen door slam, scooped up the half-done omelette from the grill and tossed it in the trash.

"Mrs. Fortune?"

"Speakin'."

"This is Beany Boyle, in New Orleans? Lula's friend.

Used to be I was Beany Thorn?"

"I remember you. Why are you callin' me? Has somethin' happened to Lula?"

"No, ma'am, not to Lula, but I got some terrible news."

"Go on."

"Pace been kidnapped, Mrs. Fortune. We was all takin' a walk in the park and the boys, Pace and my son, Lance, took off outta Lula's and my sight—I was carryin' my baby, Madonna Kim?—and someone snatched Pace."

"I knew somethin' awful'd happen if Lula left home! Put her on the line!"

"She's kinda out of it right now, Mrs. Fortune. She asked me to call you."

"You put Lula on the line right now, dammit!"

"I really can't, she's too broke up to talk to you. The police are handlin' it and Sailor's here."

"*He's* there?! Satan takes a holiday!"

Marietta hung up.

"Mrs. Fortune? Mrs. Fortune, are you there?"

Beany hung up.

As soon as she'd cut Beany off, Marietta dialed Santos's private number. A man answered on the third ring.

"Bayou Enterprises."

"This is Marietta Pace Fortune, Clyde Fortune's widow. I got to speak to Marcello Santos right away! It's urgent!"

"Wait," the man said.

Two minutes later, Santos came on the line.

"Yes, Marietta. How pleasant to hear from you."

"Marcello, somethin' real *un*pleasant's happened. My grandboy, Pace—you met him at my birthday party. Remember, he asked you about your thumb?"

"I do."

"He's been kidnapped, in New Orleans!"

"When did this happen?"

"Yesterday, I believe. I just got the call. You gotta help find him! Lula's there and that horrible Sailor Ripley's with her. I'm gonna be about flat outta my mind in a New York minute!"

"Calm yourself, Marietta. I will do everything I can, of course. As it happens, I am about to leave very shortly for New Orleans. Before I go, I will contact people there who may be able to help. I will call you from Louisiana as soon as I have any information."

"He's my only grandchild, Marcello! Lula knew how to raise him, this wouldn'ta happened."

"Do you know how the kidnap occurred?"

"Someone stole Pace out of a park is all I know."

"The police have been notified?"

"I suppose, yes. But you gotta get him back for me, Marcello, please!"

"I will make a call right away. Do you want me to send someone to stay with you?"

"No, no, I'll get Dal. You need the number where Lula's at?"

"It won't be necessary. Goodbye, Marietta. We will talk again very soon."

"I appreciate this, Marcello. I wouldn't ask if it wasn't so important."

"I know, Marietta, I understand. Goodbye."

Marietta called Dal next.

"Dal? Pace been kidnapped in New Orleans by God knows who and Sailor's there reattachin' himself to Lula! Can you believe my life?! Who'd I kill, Dal? I ask you! What'd I do to deserve this?"

"Slow down a sec, peach. You're sayin' Pace been kidnapped and Sailor'n Lula're back together in N.O.?"

"That's it! That's the package."

"What's bein' done?"

"I just now got off the phone with Santos. He's goin' there himself today. That slut friend of Lula's, Tap Thorn's daughter, called me, said they got the police workin' on it."

"What'd Lula say?"

"She didn't. The Thorn girl wouldn't let her come to the phone. Said Lula was in a faint, or somethin'."

"Wouldn't doubt it. I'll be over in a minute, Marietta. Is the back door unlocked?"

"Good, Dal, yes. Bye!"

Marietta dialed the number of Johnnie Farragut's office in Charlotte.

"JF Investigations. Farragut talkin'."

"Crazed animal stole Pace in N.O. and Lula's back with Sailor!"

"Marietta? What?"

"Pace been kidnapped! Lula and him went to N.O. to visit Tap Thorn's most irresponsible child, the one married a alligator wrestler, and now Sailor's there, too!"

"Have they called the police?"

" 'Course they have. I called Santos soon as I heard, and he's sendin' in the troops. Johnnie, I tell you, it's another trial! Clyde burned to death, Lula run off with a robber and killer, now my precious grandbaby been taken!"

"I'm comin', Marietta. Take me two and a half hours. You call Dal yet?"

"She's on her way."

"Good. I'm leavin' now."

Marietta hung up, staggered into the front room, where only a few days before Pace had unwrapped her birthday presents, and collapsed into Clyde's worn old leather armchair. She heard the back door open and close.

"Marietta? Where are you?"

"In here, Dal."

Dalceda Delahoussaye came in, dropped to the floor, and hugged Marietta's knees.

"Oh, Marietta, I'm so sorry. This is a nightmare."

"I ain't certain there's a God, Dal, I never been convinced. But one thing I do know, there's a Devil, and he don't never quit."

Elmer's room was ten feet by ten feet. There were two windows, both of which were half-boarded over and nailed shut; a sink; a single bed; one cane armchair; a

small dresser with a mirror attached; and a writing table with a green-shaded eagle-shaped lamp on it. The one closet was empty because Elmer had no clothes other than the ones he wore. He had been meaning to buy some new pants and shirts, but he kept forgetting. Elmer foreswore shoes; they interfered with the electrical power he absorbed from the earth through his feet. In one corner was a pile about two feet high of canned food, mostly Campbell's Pork and Beans and Denison's Chili. On the dresser were two half-gallon plastic containers of spring water and a Swiss Army knife that contained all of the necessary eating untensils plus a can opener. There was no garbage in the room, no empty cans or bottles. Elmer disliked refuse; as soon as he had finished with something, he got rid of it, depositing it in a container on the street.

Pace slept on the bed. Elmer sat in the cane armchair, twirling his hat on the toes of his left foot and looking at the illustrations in his favorite book, *The Five Chinese Brothers*. His mother, Alma Ann, had read this story to him countless times and Elmer knew every word of it by heart. This was fortunate, because Elmer could not read. He'd tried, both in the two years he'd attended school and with Alma Ann, but for some reason he found it impossible to recognize the letters of the alphabet in combination with each other. Elmer had no difficulty identifying them individually, but set up together the way they were in books and newspapers and on signs and other things confused him. He had taken *The Five Chinese Brothers* with him from the farm and he looked at the pictures in it while reciting the story to himself several times a day. Elmer was anxious to show the book to his friend, but he would wait until he was certain Pace was really his friend. Alma Ann had told Elmer that sharing something, even a book, was the greatest gift one human being could bestow upon another. It was very important, she said, to have complete and utter faith in the sharer, to know that he or she would share in return. Elmer was not yet sure of this friend, since he had never had one other than Alma Ann, though he hoped that he and Pace would become perfect companions.

The five Chinese brothers were identical to one another, and they lived with their mother. They had no father. One brother could swallow the sea; another had an iron neck; another could stretch his legs an unlimited distance; another could not be burned; and another could hold his breath forever. Elmer recited the story softly to himself as he looked at the pictures, twirling his engineer's cap for a few minutes on one foot, then switching it to the other. The Chinese brother who could swallow the sea went fishing one morning with a little boy who had begged to accompany him. The Chinese brother allowed the boy to come along on the condition that he obey the brother's orders promptly. The boy promised to do so. At the shore, the Chinese brother swallowed the sea and gathered some fish while holding the water in his mouth. The boy ran out and picked up as many interesting objects that had been buried under the sea as he could. The Chinese brother signaled for his companion to return but the boy did not pay attention to him, continuing to hunt for treasures. The Chinese brother motioned frantically for him to come back, but his little friend did not respond. Finally the Chinese brother knew he would burst unless he released the sea, so he let it go and the boy disappeared. At this point in the story, Alma Ann had always stopped to tell Elmer that this boy had proven not to be the Chinese brother's perfect friend.

The Chinese brother was arrested and condemned to have his head severed. On the day of the execution he asked the judge if he could be allowed to go home briefly and say goodbye to his mother. The judge said, "It is only fair," and the Chinese brother who could swallow the sea went home. The brother who returned was the brother with an iron neck. All of the people in the town gathered in the square to see the sentence carried out, but when the executioner brought down his sword, it bent, and the Chinese brother's head remained on his shoulders. The crowd became angry and decided that he should be drowned. On the day of his execution the Chinese brother asked the judge if he could go home and bid his mother farewell, which the judge allowed. The brother who returned was the one who was capable of stretching his legs. When he was thrown overboard in the middle of the ocean, he rested his feet on the bottom and kept his head above water. The people again became angry and decided that he should be burned.

On the day of the execution, the Chinese brother asked the judge for permission to go home to say goodbye to his mother. The judge said, "It is only fair." The brother who returned was the one who could not catch on fire. He was tied to a stake and surrounded by stacks of wood that caught fire when lit, but the Chinese brother remained unscathed. The people became so infuriated that they decided he should be smothered to death. On the day of his execution, the Chinese brother requested that he be allowed to go home to see his mother. The judge said, "It is only fair," and of course the brother who returned was the one who could hold his breath indefinitely. He was shoveled into a brick oven filled with whipped cream and the door was locked tight until the next morning. When the door was opened and the Chinese brother emerged unharmed, the judge declared that since they had attempted to execute him four different ways, all to no avail, then he must be innocent, and ordered the Chinese brother released, a decision supported by the people. He then went home to his mother with whom he and his brothers lived happily ever after.

Elmer knew that he and Alma Ann could have lived happily ever after had she not been worked to death by Hershel Burt and Emile, who would have also worked him to death had Elmer not executed them. He hoped with all of his might that this boy Pace would be worthy of his friendship and not be like the boy who accompanied the Chinese brother to the sea. Elmer put down *The Five Chinese Brothers* and looked at Pace. The boy's eyes were open. Elmer stopped twirling his foot.

"You gonna let me go home to my mama?" Pace asked.

Elmer remembered what the judge had said to the Chinese brothers.

"It's only fair," he said.

Pace sat up. "Can I go right now?"

"Problem is," said Elmer, "I don't know I can trust you yet."

"Trust me how?"

"To come back."

Pace stared at Elmer's pale blue eyes.

"You're crazy, mister," he said.

"Alma Ann said I weren't, and she knows better'n you."

Pace looked around the room.

"Guess the door's locked, huh?"

Elmer nodded. "I don't guess."

"So I'm a prisoner."
Elmer started twirling his cap on his right foot.
"You'n me is gonna be perfect friends."
"Holy Jesus," said Pace.
Elmer shook his head. "Jesus is bunk."

"I just couldn't handle it, peanut, seein' you and Pace so sudden after all them years livin' on nothin' 'cept hope. Reality's a killer, Lula, you know? That's why I

run from you like I done. Been six months now, though, and I'm gettin' used to bein' outside the walls. Might be I'm more ready to deal with things the way they are, includin' you'n Pace."

"If we ever find him."

"We'll find him sweetheart. Ain't no kidnapper gonna keep our fam'ly apart. After all, we're together again, even though the circumstances is rotten."

It was nine A.M. and Sailor and Lula were sitting at the kitchen table in Beany and Bob Lee's house having coffee. They'd been awake most of the night, not talking very much, mostly just holding and looking at one another and crying. They'd finally fallen asleep in each other's arms, fully clothed, emotionally exhausted, on the living-room floor. Lance had awakened them about an hour ago, shaking Lula, saying, "Y'all can use my bed, Aunt Lula. I'm up." The telephone rang and Beany came into the kitchen from the laundry room and answered it.

"Boyle home."

She listened for a few seconds, then handed the phone to Lula.

"Police, for you."

"This is Lula Fortune. Yes, Detective Fange, of course we can. My boy's daddy's here now, he'll be comin' with us. Soon as possible, I understand. Bye."

She handed the phone back to Beany, who hung it up.

"Detective Fange wants us to come down to the police station, Beany, see if we can recognize any faces in their suspect books we mighta noticed in the park."

"I'll go next door right now, make sure Tandy Flowers can watch the kids."

A half hour later Sailor, Lula, and Beany were on their way to New Orleans police headquarters in Beany's red 1988 Toyota Cressida station wagon. Sailor and Lula sat in the backseat, holding hands and not talking, while Beany drove. She took Bonnabel Boulevard to Metairie Road, turned left and followed it west into Orleans Parish until they hit the Interstate, which she seldom used, preferring to drive on surface streets; but today was different, they were in a hurry, so Beany braved the truck traffic and headed downtown on Highway 10.

"You don't have to come in, Sailor, you don't want to," Lula said, after Beany had parked the wagon and they were walking across the street to the station. "No need for you to be uncomfortable."

"It's okay, Lula. These kinda cops ain't much compared to them old boys at Huntsville. In there you blink more'n twice a hour and the man figures that's one too many, he'll lay your head open quicker'n grain goes through a pigeon. I'll be fine, honey, thanks for thinkin' of it."

Detective Fange gave Beany and Lula several large books of mug shots to look through. Sailor sat next to them at the table, thinking that he might recognize one or two men he'd known in North Carolina or Texas prisons. Fange was a short, stout, dark-haired man in his mid-forties. He had a deep triangular crease in the center of his forehead that twitched every few seconds, and he had a habit of smiling briefly after he spoke a sentence.

"You even think you seen one of these fellas in Audubon Park, you holler, right?" said Fange, punctuating this order by exposing his tobacco-stained teeth for a half-second.

The two women nodded.

"I'll be in my office, two doors down, you need me."

After Fange had gone, Beany said, "That triangle on his forehead? That's right where the third eye is."

"Third eye?" said Lula. "What are you talkin' about?"

"It's the mystical one allows a person to see into the soul. Read about it when I was pregnant with Madonna Kim."

"Beany, I just ain't up for that strange shit right now. Let's go over these faces."

Beany and Lula looked carefully at each photo, full-face and profile of every man and a few women, but recognized none of them. Sailor didn't see anyone he knew until they were halfway through the final book.

"I know him," he said, pointing to a particularly ugly white man who looked a lot like former President of the United States Lyndon Baines Johnson. "He bunked in Walls Unit at Huntsville, same as me. Afton Abercrombie, that's him. Everybody called him LBJ, 'cause of the resemblance. He hated bein' called that since he was convinced it was LBJ allowed the Mafia to assassinate John F. Kennedy in Texas. Claimed Johnson was in cahoots with the Dallas organized crime people who done it. Abercrombie's kind of a nut about the subject, reads all the books come out concernin' the case. Says Crazy Eyes Santos had a lot to do with it, too."

"What was he in for?" Beany asked, pointing to Abercrombie's picture.

"Multiple rape and attempted murder, I believe. Liked to screw old ladies, *real* old ladies, like in their eighties. He'd get jobs as a janitor or nurse's aide in nursin' homes and attack old women couldn't defend theirselves. Said most of 'em didn't complain, half of 'em bein' senile and not knowin' what was goin' on, and the other half thankful for the attention. What done Abercrombie in was rapin' a dyin' woman hooked up to some breathin' device. Tubes come loose durin' the assault that set off a signal and the nurses caught him in the act."

"One real sick puppy," said Beany.

"No doubt about it," Sailor said. "Abercrombie jacked off a dozen times a day, dreamin' about old ladies. Good poker player, though."

After they'd finished looking through the books, Beany and Lula stopped into Detective Fange's office. He looked up from his desk and the triangle on his forehead twitched.

"No luck, hey, ladies?" he said.

Lula shook her head no.

"What now?" she asked.

"We got bulletins out about the boy, and officers showin' copies of the photo of him you give us. Any information turns up, I'll let you know."

"We're gonna keep searchin' ourselves," said Sailor.

"Expect you would," said Fange. "Let's hope Pace just walks in the door tonight askin' what's for supper. Happens sometimes."

Detective Fange gave a quick smile and returned his attention to the papers on his desk. Sailor took Lula and Beany by the arm and led them to the elevator.

Perdita Durango was sitting in Poppy Papavero's blue BMW in front of the building when Sailor and the two women came out. She was waiting for Poppy, who had told her he had to drop into the police station for a minute in order to renew his hunting license. Poppy had laughed after he said this, and told her to leave the motor running. Perdita dipped her head as soon as she spotted Sailor, hoping he wouldn't look in her direction. He guided his female companions across the street without turning toward Perdita, and she relaxed as she watched him climb into the backseat of a red station wagon and drive away. She wanted to follow Sailor and find out where he was staying. He was the only person alive who could link her to the robbery attempt more than ten years before in Texas. Perdita thought about this while she waited for Poppy. There was only one thing to do, she decided, and that was to kill Sailor.

"Thanks for waiting, sugar," said Poppy, as he got into the car. "Eddie Fange's one serious coonass, but he's dependable as trouble. He sure is upset about this kidnapping case, though, I can tell."

Poppy steered the BMW into traffic.

"What case is that?"

"A ten-year-old boy was kidnapped out of Audubon Park. Here, Eddie gave me a photograph."

Poppy took the picture out of the left breast pocket of his jacket and handed it to Perdita.

"Boy's name and address are on the back," he said. "Some Short Eyes got him, I bet. Those are the scum of the planet. They ought to be shot on the spot and their bodies fed to the gators."

Perdita read the name, Pace Roscoe Ripley, and the address, 833 Charity Street, Metairie, Louisiana. She memorized the address and handed the photo back to Poppy.

"Yes," she said, "that's terrible."

"You partial at all to hummin'birds?" asked Elmer.

"What you mean, 'partial'?" said Pace.

Elmer Désespéré sat in the cane chair twirling his engineer's cap on the toes of his city-dirt-blackened right foot.

THE CUBAN

EMERALD

"Mean, do you like 'em."

Pace rested on his elbows, dangling his legs over the edge of the narrow bed.

"Ain't seen many, but I suppose. They just birds."

Elmer bared his mossy teeth. "One time Alma Ann and me spotted a Cuban Emerald," he said, and shifted the cap to his equally soiled left foot. "Alma Ann had her a bird book said that kinda hummin'bird don't naturally get no further north'n South Florida. But we seen it hoverin' over a red lily at Solange Creek. Alma Ann said it musta been brought up by someone to Louisiana 'cause it was too far for it to've strayed."

"What color was it?"

"Green, mostly, like a emerald, and gold."

"You ever seen a emerald?"

"No, but they's green, I guess, which is why the bird's called that."

"What's Cuban about it?"

Elmer frowned and let the hat fall off his foot.

"This'n's special, Alma Ann said. Ain't no other bird like it over the world."

"My mama and me had us a bird, but it died."

Elmer's eyes opened wide. "What kind?"

"Parakeet. It was blue with a white patch on the head. His name was Pablo."

"How'd he die?"

Pace shrugged. "We just found him one mornin' lyin'

on his side on the floor of his cage. I took him out and looked in his mouth."

"Why'd you do that?"

"What the doctor always does to me when I'm sick, so I done it to Pablo."

"See anythin'?"

"Not real much. Pulled out his tongue with my mama's eyebrow tweezer. It was pink."

"You bury him?"

"Uh-uh. Mama wrapped Pablo in a ripped-up dishtowel and put him in the freezer."

"Why'd she do that?"

"We was gonna burn him later, but we forgot. Mama says throwin' a body on a fire's the only way to purify it and set free the soul. The kind of Indians they got in India do it, Mama says. But we just forgot Pablo was in the freezer till a bunch of time later when Mama was cleanin' it out and found the dishtowel all iced up. She run hot water over it and unrolled it and there was Pablo, blue as always."

"What'd she do?"

"Stuffed him down the disposal and ground him up."

Elmer whistled through his green teeth. "Don't guess that done heck for his soul."

Pace lay back on the bed and crossed his arms over his chest.

"I reckon his soul had pretty well froze solid by then," he said.

"If I ever had a Cuban Emerald died on me, I wouldn't burn it, or stuff it in no disposal, neither. I'd eat it."

Pace closed his eyes. "The beak, too? Bird beaks is awful sharp."

"Yes, I believe I would. I'd swallow it beak and all, so my insides'd glow emerald green."

"Don't know how I ever coulda thought you was crazy, Elmer. I apologize."

Elmer nodded. " 'Preciate it."

Santos looked in the mirror over the washbasin in the restroom of his office on the top floor of the Bayou Enterprises building on Airline Highway in Kenner and

KEEPING

THE FAITH

adjusted his hairpiece. He used a wet tissue to scrub off the excess mucilage that had trickled down and dried on his forehead. Santos took off his yellow-framed dark glasses and stared at himself. He hated the nickname Crazy Eyes, but he had to agree with the old Don, Pietro Pericolo, who had given it to him when he was the Don's driver, that his eyes were indeed very strange. The red pupils spun and danced inside the green irises, which were surrounded by yellow sparks. Santos put his sunglasses back on. The old Don had been dead for many years now, and Marcello still missed him. Don Pericolo had kept his word and made certain that Santos was in position to take over the organization when the stomach cancer claimed him. On his deathbed, the old Don had motioned for Santos to come closer, and whispered in his ear, "*Che cosa viene appresso,* Marcello?" Then Don Pericolo had died, his last taste of life softly settling on Santos's face.

"What comes next, Don Pericolo?" Santos said to his own reflection.

He went into his office and sat down behind the gigantic oak desk that had been built in Palermo more than one hundred years before for Lupo Sanguefreddo, Don Pericolo's predecessor. Santos pressed a button that was on the underside of the right top drawer and the door to an outer room opened, admitting Carmine Papavero.

"Marcello, you look *meraviglioso!*" said Carmine.

"Sit," Santos said, motioning with his right hand to a chair on the opposite side of the desk. "There is a serious matter that I would appreciate your trying to do something about. A young boy has been kidnapped here in New Orleans, the grandson of an old friend of mine. I want you to find him, if possible."

"Marcello, I know of this situation already. I have a photograph of the boy."

Carmine took the photo out of his pocket and put it on Santos's desk.

"Is this the grandson of your friend?" he asked.

"It is. How did you get this?"

"From Eddie Fange, the detective who takes care of the Orleans Parish payoffs. It's his case."

"Very good, Carmine. My friend is very worried about the boy, as you can imagine."

"Of course, Marcello. It's a horrible thing, the theft of a child."

"*Tutto ciò mi preoccupa*. The way the world is today worries me. With all these *pazzi* running loose, nobody is safe, not even a small boy."

Carmine nodded. "I have a description of the kidnapper. He was *scalzo*, barefoot. An insane person."

Santos sighed deeply. "I must call the child's grandmother now and comfort her. Go and find out what you can."

Carmine stood, picked up the photo and replaced it in his coat pocket.

"Please convey to her my sympathies," he said, and left the room.

Santos nodded and began dialing Marietta's number. She answered before the second ring had ended.

"Lula?" Marietta shouted.

"It is I, Marietta, Marcello."

"Oh, Marcello, I'm frantic. There ain't been no word yet."

"I just wanted to inform you that my people are doing everything they can."

"Dal and Johnnie are helpin' me get through this. They're lambs."

"Marietta, you know I think a great deal of you. Had it not been for my respect for Clyde, things could have been different."

"Let's not talk about that kind of thing now. I'm way too upset to consider mighta-beens. I appreciate your efforts on behalf of my family. I'm in your debt."

"No, Marietta, where we are concerned there is no debt, only friendship."

"Marcello, if some maniacal creature's harmed my beautiful grandboy I'll just die!"

"It is at such moments that my old friend Don Pericolo would say, *non bisogna abbattersi così facilmente.* One should not get discouraged so easily. You must remain strong."

"Yes, Marcello, you're right, of course."

"We will speak soon, Marietta. Goodbye."

"Bye."

Marietta hung up and wiped the tears from her eyes with a vermilion silk handkerchief that had belonged to her grandmother, Eudora Pace.

"The gangster got a line on the case yet?" Johnnie asked.

Marietta stared hard at him, then said, "Who ain't a gangster these days, Johnnie Farragut? The whole world's nothin' but a big racket, with one murderin', thievin' bunch tryin' to horn in on another. Least Santos is on our side, and I'm glad we got him."

"Amen," said Dalceda. "Anybody ready for another cocktail?"

"My daddy murdered a man once," Pace said. "I heard my grandmama talkin' about it with her friend Johnnie, who's a private investigator and carries a gun. Mama

NIGHT IN

THE CITY

thinks I don't know Sailor really killed Bob Ray Lemon, but I do. He'll get you, too, soon as he finds out what's happened and where I am, which'll be any minute. Him or Crazy Eyes Santos, Grandmama's other man friend, who's a big gangster and kills people all the time. Won't bother him a bit to twist your puny chicken head clean off the neck. You'd best just let me go and run for it, or you'll be fish scum, you'll see."

Elmer Désespéré was beginning to realize his mistake. He had grabbed an unworthy boy, someone not suited to be his perfect friend, and he was in a fix over what to do about it.

"I done murdered *two* men," said Elmer, who was sitting in the cane armchair across from where Pace sat on the floor next to the bed. Elmer had tied Pace's hands together behind his back after the boy had attempted to put out Elmer's eyes with the fork part of the Swiss Army knife. "And prob'ly I'll have to murder a mess more before I'm through, includin' you, it looks like."

"Let me go and you won't have to kill me. I won't tell anyone where you live. You don't let me go, they'll find us and kill you sure. Least right now you got a choice."

Elmer stood up. "I got to go out, get some fresh water. I'll figure out later what I'm gonna do, when I talk to Alma Ann. She'll guide my hand."

Elmer took hold of Pace, dragged him into the empty closet and shut the door.

"I wouldn't be surprised she instructs me to twist *your* puny chicken head," Elmer shouted. "Clean off the neck!"

He went out into the street and headed for the Circle K convenience store. This child was a puzzlement, Elmer thought. He would have to be more careful of who he snatched next. Follow him for a while, maybe, see if he acted right. This one weren't no good at all and likely never would be. Can't trust a pretty face, ain't *that* the truth!

Elmer had been thinking so hard about Pace that he did not realize he'd turned the wrong way off Claiborne. Somehow he had wandered onto a street called St. Claude and he was lost. It was very late at night and Elmer missed Alma Ann. He wished she were here and he was tucked into bed with her reading to him. He saw some men gathered up ahead at the corner and he walked toward them. Before Elmer had gone halfway, he noticed that three men were walking toward him, so he stopped where he was and waited, figuring if the direction he needed to go in was behind him then he wouldn't need to cover the same ground. The three men, all of whom were black and no older, perhaps even younger, than Elmer, surrounded and stared at him.

"Come you ain't got no shoes on?" asked one.

"Don't make no connection otherwise," said Elmer.

"Feet's black as us," said another of the men.

"You heard of the Jungle Lovers?" the third man asked.

Elmer shook his head no.

"We them," said the first man. "And this our street."

"You a farm boy?" asked the second.

Elmer nodded. "From by Mamou," he said. "Road forks close the sign say, 'If It Swim I Got It.' "

"Where that?"

"Evangeline Parish."

The three men, each of whom was wearing at least one gold rope around his neck, began moving around Elmer, circling him, glancing at one another. Elmer stood absolutely still, unsure of what to do.

"You got any money, hog caller?" said one of the men.

"No," said Elmer.

The man behind Elmer pulled out a Buck knife with a six-inch blade, reached his right arm around Elmer and slit his throat completely across, making certain the cut was deep enough to sever the jugular. Elmer dropped to his knees and stuck all four fingers of his left hand into the wound. He sat there, resting back on his heels, blood cascading down the front of his overalls and on the sidewalk, for what seemed to him like a very long time. Elmer looked up into the dark eyes of one of the men and tried to speak. He was asking the man to tell Alma Ann he was sorry to have failed her, but the man did not try to listen. Instead, he took out a small handgun, stuck its snub nose all the way into Elmer's mouth and pulled the trigger.

THE EDGE

OF LIFE

"Don't worry about it, Sailor," said Bob Lee, "I can afford to take the day off. This ain't no small matter, after all, and the police can't be expected to exercise a whole lot of manpower over one more stole child."

"Want you to know I 'preciate it, Bob Lee," Sailor said, "extra much. What you and Beany's doin' for me and Lula's special. I mean, you got your own two kids and a new business to worry about. I ain't about to forget it."

Sailor and Bob Lee were preparing to hit the streets together and search for Pace.

"Just let me kiss Beany goodbye and we can get movin'."

Sailor waited for Bob Lee in the living room. Lula was still asleep, having taken a medication Beany's doctor had prescribed to help her relax. How he, Sailor, could have been so selfish, so stupid, so cowardly, astounded him. Had he acted like a man six months ago, Sailor thought, this wouldn't have happened. It had been his opportunity, after wasting the dime, to take care of Pace and try to make things up to Lula. They were his responsibility and he'd failed them and himself as well. Sailor prayed now for another chance. Ten years in the joint had proven to him that it wasn't every man who had a choice in life. The fact that he'd blown it twice before with Lula ate at Sailor. It was his fault, he'd decided, that their precious son was in this unholy circumstance. If anything terrible happened to Pace, Sailor knew he would be unable to go on living.

In Huntsville, Sailor had come in contact with the most hard-luck boys he ever could have imagined. Most of them were murderers or had been involved, as he'd been, in the commission of crimes during which one or more persons had died. One fellow, Spook Strickland, a tough nut from Anniston, Alabama, where he'd been a Grand Dragon or Imperial Wizard in the Ku Klux Klan, had told Sailor his belief that God's message was that nobody *deserved* to live. The gospel according to Spook Strickland maintained that staying alive was an option not available to everyone, and that's why people like him existed, to destroy the least worthy among them. Sailor had asked him why God had created billions of people in the first place, and why He continued to produce more, a question that gave Spook Strickland a good, long laugh. After he'd settled down, Spook had told Sailor that most human beings were provided for target practice. Those people were slaves, Spook said, disposable and without redeeming value. Organizations such as the Klan and the Great Whites, the prison gang Spook led at Huntsville, were placed on earth as reminders of the true nature of homo sapiens, and to maintain a necessary order. Each member of the Great Whites had on the underside of their upper right arm a tattoo of a shark with the words ORDER AT THE BORDER OF HELL etched around it. Spook Strickland had tried to get Sailor to join but Sailor resisted, even though things might have gone easier for him while he was inside, since Spook's gang controlled many of the more worthwhile and profitable functions in the prison, including drugs, cigarettes, and the machine shop. Sailor had hung out with the Great Whites, though, more for protection from the Mexican Mafia and Uhuru Black Nation than out of subscription to their ideas. He had needed to stay alive, that's all. He had, and now it was up to him to act right.

"Ready to roll, fella," said Bob Lee, putting a hand on Sailor's right shoulder. "Beany'll make sure Lula's all right while we're gone. Told her we'd call in a couple of hours or so."

Perdita Durango had parked a few houses away behind a silver Plymouth Voyager. She watched Sailor get into the passenger side of Bob Lee's black and tan Lincoln Town Car, and started the engine of Poppy's BMW as Bob Lee backed down the driveway into the street. She followed the Lincoln onto Veterans Memorial Boulevard and headed east two cars behind, turning right on Pontchartrain, then going east again on 610. Bob Lee got off the Interstate at Gentilly Boulevard and backtracked to St. Bernard Avenue, where he pulled into a shopping center and parked in front of a storefront office that had the words GATOR GONE, INC. stenciled on the tinted window glass. Perdita brought the BMW over near the shopping center entrance and kept the engine idling. Bob Lee got out of the Town Car and went into the office of Gator Gone, Inc. Sailor stayed in the car.

Perdita picked up the Smith & Wesson .357 Magnum from the floor between her feet, shifted the BMW out of neutral into first gear and glided toward the black and tan Lincoln. She pulled into the parking space to the right of Bob Lee's car, shifted the BMW into reverse, keeping the clutch and brake depressed, and lowered her window. Sailor was staring straight ahead as Perdita raised the gun with both hands and aimed at his right ear. The instant she pulled the trigger Sailor leaned forward to pull his left pantsleg over his boot. The bullet went behind Sailor's head through the Lincoln's windows into the roof of a pink Acura parked on the other side, ricocheted off the Acura and to the right into the yellow wood facing of the building. Sailor hit the deck and kept his head covered with his arms while Perdita peeled the BMW backward out of the parking space, spun a one-eighty, braked hard, shifted furiously into first and floored the gem of Bavarian engineering, fishtailing her way out of the shopping center. Sailor opened his door, rolled on the pavement and looked up in time to see its blue butt with the words PAPA UNO on the license plate streak away.

Bob Lee came running out of Gator Gone, Inc., saw Sailor stretched out on the ground, and yelled, "Ripley! You all right?"

Sailor rolled over on his back, saw the frightened look in Bob Lee Boyle's big brown eyes, and closed his own.

"I'm fine, Bob Lee," he said, and grinned, feeling the sun on his face. "Just never know what part of your life's liable to open up again at any particular time."

Sailor opened his eyes and saw the crowd of people gathering around him. He scrambled to his feet and brushed himself off.

"Come on, Bob Lee," he said, "let's go find my boy."

Guadalupe DelParaiso had lived at the same address all of her life, which was seven months more than eighty-six years. She had never married, and had outlived each

OUT OF THIS

WORLD

of her sixteen siblings—nine brothers, seven sisters—as well as many of her nephews and nieces, and even several of their children. Guadalupe lived alone in the down-stairs portion of the house her father, Nuncio DelParaiso, and his brother, Negruzco, had built on Claiborne Avenue across the street from Our Lady of the Holy Phantoms church in New Orleans. The neighborhood had undergone numerous vicissitudes since Nuncio and Negruzco had settled there. At one time the area had been home to some of the Crescent City's most prominent citizens, but now Our Lady of the Holy Phantoms, where the DelParaiso family had worshiped for forty years, and where Guadalupe and her sisters and brothers had attended school, was closed down, and the street was littered with transient hotels, beer and shot bars, pool halls, and the drunks, junkies and whores who populated and patronized these establishments.

Guadalupe rented the upstairs rooms in her house by the week. She made sure to get the money in advance and kept a chart on the wall in her kitchen listing the dates the rent was due for each room. Guadalupe would rent to singles only, and not to women or blacks under the age of fifty. She had not left the house in four years, depending on her bachelor nephew, Fortunato Rivera, her sister Romana's youngest son, who was now fifty-two years old, to bring her groceries and other supplies twice a week. She paid Fortunato for what he brought

183

her on Wednesdays and Sundays, and gave him a shopping list for the next delivery. Guadalupe had not been sick since the scarlet fever epidemic of 1906. The doctor who attended her at that time told her mother, Blanca, and Nuncio, that Guadalupe's heart had been severely damaged by the fever and that he did not expect her to live beyond thirty. It was Guadalupe's oldest sister, Parsimonia, however, who succumbed to a weak heart at the age of twenty-nine. As the years passed, Guadalupe only became stronger in both body and mind.

Guadalupe was making up her list for Fortunato, who would be coming the next day, Wednesday, when she heard a pounding noise, like the stamping of feet, coming from the room above the kitchen. She had rented the room almost a week before to a soft-spoken, polite but bedraggled-looking young man whom, she believed, worked for the railroad. The young man had seen the ROOM FOR RENT sign in the front window and had taken what had once been her brothers Rubio, Martin, and Danilo's room immediately. He paid Guadalupe a month's advance because, he told her, it looked like the kind of a place his mama, Alma Ann, would have been pleased to occupy. Guadalupe had not seen the young man since the day he'd rented it.

This pounding disturbed Guadalupe; she could not concentrate on her grocery list. She went into the pantry, picked up her broom, brought it back with her to the kitchen and bumped the end of the handle several times against the ceiling.

"You stop!" she shouted. "No noise in Nuncio's house or you get out!"

The pounding did not stop, so Guadalupe put down the broom, left her part of the house and walked slowly up the stairs. She stopped at the door to the young railroad worker's room and listened. She could not hear the pounding as distinctly from the hallway as she could in her kitchen, but she heard it and knocked as hard as she could on the door with her left fist.

"You stop! You stop or leave Nuncio and Blanca's house!"

The pounding continued and Guadalupe removed her keychain from the right front pocket of her faded rose-colored chenille robe and unlocked the door. The single overhead sixty-watt bulb was burning, but there was nobody in the room. The noise was coming from the closet, so she opened it. A body hurtled past Guadalupe so fast she did not see who or what it was, and by the time she turned around, it was gone. Guadalupe had been tremendously startled; suddenly she felt faint, and staggered to the cane armchair. She sat down and attempted to calm herself, but she was frightened, thinking that the shadow that had rushed out of the room had been the ghost of her severely disturbed brother

Morboso, the one who had hanged himself in that closet. It had been Parsimonia who discovered Morboso swinging there, and it was this incident, Nuncio and Blanca believed, that had damaged Parsimonia's heart and led to her premature death. The ghost of Morboso DelParaiso was loose, Guadalupe thought. Perhaps he had driven away the young railroad man, or even murdered him as he had the pretty young nun, Sister Panacea, whose body Nuncio and Negruzco and Father Vito had secretly buried after midnight on October 21, 1928, in the garden of Our Lady of the Phantoms. Guadalupe rested and remembered, seeing again what she could not prevent herself from seeing.

Pace ran down the stairs and managed to turn the big gold knob on the front door by holding it between the bottom of his chin and his neck. He ran a block down the street before he stopped in front of an old Indian-looking guy who was leaning against the side of a building sipping from a short dog in a brown paper bag.

"Untie me, mister!" Pace shouted at him. "Get my hands loose, please!"

The Indian's eyes were blurry and he seemed confused.

"A crazy man kidnapped me and tied me up!" Pace yelled. "I just ran away! Help me out, willya?"

The Indian held out his half-pint of wine, as if he didn't know what to do with it if he assisted Pace.

"Put your bottle down on the ground and undo this here knot," said Pace, turning around and showing the Indian his hands.

The old guy bent over and carefully deposited his sack on the sidewalk, then straightened up and tugged on Pace's hands until they were freed.

"Thanks a lot, mister," said Pace, tossing away the strip of bedsheet Elmer had used to bind him. He reached down and picked up the Indian's short dog and handed it to him. "Don't know if God loves ya," Pace shouted, "but I do!"

Pace ran along Claiborne until he saw a police car parked at the curb. He went over to the car and stuck his head in the open window on the passenger side.

"Evenin', officer," Pace said to the policeman sitting behind the steering wheel. "I'm Pace Roscoe Ripley, the boy got kidnapped in the park the other day? Are you lookin' for me?"

Federal Bureau of Investigation agents Sandy Sandusky and Morton Martin stopped into the Lakeshore Tap, a tavern on Lincoln Avenue about a mile from Wrigley

THE OVERCOAT

Field. In another hour or so, when the Cubs game ended, the place would be packed; at the moment, the two agents were the only customers. They sat on adjoining stools, ordered drafts of Old Style, and drained half of their beers before Sandusky said, "Is there a field office in North Dakota?"

"Where in North Dakota?" asked Martin.

"Anywhere."

"Why do you ask?"

"Because that's where we're going to be transferred to unless we can nail whoever ordered the hit on Mona Costatroppo, that's why."

Both men took another swig of beer.

"We know it was Santos," Martin said.

"The man hasn't had a rap pinned on him once. Never done time, Morty, never had a speeding ticket."

"If we can locate the shooter, we got a chance."

"He's in the sports book at Caesar's Palace right now, a hooker on each arm, betting trifectas at Santa Anita with the fee."

"So what do we do, Sandy?"

"Buy bigger overcoats."

Sandusky swallowed the last of his draft and climbed down from his stool.

"Order me one more, Morty. I'll call the office."

Sandusky came back five minutes later, a big grin on his ruddy face, and slapped Morton Martin on the back.

"Give us a couple shots of Chivas," Sandusky said to the bartender.

"What's up?" asked Martin. "Santos turn himself in?"

"Not quite, but Detroit picked up the hammer."

"No kiddin'. I thought you told me he was in Vegas juggling bimbos."

"Where I'd be."

The bartender brought two Scotches and Sandusky slapped down a ten.

"Keep the change," he said. "Looks like I won't need a new overcoat, after all."

Sandusky handed a glass to Morton Martin, tapped it with his own, and said, "To Tyrone Hardaway, a.k.a. Master Slick, resident of Chandler Heights, Detroit, Michigan, product of the Detroit public school system, who just couldn't keep his mouth shut or the blood money in his pocket for more than twenty-five minutes."

Sandusky and Martin knocked down the Chivas.

"Apparently, this Hardaway was letting all of his homeboys know what a big man he was, working for the guineas. He was buying gold chains, leather jackets and primo drugs for everyone in the neighborhood while bragging about the fresh job he'd done in Chicago for the famous Mr. Crazy Eyes. Somebody snitched on him, of course, and the Bureau brought him in no more than an hour ago. They say he told them that Santos's people forced him to whack the broad; otherwise, Tyrone said, the organization was going to move him off his turf and let another gang handle the crack trade."

"I know J. Edgar Hoover always said there was no such thing as organized crime in this country, but I'd bet Tyrone is telling the truth."

Sandusky laughed, and motioned to the bartender. After both men had refills, Sandusky held up his glass and admired its amber contents.

"To the truth!" he said.

"Yes, Mama, he's here with us now, and he's doin' fine."

"Put the boy on the line, Lula."

IN THE WAKE
OF THE NEWS

Lula handed the phone to Pace.

"Hi, Grandmama. Marietta, I mean. How you?"

"Pace, darlin', you call me Grandmama all you want. We been so worried! Your Auntie Dal and Uncle Johnnie been with me the whole time, waitin' for news. Your mama says you ain't got a hair out of place. Tell me what happened."

"I escaped, is all. The man left me tied up in a closet and when someone opened the door I ran out of there fast as I could. Bo Jackson couldn'ta caught me. I was flyin'!"

"Who was this man? Did he harm you?"

"Crazy kid, not too much older'n me, really. Name was Elmer Désper-somethin'. He was searchin' for a friend, he told me. His mama died on their farm and after he didn't get along with his daddy and brother, so Elmer killed 'em. Least that's what Sailor said. Elmer's dead, too. Found him this mornin' with his head blowed off. He didn't really hurt me none, only tied up my hands when he put me in the closet. I got a wino to undo me after I escaped."

"What a terrible time for you! Is Sailor intendin' to stay with y'all for a while?"

"I hope so, Grandmama. He's my daddy."

"I'm just so pleased you're safe, sweetie pie. I'll see you real soon. Let me have your mama again. Love you."

"Love you, Grandmama."

Lula took the phone.

"Mama, I want you to know Sailor and I've decided to try to stay together. We got a lot of talkin' to do and things to work out, we know, but we both think it'd be best for us and Pace if we can be a fam'ly."

"Lula, you know I only want what's best for you and my grandboy, so I hope you know what you're doin'. This ain't the proper moment for us to get into this, what with Pace just bein' found and all, but I got a strong opinion on the matter, as you could imagine."

"Yes, Mama, I can. We're all gonna stay here with Beany and Bob Lee while Sailor and I figure out what to do. Bob Lee's offered Sail a job at the alligator repellent factory, and Beany'd like me to take care of Madonna Kim and Lance when she enrolls in the St. John the Baptist College of Cosmetology in Arabi. There's plenty of room here, and if things work out between me'n Sailor, we'll find our own place."

"Well, Lula, I've promised Dal I'd hold my tongue until we're all calmed down from the kidnappin', so I will."

"Mama, it *is* my life."

"Johnnie got some business to attend in N.O. next week and he's asked me to come with him. You can't believe what a rock Johnnie's been for me these last few days."

"You oughta marry him, Mama, before you get too old to enjoy yourself."

"Lula, hush. I expect we'll be stayin' at the Sonesta."

"Separate rooms?"

" 'Course, separate rooms. Listen, Lula, I'm thinkin' I'll attend the Daughters meetin' this afternoon, now we got Pace safe, so I'll say bye. I'll let you know when Johnnie and I'll be in."

"Okay, Mama."

"Keep a eye on my grandboy, now. Love you, Lula."

"Love you."

Marietta was hanging up when Dalceda Delahoussaye came in through the back door like a fireball.

"Marietta! I been dialin' you like mad!"

"I was talkin' to Lula, honey, and Pace. He ain't hurt and he sounds fine. Man who took him's dead."

"Lula told us he was fine last night!" Dal shouted as she raced through the kitchen into the front room.

"Needed to hear his precious voice. Dal, what are you doin'?"

Dal had switched on Marietta's nineteen-inch Sony Trinitron and was flipping the dial.

"What I was callin' you about was Santos. What number's that all-news channel?"

"Eleven, I believe. What about Santos?"

"He's been arrested! Look, here it is."

"Arrested? What are you ravin' about?"

"Hush and listen!"

"In New Orleans this morning," said the television news reader, "federal agents took into custody reputed organized crime king Marcello Santos on charges of conspiracy to commit murder and murder of his alleged mistress, Mona Costatroppo, in Chicago last week."

Videotape came onscreen showing Santos, his hands cuffed in front of him, being taken out of the backseat of a black car and led by FBI men up the steps of a courthouse. His sunglasses were askew, as was his toupee. He was obviously shouting something at the reporters following him, but it was impossible to hear what he said. The news reader continued:

"Santos, known as 'Crazy Eyes' because of an unusual congenital opthalmic condition that causes his eyes to frequently change color and appear unstable, became the head of the Pericolo crime family following the death of Pietro 'The Sicilian Salmon' Pericolo in 1962. According to noted organized crime authority Hieronymous Bernstein, author of the best-selling book, *From Fear to Uncertainty: Behind the Breakdown of the Mafia*, the Pericolo family, which controls rackets across the southern United States, especially along the Gulf Coast, had its foundation in Palermo under the leadership of the legendary gangster Lupo Sanguefreddo, who was assassinated while having a shave in the barbershop of the Egyptian Gardens Hotel in Miami Beach in 1939. Sanguefreddo was fighting a deportation order at the time of his death."

Marietta turned off the set.

"Don't know how they can get away with sayin' all that stuff about a man never been convicted of a thing!" she said. "Do you believe he done it, Dal?"

"You mean had Mona Costatroppo killed?"

Marietta nodded.

"Hard to say. That kind of woman digs her own grave."

The telephone rang and Dal picked it up.

"Hello, Johnnie. Yes, we just watched it on the news. She's all right. Yes, I will. She talked to Pace and he's fine. Yes, okay. Bye."

Dal hung up and said, "Johnnie wanted to know if you'd heard about Santos. Says he'll be back around six. I'm goin' to the Daughters at two. You comin'?"

"Might as well. They'll all want to know about Pace."

"Don't be worryin' too much about your old buddy Marcello. He'll find a way out, like always."

"Ain't it somethin', though, Dal, how it's just one weird thing happens after another?"

"Stay tuned," said Dal, opening the front door. "I got a powerful hunch there ain't never gonna be a end to it."

"It's the terrible truth, Jimmie. They are transferring Santos to Chicago tomorrow for the arraignment. No bail is
being allowed until after the charges are brought. And

A WELL-RESPECTED

MAN

even then, who knows? Our
attorney here in New Orleans,
Irving Bocca, says there is no
guarantee the Chicago judge
will grant bail, no matter what amount. The government
wants him bad, and they figure this is their best shot. I
don't blame them, either, for thinking that. You know
Marcello wanted to take care of this business himself,
and I believe he acted too hastily, though I know nothing
of the details."

"Who is handling the case in Chicago for him?"

"Louis Trifoglio. The father, not the son."

"Good. So, you know how to proceed?"

"*Conte pure su di me*. Jimmie, you can count on me."

"You have my blessing, Carmine. Have you settled
things yet with Tiger Johnny?"

"Yes. *Ci comprendiamo*. I am certain we understand
each other."

"You know, as far as I am concerned, *è un buon' a
nulla*. He is good for nothing, like all of the Ragusas."

"*C'è voluto del bello e del buono per convincerlo*. It
took some convincing, but things will be all right."

"If you say it, it must be so. *Ciao*, then, Carmine. You
will keep me informed of Marcello's circumstances."

"Of course, Jimmie. I will. I am grateful for your blessing. *Ciao*."

Both Jimmie Hunchback, in New York, and Poppy
Papavero, who was sitting in Santos's chair in the office
of Bayou Enterprises, hung up. Poppy had been entrusted

to run the organization in Marcello's absence, regardless of how long that might be, and he was pleased with the knowledge that Santos's associates had agreed without debate about his capability. He picked up the receiver again and dialed Perdita's number.

"Yes?"

"Perdita, my pet, things are good, under control. While Marcello is away, I am in charge. Now listen, I've been thinking about us, what we should do."

"Do about what?"

"I think we should get married. What do you think of that idea?"

"Heard worse."

Poppy laughed. "Does that mean you say yes?"

"Sure, it's what you want."

"It is. I know of a good house to buy, in a good place; a modest yet spacious house in a convenient location. It belongs now to Irving Bocca, who is willing to sell."

"Where's this house?"

"Metairie. It will be perfect, Perdita. We won't know anybody there, and nobody will know us."

After an unusually late supper, Bob Lee excused himself
and said he had to go back to the office to take care of
the paperwork he'd ignored during the excitement of the

last few days, and Beany took
Lance and Madonna Kim up-
stairs to put them to bed, leaving Lula, Pace, and Sailor
at the dining-room table. Lula had told Beany not to
worry about the dirty dishes, she'd heated up more of
the Community coffee Sailor had taken such a liking to,
and poured them each another cup. During the time
Lula had gone into the kitchen for the coffee and come
back, Pace had put his head down on the table and
dozed off. Lula sat next to Sailor and together they
watched their son sleep.

"Well, peanut, I'd like to believe we got us a fightin'
chance."

"You'd best believe it, Sail. Look at that little boy
breathin' there. If he ain't worth the effort won't never
nothin' will be. Pace and us both just come through the
worst scare we've ever had, and I guess to hell we've
had a few in our short lives. It's one thing your gettin'
yourself in deep shit with bad actors like Bob Ray Lemon
in North Carolina and Bobby Peru in Texas, but now
you got a fast-growin' son needs you. Reverend Willie
Thursday back home in Bay St. Clement says a boy
without a father's a lost soul sailin' on a ghost ship
through the sea of life."

"It ain't my intention to let you and Pace down, and
I won't be playin' no chump's game again, neither.
Speakin' of the past, though, I seen Perdita Durango."

"Here in New Orleans?"

Sailor nodded. "Didn't figure on tellin' you this, but

someone took a potshot at me in the shoppin' center by the Gator Gone office the other day. I'm pretty sure it was Perdita. I made Bob Lee swear he wouldn't say nothin' about it."

"But, Sail, why would she want to shoot you?"

"Maybe she thinks I'm out to get her for runnin' out on me and Peru. I'm the only one could I.D. her for the caper. I also spotted her on the street last week when I was leavin' Hattiesburg. She was with the same blue BMW squealed away from the shootin' in the shoppin' center."

"Sweet Jesus, honey. What're we gonna do about this?"

"Don't panic, peanut. I'll just have to keep the eyes in the back of my head open. Prob'ly Perdita was aimin' to warn, not kill, makin' sure I knew it was her had the drop on me. I wouldn't say nothin' to the cops, anyway."

"Sail, this unpredictable scary behavior don't almost improve my peace of mind."

"I know it, but you're my baby Lula, and at least we're in it together again. You, me, and Pace, that is. Reverend Willie Thursday won't be preachin' no ghost ship sermon concernin' our son."

Lula leaned over and kissed Sailor below his left ear.

"I love you, Sailor Ripley. I always figured we'd find our way."

Sailor grinned and put his left arm around Lula, pulling her closer to him.

"Peanut, it was just inevitable."

EVIDENCE

O

1
9
5

III

SULTANS

OF AFRICA

"Piero Aldobrandi, unhelmeted, was wearing the black cuirass and the red commander's scarf and carrying the baton which linked him forever to this scene of carnage. But the figure, turning its back to the spectacle, relegated it to the mere status of landscape, and the face, strained by a secret vision, was the emblem of a supernatural detachment."

JULIEN GRACQ,
LE RIVAGE DES SYRTES

"The best thing you can hope for in this life is that the rest of the world'll forget all about ya."

Coot Veal shifted his shotgun from right to left and

SULTANS OF

AFRICA

checked the fake Rolex on his right wrist. Buford Dufour had bought the watch for forty bucks in Bangkok when he was in the air force and sold it later to Coot for fifty.

"Half past four," he said. " 'Bout time to give it up, I'd say."

Pace Ripley pulled a brown leather-coated flask from the left hip pocket of his army surplus field jacket, unscrewed and flipped open the top and took a swift swig of Black Bush that he'd filched from his daddy's bottle.

"Want 'ny?" he asked Coot, holding out the flask.

"Naw. I'll get mine shortly."

Pace recapped the flask and put it back in his pocket.

"What you mean, Coot, hopin' you get forgot?"

Coot Veal, who was fifty-eight years old and had never been farther away from South Louisiana than Houston, Texas, to the west; Mobile, Alabama, to the east; and Monroe, Louisiana, to the north; who never had married or lived with a woman other than his mother, Culebra Suazo Veal, who had died when Coot was forty-nine; grinned at the fifteen-year-old boy, his friend Sailor Ripley's son, and then laughed.

"Mean it's not in a man's interest to let anyone interfere with or interrupt what's there for him to do."

Coot pulled out a pistol from his hip holster and held it up.

"This here's a single-shot Thompson Contender loaded with .223 rounds. Not the biggest gun in the world, not the best, either, but it suits me. Read about a Seminole brought down a panther with one in the Everglades."

Coot replaced the pistol in its holster.

"Zanzibar slavers over a century ago called the gun the Sultan of Africa. The world's still ruled by weapons, Pace. They're what separates the operators from the pretenders."

Pace looked out over the marsh. He and Coot hadn't had a fair crack at a duck all day. Water had somehow leaked into his high rubber boots and soaked his woollen socks.

"Okay, Coot," he said, "let's hit it. Gettin' skunked like this is insultin'."

Pace and Coot were riding in Coot's 1982 Dodge Ram pickup, headed home to New Orleans.

"You think I should go to a hooker, Coot? I mean,

before I start in on regular girls. To have me some experience."

Coot laughed and spit out his open window. Pace uncorked the flask and swallowed some Bush.

"Tough call, kid," said Coot. "Only time I used one I was about your age, maybe a year older. My daddy, Duke Veal, had fashioned me a shoulder holster to wear when I was playin' Chicago gangster. I had a old Chinese target pistol was missin' the firin' pin and stuck it in the shoulder holster. Put on my Sunday suit coat over it and marched down to Rampart Street. Wanted to take off the coat in front of a woman, impress her, so she'd think I was a real racket boy.

"I found me a big, tall red-headed gal and followed her upstairs to her crib. Price was three dollars, plus one or two for the room. Four or five dollars altogether. It was about all the dough I had at the time, but I was convinced this was my best idea to date and I was goin' through with it, hell or high water. Made damn sure she saw me take off my jacket, but she was a seasoned whore. Didn't bat an eye or laugh at me, neither one. Just laid there on the bed with no kind of look at all on her face. I left the holster on, only took off my pants. Did the deed, stood up, put my pants and coat back on and got out of there. Woman never said a word about the gun or nothin' after I give her my money. Haw! How's that for a backfire?"

"You ever tell your daddy 'bout it?"

"Duke? Hell, no. I had, he woulda kicked my sorry ass to Memphis. Duke Veal didn't take kindly to throwin' away good money on bad women."

"Guess you're sayin' I oughta save mine."

Coot nodded and turned on the headlights.

"Might be best," he said. "But I think I still got that old shoulder holster around someplace, you decide you need it."

"That you, Sail?" Lula shouted.

Sailor Ripley let the screen door slam shut behind him.

"No," he said. "It's Manuel Noriega."

THE MIDDLE

YEARS

Lula came into the front room from the kitchen and saw Sailor slump down into the oversized, foam-filled purple chair that Beany and Bob Lee Boyle had given them last Christmas.

"Who'd you say? Barry Manilow?"

"No. Manuel Noriega, the *de*posed president of Panama."

"Uh-uh, you ain't him. You got too good a complexion."

Lula went over and kissed Sailor on the top of his head.

"Long day, huh, Sail?"

"You know it, peanut. Gator Gone's goin' great guns since the envir'mentalists got that new reptile protection law passed. Ever' fisherman in the state of Louisiana needs it now. You up to fetchin' me a cold Dixie?"

"*No hay problema, esposo*," Lula said, heading toward the kitchen. "Bet even Bob Lee never figured his gator repellent'd go this good."

"Yep. That one ol' formula 'bout to make him a rich man. He's talkin' about settin' up a Gator Gone Foundation that'll make funds available to poor folks been victims of gator and croc attacks who're in need of ongoin' medical treatment."

Lula returned with the beer and handed it to Sailor, who drank half of it right away.

"Thanks, honey," he said. "Sure build up a thirst

overseein' that shippin' department. You know we're gonna build us our own warehouse in Gretna?''

Lula sat down on the zebra-striped hideaway.

"First I heard. Beany ain't said nothin' about it."

"Yeah, the Algiers location can't hold us, and besides, makes more sense to own than rent."

"Best thing we coulda done is settle here, Sail. New Orleans give us a whole bunch more opportunity than we ever coulda got back in North Carolina."

Sailor took another swig of Dixie.

"Not the least of which is bein' a thousand miles away from your mama. We never woulda had a chance in Bay St. Clement, peanut. Not with Marietta on my case."

"She's calmed down now, darlin', since she seen how swell a daddy you been to Pace. Also your workin' so hard for Bob Lee and everythin'."

"Wouldn'ta made it this far is all I know."

The telephone on the front hall table rang. Lula got up and answered it.

"Ripley home. Hi, Beany. Uh huh, Sail too. God don't make men the way He used to, like Mama says. Madonna Kim got over her cold yet? Uh huh. Suppose I might could. Lemme ask God's almost-best piece of work."

Lula tucked the receiver into her breast and turned toward Sailor.

"Honey? Beany'd like me to 'comp'ny her to Raquel Lou Dinkins's house for about a hour? See her brand new baby, Farrah Sue. You-all be able to survive without me that long?"

Sailor tipped the bottle and drained the last bit of beer, then nodded.

"Hell, yes. Me'n Pace'll get us a pizza or somethin'. Where is that boy, anyway?"

"Went huntin' this mornin' with Coot Veal, your buddy married his mama."

Lula put the phone back to her mouth and left ear.

"Want me to drive?" she asked Beany. "Uh huh. See ya in a minute."

Lula hung up, picked up her purse and car keys from the table, went over to Sailor and kissed him again on the top of his head.

"Sweetheart, you know what?" she said.

"What's that?"

"You losin' some hair right about there."

"Where?"

"Kinda in the middle toward the back."

Sailor felt around on his head with the fingers of his right hand.

"I can't feel nothin' missin', Lula. Anyway, it can't be. Nobody in my fam'ly went bald. Not my daddy or his daddy or my mama's daddy."

"None of 'em lived long enough to go bald, darlin'. Don't worry about it, just a small patch is all. I gotta go."

Sailor jumped up and dropped the beer bottle on the floor.

"Goddammit, Lula! You just gonna run out and leave me after tellin' me I'm goin' bald?"

"Bye! Back soon!"

Sailor watched Lula go out the front door, heard her open and close the door of her new Toyota Cressida station wagon and start the engine. He went over to the hall mirror and leaned his head forward while attempting to look up into the glass, but he couldn't see the top of his head. He turned sideways, tilted his head toward the mirror and rolled his eyes all the way over, but that didn't work, either. The front door slammed and Pace came in.

"What you doin', Daddy?" he said. "And where's Mama goin'? What're you all twisted around for?"

Sailor bent forward toward the mirror again, angling off slightly to the right.

"Take a look, son. Am I losin' my hair?"

Pace stared at Sailor, then shook his head slowly.

"More likely you're losin' your mind, Daddy. We gettin' a pizza for supper?"

The Rattler brothers, Smokey Joe and Lefty Grove, non-identical sixteen year old twins who were named by their daddy, Tyrus Raymond Rattler, after the two men his daddy, Pie Traynor Rattler, considered to have been the

two best pitchers in major league history, tooled through Gulfport along Old Pass Christian Road in their Jimmy, trading swigs off a fifth of J. W. Dant. They were headed back to New Orleans from Biloxi, where they had gone to pay their respects to the memory of Jefferson Davis on his birthday. Smokey Joe and Lefty Grove had taken advantage of the school holiday to visit Beauvoir, the last home of the Confederate president. The federal holiday officially honored the birth of the Reverend Martin Luther King, Jr., who happened to have been born on the same day as Jeff Davis, a convenience appreciated by the Rattlers.

Their mother, Mary Full-of-Grace, had been institutionalized for the past six years in Miss Napoleon's Paradise for the Lord's Disturbed Daughters in Oktibbeha County, Mississippi, and the Rattler boys had considered visiting her but decided the drive was too far for the short time they had. Besides, Lefty Grove reasoned, she wouldn't recognize them for who they were. The last time they'd gone up with their daddy, six months before, she'd called them the apostles James and John, sons of Zebedee. Sometime during the twins' seventh year, Mary-Full-of-Grace became convinced that she was in fact the Holy Virgin, mother of Jesus. She'd insisted that the people about her were not who they pretended to be and that every man she encountered desired to sleep with her. Tyrus Raymond took her to several doctors during the following two years, but her condition worsened, resulting finally in the diagnosis of a breakdown of a schizoid personality, with the recommendation that she be institutionalized as a hopeless case.

"What you think about Mama?" Lefty Grove asked Smokey Joe, who was behind the wheel.

"What you mean, what I think?" said Smokey Joe, reaching out his right hand for the bottle.

"Mean, you got a notion she ever gonna recover her mind?"

"Ain't 'xactly likely, how Daddy claims."

Smokey Joe took a quick swallow of Dant and handed the fifth back to his brother.

"You finish it, Lef'. I be dam see the road."

"Want me to drive? I feel good."

"Feelin' good and drivin' good ain't the same. I'll handle her home."

Lefty Grove put his red and yellow L.A. Gear high tops up on the dashboard and sucked on the bottle.

" 'Bout Ripley?" said Smokey Joe. "Figure to trust him?"

"You mean on the deal, or just keep his mouth shut?"

"Either."

"Need a third, Smoke, you know? Pace a good boy."

"Mama's boy, you mean."

"Least he got him a almost sane one."

Smokey Joe snorted. "What you mean, almost sane?"

"Like Daddy said when he come home after deliverin' Mama to Miss Napoleon's, 'Ain't one of the Lord's daughters got a firm grip on life.' He put a extra pint of fear in their blood, makes 'em more uneasy than men."

"Daddy ain't naturally wrong."

"Uh-uh," said Lefty Grove. "He's a Rattler, by God."

Pace stared out the window of his room at the maple tree in the backyard. A blue shape flashed from branch to branch. Pace raised his right hand, formed his fingers

IN BED WITH

THE RATTLERS

into a gun and pointed the barrel at the flitting patch of blue.

"Bam!" he said, bouncing the tip of his index finger off the glass. "You done bought the farm, Mister Jay."

Pace lowered his hand and relaxed his fingers. He heard the downstairs telephone ring.

"Son!" Sailor shouted. "Phone for you!"

"Comin', Daddy!"

Pace stood up, pushed his feet into a pair of thongs, walked downstairs and picked up the telephone receiver from the hall table.

"Pace Ripley speakin'."

"Hey, boy, how you?" said Lefty Grove Rattler. "What you been up to?"

"Oh, hi, Lefty. Nothin' special. Went duck huntin'."

"Got you a few birds, huh?"

"Naw. Weren't a good day."

"Been thinkin' 'bout what we discussed?"

"Haven't had time, tell the truth."

"You still like the idea, though, don't ya? Better'n workin' at Popeye's."

"Know that, Lefty Grove. I like it, sure. Mean I'm in, I suppose."

"Knew we could count on you, Pace. Smokey Joe'll be glad to hear it."

"Thought he don't like me."

Lefty Grove laughed. "He don't like nobody much, even me. Ain't to worry."

"I guess I won't, then."

"There you go. Meet us at Nestor's Sandwich City on Magazine, to-morrow evenin' at six."

" 'Cross from Jim Russell's Record Shop?"

"Got it right and tight tonight, Pace Roscoe."

"How you know my middle name's Roscoe?"

"Us Rattlers is straight from the gate to the plate, boy. Got to know who you're dealin' to, well as with. Abyssinia."

Lefty Grove hung up and Pace stood in the hallway holding the phone to his left ear.

"You still on the line, son?" Sailor shouted from the kitchen.

Pace put the receiver back in the cradle.

"All through, Daddy."

"Come on in, then," said Sailor, "have a piece of your mama's pecan pie. You been lookin' skinny."

Pace massaged the back of his neck with his right hand. His head ached and he needed a drink.

"Back in a minute, Daddy," he said, and went out the front door.

Pace sat down on the bottom step and rested his head and arms on his knees. The Rattlers were dangerous, sly boys, all right, and now he was about to climb into bed with them. At first Pace had thought they were joking when they proposed that he join them in knocking off the shakedown drop in the Quarter. Lefty Grove explained to him how each Thursday afternoon at three o'clock the weekly protection money from the businesses in the French Quarter was delivered to an idle caboose on a sidetrack near the Bienville Wharf. The collection remained there, cared for by two men, until approximately three forty-five, when a private armored car came to fetch it. Pace was both scared and excited by the idea of committing a crime. Something inside him wouldn't allow Pace to resist the promise of the thrill.

A cousin of the Rattlers, Junior Broussard, had worked for Carmine "Poppy" Papavero, the Gulf Coast rackets boss, for four years until Ju-nior's death a couple of months back. Junior's wife, Manuela, had shot him, Lefty Grove said, during an argument about Junior's friendship with a woman named Jaloux Marron, a hostess at one of Papavero's nightclubs. Until then Junior had been in charge of the protection haul. Lefty Grove and Smokey Joe had overheard their cousin talking about the setup with their daddy, Tyrus Raymond, and decided to snatch the cash if they could. Junior being out of the way made things easier, Lefty Grove explained, because they wouldn't have to kill their own cousin if they were forced to. Three guns were better than two, the Rattler brothers figured, and Lefty Grove had tapped Pace to complete the trio. The deal was set to go down next Thursday. Today was Sunday. Pace had four days to make up his mind.

"What you doin' sittin' out here?" Sailor asked from behind the screen door.

Pace lifted his head. "Just thinkin', Daddy." He stood up. "Guess I'm a little tired. Me and Coot got out early this mornin'."

"Well, come have some pie. Your mama'll be insulted we don't make a major dent in it."

"Daddy?"

"Yes, son?"

"You never have talked much about the time you done

DOWN TIME

in prison."

Sailor sliced into his wedge of pecan pie with one side of his fork, scooped up the piece, delivered it to his mouth, chewed and swallowed. Pace sat across the table from him, holding a fork in his right hand, ignoring his own piece of pie.

"Not much to say, I guess, Pace. Jail time is down time far's I'm concerned. You don't come out any different than how you went in, 'cept older. That's if you come out at all."

"How many times you been in, Daddy?"

"Twice."

"Once for manslaughter and the other for armed robbery, that right?"

"Correct. Didn't mean for the first to happen. Just a bar fight with a slime-bucket named Bob Ray Lemon was botherin' your mama. I was nineteen years old and didn't know no better'n to knock the sorry son of a bitch cold. He didn't get up and they stuck me in a work camp up on the Pee Dee River for two years. I'd had me any kind of lawyer I wouldn'ta done a minute."

"What happened the other time?"

Sailor put down his fork and shook his head.

"That was my mistake. Lucky I'm even here to talk about it. Your mama and me was tryin' to get to California from North Carolina, runnin' from your grandmama, Marietta, and her detective friend, Johnnie Farragut, who she'd signed on to track us down. Marietta didn't like the idea of her fine and only daughter takin' up with a ex-con such as myself. Lula met me at the gate the day I got my walkin' papers from Pee Dee, and we took off in her old white Bonneville convertible. Made it as far as West Texas when we about run out of funds. That's where I went over the line.''

Sailor stood up and walked over to the refrigerator, opened it, took out two bottles of Dixie beer, shut the door, came back over to the table, handed one to Pace and sat back down. He popped his open and took a long swallow.

"How you mean 'over the line,' Daddy?"

"Your mama was pregnant with you and we was stuck like bugs in a bottle, stranded in a podunk town called Big Tuna. Met a mean fella there named Bobby Peru. Lula said he was a black angel and told me I should stay away from him, but of course I didn't pay no attention and got hooked in on a plan to rob a feed store over to the county seat, Iraaq. We went ahead and done it and Bobby got his head blowed off. I got caught, of course, and Peru's girlfriend, a strange Tex-Mex gal named Perdita Durango, who was drivin' the getaway car, escaped. They sent me to Huntsville, where I put in ten years down to the hour."

"Whatever happened to Perdita Durango?"

Sailor smiled, lifted the brown bottle to his lips and took a sip.

"Oh, she's around somewhere, I suspect. A Grade-A piece of work like her don't just fade away."

"What was it like inside the walls, Daddy? How'd you get by?"

"Remindin' myself every minute of every day how stupid I was to end up there in the first place. Knew if I was still alive when I got out I'd do anything, any kind of straight job, not to go back again. And I thought about your mama and you, how you-all were gettin' along. Figured you both were better off without me, the way I'd been goin', but knew if I had the chance to change, I would. Until I could prove it to myself, though, it wouldn't do to make you and your mama suffer my ignorance. That's why it took a little while after I got sprung for us to get back together. I had me some serious readjustin' to do."

"Bet there's some lost souls behind them bars."

"The lostest, son. Now eat your pie and drink that beer and we'll get us some rest. Tomorrow's already feelin' like it's gonna be longer'n today."

Sailor flopped down into the Niagara, levered the foot-
rest chest high, fingered the space command and flipped
on the new RCA 24-inch he'd bought at Shonga-

loo's Entertainment Center
right after his recent raise from
Gator Gone. He dotted the i across cable country until
it hit channel 62, when the sound of CCR's "Bad Moon
Risin' " stopped him. It was past one o'clock in the morning. Pace was asleep upstairs and Lula was at Beany's,
baking cakes for the Church of Reason, Redemption and
Resistance to God's Detractors fundraiser. Sailor ticked
the volume up a couple of notches. Suddenly the music
faded out and a man's face in close-up came on the
screen. The man was about forty years old, he had blond,
crew-cut hair, a big nose that looked like it had been
sloppily puttied on, and a dark brown goatee.

"Howdy, folks!" said the man, his duckegg-blue eyes
blazing out of the set like laser beams. "I'm Sparky!"

The camera pulled back to reveal Sparky standing in
front of an old-fashioned drugstore display case. Behind
the counter and just to the side of Sparky's left shoulder
was another man of the same approximate age but four
inches taller. This man had thick, bushy black hair with
a severe widow's peak and a discernibly penciled-in
mustache under a long, sharply pointed nose.

"This asparagus-shaped fella behind me's my partner,
Buddy," Sparky said, and Buddy nodded. "We'd like to
welcome you-all to Sparky and Buddy's House of Santería, the store that has everything can make that special
ceremony just right."

The words SPARKY & BUDDY'S HOUSE OF SANTERIA 1617
EARL LONG CAUSEWAY WAGGAMAN, LOUISIANA flashed on

the screen in giant red letters superimposed over the two men. The letters stopped flashing and Sailor sat up and took a closer look. Blood root suspended from the ceiling and dozens of jars filled with herbs, votive candles in a variety of colors, and various unidentifiable objects lined the rows of shelves behind Sparky and Buddy. Sparky raised his arms like Richard Nixon used to, the fingers of each hand formed in a V.

"We've got the needs for the deeds, ladies and gentlemen. We've got the voodoo for you! Oh, yes! We've got the voodoo, hoodoo, Bonpo tonic, Druid fluid, Satan-ratin', Rosicrucian solution, Upper Nile stylin', Lower Nile bile'n Amon-Ra hexes, Tao of all sexes, White Goddess juice'll kick Kundalini loose, the Chung-Wa potion'n ev'ry santería notion!"

Sparky lowered his arms, walked forward past the camera eye, then returned carrying two twisting snakes in each hand.

"Get a load of the size of these rattles, Pentecostals!" he shouted, raising his right arm, the one draped with a pair of diamondbacks. "And ladies, check out these elegant coachwhips!" Sparky raised his left arm to show them off. "Hey, Buddy! Tell the good folks what else we got!"

Sparky walked off-camera again and Buddy leaned forward over the counter, pointing to the floor with his right hand.

"Take a good look here, people," he said, and the camera eye dipped down, closing in on a one-hundred-ten-pound brindled pit bull stretched out on the floor, his head resting between his front paws, a seeing-eye harness strapped to his barrel chest. Next to his enormous head was a black water bowl with the name ELVIS stenciled on it in raised white letters. "We got a good selection of man's best friends, too."

Sparky's legs came back into view and the camera panned back up.

"Mullahs, mullahs, mullahs!" Sparky intoned. "You got trouble with the Christian Militia? Come on down! And hey, troops! Them mullahs makin' you a cardiac case? Those Ayatollah rollers got you grittin' your bicuspids? You-all come on down, too! We are a hundred and five percent bona fide non-sectarian here at Sparky and Buddy's!"

Again the giant red letters spelling out SPARKY & BUDDY'S HOUSE OF SANTERIA 1617 EARL LONG CAUSEWAY WAGGAMAN, LOUISIANA flashed on the screen.

"Right, Buddy?" Sparky said, and the flashing letters blinked off.

"Affirmative, Sparky!"

"And, Buddy, we got a special I ain't even told my mama about! This week only we discountin' mojos. Mojos for luck, love, recedin' hairlines, bald spots, money honey and—my own favorite, works like a charm—irregularity. This one's guaranteed to get you goin' and flowin'!"

Sailor watched as from behind the counter Buddy lifted up two wine glasses filled to the brim with amber liquid. He handed one to Sparky and together they raised the glasses high.

"Well, Buddy, as our old pal Manuel used to say in Tampa many years ago, *salud* and happy days! This is the four-hundred-sixty-sixth appearance we've made for Sparky and Buddy's House of Santería. Remember, we're at 1617 Earl Long Causeway, in the community of Waggaman, servicin' all of south Louisiana. Y'all come on down!"

"Bad Moon Risin' " started up again and the giant red letters reappeared for several seconds before the station segued into the video of L.L. Cool J's "Big Ole Butt." Sailor pressed the OFF button on his space command. He sat still for a minute, then lifted his left arm and with his fingers explored the crown area of his head where Lula had told him his hair was thinning. He got up and went over to the hall table, picked up the pencil and pad next to the telephone and wrote down Sparky and Buddy's address.

"They do it different now, Lula. Ain't hardly no cuttin' to speak of. Drop a line in through the navel and reel the creature out. Stick a Band-Aid on it. Make two tiny incisions on the sides, is all."

SNAKES IN THE
FOREST

"But, Mama, you gotta stay in the hospital least one night. The doctor told you that."

"Don't know why. I might could take off right out of there, I feel good enough."

"Doctor says if there's a stone they gonna have to cut it out the regular way. That happens, you'll be in there three, four days."

"There ain't no stone and I ain't lettin' 'em run no tubes through me."

"You'll let 'em do what's necessary, Mama. This is your gall bladder we're discussin' now, not no perm job. I'll be into Charlotte tomorrow at noon, so I'll see you about one-thirty, all goes well. Dal's pickin' me up."

"You already talked to her?"

"Of course, Mama. We got it worked out how to take care of you."

"You're still the one needs takin' care of, Lula. How's my grandboy doin', anyway?"

"Pace is just fine, and so's Sailor. He got him a raise a couple weeks back. Bob Lee's Gator Gone repellent's sellin' better'n ever."

"Sailor throw the new money away on a TV or a truck?"

"Oh, Mama, you ain't never gonna give him a chance to redeem himself, are you?"

"Guess you're still attendin' that crackpot church, else you wouldn't be usin' that word."

"The Church of Reason, Redemption and Resistance to God's Detractors ain't no kinda crackpot outfit, Mama, and you know it."

"Know nothin' of the kind. Saw where that preacher of yours got arrested for havin' a video camera hid in the ladies' restroom at the church buildin'."

"It wasn't Reverend Plenty put it there, Mama. There's always snakes in the forest."

"With that type of weird individual leadin' the flock, Lula, you can't expect no better. Reverend Willie Thursday spoke here in Bay St. Clement last Sunday about false prophets like Goodin Plenty, sayin' how the world depends on them to save it. That's stupid talk, Lula. No way the world's welfare revolves around any one person. You'd best get shut of that nut case soon as now."

"The Three R's is right thinkin', Mama. Goodin Plenty just got a different way of gettin' his point across."

"Such as when he run off to Barbados with his twelve-and-a-half-year-old stepdaughter and she said after how he made her do them disgustin' things with chicken parts!"

"Mama, Rima Dot Duguid done long since been committed. And you tellin' me now you believe what you read in the *National Enquirer?*"

"If she's in the bin, it's no thanks to that perverted sinner."

"Mama, let's stop this. You gotta get your mind right for the comin' ordeal. I'll see you tomorrow."

"Just as well. Here's Dalceda now, comin' in the back door."

"Bye, Mama. Love you."

"Love you, Lula. Dal says for me to assure you she'll be at the airport on time. That is if Monty, her new Lhasa apso, don't play sick again."

"I'm sure everything'll be fine, Mama. Bye."

Pace got up late. He didn't want to go to school. He lay in his bed, listening for noises in the house. Lula had delivered her cakes to the church and then had Beany

drive her to the airport. Sailor was at the Gator Gone ware-

house. Pace opened the drawer of his bedside table, took out a pack of Camels and shook one loose. He reached back into the drawer and found a book of matches that had the words WHATEVER HAPPENED TO SEAN FLYNN? printed on it, struck one and lit up the cigarette.

He thought about this deal with the Rattler brothers, and the more he thought about it the less he liked it. Now that he knew the score, however, there would be no easy way to back out. The Rattlers, Smokey Joe in particular, would not take kindly to the idea of Pace's walking around with this information in his head. Either they'd have to alter their plans and choose another target, or do something about Pace, and Pace figured the Rattlers didn't take full possession of more than one idea at a time.

The other night Pace had watched a movie on TV with Sailor called *Bring Me the Head of Alfredo Garcia*. It was about an out-of-luck American piano player in Mexico who searches for the body of a guy who'd impregnated the daughter of a wealthy *patrón*. The American must cut off the corpse's head and bring it to the *patrón* in order to earn a reward. The movie, Pace remembered, got progressively weirder and wackier, with the American doublecrossing and being doublecrossed by everyone he meets. There was a lot of killing, so much killing that the movie became kind of a comedy, with mutilation upon mutilation. The last part was the best, he thought,

2
2
2

when the American has the head in a sack covered with flies as he drives his battered old convertible through the sun-baked, scabrous Mexican countryside, swatting away the flies that threaten to engulf him. Pace wondered why the American didn't just put the head in the trunk of the car.

The Rattlers weren't about to let him beg off. Better to tough it out, Pace decided. Lefty Grove and Smokey Joe didn't fool around, and *Bring Me the Head of Pace Roscoe Ripley* was one movie Marietta Fortune's only grandboy was insufficiently prepared to appreciate. Pace lolled around the house most of the day, reading around in one schoolbook and another without retaining much of anything. He didn't so much dislike school as he disliked having to show up there every weekday. If attendance were voluntary, he thought, then school wouldn't be so bad. He could quit in another year, when he turned sixteen, but he knew that his parents wouldn't like it. Sailor hadn't finished grammar school, so of course he expected Pace to go to college and go on to become president of the United States or something. Pace wondered how many presidents had been the son of a twice-convicted felon.

At four o'clock the telephone rang and Pace answered it.

"Pace, honey, that you?"

"Yes, Mama. You at Grandmama's?"

"I am. Just wanted you and Daddy to know I made it safe and sound. Auntie Dal picked me up at the Charlotte airport and we drove through a absolute terror of a rainstorm all the way to Bay St. Clement. Started pourin' the instant our plane landed and it's still comin' down like a shower of Pygmy darts on a safari. Lightnin', too. Sky's blood red. How's it there?"

Pace looked out a window.

"Nothin' special. Sorta gray."

"How was school today?"

"Same as ever."

"Okay, sweetie pie. You need somethin' and Daddy ain't around, go to Beany, you hear?"

"I'll be fine, Mama. Tell Grandmama hello and hope she comes through."

"Hush, 'course she will. Take care now, Pace. Love you."

"Love you, Mama."

"Be home soon's I can."

"Bye, Mama."

"Bye."

Pace hung up and checked his pockets to make sure he had some money, then left the house and headed for Nestor's Sandwich City to meet the Rattlers. He took a bus to the corner of Canal and St. Charles, got off, walked one block down Canal to Magazine, turned right and continued walking. At the northeast corner of Felicity and Magazine, an obese black woman with the largest bosom Pace had ever seen was sitting on the curb with her legs in the street, singing "Give Me That Old-Time Religion."

"It was good for the Baby Jesus," she sang, "it was good for the Baby Jesus. It was good for the Baby Jesus and it's good enough for me!"

Pace kept walking, wondering how in the world a woman's breasts could grow that large, and he picked up the tune. He began singing, half to himself, half out loud, inventing verses as he headed to the rendezvous.

"It was good for Elvis Presley," Pace sang, "it was good for Elvis Presley. It was good enough for Elvis Presley but it weren't good enough for me."

Pace used Stonewall Jackson, Jimmy Swaggart, Paula Abdul, Magic Johnson, Jimmie Rodgers, and the Ninja Turtles in his altered version of the hymn before he reached Nestor's. He entered Sandwich City and stopped singing when he saw Lefty Grove and Smokey Joe sitting on stools at the counter eating fried oyster po'boys.

"Isn't that Pace goin' into Nestor's?" Beany Boyle asked her son, Lance, as she turned right off Napoleon Avenue into Magazine.

Lance leaned forward over the front passenger seat of his mother's Taurus station wagon and took a look.

"Yeah, that's Pace," he said, and flopped down on the backseat next to his sister, Madonna Kim.

"That Nestor's supposed to be some kinda drug den, ain't it?" said Beany.

"I guess," Lance said. "The Rattlers hang out there, I know."

"The who?"

"Rattlers, Mama. They're brothers."

"Them the ones their daddy set fire to the high school in Cut Off after they quit teachin' Creationism? And the mama's stuck away in some Mississippi home for the depraved?"

"Think so. They're mean ol' boys."

"Wonder if Sailor and Lula know where their boy's spendin' his time."

On his way home from Nestor's, Pace stopped to read a handbill posted on a telephone pole in front of Panther Burn Items.

BLACK PLANET

A CHALLENGE TO WHITE PEOPLE
ARE YOU TIRED OF . . .

Affirmative action quotas that discriminate against Whites in hiring, promotion, and admission to colleges?

A non-enforced immigration policy that has flooded our country with millions of scab-laborers and welfare parasites?

The brain-washing, by the schools and the media, of White Youth with racial self-hatred and genocidal race-mixing propaganda?

A non-White crime wave which makes our cities unsafe for our families?

Sham elections that allow only the lying toadies of the criminal ruling class to enter the halls of government?

The turning of this once-great White Nation into an impoverished banana republic ruled by traitors and criminals, owned by foreign corporations and populated by mongreloids?

If so, why not join with the thousands of your White kinsmen and kinswomen of the Third Position who are fighting for White survival?

JOIN THE WHITE ARMED RESISTANCE! IF YOU ARE INTERESTED IN OUR IDEAS PLEASE WRITE OR CALL . . .

WAR, P.O. Box 2222, New Orleans, LA 70115
Recorded Message (555)MAKE-WAR

When he'd finished reading and turned to go, Pace was startled to see a tall, thin, red-faced man in his mid-thirties wearing a yellow straw cowboy hat, plain long-sleeved white shirt with the cuffs and collar buttoned, and sharply creased black slacks standing directly behind him reading the same handbill over his right shoulder.

"Knew a fella worked derrick with told me his wife started complainin' once, ridin' in the car," said the man. " 'Life with you's just terrible,' she said to him, and threatened to throw herself right out of the car onto the road. 'Hold on just a minute,' this fella told her, 'let me see I can get up some speed.' He guns it up toward eighty, then cuts the wheel hard into a hundred-eighty degree spin, car rolls over four times and somehow they both survive without even one broken bone between 'em. Fella said after that whenever they was drivin' and he started goin' a little too fast, she just quit talkin' and clamped on her seat belt."

Pace slid away from between the pole and the man, nodded at him and walked off without feeling compelled to reply.

"It's awful what's goin' on in the world, Lula, and it ain't about to stop until the worst. Am I right, Dal?"

Marietta was lying in her hospital bed, reading the

KILLERS

Charlotte *Observer*, and talking to Lula and Dalceda Delahoussaye, each of whom were seated on chairs on opposite sides of the bed. They were waiting for the doctor to stop by before having Marietta taken to the operating room.

"Looks it," said Dal. She and Marietta had been friends since their days together at Miss Cook's in Beaufort, more than forty years before. Since that time they had never lived farther apart than a ten-minute walk.

"Whole planet's come unhinged," said Marietta. "Look at this: 'Uniformed Gunmen Kill 8 at Cockfight.' That's the headline. 'Men in military uniforms sprayed gunfire at a group of people attending a cockfight in central Colombia late Saturday, killing eight people, local news accounts said yesterday. The private Radio Cadena Nacional and the domestic news agency Colprensa said the gunmen killed eight people and wounded four in Yacopi in Cundinamarca state, 60 miles north of the capital of Bogota.' Dal, ain't that where Louis used to do business, Bogota?"

"No, Marietta, it was La Paz, Bolivia, but it weren't no better there. Had them a brewery Louis sold 'em parts for. The company needed their own army to protect it and the workers. Louis stayed down there three months once, settin' it up and makin' sure it run right. You remember, Marietta, that's the time I took advantage of his absence to redecorate the livin' and dinin' rooms? He come back and didn't even notice."

"Some husbands is like that, Dal."

"*Some* husband is right."

"Mama, did you take that yella pill the nurse give you?"

"Yes, Lula, dear, I took the yella pill."

"Suppose to calm you."

"I'm calm."

The doctor came in, followed by a nurse.

"How we doin', Mrs. Fortune?" he said. "You ready?"

Marietta folded the newspaper and handed it to Lula.

"Been ready for two hours, Dr. Bonney. Been borin' Mrs. Delahoussaye here and my daughter to death. Don't think you know Lula, do you? Lula, this is Dr. Bonney, a descendant of Billy the Kid. Don't he have the most beautiful wavy black hair and blue eyes? Doctor, this is my favorite daughter, Lula Pace Fortune."

"Lula Ripley, now," Lula said, extending her right hand to the doctor. "How do you do?"

They shook hands.

"You live in New Orleans, your mother's told me."

"Yes, with my husband and son. He's fifteen."

"It's my grandboy's fifteen," Marietta said. "And his daddy that acts like it."

"Mama, stop! Sailor's providin', and he ain't been in no trouble for years."

"Mrs. Fortune," said Dr. Bonney, "I'm gonna let Nurse Conti here prepare you for surgery, if you don't mind. Ladies, I'm afraid you'll have to leave now."

Dal stood up and kissed Marietta on the cheek.

"You be fine, love," said Dal. "I'll talk to you tonight."

Lula leaned over and kissed her mother on the forehead.

"Be tough, Mama."

"Ain't it strange how I always think of your daddy at moments like this?" said Marietta. "Clyde's face slides right into focus whenever I have a serious situation to consider."

"Don't worry, Mrs. Fortune," Dr. Bonney said. "You won't hardly be able to tell we touched you."

"Didn't think Billy the Kid fathered any children," said Lula.

"I'm not a direct descendant of his, Mrs. Ripley, but we are of the same stock."

"Every family's got its killers, Doctor," said Marietta, staring straight at Lula. Then she turned and smiled at Dr. Bonney. "It ain't as if there's anything you could do about it."

"Pace, buddy? Bob Lee mentioned to me today that Beany told him she saw you goin' into Nestor's Sandwich City yesterday down on Magazine. That right?"

LIVES OF THE

HUNTED

Pace looked at Sailor, then away. They were in the kitchen and Pace was eating a bowl of cereal. The Wheaties box with a picture of Michael Jordan on it was on the table between them.

"I guess."

"What you mean, you guess? Either it was you Beany seen or it wasn't. Which?"

"Mean I guess it was me, she says so."

"So what's happenin' in Nestor's these days other'n dope deals?"

Pace scooped up a tablespoonful of Wheaties and crammed it into his mouth. He couldn't answer while he chewed. The telephone rang and Sailor picked it up.

"Ripley home, Sailor speakin'. Hi, peanut, how you? That's good. Told you she'd pull through. Your mama's like a big dog on a red ant. How long you figure? Uh huh. Well, do what's needed. I know. Oh yeah, we're fine. Pace is sittin' here wolfin' his Wheaties like any other All-American pup. We're busier'n blazes at the factory. Okay, I will. Love you, too, peanut. Bye now. Uh huh. You bet. Bye."

Sailor hung up.

"Mama says to tell you she loves you and that both Grandmama and Auntie Dal send their love. Mama's got to stay with your grandmama for several days, until the doctor says Marietta can get around on her own. Now, what's news at Nestor's?"

"Nothin', really, Daddy. Met up with some boys there, is all."

"You in any kinda fix, son?"

"No, Daddy, I ain't."

"You'd tell me, you was, wouldn't you?"

" 'Course."

"Come to me anytime 'bout anything, you understand? Ain't nothin' can upset me 'less you're less'n straight about it."

"I hear you, Daddy. Thanks."

There was a knock on the back door and then it opened. Coot Veal came in.

"Hey, Sail!" Coot said. "Hey, Pace!"

"Hello, Coot," said Sailor. "*Que paso?*"

Coot had on a yellow and blue LSU baseball cap with a drawing of a tiger on it and a white tee shirt with the words BUBBA'S BILOXI PORK BAR printed on the front and WE MIGHT BE CLOSED BUT YOU'D NEVER KNOW IT on the back. He took a clean bowl and a spoon out of the dish tray, sat down at the table and poured himself some Wheaties.

"I was a kid," Coot said, "they had Bob Richards on the box. Bet you don't know who Bob Richards was," he said to Pace.

"Right again," said Pace.

"O-lympic pole vault champ, I believe. And a good Christian. Hollywood even made a movie about him. Or was that Bob Matthias? Maybe they made movies about both of 'em. Matthias was a O-lympic athlete, too. And prob'ly not a bad Christian, either, though I don't know for sure. What I do know for sure is I ain't partial to this new deer dog law they're tryin' to put through in Mississippi. The rich folks there get it in and next week the sonsabitches in Baton Rouge be hollerin', too."

"What law's this?" asked Sailor.

"Seems the Miss'ippi Property Rights Association's lookin' to outlaw huntin' with dogs, only allow still-huntin'."

"They can't do that," Pace said.

"Hell, they can't!" said Coot. "Look what they done about abortion and taxes. Ask your daddy, he knows. Landowners want the territory to themselves, and there ain't much open territory left. No more road huntin' at all, they say, from trucks or standin'. Wanna do away with dogs altogether. You 'magine not allowin' blue ticks or runnin' walkers in the woods? Only place you'll be able to see 'em is up in the Madison Square Garden prancin' around with a tube pushed up their asshole."

"Why they doin' this?" Pace asked.

"What begun it was a old boy in Petal, I think it was, got shot by a hunter after he chained up the hunter's dogs runnin' loose on his property."

"I used to work over in Petal," said Sailor.

"Didn't know that," said Coot.

"For a short time, in a lumberyard. After I weren't required by the Texas state prison system to stay close to home no more."

"Some bad apples, no question, could ruin the sport for ev'ryone. Let their hounds run wild, kill people's pet ducks, scare children. But it ain't most of us can't control our dogs. Hell, a man's dogs is part of his fam'ly. Problem is the landowners who do their huntin' in private clubs. They buy up all the land in the first place and don't leave nothin' for the common man. People should be let to hunt the way they like to hunt. Miss'ippi state legislature done already passed a bill bans huntin' from within one hundred feet of the center line of a road. Now they mean to regulate firearms, too."

"It don't sound good," said Sailor.

"Pretty quick this whole country'll be nothin' but a suburb of Tokyo, anyway. We're lucky, they'll let us out on Sunday to take a leak. Other six days we'll be too worried or busy bendin' over to risk it."

Sailor laughed. "Got a point there, Coot."

Coot stood up. "Gotta take a leak, too," he said, "while I still got the chance. How you doin', Pace? Stayin' out of trouble?"

"Mostly."

"All a man can do," said Coot.

Inez's Fais-Dodo Bar had been a fixture on Toulouse Street in the Quarter for more than thirty years. The original owner, Inez Engracia, had been shot to death

by a jealous lover six months after the place opened. Inez's heir, her sister Lurma, sold out to Marcello "Crazy Eyes" Santos, the organized crime king of the Deep South, who was now serving a life sentence in the Federal Correctional Institution at Texarkana for conspiracy to commit murder and the murder of his mistress, Mona Costatroppo. Mona had been killed in a hotel room in Chicago, where she was waiting to testify against Santos as part of her participation in the Federal Witness Protection Program. The Crazy Eyes Gang and its holdings, legitimized as Bayou Enterprises, were being overseen in Santos's absence by Carmine "Poppy" Papavero. Papavero had invited Bob Lee Boyle to have a drink with him at Inez's to discuss the possibility of Bayou Enterprises becoming involved in the distribution of Bob Lee's Gator Gone repellent and related products. Bob Lee knew better than to reject outright Papavero's overture, so he accepted the meeting and asked Sailor to accompany him.

"You know more about this kind of thing than I do, Sail, that's why I wanted you to come along."

Bob Lee and Sailor were walking along Toulouse toward Inez's at nine o'clock in the evening. They'd left Bob Lee's Grand Prix in the parking lot of Le Richelieu on Barracks Street, where Sailor knew the attendant, Fudge Clay. Fudge's brother, Black Henry, had been at Huntsville with Sailor for two years until another inmate had carved up Black Henry in the shower room, the result of miscommunication concerning a sexual question.

"What the hell I know, Bob Lee? Only thing is to listen to the man, hear what he has to say and take it or don't take it from there."

The two Gator Gone representatives turned into the Fais-Dodo and Sailor immediately spotted Carmine Papavero. The Gulf Coast mob boss, wearing his signature burgundy blazer, was seated at a large corner table with three other men. Papavero's photograph had appeared often enough in the local newspapers and on television since he'd replaced Marcello Santos that even Bob Lee, who made no effort to keep up on current events, recognized him. As Sailor and Bob Lee approached his table, Papavero rose to greet them. He was a large man, his belly strained at the single-buttoned sports coat, and he wore a wide yellow tie decorated by a hand-painted pink flamingo.

"Mr. Boyle, I believe," said Carmine Papavero, reaching his thick right hand toward Bob Lee, who took it quickly into his own and participated in a solid shake.

"Yes, sir," said Bob Lee. "And this is my colleague, Mr. Sailor Ripley."

Papavero withdrew his right hand from Bob Lee's and thrust it at Sailor, who reciprocated.

"A pleasure, Mr. Ripley. Please, sit down both of you."

Two of the men who had been seated at Papavero's table got up and walked away, allowing Bob Lee and Sailor to take their chairs. Papavero did not bother to introduce the man who remained, an extremely thin, blue-skinned individual with a pinhead and creaseless ears the size and shape of dieffenbachia leaves. Bob Lee looked once at the man and did not look at him again. Sailor recognized the man instantly as the former inmate at Huntsville who had stabbed Black Henry Clay, Fudge Clay's brother, to death in the shower room. He was not certain if the man, whose name was Zero Diplopappus, recognized him.

"You fellas need drinks," Papavero said, and signaled a waitress who stood near the table, her only duty while it was occupied by Carmine and his group.

"Dixie," said Bob Lee.

"Two," said Sailor.

"Two Dixies," said the waitress. "Anybody else need anything?"

Zero Diplopappus's ears waved once, as if a sudden breeze had sliced through the room, but he did not speak. Papavero did not reply and the waitress walked away.

"Mr. Papavero, sir," said Bob Lee.

"Please, call me Poppy. All of my friends do."

"I just want you to know, sir, that I agreed to meet with you out of respect, not because I'm interested in changing my arrangements for product distribution."

"That's fine, Mr. Boyle—Bob Lee—I understand, and I appreciate your candor. But I am in a position to make you an offer, a generous offer, on behalf of Bayou Enterprises for fifty-one percent of the Gator Gone Corporation. You would be retained, of course, as director of the company. Name your price."

"Can't do it, Mr. Papavero."

"Poppy, please."

"I just don't want to sell Gator Gone. It's all I have. I invented the repellent and started by manufacturing it and shipping it out of my garage. I worked real hard, along with Sailor here, to build up the business. We just now got it goin' good, and I ain't ready to give it up. Don't know that I'll ever be."

The waitress brought the two beers, placed them on the table along with two glasses and left.

"Mr. Ripley, is it?" Papavero said to Sailor.

"Yes, sir."

"Why don't you take your beer over to the bar and drink it there. I'd like to discuss this business in more detail with Bob Lee here, a little more privately, if you don't mind."

"I don't mind," said Sailor. "Okay with you, Bob Lee?"

Bob Lee nodded and Sailor stood up, picked up his Dixie and went over to the bar. Zero stayed in his seat.

"You a friend of Poppy's?"

Sailor turned around and saw a young woman, no more than twenty-two, with short, white-blond hair, wearing long purple and pink parrot earrings. Her small cat's eyes were clear green.

"Just met him."

"I'm Jaloux Marron. How about you?"

Sailor smiled. "I'm nothin' of the kind. But my name's Sailor."

Jaloux Marron smiled, showing uneven, very white teeth.

"Hey, Sailor, buy me a drink?"

"Buy you a beer's about it. I ain't rich."

"Good enough."

Jaloux gave the high sign to the bartender, caught his eye and pointed to Sailor's bottle, then at herself. The bartender nodded, cracked open a cold Dixie and set it in front of her.

"How you like N.O.?" she asked Sailor.

"Pretty much. I live here."

"No kiddin'? You look too decent."

"First time anybody accused me of that."

"Guess there's more to you than meets the eye."

"You meet my eye just fine, Miss Marron."

"Just Jaloux'll do."

"Everybody's damn informal around here."

"It's that kinda place. You want to go someplace else, get some room service?"

Sailor laughed. "Can't do it."

"Guess you really are decent."

"Really married, anyhow. You know Papavero?"

"Sorta. I work for him, just like everyone else."

"I don't."

"Yeah, you-all're too decent."

Bob Lee came over and touched Sailor's arm.

"Let's go, Sail," he said, and headed for the door.

Sailor took a long drink of Dixie, then said, "Been swell meetin' ya, Jaloux. You're a good-lookin' lady, if you don't mind my sayin' so."

"Don't never mind that kinda talk, Sailor. Be nice to see you again, especially when you ain't feelin' so decent."

Jaloux took a card from a small sequined handbag and held it out to Sailor.

"Don't lose this, okay?" she said.

He took the card and read it. The words NIGHT TALK and a telephone number were printed on it. Sailor looked into her little green eyes.

"Try not to," he said, and walked out of the bar.

"What d'ya think?" Sailor asked Bob Lee as they headed toward Barracks Street.

"Think it's time to go home, watch 'Fishin' Hole' on ESPN."

At the parking lot, Sailor decided not to say anything to Fudge Clay about seeing Black Henry's slayer in the Fais-Dodo, and he didn't exactly know why.

J
A
L
O
U
X

o

"We ain't gonna need no masks," said Smokey Joe, "because they ain't gonna be nobody left over to identify us."

DOWN TO ZERO

"Don't mention that little fact to Ripley, brother. Might could weird him out."

Lefty Grove and Smokey Joe Rattler were sitting in their Jimmy, which was parked on Decatur Street near the corner of Esplanade, waiting for Pace. Lefty Grove zipped open the green Tulane Wave athletic bag that was on the floor between his feet, removed a Black Magic sheath-sprung switchblade and put it into his pants pocket. He took out two Colt Pythons, stuck one in his belt and handed the other to Smokey Joe.

"Where'd ya find these nifty partners?" Smokey Joe asked.

"Skeeter McCovery brung 'em back from Mobile last month. Skeeter says there's more weapons per square mile in Alabama than there are wanted men in Florida, which is sayin' somethin'."

"Well, he ain't no liar and he done a job or two. You figure on Ripley packin'?"

"Don't see a need for it. We got enough to put out all the lights."

The Rattler brothers sat and smoked Marlboros. Lefty Grove was wearing a powder blue tank top with the words HAVE YOU HUGGED A COONASS TODAY? stenciled on the front, black Levi's with the bottoms rolled twice, and a pair of brand new Head tennis shoes without socks. Smokey Joe wore a black tee shirt emblazoned with a rubberized image of Michael Jordan executing a reverse dunk, the rubber part of Jordan's dangling tongue torn off, faded Lee Riders ripped at both knees, and green Converse high tops without socks. Both boys planned to wear red and white cotton hand-kerchiefs tied around their heads to cover their hair. Tyrus Raymond, their daddy, had told them that people are more easily identified by their hair, both color and style, and by whether or not they have any, than by any other common characteristic.

"How many years Daddy been considered dead now?" asked Smokey Joe.

" 'Bout twenty, I believe. Why?"

"Don't know. Just thinkin' how his name bein' engraved on that Viet-nam Memorial in Washin'ton is kinda spooky."

"Daddy don't mind. Far's the government knows he's long gone, so he don't have to pay no taxes or nothin' forever. Pay for ever'thin' with cash the way he does, use out-of-state driver's licenses and not registerin' nothin' in his name means he's about free as any man can be. Bein' declared legally dead has all the advantages of bein' really dead without none of the drawbacks, such as *bein'* dead. Long as you're alive, you ain't got nothin' to worry about."

"Seems to me, only way a man got nothin' to worry about is if he *is* dead. Long as you're alive you got problems, Lef', even if all the governments of the world got your account cancelled. Devil got your name down's a differ'nt story."

"How's that?"

"That ol' boy make you wish you was back on earth payin' your neighbor's taxes, I'm right convinced."

"Ain't wise makin' reference to no devil around Daddy, you know. He'll think it's Mama's blood talkin'. There's Pace Ripley comin' now."

Pace walked up to the passenger side and nodded.

"Nice afternoon for a armed robbery, Ripley, don't ya think?" said Lefty Grove.

"Cloudy day like any other."

The Rattlers wrapped the red and white kerchiefs around their heads, knotted them at the back and got out of the truck. Pace had on a plain white tee shirt, an unzipped beige windbreaker, blue Wranglers and red Air Jordans with tube socks.

"You carry this," said Smokey Joe, handing Pace a canvas mail sack. "Just do what we talked over and one day we'll three be eatin' Big Macs on Mars."

Lefty Grove slapped a black Baltimore Orioles baseball cap on Pace's head.

"Wear this," Lefty Grove said, "so they can't see your hair."

The Rattlers carried the Pythons stuffed into the front of their pants with their shirts over them. Pace followed behind as they made their way across the railroad tracks by the wharf. It was three-twenty-five on a Thursday afternoon when they boarded the discarded brown caboose. Zero Diplopappus saw them first, but there was no conversation. Smokey Joe shot Zero in the head at point-blank range and didn't wait for him to go down before facing the other protector of the take and holding the Python in front of his eyes. The money was on a table in large, brown paper shopping bags. Pace shook the contents of each bag into the canvas mail sack while Lefty Grove guarded the door. Nobody spoke. When all of the money had been collected, Pace slung the sack over his right shoulder and exited the caboose with Lefty Grove. Smokey Joe grinned at the man he had covered.

"You're all dead," croaked the man, whose name was Dewayne Culp. Dewayne Culp's skin was yellow and heavily wrinkled, and he had an enormous Adam's apple that ascended and descended inside his thin, withered neck like a rickety elevator in a decrepit hotel.

"Uh-uh," said Smokey Joe, before he pulled the trigger again, "you are."

The three boys were in the Jimmy headed east on Chef Menteur Highway when the two armored car guards entered the caboose. One of them bent over Dewayne Culp, took one look and stood up. The other guard helped Zero Diplopappus to his feet and handed him a handkerchief, which Zero used to wipe away the blood on his face from where he'd been grazed by Smokey Joe's bullet.

"It was them two punk cousins of Junior's," said Zero, "the Rattlers, with another kid. They thought I was dead."

Zero's massive ears flapped a couple of times, then he laughed.

"Third kid was the likeness of a fella I run into the other day," he said, "an ex-con I done time with in Texas, name of Sailor Ripley. Would be somethin' if it turned out to be his boy, wouldn't it?"

"Know why the Good Lord created women?"

"Why's that?"

"Sheep couldn't do the dishes."

HOMAGE TO

PROMETHEUS

The Rattler brothers both laughed hard. They were sitting in the pickup cab. Pace was riding in the back of the truck, his black cap pulled down as far as it would go. The plan was to hide out in Mississippi for a spell, close to Miss Napoleon's Paradise, so Smokey Joe headed the Jimmy north on Interstate 59 toward Meridian, where they'd connect to Highway 45 and shoot straight into Lookout World. Nobody would figure on their being with the Lord's Disturbed Daughters, the Rattlers thought, and this way they could spend some time with Mary Full-of-Grace.

"We'll stash the money with Mama," said Lefty Grove. "It'll be safe there."

"You sure, Lef?" said Smokey Joe. "She finds out, she'll just give it away."

"I'll make sure she don't know she even has it. Hide it when she ain't lookin' in that old trunk from Grammy Yerma ain't been taken out from under her bed since she come there."

Pace watched the Sportsman's Paradise roll away from under him. He considered the situation, not quite comprehending the fact that he and his semi-moronic compañeros were now officially fugitives from Gulf Coast Criminal Central. Pace had gotten into the deal in the first place based on his notoriety as the son of Sailor Ripley, the Texas killer and bandit. That was a sure-enough hoot, seeing as how Sailor had been caught during his first attempted robbery and the only killing he'd done had been an accident in North Carolina. Pace's daddy had never gotten away with a thing, but his reputation as a hard case, false though it was, had tainted his boy and pressured Pace into acting stupid. Maybe that was it, Pace thought, us Ripleys is simply dumb as they come. No good reason I should be speedin' away with these backyard chicken fuckers. Ought to be life weren't always more ornery a animal.

Pace wished he'd taken along his flask. A healthy hit of Black Bush would drop him over the edge just now. WELCOME TO LOUISIANA flashed by and Pace knew they'd crossed into Mississippi. Suddenly the sun faded and Pace looked up. Black clouds formed like Mike Tyson's fists were about to batter the planet. He pulled his windbreaker up over his head and closed his eyes. Is this what it felt like to you, Daddy, Pace whispered, when you were in the deep shit?

Poppy Papavero and Zero Diplopappus sat in the front seat of Poppy's powder blue BMW, which was parked next to the curb outside ARRIVALS at the New Orleans

TALK TURKEY
TO ME

International Airport. Zero's head had a white bandage wrapped around it that pinned back his elephantine ears so that he looked like Chuck Connors as Geronimo in the movie based on the life of the Apache chief. Both Connors and the gangster had blue eyes, however, rendering any actual resemblance to Geronimo extremely dubious. Poppy puffed on a Monte Christo while they waited for his wife, Perdita, to arrive on a connecting flight from New York. She had been in Europe for three weeks, shopping and sight-seeing.

"Don't worry, Poppy," said Zero, "we'll find these guys and get the money back. I got a good idea where they are."

"Yeah? Where's that?"

"Up by Starkville. The Rattler mother's a crazy, been locked up in some home there for years."

"What makes you think that's where they've gone?"

"They're kids. If they ain't with the papa, which they ain't—'cause we checked, and that guy's plenty crazy, too—then they're with the mama. My guess is they go see her before goin' anywhere else."

"Ah, they could be in Memphis by now, or Chicago."

"I'll get 'em, Poppy, believe me."

Poppy looked at Zero, took the cigar out of his mouth and grinned.

"I do, Zero, I believe you." He tossed what was left of the Monte Christo out the window.

2
4
1

Zero's eyes narrowed and half closed.

"I'm gonna fillet all three of 'em," he said.

"Mm, mm," said Poppy. "I can smell that deep-fried boy cookin' right now."

At his house in Metairie, Sailor put the card Jaloux Marron had given him on the table by the telephone and dialed the number printed on it. Someone picked up after three rings.

"Night Talk. This is Cindy speakin'. Call me Cin. And what do you want to talk about?"

"Hello," Sailor said, "I'd like to speak to Jaloux, please."

"She's on another line at the moment. Would you like to talk to me, or would you prefer to wait? I'm sure I can tell you whatever it is you need to hear."

"I'm sure you can, but I need to speak with her."

"Hang on, then, honey."

A radio station came over the line while Sailor was on hold.

"In other news, the state of Nevada has six hundred to seven hundred fifty new residents who are multiplying rapidly, but many of them may not live out the year. The Nevada Department of Wildlife has transplanted wild turkeys to western and southern parts of the state to establish the birds, which are not native to Nevada, in an effort to increase the population for hunting, a biologist involved with the project said today.

" 'The population is growing so fast I expect we might have a hunt by next year,' he said. 'We'll probably set up isolated hunts. In the meantime, the birds are relatively visible and are tremendously spectacular to watch, especially during mating. When the male turkey struts, his tail feathers fan out with very colorful displays. And they're darn fast birds, too,' he added, 'able to run as fast as a horse and fly as rapidly as smaller ducks.'

"According to this report, the transplanted turkeys are mostly of the Rio Grande variety, and they thrive on river bottom lands instead of the forests the birds usually enjoy. Most of these turkeys came from Amarillo, Texas.

"Nationwide, the turkey population has grown to four million after a low of thirty thousand at the turn of the century, when unregulated hunting, clearing and burning of native hardwood habitat and human encroachment threatened the species. By all accounts, the wild turkey has made quite a North American comeback.

"From New York City, where the only Wild Turkey you can find is in a bottle, comes another kind of news. A twenty-three-year-old woman, who was raped and robbed when she was trapped between a subway revolving-gate exit and a locked fence blocking the stairs to the street, won the right to sue the Transit Authority for negligence. The woman, a television makeup artist, was on her way home at ten P.M. last July nineteenth, when she left the station through a one-way revolving turnstile and found the stairs to the street barred and locked. A man she asked for help came through the turnstile, produced a knife, and robbed and raped her. It is not clear how he got out, but police believe he had a key or squeezed over the gate.''

"Hi, this is Jaloux. We can talk now."

Sailor was startled by the sudden switch from the radio to reality.

"Uh, hello, Jaloux. This is Sailor Ripley. We met the other evenin' in Inez's Fais-Dodo Bar and you give me your card."

"Uh huh. What you want to talk about, Sailor?"

"I need some information, Jaloux, about my son, and I thought you might could help me get it."

"What's his name?"

"Pace. Pace Roscoe Ripley. He's fifteen and I found out from a note he left me that he was involved in a robbery of funds belongin' to your boss, Mr. Papavero. I was hopin' to find out where Pace is now, if Papavero and his bunch got it figured out yet."

"Honey, this is somethin' I *can't* talk about. I'm sure you understand."

" 'Course. I was just hopin' we could make a date to meet some-where—anywhere, anytime—long as it's soon."

"Give me your number, Sailor. I'll ask around and call you back."

"Fine. It's 555-8543. I was thinkin' about callin' you anyway, Jaloux, you know? I mean, I had you on my mind."

"Talk to you later, Sailor Ripley. You can tell me what I had on when you had me on your mind. Bye."

She hung up before he could say, "Thanks, Jaloux."

The boys stopped at Scooba's Cafe in Lookout World, population 444, to have something to eat after a long night on the road and before visiting Miss Napoleon's

S C O O B A ' S

Paradise. Lookout World had been named by the daughter of Fractious Carter, Metamorphia, after his death in 1962 at the age of 101. Until then, the town was called Carter, having been owned, operated and maintained by him since its incorporation. Metamorphia was fifty-nine years old when her father died and she was his sole heir. She'd never married and had waited all of her life to get away. Before taking off, Metamorphia changed the town's name to what she shouted out at Fractious's funeral. "Look out, world!" Metamorphia cried as she walked away from the grave. "I ain't sixty yet!"

Nobody in Lookout World had heard from her for forty years, except for a picture postcard of the Halliday Hotel, Ohio and 2d streets, "Grant Stayed Here," postmarked Cairo, Illinois, and dated October 2, 1969, which was received by Leander Many, Fractious Carter's lawyer, who was at that time ninety-four and about to be a terminal victim of emphysema, brought on, Many believed, by his lifelong penchant for the practice of onanistic asphyxia. Metamorphia wrote: "Bet you Bastards think I am Beyond Hope. Maybe your Right. Lester says I got a Head Start to Satan." Neither Leander Many nor anyone else in Lookout World knew who Lester was.

Lefty Grove and Smokey Joe each automatically ordered hotcakes, grits with gravy, and chicory coffee, the same meal Tyrus Raymond Rattler ate every morning of his life since his sons could recall. Pace stared at the counter girl. She was about his age, under five feet tall, too skinny to lie on, with messy mud-red hair and bad acne. She looked like he felt.

"Come, boy," she said, "already sunup in Lowndes County."

"Grits 'n' gravy, is all," Pace said. "And a Coke, you got one."

"Got it."

She went off to put in their order and Pace picked up a day old *Delta Democrat-Times* that was lying on the stool next to him. Sailor had told Pace how it had been his own daddy's practice to turn to the Obituaries page first thing; it had become Sailor's habit, too, and now Pace searched for the death column. It was always interesting to read about other people's lives, Sailor said. It took your mind off your own.

JOE SEWELL, 91, HALL OF FAMER TOUGHEST TO STRIKE OUT was the top line. "Joseph Wheeler Sewell, the eagle-eyed batter who struck out only 114 times during a fourteen-year major league career, died on Tuesday at his home in Mobile, Alabama," Pace read. "He was elected to the Baseball Hall of Fame in 1977 and was ninety-one years old when he died. Over eleven seasons with the Cleveland Indians and three with the New York Yankees, from 1920 to 1933, Joe Sewell struck out only three times in two seasons and only four times in two others. Umpires deferred to his judgment to the point where if he chose not to swing at a pitch, they would virtually always call it a ball.

"Mr. Sewell, who was born in the town of Titus on October 9, 1898, said that he developed his batting skills as a youngster in rural Alabama by repeatedly tossing rocks and lumps of coal into the air and belting them with a broomstick. No one in major league history who played as much struck out less, and Mr. Sewell played a lot. He entered the American League as a twenty-one-year-old replacement for Ray Chapman, the Indian shortstop who became the only big-leaguer to die in a game when he was struck in the head by a pitch thrown by Carl Mays of the Yankees. From September 7, 1920 until May 2, 1930, when he was kept in bed with a brain fever, Mr. Sewell played in 1,103 consecutive games.

"At five feet, six-and-a-half inches tall and 155 pounds, Joe Sewell compiled a career batting average of .312, including a high of .353 in 1923 and nine other .300 seasons. Most of his 2,226 hits were singles, but none was of the broken-bat variety. Aside from his record of 115 straight games without striking out in 1929, the most compelling evidence of Mr. Sewell's uncanny ability to put wood solidly onto the ball was that *he used only one bat during his entire major league career.* It was a thirty-five-inch, forty-ounce Ty Cobb model Louisville Slugger he kept in condition by seasoning it with chewing tobacco and stroking it with a Coca-Cola bottle.

"Mr. Sewell was a star football and baseball player for the University of Alabama, and led the school baseball team to four conference titles before joining the minor league New Orleans Pelicans in 1920. Before that summer ended, he was on a World Series championship team as Cleveland beat the Brooklyn Dodgers.

"After his career ended, Mr. Sewell worked for a dairy and was a major league scout. In 1964, at the age of sixty-six, he became the Alabama baseball coach, winning 114 games and losing ninety-nine in seven seasons. His two younger brothers, Tommy and Luke, both of whom are dead, also played in the major leagues. Mr. Sewell is survived by a son, Dr. James W. Sewell of Mobile, a daughter, L.C. Parnell of Birmingham, ten grandchildren and fourteen great-grandchildren."

The waitress brought the boys' breakfasts and set the plates down on the puce Formica counter.

"Need anythin' else, y'all holler," she said.

"What's your name?" asked Smokey Joe.

"Hissy. Mama's Missy, sister's Sissy."

"What's your daddy's?"

"Ever'body calls him Bird-Dog, but his real name's Buster. Buster Soso."

Pace put down the newspaper and picked up the can of Coke Hissy Soso had brought him and studied it.

"What you eyeballin' that can for?" asked Lefty Grove.

"Wouldn't do to rub a old wood ball bat with this, would it?" said Pace.

"Hi, Sail, sweetie. How're my boys?"

"Oh, Lula, it's you."

"Who were you expectin' to call? Ann-Margret,

LULA'S PLANS

maybe?"

"No, honey, I thought it might be Pace. How's Marietta?"

"Mama's recoverin' faster'n they'd like, as if we couldn'ta guessed she would. Dal and I can't no more keep her down than Imelda Marcos could quit buyin' shoes. I'm thinkin' I might stay another couple days, though, just to make certain her heart don't start flutterin', like after she had that bad fall last summer."

"Whatever's best, peanut."

"Then, of course, Reverend Plenty's appearin' in Rock Hill on Monday? I'm also thinkin' it could be a excitin' deal to go hear him at the openin' sermon of the first South Carolina branch of the Church of the Three R's. I could stay over in Charlotte with Bunny Thorn, Beany's first cousin once or twice removed? The one lost her left arm, most of it anyway, in a car wreck at the beach in Swansboro when she was eighteen? You remember my tellin' you about her? I ain't seen Bunny in years. She owns a laundromat out by the Speedway. Wonder if Bunny'd go hear Goodin Plenty with me."

"Sounds all right to me, Lula. Stay as long as you need."

"How's Pace? He gettin' to school on time and eatin' proper?"

"He's been keepin' busy."

"You got a eye on him, Sail, don't you?"

"Don't be worryin' about us Ripley males, honey. We're survivors."

2
4
7

"Glad to hear it. Sailor?"

"Yes, ma'am?"

"You love your Lula?"

"I do, peanut. Always will, too."

"*Hasta siempre*, darlin'."

"*Hasta siempre.*"

"Glad you could make it, Coot," said Sailor. "This'd be a tough one to face alone."

"Got plenty of food, weapons and ammo and the

THE SHINING

PATH

Ram's gassed to the gills. Figure we can work the give-and-go, you'n me's all we got, like them Shinin' Path people in Peru. You heard of 'em, haven't ya? The Cocaine Commies? Good Chinese-style guerilla fighters, though. What's your idea on the procedure?"

Coot Veal was decked out in his best cammies, black lace-up Red Wings, green Semper Fi hat, and double-reflector wraparounds. He took a small black leather pouch containing an Urban Skinner out of a pocket of his field jacket, clipped it on to his belt and twisted it front to back. The telephone rang and Sailor lifted the receiver.

"Ripley."

"Sailor, I got bad news." It was Bob Lee Boyle.

"What now?"

"Bomb blew out the front door and some windows of the new warehouse."

"When'd this happen?"

"About a half hour ago. Guess Papavero don't take no like a man."

"Not many do."

"I ain't changin' my mind, though, Sail. I mean, Gator Gone's *mine*."

"I'll back you, Bob Lee, whatever you decide."

" 'Preciate that, Sailor Ripley. Knew you would. I'm goin' over to assess the damage now. Comin'?"

"Can't, Bob Lee. Pace is in some trouble and I got to attend to it first. I'm sorry but it's priority."

"Understand. Anything I can do?"

"Make sure you don't say nothin' to Beany or it'll likely get back to Lula. Coot Veal's here. Think we can handle it, thanks the same."

"Okay, good buddy. Let's each check in later."

"You got it, Bob Lee. *Cuidado*, hear?"

"I'll try."

"And give me a holler you hear direct from them boys."

"Sail?"

"Uh huh?"

"This what's called a hostile takeover bid?"

Sailor hung up and told Coot what had happened.

"This sad ol' life's becomin' a tougher proposition all the time," Coot said. "I had me a terminal disease no tellin' what I'd do. As it is my short list is gettin' longer all the time."

"Figure it'll be any better in the next?"

"You turnin' Hindu?"

"Heard a piece on the news earlier about a sixteen-year-old boy, not much older'n Pace, escaped from Cuba on a surfboard."

"A surfboard?"

"Yeah. Seems a East German tourist bought the kid a windsurfin' board and he took off for Florida. Made it thirty miles before the boom broke, which he managed to re-rig somehow, well enough to go another thirty miles when the thing give out for good. Got picked up by a Bahamian freighter crewed by Koreans couldn't speak Spanish or English. They notified the U.S. Coast Guard, who took the boy the last thirty-mile stretch into Key West. Kid said he was goin' to live with relatives in Miami. Didn't seem to think what he done was so remarkable. Just wanted to be free, is all."

"Desperate people do all kinds of incredible things."

Sailor nodded. "Made me wonder about Pace. What made him so damn desperate that he'd do this fool thing with them worthless Rattlers?"

Coot shook his head and said nothing, just took off his shades, checked them for smudges and put them back on. The doorbell rang and Sailor answered it.

"Hi, Sailor man."

"Thanks for comin' by, Jaloux. You find out anything?"

Sailor let her in.

"Poppy's wife—sometimes I go shoppin' with her?—she told me they figure the boys is headed north into Mississippi."

"What's there?"

"Rattler brothers got a insane mama locked up in a place called Miss Napoleon's Paradise for the Lord's Disturbed Daughters. Perdita says Zero, Poppy's top gun, is goin' after 'em with some pistols. Zero was wounded durin' the takedown and he won't be lookin' to take no prisoners."

"You say Perdita?"

"Yeah. Poppy's wife. Why?"

"She a Tex-Mex woman, last name of Durango?"

"Don't know that I ever heard her own last name, but yeah, she's from Texas and looks Mexican, all right. You know her?"

Sailor nodded. "I did. Listen, Jaloux, you been a big help. Anything I can do for y'all, let me know."

"There is, Sailor man. Definitely is somethin' you can help me with."

"I got to get goin' now, Jaloux. My boy's in tough and I got to find him before this Zero does."

"I'm goin' with you, then."

"Really, Jaloux, you don't want to get mixed up in this, 'specially as how you're an employee of Mr. Papavero's. Me and my pal Coot here can handle it, I hope."

"I'm comin' along, Sailor. I know right where Miss Napoleon's is, 'count of I used to live nearby in Starkville for two years when my mama was married to her third husband, man named Dub Buck owned a Buick dealership. Had him a string of signs on old Highway 82 from Eupora to Mayhew said, 'Buy Buck's Buicks.' Dub had did some small piece of time before Mama met him, for exposin' his self in a public park up in Greenville. I liked him, though. Dub died of food poison in Nogales one weekend when I was fourteen. Least that's what Mama said when she come home without him. She and me moved to N.O. right after."

"Coot, this here's Jaloux Marron," said Sailor. "She's gonna show us the way."

"Semper Fi, Miss Marron," said Coot, tipping his cap.

"Can't say the same, Mr. Veal."

Smokey Joe pulled the Jimmy up to the premium pump at the self-serve Conoco in Meridian and cut the engine.

"Be right back," he said to Lefty Grove, as he got out and headed for the pay-in-advance window.

BACK TO

BUDDHALAND

As he approached the pay window, Smokey Joe could see that there was a problem. A medium-sized black man in his thirties, with long, slanted, razor-shaped sideburns, wearing a camel hair sportcoat, was arguing with the Vietnamese kid behind the bulletproof pane.

"Pay for cigarettes!" said the Vietnamese kid, nodding his head quickly, causing his lank, black forelock of hair to flop forward almost to the tip of his nose.

"I paid you for 'em, motherfucker!" the black man shouted. "You already got my money!"

"No, no! Pay now! You pay for cigarettes!"

Standing off to one side, about eight feet from the man, was a young black woman wearing a beige skirt that ended mid-thigh of her extraordinarily skinny legs, and a short brown jacket that she held tightly around her shivering body despite the intense heat.

"Pay him or let's go!" she shouted. "I ain't wastin' street time on no cigarettes!"

"Keep the damn cigarettes, then, chump monkey!" the man yelled at the kid, throwing a pack of Winstons at the window. The pack bounced off and fell on the ground. "And go back to Buddhaland! Leave America to us Americans!"

The man turned away from the window and saw Smokey Joe approaching.

"Hey, man," he said, "you familiar with this area?"

"Why?" asked Smokey Joe.

"My wife and me got a problem with our car, see, and we need—"

"Sorry," Smokey Joe said, "I don't have any money to give away today."

"No, man, I don't want no money. All we need is a ride. We got to get our car towed."

"Call a tow truck."

"That's the problem, see, we don't know our way around here and we got to get the car fixed."

There was a large sign next to the garage door in the station that said MECHANIC ON DUTY 24 HOURS. Smokey Joe pointed to it.

"There's a mechanic right here," he told the man.

"Wouldn't let no chump monkey from Buddhaland touch it!"

"Come on!" shouted the woman, her thin naked knees shaking. "Turn loose, Chester. It ain't happenin'!"

Smokey Joe saw the man's eyebrows twitch and his face contort, twisting up on the left side, his nostrils flaring. The man hesitated for a moment and Smokey Joe braced himself, thinking that the man might attack him. But the man turned his back to Smokey Joe and followed the woman into the coffee shop of a motel next door.

"Ten bucks premium," Smokey Joe said to the kid, sliding a bill on the metal plate beneath the window.

As Smokey Joe pumped the gas, a well-dressed, overweight, middle-aged black woman, who had just finished fueling her late-model Toyota sedan, said, "Shouldn't be treatin' nobody like that. Ain't no way to be treatin' people here. This ain't no Asia."

She got into her car and drove away. One of the Vietnamese attendants, dressed in a clean, crisp blue uniform, walked out of the garage and over to Smokey Joe.

"This is bad neighborhood," he said, shaking his head. He took the fuel hose from Smokey Joe, who had drained his ten dollars' worth, and replaced it on the pump.

Smokey Joe slid behind the steering wheel of the Jimmy and started it up.

"You hear any of that?" he asked Lefty Grove.

Lefty Grove nodded and said, "Even gettin' gas nowadays reminds me of what Ray L. Menninger, the veterinarian-taxidermist, who Daddy said was the most honest man in Iguana County, Texas, used to say: 'With me, one way or the other, you get your dog back.'"

Nell Blaine Napoleon had moved into The Paradise eighty-two years ago, when she was four and a half years old. Her father, Colonel St. Jude Napoleon, a career

THE PARADISE

army man, and her mother, Fanny Rose Bravo, had designed and had the twenty-six-room Paradise house built for them, and they had both lived and died there. Nell was their only child. By the age of twelve, Nell had decided to devote her life to the well-being of others. She was initially and forever inspired by a local black woman called Sister Domino, who spent each day administering to the sick and needy. Sister Domino allowed the young Nell to accompany her on her rounds of mercy, and taught her basic nursing skills, which Sister Domino had acquired at the Louise French Academy in Baltimore, where she had lived for eighteen years before returning to her Mississippi birthplace. Sister Domino's ambition had been to assist Dr. Albert Schweitzer at Lambarene, in Africa, and she read everything she could about him and his work, constantly telling Nell what a great man Schweitzer was and how there could be no higher aspiration in life than to work to alleviate the suffering of those persons less fortunate than themselves. The "Veritable Myriad" Sister Domino called the world's population.

Nell's parents never attempted to dissuade their daughter from her passion, or to turn her away from Sister Domino. Both St. Jude Napoleon and Fanny Rose Bravo were great believers in self-determination, and if this was the path Nell chose to follow, it was her business and no one else's. Their feeling was that there were certainly worse directions a life could take, and they let

2
5
4

her be. The only time Nell had unwillingly had to separate herself from Sister Domino was the period during which she was required by her parents to attend Madame Petunia's School for Young Women in Oriole, between the ages of fourteen and seventeen. During her holidays, however, Nell would be back at Sister Domino's side, going from home to home among the poorest residents of Oktibbhea, Lowndes, Choctaw, Webster, Clay, Chickasaw, and Monroe counties. Following graduation from Madame Petunia's, Nell never wavered, dedicating herself fully to Sister Domino's work, which became her vocation also.

After her parents were killed by a falling tree that had been struck by a double bolt of ground lightning during a late-August electrical storm, Nell, who was then twenty-four, inherited The Paradise and invited Sister Domino to live there with her, which offer Sister Domino accepted. Eventually, Sister Domino and Miss Napoleon, as Nell came to be called, succeeded in converting the house into a combination hospital and retreat for those individuals incapable of dealing on a mutually acceptable basis with the outside world. Sister Domino's mandate, however, held that those residents of The Paradise be *serious* Christians. No blasphemy was tolerated and no waffling of faith. This policy, though, extended only to The Paradise; those persons she and Nell treated outside the house were not required to adhere to Christian tenets, the Lord's beneficence being available to the Veritable Myriad.

Sister Domino never did get to the Congo to assist Dr. Schweitzer, though Nell offered to pay her way. There was always too much work to be done at home, Sister Domino said, and when news of Dr. Schweitzer's death reached her, Sister Domino merely knelt, recited a brief, silent prayer, arose and continued scraping the back of a woman whose skin was inflamed and encrusted by eczema. Sister Domino died three years later, leaving Nell to carry on alone. As the years passed, however, Nell limited her ministrations to women, preferring their company to that of men, whom, Nell concluded, tended toward selfishness in their philosophy, which displeased her. Once made, Nell's decision was irreversible, and her devotion was further refined by her increasing acceptance of nonviolent, mentally disturbed women. A decade after Sister Domino's death, Nell officially registered her home with the county as Miss Napoleon's Paradise for the Lord's Disturbed Daughters. A large oil portrait of Sister Domino, painted from memory by Nell, hung on the wall opposite the front door so that the first sight anyone had upon entering was that of Miss Napoleon's own patron saint.

Mary Full-of-Grace Crowley Rattler fit in perfectly at The Paradise. As the mother of Jesus Christ, it was simply a matter of being acknowledged as such that contented her. At no time during her stay had Mary Full-of-

Grace caused Miss Napoleon the slightest difficulty, not even when another woman, Boadicea Booker, who also believed she was the mother of the Christ child, lived at The Paradise. Boadicea had died within three months of her coming, so it was possible, Miss Napoleon believed, that Mary Full-of-Grace had no knowledge of her existence. When Tyrus Raymond Rattler and his sons came to visit Mary Full-of-Grace, Miss Napoleon was pleased to welcome them, as they were unfailingly polite and well-behaved. Even when Lefty Grove and Smokey Joe were small children, Miss Napoleon noticed, they had minded their father precisely and comported themselves properly in the presence of their mother. Therefore, when Mary Full-of-Grace's sons and another boy appeared on the front porch of The Paradise one windy afternoon, Miss Napoleon welcomed them inside.

"Afternoon, L.G.," she said. "Afternoon, S.J. Your mother will be pleased to see you. And who is this young gentleman?"

"Hello, Miss Napoleon," said Lefty Grove. "This is our friend, Pace Ripley."

Pace set down the sack he'd been carrying and nodded to the old woman, who was barely more than four feet tall. Pace figured her weight at about seventy-five pounds. His daddy could lift her off the ground with one hand, he figured, dangle her by her ankles with his arm stretched straight out.

"Hello, ma'am," Pace said. "Beautiful place you got here."

"My parents, Colonel St. Jude and Fanny Rose Bravo, built it and left it in my care so that I might care for others. You boys can go right up, if you like. Mary Full-of-Grace is in her room. She never leaves it until dark."

"Thank you, Miss Napoleon," said Smokey Joe. "We 'preciate all you done for Mama."

"The Lord prevails and I provide," said Miss Napoleon, as the Rattler brothers, followed by Pace, who carried the sack, filed up the stairs.

Mary Full-of-Grace was sitting perfectly still in a high-backed wing chair next to the windows when the boys entered her room. Her long, silver-blue hair hung in two braids, one on either side of her V-shaped head. She wore a white, gauzy robe with a golden sash tied at the waist. Pace noticed that she had almost no nose, only two air holes, and hugely dilated brown eyes. She kept her long, thin hands folded in her lap. Her fingers looked to Pace as if they were made of tissue paper.

"Hello, Mama," said Lefty Grove, who kissed her forehead.

"Hello, Mama," said Smokey Joe, who followed suit.

The brief, soft touch of their lips left dark marks on her skin.

"This boy here's our associate, Pace Ripley," Lefty Grove said.

"Hello, Mrs. Rattler," said Pace, trying to smile.

Both brothers looked quickly and hard at Pace.

"This here's the mother of Baby Jesus," said Smokey Joe.

Mary Full-of-Grace stared out the window to her left.

"My son is soon in Galilee," she said. "I keep the vigil."

Smokey Joe motioned to Pace and Pace slid the sack containing most of the money from the robbery under the light maple four-poster bed.

"Well, Mama, we don't mean to disturb you none," said Lefty Grove. "We'll just come back by and by."

Smokey Joe headed out the door and Pace followed.

"By and by," said Mary Full-of-Grace. "He will be by, by and by." She continued to stare out the window.

"So long, Mama," said Lefty Grove, closing the door behind him.

They did not see Miss Napoleon on their way out but Pace spotted the portrait of·Sister Domino.

"Who's that?" he asked, walking over to take a closer look. "And what does this mean?" he said, reading the words carved into the bottom of the frame. "God's Gift to the Veritable Myriad."

"Must be was Miss Napoleon's mammy," said Smokey Joe. "What the hell you think?"

Pace trailed the Rattlers out of The Paradise, wondering about those words carved into the frame. A hunchbacked old woman was coming carefully up the steps of the porch, holding a large, blue plastic fly swatter.

"Suck cock!" she spat at them. "Suck cock! Suck cock! Suck cock!"

"You won't regret goin', Bunny. Reverend Plenty puts on a show and a half."

"I'm lookin' forward to it, Lula. Been needin' to get away from the laundromat anyway. More'n even a two-armed woman can handle there."

RIOT AT

ROCK HILL

Lula and Bunny Thorn were riding in Lula's rented T-bird from Charlotte to Rock Hill to witness Reverend Goodin Plenty's first-ever sermon in South Carolina. His Church of Reason, Redemption and Resistance to God's Detractors had been running ads in every newspaper within two-hundred-fifty miles of Rock Hill for a month.

"How's your sex life, Lula? You don't mind my askin'."

Lula laughed, looked quickly at Bunny, then back at the road.

"Well, okay, I guess," she said, and with her right hand shook a More from an opened pack on the seat next to her, stuck it between her lips and punched in the dashboard lighter. "How's yours?"

"Lousy, you don't mind my complainin'. Guys'll do it once with a one-armed woman, just for a kick, 'cause it's kinda unusual, you know. That's it, though. They don't come lookin' for seconds. I been wed to a rubberized dick for a year now. Least it don't quit till my arm give out. I'm considerin' joinin' some women's group just to meet some queer gals. Maybe they won't mind a two-hundred-twenty-pound washerwoman with one musclebound arm. And I almost lost it, too, tryin' to unjam a Speed Queen the other day."

The lighter popped out and Lula lit her cigarette, took a couple of powerful puffs and laughed again.

"Bunny, you're somethin' fresh, I tell you. Sailor'd love you to death."

"Yeah? Think I oughta come visit, stay at your house? Maybe get Sailor to give me a workout or two?"

Lula coughed hard and tossed the More out the window.

"Just jokin', hon'. Tried to get Beany to ask Bob Lee if he'd do it, but she didn't go for the idea. And she's my cousin! Guess I'll have to stick with Big Bill."

The parking lot at the Rock Hill church site was full by the time Lula and Bunny arrived, so Lula parked the T-bird across the road. Since groundbreaking for the church building had not yet commenced, a giant tent had been set up and filled with folding chairs. Lula and Bunny managed to find two together at the rear. The tent was filled to capacity by the time Reverend Goodin Plenty, dressed in a tan Palm Beach suit with a black handkerchief flared out of the breast pocket, walked in and strode down the center aisle, hopped up on the platform, grabbed a microphone and faced the audience.

"My goodness!" Goodin Plenty said as he smiled broadly and sized up the crowd. "Ain't this just somethin' spectacular! My, my! Not a empty seat in the Lord's house tonight. Ain't it grand to be alive and holdin' His hand!"

"Yes, sir, Reverend!" someone shouted.

"Tell us about it, Reverend!" said another.

Reverend Plenty smoothed back his full head of prematurely white hair with both hands, making the microphone squeal, then raised up his arms as if he were a football referee signaling that a touchdown had been scored.

"I am gonna give you somethin' tonight, people! The Church of Reason, Redemption and Resistance to God's Detractors is here in the great state of South Carolina, first to secede from the Union, to stay!"

"Maybe so," shouted a tall, skinny, bald-headed man wearing a blue-white Hawaiian shirt with red and yellow flowers on it, who jumped up from the front row, "but *you* ain't!"

The skinny man held out a Ruger Redhawk .44 revolver with a seven-and-one-half-inch scoped barrel and pointed it straight at the Reverend's chest.

"This is for Marie!" the man yelled, as he held the gun with both hands and pulled the trigger, releasing a hardball round directly into Goodin Plenty's left temple as he attempted to dodge the bullet. The shell exploded inside the Reverend's brain and tore away half of the right side of his head as it passed through.

A riot broke out and Lula and Bunny got down on their knees and crawled out of the tent through a side flap. As soon as they were outside, they stood up and ran for the car.

"Holy shit!" said Bunny, as Lula cranked the engine and sped away. "That was better than the Hagler-Hearns fight! Only thing, it didn't last as long."

Lula put the pedal down and drove as fast as she dared.

"Uh-uh-uh," Bunny uttered. "That Marie must be some *serious* piece of ass!"

Wendell Shake watched the Jimmy's oversized tires crawl through the mud ruts toward his farmhouse. He lifted the 30-06 semi-automatic rifle to his right shoulder

SHAKE, RATTLE

& ROLL

and sighted down the four-power Tasco scope. At his feet, propped on end under the window, was a loaded eleven-and-three-quarter inch, forty-pound draw Ninja pistol crossbow with a die cast aluminum body and contoured grips. Wendell had come home to Mississippi and the Shake family farm two months before, after the fifth severed head had been found in a garbage can in the Bronx. That was the last of them, Wendell decided, one for each borough of New York City, to show the Jews, Catholics, and coloreds what he thought of their so-called civilization. Armageddon was about to commence, Wendell believed, and he was an operative of the avant-garde. It was his Great Day in the Morning, as he liked to call it, at last, after forty-eight years of silent suffering, witnessing the slaughter of the innocents. Now, however, the rest of the avenging angels were poised to strike, and the message Wendell had delivered was being read and discussed. Perhaps, Wendell thought, as he watched the Rattler brothers and Pace disembark from their vehicle, he was about to receive an acknowledgment of his effort.

"This place been abandoned for years," Lefty Grove said to Pace, as the three boys walked up the path to the house. "Daddy and us used it lots of times when we come up to visit Mama. Been about three, four months since we been here, I guess. Right, Smoke?"

" 'Bout that, Lef. You remember this gate bein' wired shut like this?"

Smokey Joe placed his left hand on the post and vaulted himself up in the air.

Before Smokey Joe had cleared the top rail, a bullet smacked into the center of his forehead, knocking him backward, so that his legs looped over the front of the rail by the backs of his knees, leaving the upper half of his body dangling upside down on the opposite side.

Lefty Grove and Pace both hit the ground and covered their heads. They heard the screen door of the house open and slam shut, footsteps coming down the porch steps and then on the path toward them. Neither of the boys dared to move. The footsteps stopped at the gate.

"Charity, gentlemen," said Wendell Shake, "ain't got nothin' to do with mercy. Even in a foreign land."

Lefty Grove raised his head and saw a middle-aged man about six feet tall and two-hundred pounds, wearing a red and gray flannel shirt, red suspenders, black pants and low-cut, steel-toed, brown work shoes. His hair was almost completely gray, with dark patches at the front, worn very long, touching his shoulders. It was difficult to see the man's face because of his heavy red beard and the way his head was pressed down close to the rifle. The man's eye sockets seemed devoid of white.

"Suppose you say somethin'," Wendell said to Lefty Grove, "and they ain't the right words?"

Wendell rested the rifle barrel on Smokey Joe's right knee, keeping the business end directed at Lefty Grove's head.

"Could be there'd be repercussions."

Pace looked up and saw Wendell standing at the gate. A light rain was falling.

"Both you boys stand up," Wendell ordered, and they obeyed.

Wendell flipped Smokey Joe's legs up with the barrel, causing the corpse's head to hit the ground before the rest of it pretzeled over. Lefty Grove and Pace got to their feet.

"Come in, gentlemen," said Wendell, unfastening and opening the gate to admit them.

Wendell marched the boys up the steps into the house, where he motioned with the gun to a wooden bench against a wall of the front room.

"Sit yourselves down there, gentlemen, and tell me what's brought you this far."

Pace sat down and Lefty Grove remained standing.

"Look, mister," said Lefty Grove, and Wendell shot him through the heart.

The last Rattler brother collapsed on the floor next to Pace's feet, made one slight lurch after he was down, then lay perfectly still. Pace closed his eyes.

"Didn't exactly sit, did he?" said Wendell, looking down at Lefty Grove's body, then up at Pace. "That's a rhetorical question, son. You needn't answer. Open your eyes."

Pace looked at the man. Wendell Shake had mud puddles where his eyes ought to have been, and he was grinning, exposing gums that matched his suspenders and a dozen crowded, yellow teeth.

"We'll wait together, son," Wendell said. "There are terrible things soon to be revealed, and man craves company. That's but one flaw in the design. Do you love the Lord, boy?"

Pace said nothing.

"Please answer."

"I do, sir," said Pace. "I surely do love the Lord."

"Then the Lord loves you."

Wendell pulled up a goose-neck rocker and sat down, resting his 30-06 across his knees. He began to sing.

"I'm goin' to take a trip in that old gospel ship, I'm goin' far beyond the sky. I'm gonna shout and sing, till the heavens ring, when I kiss this world goodbye."

Pace saw the pistol crossbow lying on the floor beneath a window on the other side of the room.

They decided to take two vehicles, Coot riding alone in his red Dodge pickup and Sailor with Jaloux in her metallic blue Chevrolet Lumina.

NEWS ON THE

HOUR

"All the top stock racers back home use these," said Sailor, as Jaloux drove, following four car lengths behind Coot Veal's Ram.

"These what?" Jaloux asked. "And where's back home?"

"North Carolina, born and raised. Luminas, they all run 'em. Quick, light, and powerful."

"Kinda like me," said Jaloux, laughing, "only you don't know it yet."

Sailor looked over at her. Jaloux was short, about five-three, with a sweet little figure that tempted Sailor to suck on her like he would a piece of hard candy, rub her smooth with his tongue until she disappeared. It wouldn't happen, though. There was no way Sailor wanted to risk breaking the bond between him and Lula. All he needed from Jaloux Marron was her help in finding his and Lula's son. This wasn't the time to get complicated.

"Mama's second husband, he was a welder," said Jaloux. "Kind of a criminal, though."

"Yeah, what kind?"

"All I know's what Mama says, but Terrell—his name was Terrell Vick—he'd need somethin' extra, Terrell'd just go out at night and knock somebody over the head and take it. Never nothin' big, I guess, small-time. Maybe that's what prompted Mama to get rid of him."

"What about your own daddy?"

"He was French. Not Cajun, real French, from France. Belgium, really, which is a place close to France. His family was all from there. Marcel Marron. *Marron* means chestnut, you know."

"I didn't."

"Yeah, he was livin' in Antwerp before he come to the States. Started sellin' hosiery for some New York company and wound up in New Orleans at a convention, where he met Mama. She was on her own by then, nineteen years old, and was sorta hard up for cash, I guess, workin' as a party hostess for this bunch of conventioneers at the Monteleone. 'Course all them boys, they just after a quick dip, and why not? That's how Mama met Marcel Marron and he got her pregnant, married her, and hung around N.O. until about two months after I was born, then run off. Mama says she never knew where to, and ain't never heard. Maybe back to New York, or Antwerp. Least I'm legal."

"You mean legitimate."

"Can't have it both ways, huh?"

"How'd you get started at the Fais-Dodo?"

"After high school, which I went three years, only work I could find was fast food places or checkin' in grocery stores. That weren't no decent money, so a guy I knew, Jim-Baby Fitch, tended bar at Inez's for a while, introduced me to the manager, Blackie Caddo, happens to be from Plain Dealin', where Mama grew up partly. He hired me and there you go."

"Strange how them things turn out."

Sailor switched on the radio and they listened to Eddie Floyd sing "Knock on Wood" before the news on the hour.

"In Baton Rouge today, a man who two days ago shot and killed another man who had just shot and killed a woman in a shopping mall, turned himself over to the police.

"Enos Swope said he acted on impulse after seeing Kirkland Ray kill his former fiancée, Yvette Vance. Lieutenant Frank LeRoi, of the Baton Rouge police department, said, 'Ray murdered this woman. She's down, she's wounded, and he goes and shoots her in the head again after she's down.'

"Swope said that as he pulled into the mall's parking lot he saw Ray chase Yvette Vance, waving a revolver in the air. Swope took out his own gun, a forty-four caliber pistol, and shot at the back of Ray's car as Ray was pulling away, hoping to disable it. His second shot penetrated the door and struck the fleeing man, who slumped down in his seat. Ray's car went out of control and crashed into a light pole, toppling it over onto the top of a 1958 Cadillac Coupe De Ville, trapping seventy-eight-year-old Johnson Buckeye inside. Both Buckeye and Kirkland Ray were taken by ambulance to a hospital, where Buckeye is listed in stable condition. Kirkland Ray was pronounced dead on arrival.

" 'I didn't want to kill him,' said Enos Swope, a twenty-five-year-old washing machine repairman. 'I was just trying to help a lady.'

"Swope fled the scene, he told police, because he was afraid of being treated like a criminal. After reading in the newspaper that police were searching for a third person believed to have been involved in the incident, he came forward.

" 'My life is a mess now,' Swope said today. 'I could lose my job, everything I own. I don't want to lose my gun. I paid dearly for it. I don't want my gun marked up. It's such a pretty gun. I love that gun.'

"Police have decided not to file charges against Enos Swope, pending a grand jury's review of the case."

Jaloux followed Coot Veal off the highway to a Short Stop convenience store.

"Hey, Sailor," Coot said, before they went in for a coffee break, "forget what I was sayin' before about them Shinin' Path people in Peru."

"Why's that, Coot?"

"Well, I was just listenin' to the radio news?"

"Yeah, so was we."

"Had a report that them guerrillas shot and killed nineteen peasants, nearly all of 'em women and children, in a small village up in the Andes. These peasants went there to escape the rebel attacks down below. Said some of the kids weren't no more'n two or three years old. Just like Nam."

A young black woman, no more than fifteen years old, a bright yellow scarf wrapped around her head, holding an infant with one arm and a bag of groceries with the other, was coming out of the Short Stop. Sailor held the door open for her.

"Thanks, mister," she said, passing Sailor without looking at him.

"No problem," said Sailor.

Carmine Papavero and Zero Diplopappus left the office of Bayou Enterprises at seven-forty-five A.M. Poppy slid behind the wheel of his powder blue BMW and punched

WORKING IN THE

GOLD MINE

up his home number on the cellular phone as he pulled into the commuter traffic on Airline Highway.

"H'lo."

"*Buona mattina*, Perdita *mia*. I wake you up?"

"Uh huh."

"Sorry, sweetheart, but I figured if I didn't call now I might not get another chance until late."

"Got a busy day, huh?"

"Zero and I are going to Mississippi today, after we make a stop in town. We might not be back until tomorrow, tomorrow night."

"I'm still pretty beat from all that flyin', honey, so I'll be sleepin' mostly. That Europe's okay, but it's too damn far away. Think from now on I'll just stick to Dallas or Palm Beach, I need somethin' special."

"Whatever pleases you, honey. Get your rest and we'll have some fun when I return."

"Hold ya to it."

Poppy laughed. "Sleep tight, baby," he said, and hung up.

"You ought to get married, Zero. Change your outlook."

"Only one I'm lookin' out for is me. Besides, I was married once."

"Oh yeah? What happened?"

"Back in Tarpon Springs, when I was eighteen. A local girl, Flora Greco. She drowned on our honeymoon in Mexico."

"I'm sorry, Zero. I didn't know."

"I don't look back. Where we stoppin'?"

"Sonny Nevers needs a visit. We'll catch him at his jewelry store right when he opens at eight."

Poppy guided the Beamer off Interstate 10 onto Claiborne and turned down Elysian Fields. He pulled in front of The Gold Mine and parked. He and Zero waited until Sonny Nevers pulled up the doorshade, then they got out and rang the bell next to the store entrance. Nevers recognized Zero and Poppy and buzzed them in.

"Don't even say it!" said Sonny, edging his five-feet four-inch, three-hundred-pound body around from behind the counter to greet the two men. "I'll have it tomorrow, no problem."

Poppy accepted Sonny's handshake and waved away the smoke from what was already the jewelry salesman's second Partagas Topper of the day.

"Wasn't expecting there'd be one," said Poppy. "You've always been a man of your word, Sonny."

"Had a small cash flow difficulty here, just straightened it out. You can count on it. Want a cigar?"

"I know I can. No, thanks."

The doorbell rang. Sonny looked out and saw two men in blue sports coats carrying briefcases.

"Salesmen," said Sonny, who went back behind the counter and pressed the buzzer.

"What can I do for you gentlemen?" he asked, after they'd entered.

Both men were more than six feet tall, well-built, had blond hair and wore Carrera sunglasses. Each man pulled a .45 automatic from his briefcase and pointed it at Sonny and Poppy and Zero.

"We'll kill all three of you," said the slightly taller of the two men in a calm voice, "unless you give us what you've got in the safe."

Nobody said a word as the taller man followed Sonny into the rear of the store. The other man kept Poppy and Zero covered while he pulled down the doorshade and reversed the OPEN sign to CLOSED. In less than five minutes, the taller man emerged from the back, carrying a large black satchel filled mostly with twenty-four-karat gold used for the manufacture of gold chain.

Sonny ran out and hurled his huge body at the man with the satchel. The other blond man turned and shot Sonny in the face, the slug going in under the nose, lifting off the top of the fat man's head. Sonny's corpse belly-flopped on the floor as an umbrella of blood spread around him.

Zero and Poppy plastered themselves against the wall. The taller blond man turned toward them and fired twice. One round entered Poppy's open mouth, killing him instantly. Zero dropped to his knees, so the man's first shot missed entirely, shattering the plaster above his head. The second shot, however, was on target, gouging a large opening in the left side of Zero's neck, causing his oversized ears to flap furiously as he crumpled over on the cool, black-and-white-tiled floor.

The two blond men put their guns into the briefcases and left the store, the shorter man making certain that the door was closed securely behind them. The men walked swiftly to a new black Cadillac Fleetwood, put the satchel, containing nearly seventy-five pounds of gold worth three quarters of a million dollars, and the briefcases into the trunk, locked it, got into the car and drove away at a moderate speed. Inside The Gold Mine, Zero Diplopappus watched a ribbon of sunlight wriggle slowly through the front window and settle on what was left of Sonny Nevers's face. Zero did not live long enough to close his eyes.

"You don't have to be afraid to talk to me, boy," Wendell Shake said to Pace. "Got somethin' to say, say it."

"I ain't," said Pace.

"This world's an awful cruel place, son. Worst place I ever been."

"You remind me of a person I met once, named Elmer Désespéré," said Pace, "hailed from Mamou. He weren't so crazy for it, neither."

"There's a few of us is sensitive to more'n the weather. Where's this Elmer now?"

"He was killed on the street in New Orleans."

"Mighta guessed. It's the good go young, like they say. But there'll be one Great Day in the Mornin' before it's finished, I guarantee."

"Sir?"

"Yes, son?"

"What is it exactly gripes you, you don't mind my askin'."

Wendell grinned. "Ain't worth explainin'. Best repeat what Samuel Johnson said: 'Depend upon it that if a man talks of his misfortunes there is something in them that is not disagreeable to him; for where there is nothing but pure misery there never is any recourse to the mention of it.' "

Pace stared at Wendell, who sat stroking his red beard.

Wendell stood up and said, "Time to tend the garden. You'll stay put, won't ya?"

Pace nodded and watched Wendell walk out of the room. As soon as the madman was out of sight, he scrambled to his feet, ran over to the pistol crossbow and picked it up. Pace heard Wendell relieving himself in what he assumed was the toilet. He crouched under the window and waited. When Wendell reentered the room, Pace pressed the trigger that released a black dart into his captor's left eye. Wendell fell down and Pace dropped the crossbow and ran out of the house, headed on foot the four miles to Miss Napoleon's Paradise.

Wendell Shake carried no identification of any kind, and when his body was found, along with those of the Rattler brothers, the only item discovered in his pockets by police was a personal ad torn from a newspaper.

> If any open-minded, good-humored men
> of any race wish to write, I'm here and
> waiting. BF doing a 60-year term for
> something that just came out bad.
> Lamarra Chaney #1213 P-17
> Women's Correctional Facility
> Box 30014, Draper, UT 84020

P
U
R
E

M
I
S
E
R
Y

o

Miss Napoleon, Jaloux, and Sailor were sitting in rocking chairs on the front porch at The Paradise, drinking iced tea. Coot had driven into Starkville to see if he could

dig up any information on the whereabouts of Pace and the Rattler brothers. It was late afternoon, siesta time for the Lord's disturbed daughters, and things were quiet.

"It's the kind of thing happens if you hold the faith," said Miss Napoleon. "Tell the truth, I was worried about paying the bills for the first time in my life. We live modestly here at The Paradise, as Sister Domino insisted, but even so we had begun to struggle. When Mary Full-of-Grace came down those stairs last night and delivered into my hands that money, it was the answer to our prayers. Now we'll be able to continue as we've always done, and provide for more than just ourselves. I've thought about opening a haven for the homeless, which until last night didn't seem possible. The Lord has plans for us we cannot even imagine."

"You always been the kind of woman make God or any man do for, Miss Napoleon," said Jaloux.

"Child, don't you know the Lord's not a man? He's all things to all manner of people, and He provides best for those who provide for others. In this case, Mary Full-of-Grace was His instrument of mercy. Praise be."

Just then, Coot Veal's Ram came tearing up the drive, and Sailor could see that Coot had a passenger with him. The truck stopped and Pace jumped out. Sailor dropped his iced tea, hopped down off the porch and embraced him.

"Boy was runnin' down the road, Sail," said Coot,

coming around the front of the truck. "Couldn't believe it myself when I saw who it was. And you won't believe this, neither. Heard on the radio that Papavero and his henchman, Zero the Greek, been shot and killed in N.O. under mysterious circumstances. Their bodies was found in a jewelry store on Elysian Fields."

"The Rattlers is dead, too," said Pace. "We was gonna hide out at a abandoned farmhouse—least the Rattlers thought it was abandoned—and turned out a crazy man with a red beard was there. He shot both Lefty Grove and Smokey Joe. I was gonna be next, but he got to talkin' with me, all kindsa strange talk, and when he went to the head I got the drop on him with a pistol crossbow and let him have it. Then I run outta there fast as I could. Daddy, it was worse than what happened to me that time with the wild boy from Mamou."

Sailor and Pace stood and hugged each other.

"It's okay now, son," said Sailor. "Looks like the Lord done pulled off another one."

Miss Napoleon nodded and smiled and rocked in her chair.

"Come on up here, you two," she said to Coot and Pace, "and have a cold glass of tea."

"Guess this means whatever's between us is gonna have to wait," said Jaloux.

Coot and Pace were waiting in the truck while Sailor

said goodbye to Jaloux in front of Inez's Fais-Dodo Bar.

Sailor grinned and brushed back his silvery black hair with both hands. Jaloux reached her right hand under the left sleeve of his white tee shirt and traced the large vein in his bicep with her index finger.

"Guess it'll have to, Jaloux. You been a giant help to me and my boy, and I ain't forgettin' it. I know I owe you."

"Rather have it be voluntary, you know what I mean."

Sailor laughed, leaned forward and kissed her above her left eyebrow.

"I do," he said.

Coot drove the Ripleys home and they were surprised to see Lula's red Cressida wagon in the driveway.

"Jesus, Mama's home," said Pace.

They got out of Coot's truck, and Pace ran into the house.

"Comin' in, Coot?" Sailor asked.

"No, Sail, thanks. I'm pretty well bushed, all this drivin'. Talk to y'all later'd be best."

"Thanks, buddy. Couldn'ta done it without ya."

Coot grinned, saluted and drove off.

"Sailor, honey!" Lula shouted, as soon as he walked in the door. "You won't believe what happened! Reverend Plenty got assassinated in Rock Hill and Bunny and I barely escaped with our own lives! I been tryin' to call you-all but there ain't been no answer. I been wild!"

Lula rushed into Sailor's arms and held him tight. Pace was lying on the couch with his eyes closed.

"Sail," Lula said, "I'm afraid the devil got this world by the tail and he ain't lettin' go."

Sailor smiled and kissed the top of Lula's left ear.

"Maybe so, peanut, but I ain't lettin' go of you, either."

Lula almost swooned. "Oh, Sail, that's what I needed to hear."

CONSUELO'S KISS

"There are two kinds of women: those who move to make room when you sit on the bed and those who remain where they are even when you have only a narrow edge."

EDMUND WILSON

III

Consuelo Whynot licked idly at her wild cherry-flavored Tootsie Pop while she watched highway patrolmen and firefighters pull bodies from the wreckage. The Amtrak

CONSUELO'S KISS

Crescent, on its way from New Orleans to New York, had collided with a tractor-trailer rig in Meridian, hard by the Torch Truckstop, where Consuelo had stopped in to buy a sweet. The eight train cars had accordioned on impact and the semi, which had been carrying a half-ton load of Big Chief Sweet 'n' Sour Cajun-Q Potato Chips, simply exploded.

"The train's whistle was blowin' the whole time and, Lord, it sounded like a bomb had went off when they hit," said Patti Fay McNair, a waitress at the Torch, to a rubbernecker who'd asked if she'd seen what happened.

Consuelo Whynot, who was sixteen years old and a dead ringer for the actress Tuesday Weld at the same age, stared dispassionately at the carnage. The truck driver, a man named Oh-Boy Wilson from Guntown, near Tupelo, had been burned so badly over every inch of his body that the firemen just let him smolder on the spot where he'd landed after the explosion. His crumpled, crispy corpse reminded Consuelo of the first time she'd tried to make Roman Meal toast in the broiler pan of her cousin Vashti Dale's Vulcan the summer before last at the beach cottage in Ocean Springs. She never could figure out if she and Vashti Dale were once or twice removed. That was a result, Consuelo decided, of her unremarkable education. Venus Tishomingo would fix that, too, though, and the thought almost made Consuelo smile.

Four hospital types dressed in white and wearing plastic gloves slid Oh-Boy Wilson into a green body bag, zipped it up, tossed it into a van, and headed over to the wrecked Crescent, which had passenger parts sticking out of broken windows and crushed feet, hands, and heads visible beneath the overturned cars. Consuelo didn't think there'd be anything more very interesting to see, so she turned away and walked back to the truckstop.

"You goin' north?" she asked a man coming out of the diner.

The man looked at the petite young thing wearing a red-and-white polkadot poorboy that was stretched tightly over her apple-sized breasts, black jean cutoffs, yellow hair chopped down around her head like somebody had given it the once-over with a broken-bladed lawn mower, red tongue still lazily lapping at the Tootsie Pop, and said, "How old're you?"

"I been pregnant," Consuelo lied, "if that's what you mean."

The man grinned. He had a three-day beard, one slow blue-green eye and a baby beer gut. Consuelo pegged him at thirty.

"West," he said, "to Jackson. You can come, you want."

She followed him to a black Duster with mags, bright orange racing stripes, Moon eyes and a pale blue 43 painted on each side. She got in.

"My name's Wesley Nisbet," he said, and started the car. The ignition sounded like thunder at three A.M. "What's yours?"

"Consuelo Whynot."

Wesley laughed. "Your people the ones own Whynot, Mississippi? Town twenty miles east of here by the Alabama line?"

"Sixteen, be exact. You musta passed Geography."

Wesley whistled softly and idled the Duster toward Interstate 20.

"Where you headed, Consuelo?"

"Oxford."

"You got a boyfriend there?"

"Better. I'm goin' to see the woman of my dreams."

Wesley checked the traffic, then knifed into the highway and went from zero to sixty in under eight without fishtailing.

"This a 273?" Consuelo asked.

"Dropped in a 383 last week. You into ladies, huh?"

"One. What's the '43' for?"

"Number my idol, Richard Petty, ran with. Lots a man can do for ya a chick can't."

Consuelo bit down hard on the outer layer of her Tootsie Pop and sank her big teeth deep into the soft, dark brown core. She sucked on it for a minute, then opened her mouth and drooled down the front of her pol-kadot poorboy. Wesley wolfed a look at Consuelo, grinned, and gunned the Duster past ninety before feathering back down to a steady seventy-five.

"You ain't met Venus," she said.

"Who's gonna watch the worms?"

"Already taken care of, Sail, honey. Beany'll do it."

"She's gonna be helpin' out at Gator Gone, too, you know, fillin' in for me."

SAILOR AND

LULA AT HOME

"Beany can handle more'n one thing at a time, darlin'. She can't get by one time, Madonna Kim will. She ain't doin' much between marriages."

"Can't believe that girl, peanut. Only seventeen and put two men in the grave."

"Bad luck is all it is, Sailor. Madonna Kim ain't no spider woman. Mean, Beany and Bob Lee raised her right."

"Just glad Pace ain't never got hooked up with her."

"How could he, bein' off in Nepal since before Madonna Kim got her first period?"

"We heard from the boy lately?"

"Month ago's the most recent. He was preparin' to leave Katmandu for the place in India the tea comes from?"

"Darjeelin'."

"That's it. Was gonna be a long trek, he said, three months or so. Wanted to know when we was comin' over and go on a hike with him. Says he ain't gonna be doin' it forever."

"I seen that Abominable Snowman movie more than enough times to know I ain't ever goin' near no Tibet, and Nepal's near it."

"Don't know how Pace can take bein' in such a cold climate. Bad enough when it snows here in New Orleans once in the blue moon. Place just shuts down."

"You know 'bout blue moons, peanut? I mean, what one is, really?"

"No, what? Just sometimes the way the sky is makes the moon look blue."

"Uh-uh. It's when there's two full moons in the same month. Second one's the blue moon."

"Where'd you hear this?"

"Woman named Jaloux Marron, used to work for Poppy Papavero, told me, long time ago."

Sailor and Lula Ripley were eating breakfast in the Florida room of their house in Metairie. Sailor was on his second cup of Community and third Quik-Do raisin-nut muffin, and Lula was halfway finished with a peach, which was all she could handle before about noon. It was seven-forty-five A.M.

"Papavero was that gangster got shot in a jewelry store, right? Dozen years ago?"

"That's right, peanut."

"And who was this Jealous woman?"

"Jaloux. Gal worked the bar at Inez's Fais-Dodo before it was shut down. Believe it's a fish place now. No, antique store, that's it."

"So how'd you know her?"

Sailor sipped his coffee and looked out the sliding glass doors at the bird feeder.

"How come there ain't no seed in the feeder?" he asked.

" 'Cause there ain't no birds around."

"Might be if there was somethin' for 'em to eat."

"Didn't realize you was such a bird lover. Who was she, Sailor?"

"Told you, Lula. Girl worked for Papavero. Met her once I was at Inez's. Weren't nothin' more to it. I ain't seen her for twelve years."

Lula popped a small slice of peach into her mouth and swallowed it without chewing. She sucked on her tongue and stared blankly at a photo of Ava Gardner wearing a low-cut dress that Sailor had clipped out of the *Times-Picayune* and tacked to the wall the day her obituary had appeared in the newspaper. Ava was a homegirl, one of North Carolina's finest.

"Don't seem possible I'll be fifty years old next week, does it, peanut? Never figured on lastin' this long. Might just last a while longer, now I come this far. What do you think?"

"Might could, you will," said Lula. "Dependin'."

"Dependin'? Dependin' on what?"

"Dependin' on your keepin' the love of a certain good woman."

Sailor laughed, put down his cup, and reached his right hand across the table toward Lula.

"I ain't about to mess with true love, Lula, you know it. I never have."

She accepted Sailor's hairless hand into her own and smiled at him.

"I know that, darlin'. Just sometimes, even at forty-seven and a half years old, that ol' bug gets to squirmin' in my brain and knocks a wire loose. I love you, baby. Always have, always will. We're it, you know?"

Sailor nodded and squeezed Lula's slim left hand with the ruby ring on the third finger that she'd worn ever since Sailor had given it to her when she was sixteen years, six months and eighteen days old.

"I do know, peanut. Don't need no remindin', though it's okay you do it now and again."

The telephone rang and Lula reached over with her free hand and picked up the receiver.

"Oh, hello, Mama."

"You busy?"

"No, me'n my true love're just about to take off on a little trip to celebrate his first half-century on the planet."

"He takin' you to the Bahamas again on one of them gamblin' junkets just so's he can piss away your home improvement savin's?"

Lula laughed. "We're takin' a car trip, Mama, up to Memphis. Sailor always did want to visit Graceland, so we're goin' now. Be gone about a week."

"What about your worms?"

"Beany and Madonna Kim'll keep an eye on 'em."

"That Madonna ain't got the brains or morals of a worm. Didn't her last husband shoot himself after he come in on her screwin' his daddy?"

"That was the first one, Mama. Lonnie Wick? The Wick Wallpaper people? Second one hanged himself. Jimmy Modesta, had a beverage distribution company in Slidell. Used to get us all that Barq's and Dr Pepper for nothin'? That one weren't really all Madonna Kim's fault."

"What you mean, Lula? I recall now she shamed him with a homeless person."

"Man ran a shelter, Mama, there's a big difference. Anyway, them Modestas has a family history of chronic depression. Jimmy's brother, mother and a couple or three others took their own life before him."

"No loss to this earth, I'm positive," said Marietta Pace Fortune. "Look, Lula, I'm glad I caught you on your way out the door because I want you to know I got a houseguest."

"You call from North Carolina just to tell me you got a visitor? This another of your and Dalceda Delahoussaye's destitute Daughters of the Confederacy? Why can't Dal take in this one?"

"No, Lula, it's not. It's Marcello Santos."

"Santos?! Mama, ain't he in jail for life?"

"Released him from Texarkana day before yesterday. He's sick, Lula, real sick. Heart's about to quit. Feds figured a sick old man can't cause them no more trouble."

"Yeah, but Mama, Crazy Eyes Santos ain't just anyone. He was the crime king of the Gulf Coast since before I was born. You always said Daddy didn't trust him. What about that company of his he used as a front, Bayou Enterprises?"

"He ain't interested, Lula, really. Besides, no way after all these years the ones runnin' things'd let him back in. And he ain't got no crazy eyes no more, he's got cataracts both sides and can barely see. Your daddy didn't depend on Marcello's word, that's true, but Clyde Fortune didn't trust anyone, tell the truth, even me, probably. Anyway, Marcello had no place to go. Was stayin' at The Registry in Charlotte when he called me. I got him fixed up in my room. I'm usin' the study, had Johnnie Farragut bring over a cot. He and Marcello are in the front room together right now, watchin' 'Wheel of Fortune.' Marcello says it's the favorite show in the joint."

"Life is full of surprises, Mama, ain't it? I thought he and Johnnie hated each other."

"Johnnie been retired from the detective business ten years now, Lula. He's almost seventy-five and all he cares about is raisin' flowers. Dal and I got him comin' twice a week to the There But for the Grace of God Garden Club."

"Mama, I got to hand it to you. Talk about the lion lyin' down with the lamb!"

Marietta cackled. "Ain't no beast so fierce as time, Lula. It's time makes us all lie down in the here and now or the hereafter, one."

"I'll check in with you-all when we get to Memphis. Meantime give my love to Dal and Johnnie. Santos, too, I suppose."

Lula looked at Sailor, who was grinning. His teeth were several shades of brown from thirty-eight years of smoking unfiltered Camels. She figured his lungs must be several shades of black. Maybe if she quit smoking Mores, Lula thought, Sailor would quit Camels, and they wouldn't die of cancer or, almost worse, emphysema, where a person had to haul a machine around with him and keep tubes stuck up his nostrils so he could breathe.

"Love you, Lula," said Marietta. "You be careful on the road. There's serious enough devils every step of the way. You hear from my grandboy?"

"Pace is fine, Mama. He's off on a trek."

"Don't know why he'd want to hole himself up way behind the Bamboo Curtain like this. Boy got a mind of his own, though, I'll give him that."

"Mama, I'm goin'. I got Sailor Ripley to protect me, so don't worry."

Lula smiled at Sailor and he raised his left arm and flexed the bicep.

"He ain't always done such a spectacular job of it, Lula, or can't you remember?"

"Bye now, Mama. Love you."

Lula hung up.

"I know, peanut," Sailor said, "the world's plenty strange and not about to change."

"Might not be worth gettin' up in the mornin' it was any different, Sail, you know?"

"Your folks know where you're goin'?" asked Wesley Nisbet, as he guided his Duster into the Bienville National Forest.

THE AGE OF

REASON

Consuelo had not looked at Wesley since she'd gotten into the car. She didn't feel like talking, either, but she knew it was part of the price for the ride.

"They ain't known where I'm goin' ever since I been able to reason."

"How long you figure that is?"

"More'n seven years, I guess. Since I was nine, when me'n Venus got brought together in the divine plan."

Wesley slapped his half-leather-gloved right hand hard on top of the sissy wheel.

"Goddam! You mean that woman been havin' her way with you all this time? Hell, that's sexual abuse of a child. How is it your folks didn't get this Venus put away before now?"

"They couldn't prove nothin', so they sent me away to the Mamie Franklin Institute in Birmin'ham. I escaped twice, once when I was eleven and got caught quick, and then two years ago I stayed gone three whole months."

"Where'd you go?"

"Venus and me was shacked up in the swampy woods outside Increase. Didn't have no money, only guns, ammo and fishin' tackle. We ate good, too. Venus is about pure-blood Chickasaw. She can live off the land without askin'."

"How'd you get found out?"

Consuelo snorted. "Simon and Sapphire—those are

my parents—hired about a hundred and one detectives. Still took 'em ninety days. Venus found us a pretty fair hideout that time.''

"What's she doin' in Oxford?''

"Got her a full scholarship to study the writin's of William Faulkner, the greatest writer the state of Mississippi ever provided the world. Venus is also a writer, a poet. She says I got the makin's, too.''

"You write poetry?''

"Not yet, but Venus says I got the *soul* of a poet, and without that there's no way to begin. It'll come.''

"You ever read any books by this fella she's studyin'?''

Consuelo shook her head no. "Venus says it ain't important. 'Course I could, I want.''

Wesley kept his ungloved left hand on the steering wheel and placed his right on Consuelo's naked left thigh. She didn't flinch, so Wesley slid his leather-covered palm up toward her crotch.

"You wouldn't know what to do with my clit if I set it up for you on the dashboard like a plastic Jesus.''

Wesley's right hand froze at the edge of her cutoffs. He kept it there for another fifteen or twenty seconds, then removed it and grabbed the gear-shift knob, squeezing it hard.

"You're some kinda wise little teaser, ain't you?'' he said.

Consuelo turned her head and stared at Wesley's right profile. He had a scar on the side of his nose in the shape of an anchor.

"How'd you get that scar?'' asked Consuelo. "Bet you was doin' such a bad job the bitch just clamped her legs closed on it.''

Wesley Nisbet grinned and took the Duster up a notch.

"I'm likin' this more and more we go along,'' he said.

"You two need anything this afternoon? I'm goin' out."

"No, Marietta," said Johnnie, "thanks. Marcello and me's doin' good."

MEN IN CHAIRS

Johnnie Farragut and Marcello Santos were both seated in overstuffed armchairs with their feet up on needle-point footstools in the front room of the Fortune home, watching a talk show on the twenty-four-inch Sony. A practically naked woman was on the screen, her long, slender, tentacle-like legs seemingly about to entwine themselves around the shoulders of the show's male host, who was perched on a step below the chair in which his guest was seated. The fluffy-haired host held the microphone up in front of her dangling breasts, which were delicately contained by a slip of pink cloth.

"Who's she?" asked Marietta. "Some X-rated movie actress?"

"Concert violinist," Santos said. "Just played Brahms's 'Opus 25.' Very nicely, too."

"Never saw no violinist looked like that."

"While back there was a woman played cello in the all-nude," said Johnnie. " 'Member her?"

"I don't," said Marietta. "I'll leave the cultural events to you gentlemen, then, you don't mind. Back after the Daughters meetin'. Dal's goin' with me, so you-all're on your own if you spill your milk or need your pants changed."

"Bye, Marietta," said Johnnie.

He and Marcello sat quietly for several minutes, listening to the inane banter between the violinist, whose right breast rested on the microphone, and the unctuous host, waiting for the woman to stand up again so they could watch her parade in her skimpy dress. The show broke for a commercial and when it resumed the female violinist was gone.

"Damn," Johnnie said, "woulda appreciated seein' them stems once more. Only thing better to look at than a cluster of Cecil Brunners."

"You're an amusing man, Johnnie," said Santos, "and a most fortunate one. Before my eyes began giving me such problems, I read a great deal. In the penitentiary, there isn't much else of a savory nature to help pass the time, as you, having been in the law enforcement business, certainly know. I most enjoyed reading the bulletins and studies issued by the Justice Department, which were made available on a regular basis by the prison library. One of the last I read revealed that in the United States approximately 640,000 crimes per year are committed that involve the use of handguns. More than 9,000 people per year are killed in the process, and another 15,000 are wounded. Also committed each year are over 12,000 rapes, 200,000 robberies and 400,000 assaults by individuals possessing guns. Three quarters of the perpetrators of these crimes are strangers to the victims."

"Don't tell me that you, of all people, Marcello Santos, one of the most feared crime bosses of our time, is advocatin' gun control!"

Santos laughed. "I'm boss of nothing any longer, Johnnie. Those days are long passed. Yes, I am against the easy availability of weapons. It's the amateurs that ruin the business. In the proper hands, these kinds of things don't happen. Certainly they do not happen so often."

"There's a lot of guns in the world, but there's only one Johnny Rocco."

"What's that?"

"Line from an old movie. Anyway, you got a point, Marcello. Funny how we end up wheezin' in armchairs like this, in the parlor of a woman we both been chasin' after for decades. Though you, of course, was necessarily out of the runnin' for a spell. And after bein' on opposite sides of the fence, so to speak, in our professional lives. Kinda creeps up on a person that there ain't much he can do to influence his outcome."

Santos sat back in his chair with his eyes closed, his large, thick hands with the left thumb missing folded together in his lap.

"Tell me, Johnnie, have you had a happy life?"

"I guess so, Marcello. My regrets don't amount to much. Only thing is, I never made no mark as a writer, which is somethin' I'd always had in mind."

"Do you believe in an afterlife?"

"You mean, like heaven? Or reincarnation?"

"Call it what you like."

"No. Do you?"

Santos nodded his head slightly.

"I do. I'm looking forward to it. What I feel behind me is only pain."

The two men sat without talking, neither of them really listening to or watching the television. Johnnie thought about a cat he'd had for a while when he was a boy, an orange tom his father had named Kissass. Kissass had been electrocuted one summer evening when a bolt of ribbon lightning struck a power line that lashed down over him as he streaked across the lawn in front of the Farragut house on Stivender Street in Bay St. Clement. That was sixty-five years ago, Johnnie thought. He could remember Kissass's face an instant before the strike, and he stopped his memory right there.

Rather than take 10 into 55 around the lake, the fast way, Sailor decided to drive over the Lake Pontchartrain Causeway and head west just before Covington on In-

RUNNING INTO

DARKNESS

terstate 12, then pick up 55 north of Pontchartrain, which would take them all the way into Memphis. He and Lula had agreed to take their time, and Sailor kept the Sedan de Ville at a respectable sixty as they cruised across twenty-four scenic miles of the most polluted lake south of Erie.

"Ever tell you about the time I seen a corpse floatin' here?" he said.

Lula was adjusting her eye makeup in the visor mirror on the passenger side of the front seat. She'd had her eyelids tinted the day before and she wasn't sure that she liked the effect. They made her eyes look sunken or something, she thought. Lula studied them now and only half paid attention to what Sailor was saying.

"Tell me what, darlin'?"

"Me'n Slim Leake was takin' his nine-year old-nephew, Pharoah Sanders Leake, whose daddy—Slim's brother, Otis Blackwell Leake—teaches wind instruments at LSU, out for a boat ride, and here come a corpse up on the port side, bloated and fumin' like a abcess on a spaniel's belly."

Lula frowned into the mirror, flipped up the visor and put her beauty utensils into her purse.

"Say what about a dog?"

"No, peanut, I'm tellin' you about a dead body we come across on Pontchartrain here one mornin'."

"Whose body?"

"I don't know. Man drowned or was dumped. Looked like a purple balloon with bad air steamin' out all pores. Stank fierce."

"Delightful. What'd y'all do?"

"Went on and rowed around a while, till Pharoah'd had enough, then took it in and told the dockmaster."

"What'd he say?"

Sailor slipped a Camel from the open pack in his left front shirt pocket, stuck it between his lips, pulled out a black book of matches with a white skull-and-crossbones on it under the words PURVIS PETTY'S PIRATE LOUNGE, flipped the cover and lit the cigarette with one hand, tossed the match out the window, inhaled deeply, and dropped the matchbook back into his pocket.

"Said floaters was a regular feature of the lake and there weren't no extra charge. Didn't seem to excite him none, though before we left I noticed he'd uncovered the NO in front of the SWIMMING ALLOWED sign on the dock. Slim Leake—you remember, back then he was the Gator Gone distribution manager in Port Allen? Slim said the pollution level of the lake was checked daily, and dependin' on the readin', swimmin' was allowed or not."

"Wouldn't never get me in this sewer. Whatever happened to Slim Leake, anyway? He reminded me a little of that movie actor, the one looked like a cute bloodhound. Harry Dean Stanton."

"Yeah, I remember him. He's the one in *The Missouri Breaks* is ridin' with some old boys from Montana into Canada when they hear some horrible animal noise they can't I.D., and Harry Dean says, 'The further north you go, the more things eat your horse.' Whoever wrote that line had a real talent. Always thought that was a pretty fair analysis of the human condition, myself."

"So what about Slim Leake?"

"Not real certain. He and Nelda Bea divorced, of course, his work went to hell in a hurry, he was drinkin' a lot and Bob Lee had to let him go. Last I heard he was up north in Ohio, managin' a trailer park."

"Nice man like Slim deserved better'n Nelda Bea. She was one impatient type of woman."

Sailor inhaled and exhaled a stream of smoke from his nostrils without removing the cigarette from his mouth. Lula looked at him and wondered how many thousands of times she'd seen Sailor pull on a Camel.

"Man might be better off without what he ain't been without since he can't recall," Sailor said, "only there ain't no way he can imagine bein' without it."

Lula nodded. "You know, honey, I'm givin' up smokin'. I got a pack of Mores with me but I ain't gonna crack 'em. This trip's a good occasion to quit."

"More power to ya, peanut. You quit forty, fifty times before. It prob'ly ain't impossible."

Lula stared out the window at the water. Thirty years ago she and Sailor had been on the move like this, only then they were running into darkness. She could recall the feeling all too well, and there hadn't really been a day since that she'd been entirely free of the memory. They were rolling in the light today, though, and Lula knew she should be thankful for it, but somehow the thought of that crazy, out of control time shook her in a way nothing else could.

"Feels fine bein' back on the road, peanut, don't it?"

Sailor tossed his half-burned butt out the window.

"Ain't no substitute," said Lula. "Rest of the world other than what's outside the windshield fades right out. Like yesterday? I was readin' in the paper about a ninety-five-year-old man murdered a eighty-eight-year-old woman in her apartment in New York City."

"How'd he do it? Hammer her with his crutch?"

Lula nodded. "Knocked her out with a lead bar he used for therapy."

"Musta been he caught her with a younger man of ninety-two."

"Uh-uh. Said she'd tried to kill him on orders from the ashes of her dead husband, which she kept in a box on her bedroom dresser. Man accused her of poisonin' fifteen people and practicin' voodoo. Said she'd put a curse on him preventin' him from havin' proper sexual relations and causin' his wheelchair to rust."

"Guess there's no guarantee of goin' gentle into the good night, or however that poem says."

Lula looked at Sailor and smiled. "After all these years, Sail, darlin', you're still capable of surprisin' me."

Sailor laughed. "What you mean, sweetheart?"

"Quotin' poetry and all. I like it."

"Well, I like you."

"I know it, Sailor Ripley. I surely do. And I really do think that despite ever'thin's happened to us, we got a charmed life."

Lula reached up and tied her long, gray-black hair back into a ponytail and put on a new pair of fake tortoise-shell Ray-Bans she'd purchased the day before at the Rexall. A huge beige pelican fell out of the sky, bounced off the roof of the car and tumbled over the passenger side into the lake.

"Just want to say one thing," said Wesley Nisbet, "before we get to anywhere, and I don't mean for you to get the wrong idea."

EVERY MAN

A KING

"What's exactly a wrong idea?" asked Consuelo. "Tough enough tellin' right and wrong in doin', here you come with thinkin'. You talkin' 'bout believin' evil?"

Wesley passed a gray-primered Dodge Shadow that had the driver's flabby left arm hanging out the window.

"Only a man can make a real woman out of you, is all."

"You a medical man, I take it."

Wesley shook his head. "Was a woman in Greenville, guess it was, convinced herself the King of Sweden was in love with her. Took to tellin' everyone she met how the King of Sweden was comin' to town soon to take her away with him and they'd live in his snow palace over there in Europe. She wrote to him every day for years, even though she never got no answer. Ever'body figured she was just a harmless person and was pretty well amused by her obsession."

"How you know all this?" Consuelo asked.

"Read it in a book about sexual behavior written by a doctor. So guess what happened? The King of Sweden, she finds out, is comin' to Memphis to visit Graceland durin' a goodwill trip. Turns out he's a big fan of Elvis. The woman tells ever'one she's meetin' the King in Memphis, closes up her house, takes her money out of the bank and drives to Tennessee. On the day the King of Sweden shows up at Graceland, there she is at the gate, waitin' for him. Naturally, he don't notice her and goes right on in.''

"She couldn't go back to Greenville after that.''

"Sticks by the gate, gettin' crazier by the minute, and when the King comes out, she pulls a gun from her purse and tries to shoot him, only her aim ain't no good and the bullet hits a tourist from France.''

"They musta locked her up for good.''

"Uh-uh. She beat 'em to it. Put the pistol in her mouth and blew her brains back to Miss'ippi, right in front of the King of Sweden and ever'-body. Doctor who wrote the book said someway the woman had developed a strange condition called De Clerambault's Syndrome, meanin' she was way out of line concernin' her object of affection. I copied out the name of her disease and memorized it.''

"Why you tellin' me this, Wesley Nisbet?''

"Your feelin's directed toward this Venus ain't normal, either. There's prob'ly a name for it, too.''

Wesley sped up and passed a powder blue BMW with California license plates being driven by a woman wearing a blond wig and large, orange-tinted sunglasses. The woman gave Wesley the finger as he went by.

"Nice folks, them California people,'' he said.

"Why you so concerned about me?'' asked Consuelo. "You don't even know me, and you ain't gonna get to, neither.''

"It's Venus I'm mostly curious about. I'm thinkin' I'd like to meet her. Maybe we three can have us a party.''

"Wesley, you're givin' me a ride and all, which I appreciate, but I got to say you ain't nearly the answer to nobody's dreams.''

Wesley laughed. "Just could be we'll find out there's any truth to that, Miss Whynot, honey.''

Consuelo arched her back and stretched her arms behind her, which made her nipples perk up under the polkadots. She held the pose long enough for Wesley to notice, then relaxed.

"Death and destruction ain't never more than a kiss away,'' she said. "Woman shot at the King of Sweden knew that much.''

Sailor and Lula sat in a tan Naugahyde booth in Rebel Billy's Truckstop off 55 near Bogue Chitto, eating bowls of chili and drinking Barq's. Sailor was reading the *Clarion-Ledger* he'd bought from a box out front.

RED BIRD

"Guess we been real lucky with Pace, peanut," he said.

Lula looked over the red lumps on her tablespoon at the top of Sailor's head and noticed that the bald spot on his crown was growing larger. Sailor was super-sensitive about losing his hair. Whenever Lula said anything about it, like suggesting he get a weave or try Monoxidil, he got upset, so she ignored the urge to reiterate her feelings regarding the situation.

"Why you say that, sweetheart? I mean, you're right and all, but what made you think of it?"

Lula stuck the spoon into her mouth.

"Item here in the Jackson paper. Headline says, 'Sorrow Ends in Death,' and underneath that, 'Boy, 12, Hangs Self after Killing Red Bird.' Story's out of San Antonio."

Lula retracted the spoon. "Nothin' good happens in Texas, I'm convinced."

"Here it is: 'Conscience-stricken after he had shot and killed a red bird, Wyatt Toomey, twelve years old, hanged himself here last night. The body was found by his sister. A signed note addressed to his parents told the motive for the act.' This is what he wrote: 'I killed myself on account of me shooting a red bird. Goodby mother and daddy. I'll see you some day.' "

"Jesus, Sail, that's a terrible story."

Sailor folded the newspaper to another page.

"Hard to know what a kid's really thinkin'," he said. "Pace had himself a few scrapes, of course, but he got clean, thank the Lord."

"Thanks to you, too, Sail. You been a fine daddy. Want you to know I appreciate it."

Sailor smiled, blew Lula a kiss and leaned back in his corner of the booth and lit up a Camel.

"Hope you don't mind my smokin', peanut. I may be a good daddy but I ain't always such a clean liver."

A waitress came over carrying a pot of coffee.

"Need refills?" she asked.

Sailor covered his cup with his left palm.

"I'm peaceful," he said. "Peanut?"

Lula nodded. "Don't mind a drop."

"Folks don't drink so much coffee they used to," said the waitress, as she poured. "Don't smoke, neither."

The waitress carried a good one-hundred-eighty-five pounds on her five-feet two-inches. She was about forty-five, Sailor guessed, and she reeked of alcohol. Sailor figured her for a nighttime cheap gin drinker. Five minutes after she was in her trailer door after work, he imagined, she'd be kicked back in her Barcalounger watching the news, four fingers of Gilbey's over a couple of cubes in a half-frosted chimney in one hand and five inches of menthol in the other.

"My wife's tryin' to quit," he said.

"I got thirty years worth of tar and nicotine in me," said the waitress, "too late to stop. Anyway, I like it. This health thing's gone just about far as it can now, I reckon. What with AIDS and the Big C, not to mention heart disease and drug-related crimes, might as well let yourself go a little and get some pleasure out of life. My son, Orwell, he's twenty-two now, was born deaf and with a withered-up left arm? He won't eat nothin' but raw vegetables, no meat or dairy. Runs three miles ev'ry damn mornin' before seven, then goes to work at the telephone office. In bed by nine-thirty each night. You'd think Orwell'd want to cut loose, 'specially after the cards he been dealt, but he figures he might could live forever he don't smoke or drink liquor and sticks to eatin' greens. What for? That ain't livin', it's runnin' spooked. Can't stand to see it, but half the world's in the coward's way at present. You folks take care now. Highway's full of God's worst mistakes."

She left the check on the table.

"Gimme a drag on that Camel, willya, Sail?"

He handed his cigarette to Lula and watched her suck in Winston-Salem's contribution to the good life.

"Feel better?" Sailor asked, as she exhaled and handed it back to him.

Lula nodded. "It's terrible, but I do love tobacco. Must be it's in our blood, comin' from North Carolina."

" 'Member that woman kept a vigil out front of the Lorraine Motel in Memphis for three years, place where Martin Luther King got shot? She was protestin' it bein' made into a civil rights museum, 'stead of a medical clinic or shelter for the homeless."

"Kinda do, honey. What happened to her?"

"Cops dragged her away, finally. Don't know where she went after."

"Why you askin' now, Sailor? That was a long time back."

"Oh, I'm thinkin' it might be interestin', long as we're in Memphis, go look at the Lorraine, maybe see the spot James Earl Ray aimed from. I mean, it's our history."

"Think James Earl Ray ever shot a bird when he was a boy?"

"He did," said Sailor, "don't guess it bothered his mind none."

"Had me a buddy for four or five years named Felix Perfecto," said Wesley Nisbet, as his Duster finished off Rankin County. "Perfecto family come over to this country from Mariel, Cuba, on the boatlift in '81. Guess they musta settled in Miami or somewhere in Florida for a while before movin' to Miss'ippi, which is where we met, right here in Jackson. Felix was a good-lookin' cat, dark-skinned with blond hair and blue eyes, which he got from his mama, who was of German extraction. Think her grandaddy was a Nazi fled to Cuba end of WW Two. All the girls went for Felix Perfecto. 'Señor Perfect' they called him. Boy had more women than Madonna had push-up bras. That's why what happened to him's such a tragedy."

Consuelo shifted her left leg out from under her and folded in her right. She couldn't wait to get away from Wesley and was relieved to see the Jackson city limits sign, but she relaxed, knowing it wouldn't be long now, and decided to humor him.

"Somethin' bad happened, huh?"

Wesley whistled softly through his front teeth.

"It ain't pretty."

"*Dit-moi.*"

"*D* what?"

"French for tell me. Venus been teachin' me."

"Felix was goin' steady with a girl name of Felicity Tchula. Señor Perfect and Miss Felicity was quite the couple around here for a good while. She was a red-haired beauty, too, full of freckles with big green eyes and a figure like nothin' this side of Sophia Loren when she was young. Ever see her in that movie, *Boy on a*

Dolphin, with Alan Ladd, who had to stand on a box to be as tall as her? She don't wear nothin' but a thin, wet shirt, stays plastered to her tits. Hope Alan Ladd had a bite or two on them bullets.

"Anyway, Miss Felicity's parents weren't altogether keen on her hangin' out with Felix Perfecto, since his main source of income come from dealin' dope. Nothin' serious, mind you. Felix sold reefer, is all, and maybe some pills once in a while, but no crack or ice or hard stuff. He started dealin' in high school and just stayed with it afterward, so's he wouldn't have to work for nobody. He was a happy guy, Felix Perfecto, and didn't never hurt people. They was sorta an ideal couple. Felicity was studyin' to be a registered nurse."

"We're almost to where I'm gettin' off," Consuelo said, "so you'd best tell me the terrible part."

"DeSoto Tchula, Felicity's daddy, decided to try and persuade Felix to break off with his daughter. He went to see Felix with three or four of his employees, construction workers from off one of the Tchula Buildin' Company jobs. Felix told DeSoto to get fucked and the goons broke both of Felix's legs, ruptured his spleen and kicked him so many times in the balls that one of 'em had to be surgically removed. Felix knew it wouldn't do no good to bring charges against the man, seein' as how DeSoto Tchula was so powerful in the town, so he waited until he healed up good as could be expected before he got his revenge."

"What'd Felicity do after her daddy mangled Perfecto?"

"Felicity's mama, Pearl, took her on a long trip to Europe. When they come back, Felix was about fit, and Felicity went to see him. He hadn't wanted to see none of his friends while he was recuperatin', includin' me, and he didn't let Felicity in, neither. Told her to go home, but warned her not to ride in a car with either of her parents."

"I can guess now what happened. Real burnin' love business, like me'n Venus."

"Uh huh. First, Pearl Tchula's T-bird blew up with her in it in the parkin' lot of the Winn-Dixie on Natchez. Couldn't tell her brains from the canteloupe parts. Quarter-hour later, DeSoto Tchula bit metal in his Lincoln Town Car when he started it up to leave a construction site out at the Ross Barnett Reservoir."

"The cops catch Felix Perfecto?"

"He was already gone by the time the bombs went off. Hijacked a private plane from the airfield, a baby Beechcraft belonged to Tchula, and headed for Cuba. He got there, too, at least in the sky over Havana, but the Cubans wouldn't let him land, sayin' they'd shoot him if he did. He told 'em he was runnin' out of fuel, but they didn't care."

"He explain about his bein' born in Cuba, and all?"

"Suppose he tried, but whatever he said apparently didn't do no good, 'cause the Beechcraft went down a few minutes later in Havana harbor. Felix never got out, drowned inside the cockpit."

"What happened to Felicity?"

"Inherited her parents' money, married a banker from Memphis and moved there. Has three kids, includin' a son name of Felix."

"Fittin'," said Consuelo. "You can drop me up here, at the A&W."

Wesley pulled into the drive-in and let the engine idle.

"Sure you don't want to hang out a bit, get to know me better?" he asked.

Consuelo opened the door and got out.

"You prob'ly ain't such a bad guy, Wesley, but I got my own agenda, you know? 'Preciate the lift," she said, and walked off.

Wesley leaned over and swung the passenger door closed. Something about the girl made him twitch where it hurt but felt good at the same time, and he made the not-so sudden decision to make sure this one didn't get away.

Marietta Pace Fortune and Dalceda Hopewell Delahoussaye were in the corner nook in Bode's Diner sipping sour Cokes following the Daughters meeting. The

BANTER AT

BODE'S

nook had been their regular
spot at Bode's for more than
sixty years, since they were little girls and used to go there
with their mothers. The diminutive Misses Pace and
Hopewell had been special favorites of W. Saint Louis
Bode, the original owner. Saint Lou, as he was popularly
known, made it a habit to present a brand-new copper
penny to each child who came into his diner to spend
in the gumball machine next to the huge old National
cash register. Marietta and Dalceda once figured out that
during their girlhoods, Saint Lou had gifted them with
approximately two thousand pennies apiece.

W. Saint Louis Bode had retired when the girls reached
sixteen, and his only son, W. Cleveland Bode, known
to the residents of Bay St. Clement as Mister Cleve, had
run the place for the next forty years, until his death,
fourteen years ago. Mister Cleve, who had discontinued
the policy of passing out pennies to kids after Saint Lou's
death three years following his retirement, had never
married, and following his funeral the diner was sold by
his heirs, cousins who lived in Pensacola, Florida, to the
P. L. Ginsberg Group, which owned most of the real
estate in downtown Bay St. Clement. To the relief of
regular patrons, such as Marietta and Dalceda, who de-
spaired at the thought of doing without their sour Cokes
and quiet chats in the corner nook three or four after-
noons a week, the Ginsberg people decided to keep the
place as it always had been, at least for the time being,

which, as Marietta pointed out, was the only time one could count on.

"Clyde wouldn't mind, Dal, do you think? I mean about Santos stayin' at the house."

"Ain't worth thinkin' about, Marietta. Clyde's dead too many years now for what he mighta thought to matter. The world changes, don't it? He'd had to change his thinkin', too, along with the rest of us driftin' souls. If Louis Delahoussaye the Third was still alive, he'd have him a firm opinion, I know."

"And what might it have been?"

Dal sucked some sour up through her straw and let it slosh around her bottom teeth before swallowing.

"That you was disgracin' Clyde's mem'ry. But Louis was a fool far's them things go, Marietta. Best parts about him was his earnin' power and love of small animals."

"You don't really miss him, Dal, do you?"

"Like a old rug was always lyin' in the same spot on the floor till it got walked over so many times it needed replacin'."

"You never replaced Louis."

"Turned out the floor looked better uncovered, after all."

Both women laughed and bent to their straws.

"Amazin', though, how well Marcello and Johnnie keep company, Dal, don't you think?"

"Neither of 'em got much teeth left, Marietta. One's a widower and mistress murderer with nothin' but down-time to show for the past couple decades, and the other's a lifelong bachelor who never had the guts to take what he thought he wanted."

"You're a tough enough nut, Dal. Why I always admired you."

"Only been cracked once, which is plenty."

"You mean Truxno Thigpen?"

Dal nodded. "That boy had lived, my life mighta been a whole sight different. I ain't complainin', though. We had our moment."

"You ever visit his grave?"

"Not for fifty years, Marietta, a whole half-century. Ain't that somethin'?"

"Sailor Ripley's gonna be fifty next week. He and Lula are goin' to visit Graceland for the occasion."

"Trux done one thing for me I never will forget."

"What's that, Dal?"

"After my dog, Clark Gable, died—'member him, the golden retriever?—Trux brought one white rose to my house every day for a month and left it in front of the door."

"You never told me that."

Dal's eyes clouded up. "Never told anyone. My mama and daddy didn't even know who done it."

"How'd you know?"

"Didn't, really. I mean, I didn't see him bringin' the flowers, but I guessed it was Truxno. Couldn'ta been nobody else. Meant to ask him if he was the one, but then that bolt of ball lightnin' scorched the life out of him on the par-three golf course used to be over by the dump before Ginsberg built them apartments, and I never had the chance."

"Dal, I'm thinkin' I might marry Marcello. He ain't got long to go."

Dalceda looked at Marietta and smiled. Her eyes sparkled despite the water in them.

"I got just the dress for you," she said.

"I have a collect call for Venus Tishomingo from Consuelo Whynot. Is this Venus Tishomingo?"

"Yes, it is."

"Will   you   accept   the
charges?"

"Yes, I certainly will."

"Go ahead, please."

The operator cut out.

"Hi, Venus, I'm on my way."

"Where you, Suelo, sweets?"

"Next to a A&W in Jackson. Just hitched a ride here
from a weird dude in a nasty short. No boy wants to
believe a girl ain't simply dyin' to lick the lint off his
nuts."

"He make a attempt?"

"Not directly. Told him you was my dream woman
and I didn't need no further stimulation."

"Sapphire and Simon know you split?"

"Don't think yet. Was a big train wreck in Meridian,
I was there. Fireman on the scene said it's the worst in
Miss'ippi hist'ry. Rescue squad'll be pullin' people's
parts out of that mess for hours. Prob'ly be findin' pieces
in the woods around for days."

"I know, it's on the news here. How long you gonna
be?"

"Depends on when I can get a lift. I'm gonna have
me a root beer and a burger and catch another ride."

"What happened to the hotrod boy?"

"Made him leave me off. He'd been trouble I woulda
asked him to take me up to Oxford. Figure I'll make it
in by midnight, I'm lucky."

"Okay, precious. I'll be waitin' up. You call again, there's a problem."

"I will, Venus. Love you dearly."

"My heart's thumpin', baby. Be careful, you hear?"

They both hung up and Consuelo left the phone booth, which was on the side of the road, and walked up to the window of the drive-in.

"Cheeseburger and a large root beer, please," she ordered from the fat man behind the glass.

"Ever'thin' on it?" he asked.

"No pickles."

"Three dollars," said the fat man, as he slid a bag through the space in the window.

Consuelo dug a five dollar bill out of her shorts, handed it to him, and he gave her back two dollars, which she folded in half and stuffed into her right front pocket.

"Y'all hurry back," the man said, his gooey, small hazel eyes fixed on her breasts.

Consuelo smiled at him, tossed her blond chop and pulled back her shapely little shoulders and expanded her chest.

"Maybe," she said.

The A&W was only a few hundred yards from the on-ramp to the Interstate, and Consuelo sipped at her root beer as she headed toward it. She took out the cheeseburger, dropped the bag on the ground and ate it as she walked. Next to the on-ramp was a Sun Oil station, and Consuelo spotted Wesley Nisbet's Duster, the hood raised, parked at a gas pump with Wesley bent into it, eyeballing the engine. She hoped he wouldn't see her. She also noticed a road-smudged white Cadillac Sedan de Ville with a man and a woman in it, about to pull away from the pump opposite the one occupied by Wesley's vehicle. Consuelo wolfed down the rest of her burger, wiped her right hand on her black jean cutoffs and stuck out her thumb as the Sedan de Ville rolled her way. The car stopped next to Consuelo and the front passenger window went down.

"Where you goin'?" Lula asked.

"Oxford," said Consuelo. "I'm a student at Ole Miss and I got to get there tonight so's I can make my classes in the mornin'."

"Guess we can take you far's Batesville," said Sailor, leaning over against Lula. "You'll have to catch a ride east from there on route 6."

"Good enough," Consuelo said, and opened the right rear door and climbed in, careful not to spill her root beer.

Sailor accelerated and guided the heavy machine onto 55 North and had it up to sixty-five in twelve seconds. Wesley Nisbet watched the white Cad disappear and snickered. He gently closed the Duster's hood and slid behind the steering wheel. He wouldn't have a problem keeping a tail on that whale, Wesley thought.

"What river's this?" Consuelo asked, as the Sedan de Ville crossed a bridge just before the fairgrounds.

"The Pearl, I believe," said Sailor. "Where you-all from?"

"Alabama," said Consuelo. "I been home on vacation 'cause my grandmama died."

"Sorry to hear it, honey," said Lula, who was turned around in her seat studying the girl.

"Yeah, we was real close, me and my grandmama."

"You didn't take no suitcase with you, huh?" Sailor asked.

"No," Consuelo said, "I only been gone a few days. Don't need much in this close weather."

Lula examined Consuelo, watching her sip her drink, then turned back toward the front. She looked over at Sailor and saw the half-grin on his face.

"You let me know the AC's too strong for you, Miss," said Sailor. "Wouldn't want you to get a chill in that outfit."

"Thanks, I'm fine," Consuelo said. "And my name's Venus."

As Wesley Nisbet trailed the white Cadillac by a discreet one eighth of a mile, he thought about his family. It wasn't too often that the Nisbet clan occupied Wesley's

THE SUITOR

mind. Most of them that he'd known were dead now, anyway, buried alongside the Bayou Pierre near Port Gibson. His mother, Althea Dodu, and his father, Husbye, had been killed in a car wreck when Wesley was four years old. They'd been returning from Pine Bluff, Arkansas, where Husbye had robbed a liquor store of four hundred dollars and a fifth of Jack Daniel's. He was sucking on the Jack when the oncoming Pacific Intermountain Express truck, into whose lane Husbye had allowed his and Althea's Mercury Monarch to drift, slammed into them head-on.

Wesley had been raised thereafter by Husbye's maiden sister, Taconey, in Weevil, Mississippi, where Wesley did his best to avoid going to school and church, preferring to spend his time under the hoods of trucks and cars and exploring the nearby woods, shooting at things with his Sears .22 rifle. Aunt Taconey had died when Wesley was seventeen, and he'd left Weevil at that time, traveling first to McComb, where he worked for a few months in a filling station, then to Memphis, where he was arrested for stealing a battery out of a new Mustang. He did ninety days in the city lock-up and, following his release, drifted down to Meridian, where he got a job as a gravedigger at the Oak Grove Cemetery.

Wesley had had an argument the day before with the foreman at Oak Grove, Bagby Beggs. Beggs, whose father, Bagby Beggs, Sr., had been a guard for twenty years at the prison farm at Parchman, had reprimanded Wesley for having left the tool shed door unlocked the previous night. Even though nothing had been stolen, Beggs told Wesley, this kind of oversight went a long way, in his opinion, toward revealing a man's true character. Beggs went on to inform him that there were plenty of able bodies in the state of Mississippi willing to work and properly acquit themselves of the responsibilities attendant to the job if the challenge proved too exacting for this particular Nisbet.

At first Wesley had tried to wriggle out of it by saying that he thought someone else had already locked the shed, but when he looked directly into Bagby Beggs's square red eyes Wesley knew the foreman wasn't about to buy it, so he apologized and promised not to let it happen again. When Wesley drove away from the job after working a half-day on Saturday, Beggs's last words echoed in his cerebrum.

"There's two sides to me, Mr. Nisbet," Beggs had said, "just like there's two sides to ever'body. The side you see's the side you get, 'cause if you don't see that side you won't see any. If I tolerate you, you'll see me. If I don't, you won't."

Wesley decided as he drove that his career as a gravedigger was about done. Not necessarily because of anything Bagby Beggs had said, but because Wesley felt that life had more to offer him than a position as a caretaker of the dead. He'd enjoyed being able to pay his daily respects to Jimmie Rodgers, the Singing Brakeman, whose remains resided in Oak Grove, but it was time to move on. Maybe he could convince this vixen Consuelo Whynot to take off with him to Charlotte, where he'd begin a career at the Speedway as a stock car racer. First, though, he wanted to check out the lesbian Chickasaw. There were plenty of things his Aunt Taconey hadn't known about, and she'd been no worse off for it, he thought.

One of these days, too, Wesley promised himself, he would go back to Meridian, creep up on Bagby Beggs, and bash his head in with a shovel. Then he'd bury the foreman in an unmarked grave, whether Beggs was already dead or not. It would probably be better not to tell Consuelo about this plan, Wesley decided, at least not right away.

"There's one thing I been meanin' to ask you about, Marcello."

Santos was propped up in the fold-out bed in the study

with two fluffy pillows behind his head. Marietta was sitting in her grandmother Pace's straight-backed mahogany chair on his right side. Johnnie had gone home an hour before, after the three of them had eaten dinner and watched a rerun on television of one of the original "Twilight Zone" episodes, the one about the last man left on earth after a nuclear blast.

This story was a favorite of Johnnie's, who at one time in his life had aspired to being a writer of bizarre fiction. In it, the actor Burgess Meredith portrays a Milquetoast bank clerk whose only real passion in life is for reading, an activity for which, due to work and a nagging wife, he never has enough time or peace to enjoy. When the cataclysmic explosion occurs, he is alone in the bank's vault, and he survives. The clerk, who must wear glasses with Coke-bottle-thick lenses, stumbles out into the light and surveys a rubble-filled landscape. After a painstaking search through the city, he realizes he is the only person around. He goes to the library, is overjoyed to find that the books have been spared, and contemplates a leisurely lifetime of reading without disturbance. Reaching for a book, however, his glasses fall off, and in his effort to retrieve them, inadvertently steps on the lenses, crunching them beyond repair. Helpless without his glasses, his future is shattered, too.

Marietta thought the story was just plain mean and didn't want to hear anything Johnnie thought about irony.

"What do you mean, 'irony'?" Marietta said. "Whenever I hear that word, all I can think of is pressin' Clyde's shirts."

After so many years of friendship, Johnnie Farragut knew better than to argue an abstract point with Marietta Fortune, so he laughed it off and said good night. She'd then fixed up Santos's bed and helped him into it. His condition was worsening visibly day by day, and she didn't see how he could get much weaker and continue living at her house. He was one close step away from an I.V. feeder and a breathing machine.

"You mean Mona, yes?" Santos said, his voice no more than a tiny croak.

"I hate to ask," said Marietta, "'specially considerin' your heart and all, but I just gotta know, Marcello. Did you have Mona Costatroppo killed?"

Santos sighed heavily. He had been sent to prison for arranging the murder of his mistress, Mona Costatroppo, who had threatened to testify against him in a federal court in New Orleans regarding a variety of criminal charges. The Feds were supposed to have given her a new identity in a distant city as part of the government witness protection program, but she had been shot to death in a hotel room in Chicago by a hitter from Detroit.

"You know, Marietta, my wife, Lina, before she died five years ago, wrote me a letter telling me that she forgave me everything, all of my sins against her and the children, none of whom, of course, will now even acknowledge that I am alive, however barely this is so. I wrote her back, informing her that had I desired absolution I would have remained a Catholic and paid a priest to perform this service. Clergy do not work for nothing, you know. The larger the alleged sin, the larger the church's bite in exchange for removing an obstacle on the path to heaven."

"Marcello, honey, I ain't interested in Lina, or any letters she mighta wrote. Far's I know, she died of natural causes culminatin' in cirrhosis of the liver."

Santos nodded slightly. "That's what I was told."

"It's this other business I need to satisfy myself about, we're gonna take a step. Answer me, Marcello."

Santos's eyes, once fiery, unsettling-to-look-into combinations of red and green, now floated on either side of his nose like opaque yolks in viscous, swampy yellow puddles. He blinked them several times, causing the puddles to overflow their containers and streak stickily down the sides of his face. Marietta took a tissue from a pocket of her robe and wiped away the effluent.

"I did, Marietta. I ordered the death of Mona Costatroppo. It was a terrible moment for me, when I realized what I had done, and that it was too late to prevent it. Mona knew it would happen, sooner or later, when she agreed to testify against me. She telephoned me one night, after she had gone into hiding. 'I have always been willing to die for you, Marcello,' she said, 'and now I am willing to die because of you.' Then she hung up. Now that you know, Marietta, what difference can it make?"

"It's the truth matters to me, Marcello. You had your reasons for doin' what you done, or had done for you, and I can live with that. I was just hopin' you wouldn't lie about this, is all. Murder ain't no more or less than a imperfect act of desperation, and ain't none of us is perfect. Nothin' to forgive or forget."

Marietta leaned over and kissed Santos on the forehead. He smiled at her and covered her left hand with the four remaining fingers of his own.

"I am a happy man tonight, Marietta. For the little it is worth, you have won the undying love and respect of an old, dying gangster."

"It's worth plenty, Marcello."

Marietta kissed him again on the forehead, stood up and grinned down at the once mighty Crazy Eyes Santos.

" 'Night, killer," she said.

"Wake up, honey," Lula said to Consuelo, "we're about at the Batesville junction."

Consuelo blinked hard a few times and pinched her cheeks. Her mouth tasted dry and sour. She wished she had an ice-cold soft drink.

WEIRD BY HALF

"Had me a awful strange dream just now," Consuelo said. "I went into my brother Wylie's room in the middle of the night, to check on him and see if he was all right. He was only about six years old in the dream—in real life he's fourteen and a half—and he was sleepin' sound. But then I looked over and there was this other bed kinda perpendicular to Wylie's, a single mattress, maybe, on the floor, and there was my cousin Worth, who drowned in Okatibbee Lake when he was twelve and I was eleven. Worth looked the same as he did then, with his reddish-brown hair cut short on the sides and floppin' on his forehead. He sat up in the bed and looked at me, and I said, 'Worth, that you?' And he said, 'Who do you think it is? 'Course it's me.' And I reached out my right hand and touched him with my fingers. I really felt him, and I jumped back, 'cause it was such a spooky feelin'. Then I woke up. Worth was real as y'all. Too damn weird by half."

"I don't dream so much anymore, now I'm older," said Lula. "Least I don't remember 'em the way I used to. How 'bout you, Sail?"

"Dreamed more in the joint than anywhere," Sailor said. "Prob'ly 'cause I was always catnappin', and my thoughts stayed close to the surface."

Sailor steered the Cadillac off the interstate and stopped at the State Highway 6 intersection.

"Here you go, Miss Venus. Oxford's due east twenty-five miles. Shouldn't have much trouble gettin' a ride to the university from here."

" 'Preciate it much. Oh, by the way, my name's really Consuelo. Consuelo Whynot, from Whynot, Miss'ippi. It's my best friend's name is Venus. She's a Chickasaw Indian. Always wanted to know what it'd feel like to have someone call me by her name, not knowin' it wasn't really mine. Anyway, thanks again."

Consuelo got out of the car, closed the door and walked off. As Sailor pulled his Sedan de Ville across the road and headed down the return ramp to the Interstate, Wesley Nisbet's black Duster crept off at the Batesville exit. He spotted Consuelo, drove up alongside her, leaned over and rolled down the passenger side window.

"Don't I know you?" he said. "Them polkadots is difficult to forget."

"What in blazes you doin' here now?" said Consuelo.

"Thought I'd take me a college tour. I ain't never been to one."

"You're followin' me."

"Just goin' the same way, is all. Hop in."

Consuelo stood on the side of the road for a minute and considered the situation, then she opened Wesley's car door.

"It'll be okay, Consuelo," Wesley said. "Y' always burn a few tiles on reentry."

In Memphis, Sailor and Lula checked into the Robert Johnson Regency, where Hilda Rae, Sailor's secretary at the Gator Gone Corporation, had made them a reservation on the recommendation of Sailor's boss, Bob Lee Boyle, who always stayed there on business trips to the city. It wasn't a fancy place, but it was clean and patroled around the clock by visibly armed security guards. A large sign at the registration desk proclaimed, THE MANAGEMENT SUGGESTS THAT GUESTS LOCK THEIR VALUABLES IN THE HOTEL SAFE DURING THEIR STAY.

"Not much of a view," Lula said, looking out the window of their third-floor room. Across the street was a dilapidated row of mostly abandoned brown brick buildings.

"Didn't come to Memphis for the view, peanut," said Sailor. "Just us and Elvis's home place is all we need."

He came up behind Lula, hugged her with his large arms folded across her breasts, and kissed her gently on the nape of her neck.

"Harder, Sail, honey. Bite me there on the neck how I like it."

Sailor gnawed harder on the lower part of Lula's neck and the tops of her shoulders, which made her moan. She bent backward into him, then forward, dipping her head as she lifted her skirt and lowered her panties.

"Stick it in, Sailor," she said. "Find a hole and drill me."

After they'd made love and showered, Sailor and Lula went downstairs to find a restaurant. Sailor was about to ask the desk clerk if he knew of a good place when

Lula grabbed his arm and pointed to a man standing just inside the front entrance.

"Do you recognize him?" Lula asked. "Ain't that Sparky? You remember, he and his friend Buddy was stranded with us in Big Tuna, Texas."

"It sure is, Lula. Holy shit. You know, some years back I thought I saw him on the late-night cable TV sellin' hair restorer. Wasn't certain, though."

They walked up behind the man, who was facing the street, and Sailor tapped him on the right shoulder.

"Hey, pardner, you ever been stuck in the Big Tuna?"

Sparky, who was wearing a straw half-Stetson similar to the one he'd worn in Texas almost thirty years before, turned around and grinned broadly when he recognized the couple.

"Well, look at this! It sure is good to know some of us poor white trash has somehow survived the ravages of time."

Sparky and Sailor shook hands and Lula gave him a big hug.

"Sailor Ripley, I presume," said Sparky. "I thought we'd seen the last of you, along with Bobby Peru and Perdita Durango. Got yourself in with a tough twosome down there. Good to see you made it out."

"Barely did, but here I am. Here *we* are. Me'n Lula been together again almost eighteen years now."

"Lula, you're just as sweet-lookin' a young thing as ever. Still got that real black hair and big gray eyes with violet lakes in 'em I ain't never forgot."

Lula laughed. "I ain't young no more, and the eyes are real, okay. But I kinda have to cheat now and then on the hair, which is threatenin' to go the way of my eyes."

"Me'n Buddy used to handle hair products back when we had the House of Santería in Waggaman, Louisiana. I could still get you some good dye, you want it."

"I thought that was you and Buddy one time doin' a commercial on the TV!" said Sailor.

Sparky smiled. "We did that for a while, till the FDA come after us. Before that we owned a bar in Dallas. Never did make it back to California."

"Where's Buddy?" Lula asked.

"Waitin' for him now. Better standin' inside the Me'n the Devil Motel here than catchin' a stray slug in the street. Memphis is a unpredictable town."

"What are you-all doin' in Memphis?" Sailor asked.

"Got us a new business, prosperin', too."

Sparky took a card out of his Madras sports coat pocket and handed it to Sailor.

" 'S&B Organ Retrieval Service,' " Sailor read out loud. " 'Only the best parts.' "

"We got a 800 number, you'll notice."

"Organ retrieval?" said Lula. "What in hell's that?"

"Vital body pieces," Sparky said. "Heart, kidneys, eyes, even livers, though real useful ones is difficult to come by, given the Southern disposition toward Rebel Yell and Wild Turkey."

"Sparky, you jokin'?" Lula asked.

"Nope. We got us some steady customers in the private sector. Keep that card, Sailor. Might come in handy. What about you folks? What's been happenin' all these years? And why're you in Memphis?"

"Sailor's vice-president of the Gator Gone Corporation now, produces alligator and crocodile repellent. It's a worldwide operation, even in India."

"Sell a bunch over there, that's the truth," said Sailor.

"We have a house in Metairie," Lula said, "by New Orleans. Our son, Pace, is livin' in Nepal, leadin' expeditions in the Himalaya mountains."

"Man," said Sparky, "life fools me right and left."

"We come up to visit Graceland," said Sailor. "Never been here before."

"Tomorrow's Sailor's birthday, his fiftieth. We're celebratin'."

"Guess you know about what the King's widow and daughter're doin' with mostly all the proceeds from the estate now, don't ya?"

"No," Sailor said, "what's that?"

"All goes to the Church of Myrmidon, that mind-control cult headquartered in San Diego. The widow and the kid're whole hog in the grip of that fake prophet calls himself Myrmidon, claims to have visited Venus and Mars and wrote all them books about out-of-body experiences. Man lives on a three-hundred-foot yacht, cruises the Greek Islands and the French Riviera. Saw in the newspaper where he was at the Cannes Film Festival last week promotin' a movie about his life. Can't set foot on U.S. soil or the Feds'll feed him into the shredder."

"Heard of the Church of Myrmidon," said Sailor, "but I didn't know they was suckin' the blood out the King's afterlife."

"Yeah, the Colonel bled him while he was alive, and now this Phelps Bonfuca, calls himself Myrmidon, drains his heirs."

"You say Phelps Bonfuca?"

"Uh huh. Myrmidon's real handle."

"I was in the joint with him," said Sailor. "At Huntsville. I did a dime standin' up for that stunt with Bobby Peru, and for four of 'em Phelps Bonfuca was in the same cell block. He was in on some bunco beef. Pyramid scam, I think. Milkin' suckers."

"Still at it," said Sparky. "Only on a big-time basis."

Sailor shook his head. "This don't make me feel so good now about goin' to Graceland, knowin' the money's endin' up in Phelps's pockets."

"It don't matter, Sail, sweetheart," said Lula. "Could be worse. The fam'ly might be donatin' the proceeds to the Cath'lic Church, or the Mormons or somethin'. One cult's same as another."

"Kinda disappoints me, is all."

"Don't matter what people do with their money," said Sparky, "long as they spend it, keep it comin' around where the other guy can reach in, he gets the chance, and grab him a fistful. Say, you folks hungry? Here's Buddy now."

Sailor and Lula looked through the glass door and saw a brown Plymouth Voyager pull up in front. The words s&b ORGAN RETRIEVAL SERVICE— ONLY THE BEST PARTS were stenciled in white on the side.

"We was just about to find us a restaurant when we seen you," said Lula.

"Come on, then," said Sparky. "We'll get some ribs. I know a place they take 'em off the body for you!"

Venus Tishomingo was six feet even and weighed a solid one-hundred-seventy-five pounds. Her hands were each the size of an infielder's glove, and she wore a 12-D

PROFESSIONALS

shoe. Her hair was chestnut brown and very thick, and hung down loose past her waist. She wore at least one ring on every finger other than her thumbs. They were cheap, colorful rings she'd bought in pawn shops in Memphis. Her eyes were clear, almost colorless stones set deep in her skull. Most people had a difficult time staring into them for very long before becoming uncomfortable and having to look away. At first glance, Venus's eyes resembled pristine pebbles in a gentle, smooth-flowing stream, but then they came alive and darted toward whomever's eyes met hers. She sat in her one-bedroom cottage in a gooseneck rocking chair, wearing only a well-faded pair of Wrangler blue jeans, reading the *Oxford Eagle*, waiting for Consuelo to arrive or call. An item datelined Jackson caught her eye.

"Pearl Buford, of Mockingbird, accused of trying to sell two of her grandchildren in an adoption scam, has pleaded innocent to charges in federal court here. Buford, 34, who told authorities she used to baby-sit professionally, also pleaded innocent to six counts of mail fraud involving solicitation of offers for the children. She is currently unemployed. Her daughter, Fannie Dawn Taylor, 16, a dropout after finishing 8th grade at Mockingbird Junior High, pleaded innocent to one count of mail fraud."

Venus had it in mind to adopt a child that she and Consuelo could raise together. Maybe more than one.

It was too bad, Venus thought, that Pearl Buford hadn't contacted her about taking on Fannie Dawn's kids.

Venus massaged her left breast with her right hand, tickling the nipple with the second and third fingers until it stood out taut and long as it would go. She had large breasts that were extremely sensitive to touch, and Consuelo knew perfectly how to suck on and fondle them. Venus dropped the newspaper and slid her left hand down inside the front of her jeans and rubbed her clit. She closed her eyes and thought about a photograph of a cat woman she'd seen in a book in the Ole Miss library that afternoon. It wasn't really a cat woman but two negatives printed simultaneously, one atop the other, of a cat and a woman, so that the face was half-human, half-feline, with long white whiskers, weird red bolts for eyes and perfect black Kewpie doll lips. Venus came quickly, bucking sharply twice before relaxing and slumping down in the chair. She removed her left hand and let it drape over the arm of the rocker. Her right hand rested in her lap. Venus was almost asleep when Consuelo knocked on the door.

Venus jumped up and opened it. Consuelo threw herself forward onto her naked chest.

"I'm starved, Venie," Consuelo said. "I need your lovin'."

"Got it comin', baby," said Venus, stroking Consuelo's wheat-light hair with a large brown hand.

Venus heard a car engine idling, looked over Consuelo's left shoulder out the door and saw the black Duster in front of the house.

"Who's that?" she asked.

"Wesley Nisbet, the one I told you about. He's a pest, but he give me a lift here. Followed the ride I caught outta Jackson, picked me up again in Batesville."

"He truly dangerous?"

"Maybe, like most."

"He figurin' you're gonna invite him in?"

Consuelo swung her right leg backward and the door slammed shut.

"Just another mule kickin' in his stall," she said.

When Wesley saw the door close, he shifted the Duster into first and eased his pantherlike machine away. He drove into town, parked on the northwest side of the square in front of a restaurant-bar named The Mansion, got out of the car and went inside.

"J. W. Dant, double," Wesley said to the bartender, as he hopped up on a stool. "One cube, splash water."

A toad-faced man with a greasy strand of gray-yellow hair falling over his forehead sat on the stool to Wesley's left. The man was wearing a wrinkled burgundy blazer with large silver buttons over a wrinkled, dirty white shirt and a wide, green, food-stained tie. He wobbled as he extended his right hand toward Wesley.

"Five Horse Johnson," the man said. "You?"

"That a clever way of tellin' me you got a short dick or's it your name?"

The man laughed once, very loudly, and wiped his right hand on his coat.

"Nickname I got as a boy. Had me a baby five HP outboard on a dinghy, used to go fishin' in Sardis Lake. Can't hardly remember my so-called Christian one, though the G-D gov'ment reminds me once a year. Hit me up for the G-D tax on my soul, they do. Strip a couple pounds a year. Forty-five G-damn years old. Amazed there's any flesh left to cover the nerves. You ain't from Oxford."

"No, ain't."

"Then you prob'ly don't know the local def'nition of the term 'relative humidity.' "

Wesley picked up his drink, which the bartender had just set in front of him, and took a sip.

"What's it?"

"Relative humidity is the trickle of sweat runs down the crack of your sister-in-law's back while you're fuckin' her in the ass."

Five Horse Johnson grinned liplessly, exposing six slimy orange teeth, then fell sideways off his stool to the floor. Wesley finished his whisky and put two dollars on the bar.

"This do it?" he asked the bartender, who nodded.

Wesley unseated himself and stepped over Five Horse Johnson, who was either dead or asleep or in some indeterminate state between the two.

"Professional man, I'll guess."

"Lawyer," said the bartender.

"I known others," Wesley said, and walked out.

Sailor and Lula spent most of their first afternoon in Memphis having lunch with Sparky and Buddy in the Hound Dog Cafe on Elvis Presley Boulevard across the

SPRINKLE BODIES

street from Graceland, a place that specialized in Elvis's favorite sandwich, peanut butter and banana on white. The four of them passed on "The White Trash Blue Plate," as Buddy called it, and ate hamburgers as they listened to old Sun 45s by the Killer, the King, Roy Orbison, Charlie Rich and Carl Perkins on the jukebox, and filled each other in on their respective activities over the past quarter of a century and more. After lunch, Sailor and Lula exchanged addresses and telephone numbers with Sparky and Buddy, who went back to work at Organ Retrieval, and then browsed the Elvis souvenir shops.

Sailor was reluctant to tour Graceland now that he knew about the connection to Phelps Bonfuca, alias Myrmidon, and he told Lula he wanted to think it over some more. He was tempted to go through Elvis's private jet, the *Lisa Marie*, which was on display in the Graceland parking lot, but he resisted the urge, since that cost money, too. He did buy a few postcards and two Elvis tee shirts—both decorated with photos from *Jailhouse Rock*, his favorite Elvis movie—at a shop called The Wooden Indian, because he figured Elvis's heirs didn't own it.

Back in their room at the Robert Johnson Regency, Sailor and Lula lay on the king-size bed in their underwear, smoking and talking. Lula had fallen off the cigarette wagon in the Hound Dog Cafe, having fished a More from her purse and fired it up before she'd even realized what she was doing. She puffed happily away and put any thoughts about the possible consequences into a dark corner of her mind.

"Sail, you know, we really been alive a long time now."

"Sometimes it feels long, peanut, other times not much. Why you say that?"

"Oh, thinkin', is all."

Sailor lit a fresh unfiltered Camel off an old one and stubbed out the butt on the letters RJR in a round glass ashtray.

"Bet Robert Johnson never stayed in no hotel fancy as this," Sailor said.

"Robert who?"

"Johnson, man this hotel's named for. Blues singer from Miss'ippi died young. Record comp'ny brought him to the city, right off the plantation, I believe. Think Dallas, or San Antone. Cut some tunes then got killed, shot or knifed or somethin', so there ain't much to listen to. What he done was outstandin', though. Kinda spooky, some of it. That's what Sparky was referrin' to when he called this place the Me'n the Devil Motel. 'Me'n the Devil' was one of Robert Johnson's songs. Another good one was 'Hellhound on My Trail.' "

Lula inhaled hard on a More and then blew a big gusher of smoke into the air where it hovered over the bed like a cumulus cloud.

"Shit, Sailor, you know so much more'n me about things? I mean, strange, about unheard of details, like what happened to Robert Johnson."

"Anybody's interested in the music knows about him, honey. Ain't nothin' special."

"Not just this, Sail. You got tons of information tucked away in every part of your brain you never even gonna use. It's a gift."

Sailor laughed. "Ain't the same as bein' smart, though. I'd been smart, never woulda spent a dozen years of my life behind bars. Only real smart thing I ever done was realize you're the best, peanut. I mean that more'n anythin'."

"Sailor?"

"Huh?"

"Don't laugh at me now, okay? When I say what I'm goin' to say?"

"How do I know if I'll laugh or not? What if it's funny?"

"No, you gotta promise or I can't say it."

"Okay, peanut, I promise."

"You think when a person dies, he just fades away? Mean, there ain't really no heaven or even no hell and it's just all over? Tell me the truth now."

"Thought you figured this out back when you was part of the Reverend

Goodin Plenty's flock in the Church of Reason, Redemption and Resistance to God's Detractors."

"You know I ain't been to church since Bunny Thorn and I seen Goodin Plenty shot to death in the tent at Rock Hill. His answers didn't hold up, neither."

" 'Member that ol' Buddy Holly tune, 'Not Fade Away'?"

"Yeah?"

"There's your answer."

"Splain yourself."

Sailor raised himself on one elbow and stubbed out his cigarette.

"I'll tell you," he said, "but now you gotta promise not to laugh."

"I do."

"Well, I believe that when folks die all their energy just disperses in the air and flies off like sparks through the universe. Their spirit shoots out of their body and sprinkles back over ever'thin'. That way nobody dies, 'cause their vital self enters into what's left."

"You talkin' 'bout reincarnation, like in India, where a person can come back in another life as a insect? Or you mean that past lives stuff?"

"Uh-uh. Some people in India figure if they live holy enough, next time around they'll be an American. No, just what I said. I call it the 'sprinkle body' theory. Sometimes maybe because of the way the earth's spinnin' or somethin', more of someone gets transferred into a newborn baby or a bee or a rose, but prob'ly that's pretty rare. I figure it's sorta like tossin' a handful of sand into the sky and lettin' the grains blow into eternity."

Lula lay still and didn't say anything.

"Peanut, you think I'm crazy, thinkin' this?"

"No, Sail, I think you're smart, real smart. About some things, I mean. Mostly important things, and this is one. Wasn't totally your fault you went to prison. There's plenty of bright boys locked up for one reason or another."

Sailor lay back on his pillow, picked up his pack of Camels, shook one out and lit it.

"Can't figure it any other way," he said.

"Sprinkle bodies," said Lula.

"Yeah."

"It makes sense, don't it, Sail? It truly does."

The room was almost completely dark, and Sailor stared at the burning end of his cigarette.

"This is the only chance we got to be who we are, Lula, to have all of ourselves in one package."

"I believe you, Sailor. I believe in you, too. But I guess you must know that by now."

Lula turned toward Sailor and fit her head into his right armpit.

"I love you, too, peanut," he said. "And you know what?"

"Huh?"

"Neither of us ain't never had another choice in this world."

Lula nuzzled in even closer.

"Listen, Lula," said Sailor, "I want you to have engraved on my tombstone: 'Dear Peanut, I love you to death,' and underneath just my name."

"Oh, Sail, don't be depressin'. You ain't about to die anytime soon."

"Prob'ly Elvis, even though he was a overweight drug addict, didn't think he was gonna go at forty-two, honey. Just remember, okay?"

"Course I will, sweetheart, it's what you want. Just you remember I love you to death, too."

"Okay, peanut, guess we might just as well do it, even if Phelps gets the money."

"Don't matter anyway, Sail. This bein' your birthday

you should do what you want. It'll be fun visitin' Graceland. Elvis didn't die there, did he?"

"Yeah, he O.D.'ed sittin' there on a toilet."

"Prob'ly if he'd always stayed in Memphis, or got him a spread down in that beautiful area around Hernando, Miss'ippi, he'd've lived a whole lot longer. Elvis was outta his true element in California, I believe. Read a Elvis-on-Other-Planets Weight Chart was in a *Enquirer* or somewhere, said that since he weighed 255 when he died, Elvis woulda weighted 648 pounds on Jupiter but only 43 on the moon."

Sailor and Lula had awakened early on the morning of his fiftieth birthday. They'd each gone to the bathroom, peed and brushed their teeth, then gone back to bed and made love. Ordinarily Lula had a hard time coming when they did it so soon after waking, but today she'd been able to get the calf out of the chute so easily that it gave her the giggles.

"What's so funny?" Sailor asked.

"Nothin', honey, just feelin' nice and warm, is all. Look, bring that big bad thing up here where I can treat it right."

Lula grabbed Sailor's cock and pulled him up so that he straddled her chest. She guided him into her mouth, placed her hands on his buttocks and let him move himself forward and back until the hourglass-shaped vein on his penis swelled to bursting and her throat was flooded.

"Still works good, don't it, peanut?" Sailor said, getting off the bed.

"I'm a lucky girl, all right."

Sailor went into the bathroom to take a shower and Lula switched on the TV. The news was on and Lula cranked up the volume in order to hear over the running water.

"In Oxford, Mississippi, last night," the young, African-American woman newscaster said, "a man was shot and killed with his own gun by a half-naked woman, who was then run over and killed by the man's car when it went out of control. Police in Oxford are calling the incident the 'Lesbian Indian Murders.' The killings were apparently the result of a love triangle involving the man, who has been identified as Wesley Nisbet, address unknown, and the woman, Venus Tishomingo, a Chick-asaw Indian who was a student at Ole Miss, and a sixteen-year-old girl named Consuelo Whynot, who was present at the scene. Miss Whynot, who was unhurt, is being held in protective custody at the Lafayette County Jail in Oxford."

"Sailor! Sail, come here! You won't believe this!"

Sailor turned off the water and grabbed a towel.

"What is it, peanut?" he said, running in and dripping everywhere.

"You know that girl hitcher we picked up and drove from Jackson to Batesville?"

"Yeah?"

"She's in jail in Oxford. Near as I could make out, a man and a woman were fightin' over her and killed each other. Cops got her in custody."

Sailor ran the towel over his head, under his arms, around his back, down his legs, daubed his feet and tossed it on the bed. He started to put on his clothes.

"Let's get down there, peanut. She might could use some help."

"What could we do for her? Besides, it's your birthday and we're goin' to Graceland."

"Don't matter what day it is. Just think it's what we oughta do. Fuck Graceland, anyway. I re-decided I don't want none of our money filterin' down to no Church of Myrmidon."

Lula got up and began to pack. The telephone rang and Sailor answered it.

"Ripley speakin'."

"Sailor, this is Dalceda Delahoussaye."

"Hello, Mrs. Delahoussaye. Why you callin'? How'd you know we was in Memphis?"

"Marietta told me. Is Lula there?"

"Yeah. You rather speak to her? She's packin' 'cause we're about to leave."

"Don't really matter, I s'pose. Marietta wanted her to know that Marcello Santos had heart palpitations yesterday and is under doctor's care at the Sister Ralph Ricci Convalescent Center here in Bay St. Clement. Marietta's stayin' by his side and won't leave."

"That so? Look, lemme put Lula on."

Sailor handed her the phone.

"Dal? Mama all right?"

"Yes, Lula, Marietta's fine, but Santos is havin' serious chest pains and's in Sister Ralph's. Marietta's there with him, holdin' his hand and readin' him chapters from his favorite book, Eugene Sue's *Mysteries of Paris*."

"That's Mama. He gonna pull through?"

"Don't think he's got long to go, Lula, but he might could hang on, bein' he's one tough Sicilian. There's somethin' else, though."

"What's that?"

"Johnnie Farragut's kidneys just completely quit on him this mornin' early, and he's over at Little Egypt Baptist plugged into a dialysis machine. Marietta don't even know yet. I ain't told her since she's got her hands full with old Crazy Eyes. Doctor at Baptist says unless Johnnie gets a transplant soon he's done."

"Sweet Jesus, Dal, what a phone call."

"Sorry to be the one, Lula, but I thought you'd want to hear the news sooner'n later."

" 'Course, Dal, I 'preciate it. Sailor and I are leavin' here now. We got a stop to make in Oxford, then we'll head for home, I guess. I'll call you when we get to Metairie."

"Okay. Take care drivin'."

"We will, Dal. Bye."

"Bye, hon'."

Lula hung up and said, "Shit hits the fan, it splatters."

"You don't care 'bout Santos, do you?"

"Not one way or another, but Dal says Johnnie Farragut's got kidney failure and needs a new one or he's a goner. He's rigged to a device at Little Egypt Baptist."

Sailor picked up the telephone.

"You got that card Sparky give you?" he asked.

Lula found it in her purse and handed it to Sailor, who read the number on it and dialed. A machine answered.

"You've reached S&B Organ Retrieval Service," said Sparky's recorded voice. "Leave a message and we'll do what we can to accommodate your needs. It might cost you some, but at least we won't charge an arm and a leg! Just a little humor there, of course. We stand by our motto: 'Only the best parts!' Be talkin' to ya. Here comes the beep."

"Sparky, Buddy, this is Sailor Ripley speakin'. Listen, Lula's mama's old friend Johnnie Farragut is got kidney failure and's hooked up to a tube or somethin' at Little Egypt Baptist Hospital in Bay St. Clement, North Carolina. He needs a transplant real quick or he's gonna die. If you can help out with this, Lula and I'll find a way to pay you back. We're checkin' out of the hotel now. I'll call you again later."

He hung up, opened his suitcase and threw in his clothes. The phone rang and Sailor answered it.

"Sailor? It's Buddy."

"I just called you."

"I know, we heard the message. We never answer ourselves. Never know who it might be. Anyway, we're on the case. Sparky's contactin' our best retrieval man, John Gray, on the other line. Prob'ly we can get a part on its way to your friend by tonight. And don't worry about the price, it's free of charge. For old times' sake."

"This is awful large of you guys," said Sailor. "Awful large."

Buddy laughed. "Sparky's standin' here talkin' in my other ear now. Hold on, Sailor."

"Sailor? Sparky here."

" 'Preciate this, Spark. You guys are beyond outstandin'."

"Anything for veterans of the Big Tuna! You tell Lula's mama not to worry. We gotta run now, we're gonna get this part out."

"We're goin', too. *Adios, amigo.*"

"*Ciao!*"

Sailor hung up.

"What'd they say, Sail? Tell me!"

"Boys have it covered, peanut. They're sendin' a new kidney to North Carolina tonight."

"Gonna cost a arm or leg, I bet."

Sailor laughed. "No, sweetheart, it ain't. It's free."

"Them two're somethin' else. Shows you how much good there still is left in the world, Sail. Just gotta know where to look."

"Don't know about good, Lula, but could be Johnnie Farragut'll be able to take a real piss again one of these days."

" 'When the phantoms cease for a moment to pass and repass on the black veil which I have before my eyes, there are other tortures—there are overwhelming com-

THE PROPOSAL

parisons. I say to myself, if I had remained an honest man, at this moment I should be free, tranquil, happy, loved, and honored by mine own, instead of being blind and chained in this dungeon, at the mercy of my accomplices.'

" 'Alas! the regret of happiness, lost by crime, is the first step toward repentance. And when to this repentance is added an expiation of frightful severity—an expiation which changes life into a long sleep filled with avenging hallucinations of desperate reflections, perhaps then the pardon of man will follow—' "

"Marry me, Marietta," said Santos.

Marietta stopped reading, closed the book and looked up at him. His face was green and puffy and his eyes were closed.

"Marietta Pace, will you marry me?"

She squeezed his right hand, the one with a thumb, with her left.

"Yes, Marcello," said Marietta, "I will."

"I still ain't sure we're doin' the right thing. I mean, we ain't even relatives."

"Maybe there ain't nothin' we can do, peanut, but I got a feelin' this is a lost girl could use a hand."

POISON

Sailor had just turned the Sedan de Ville onto Highway 6 toward Oxford.

"Sail, look how these trees is bein' strangled by kudzu. Them vines strap around 'em like boas on bunnies."

"No stoppin' it, I guess. Kudzu's nature's version of The Blob."

"Wonder if Beany's rememberin' to turn my worms."

Sailor turned up the radio.

"In Miami yesterday," said a newscaster, "a man and a woman died after drinking a six-pack of a Colombian soft drink laced heavily with cocaine. Pony Malta de Bavaria, an imported beverage that has been available for sale in limited quantities in independent grocery stores in the area known as Little Havana, was removed from shelves this morning by order of the Greater Miami Board of Health."

"Used to be Co-Cola had cocaine in it, didn't it, Sailor?"

"Think maybe the first few batches did, till the government figured out a better way to make money off it."

Oxford came up fast and Sailor slowed the Cad as they entered the town. He drove in on Old Taylor Road and followed the signs to the square, where he stopped and asked an old man for directions to the police station.

"They holdin' the 'Last Kiss' girl there, you know," said the man. "I been over but they ain't lettin' nobody in."

The old man was wearing a faded, torn yellow tee shirt that had the words FREE BYRON DE LA BECKWITH on it in black block letters. The man had no hair and no visible teeth, and as he pointed across the square with his left hand, Sailor noticed that the index finger was the only remaining digit on it.

"Lafayette County Jail's just yonder, past the square. Follow around and it'll be on your right. Tickets to view a poison pelt like her'd move faster'n jumper cables at a nigger funeral, I'll guarantee."

Sailor nodded at the man, drove to the jail and parked on the street in front. In the space ahead was a Mercedes-Benz 600 sedan with a Lauderdale County personalized license plate that read WHY NOT.

"Bet that belongs to her parents," said Lula.

"We'll find out," said Sailor, as he opened his door.

As soon as Sailor and Lula entered the station, Consuelo Whynot, who was standing with a well-dressed middle-aged couple and a sheriff, shouted, "They're the ones picked me up in Jackson! They'll tell you 'bout how I was runnin' from that deranged boy!"

"That true?" asked the sheriff, walking toward Sailor and Lula.

"It's true we give her a lift from Jackson to Batesville," said Sailor, "but we don't know nothin' 'bout no boy."

"Why you here?"

"Heard about the incident on the TV news in Memphis, where we was stayin'," said Lula. "Today's my husband's fiftieth birthday, which we was plannin' to celebrate, but he thought it'd be best we drove down and see she needed help."

"You-all sure I didn't tell you 'bout that hor'ble Wesley Nisbet?" asked Consuelo.

"Not that I recall," said Sailor. "You?" he asked Lula.

"Uh-uh."

"I give him one kiss, is all," said Consuelo. "I swear. Said he'd leave me'n Venus be if I did. Had a gun, that boy. Then he told us unless we did a act of love while he watched, he was gonna kidnap me. That's when Venus took after him and the cat caught the chicken. Mama, you got a cigarette?"

The well-dressed woman took a pack of Mores from her purse, removed one and handed it to Consuelo.

"Need a blaze," Consuelo said.

Her mother produced a gold lighter with the initials sow on it and lit Consuelo's cigarette.

"Sailor, look," said Lula, "she smokes the same brand as me."

"So you folks don't know nothin' 'bout this Nisbet?" asked the sheriff.

"We don't," Sailor said.

"Look, sheriff," said the well-dressed man, "none of this really matters, does it? Consuelo will be with us if you need her. We'll make sure she don't leave home again until this case is cleared up satisfact'rily."

"You can take her," the sheriff said. "Ain't nothin' I can charge her with. It's you and your wife might have a problem, bein' she's a minor."

"Old enough to get married without nobody's permission," said Consuelo. "Though there ain't a man alive can replace Venus in my affections."

"Let's go, Sail," Lula said. "Nobody needs us here."

"Okay, peanut. So long, Consuelo. Good luck."

Consuelo took a deep drag on the More and pushed her free hand back through her brushfire of hair. She pursed her lips and exhaled, then smiled at Sailor.

"Elvis has left the buildin'," she said.

John Gray lived, ate and worked alone. He had risen only several minutes prior to the phone call from S&B Organ Retrieval, his best customer. The day had begun

well for John Gray, and he hummed the tune of "Just a Closer Walk with Thee" while he shaved. John Gray was forty-five years old, he was slightly more than six-feet three-inches tall, weighed two-hundred-ten well-muscled pounds, wore a bushy black hair weave, and a thick Mexican *bandido*-style mustache that he coated with black Kiwi shoe polish. His eyes were light green, although on a bright afternoon, when he wasn't wearing dark glasses, they turned almost yellow. He wore a three-piece, Wall Street gray Brooks Brothers suit every day, with a red handkerchief in the breast pocket, and black Reebok dress shoes.

John Gray knew where to go for product. He kept his supercharged, midnight blue 5.0-liter Mustang under control as he glided through the Memphis streets. When he arrived at the corner of Murnau and Lewton, he slid to the curb and let the engine idle while he waited. The neighborhood appeared deserted, with abandoned buildings on all sides, but within thirty seconds, two teenaged boys appeared, both wearing Bart Simpson tee shirts, black Levi's and Air Jordans. They came over to the Mustang.

"Got ice, bro'," one of the boys said, as they both leaned their heads toward John Gray, "blow you away."

"No," said John Gray, as he brought up the nine-millimeter machine pistol he'd been holding on his lap, "blow *you* away."

He shot both boys point-blank once each in their foreheads, got out of the car, picked them up, placed them carefully in the trunk and wrapped a heavy brown blanket tightly around the bodies.

As he drove at a modest speed toward the S&B office, John Gray began to sing "Angelo castro e bel" from Donizetti's *Il Duca d'Alba*. Though not a true tenor, John Gray did his best to mimic Caruso's interpretation of the piece, imagining himself as Marcello de Bruges pouring his heart out for Amelia d'Egmont, who is at that moment on her way to meet him.

Sailor and Lula stopped to eat at the Mayflower Cafe on Capitol Street in Jackson on their way home. Most of downtown Jackson had been recently torn down, in-

LIFE AS WE

KNOW IT

cluding the grand old Heidelberg Hotel, and replaced by faceless state government buildings and parking lots. Not that most of the city was that old, Sherman having torched everything that would burn on his march to Atlanta during the unpleasantness known unpopularly as the War Between the States. About the only building left standing after the Yankees left had been the old Capitol. Since the demise of Tom and Woody's Mississippi Diner, the Mayflower was pretty much the end of the line for the downtown restaurant business.

"Same two Greek brothers been operatin' this place since forever," Sailor said to Lula, as they seated themselves in a red leather booth.

He pointed to two ancient-looking, bald-headed, big-nosed men sitting at a Formica table by the cash register. Above the register on the wall was a framed photograph of a man whom both brothers resembled closely.

"That picture's prob'ly of their daddy," said Sailor. "Food's as good here as at the Acme, I recall. Ain't been in since them few months we was apart followin' my release from Huntsville. Those were dark days for me, peanut."

"I know, Sail. They were for me, too."

Sailor shook his head. "Never will forget workin' in that lumberyard in Petal, and livin' in that crummy furnished room over the St. Walburga Thrift Store in Hattiesburg. Whew, that was a bad deal. Come through here and stayed a few days after I left you and Pace in N.O.''

"Let's not talk about it, Sailor. Them days is long gone. Look at the good life we created together since then."

Sailor reached across the table and put his hands over Lula's.

"I'm fine, peanut. You don't hear me complainin'. Hate seein' a bad fam'ly situation like the Whynots, is all."

"Won't be no easy road for that Consuelo. Least not for a while."

"She's wild in the country, okay."

A waitress came over and Sailor ordered fried oysters, shrimp, onion rings, fries and two glasses of iced tea.

"That should do it," he said. "What you gonna have, Lula?"

After they'd eaten, Sailor suggested that they not drive all the way home that night, and Lula agreed. They got a room at the Millsaps Buie House on North State Street, a Victorian relic that had originally been the residence of Confederate Major Reuben Webster Millsaps, founder of the local Methodist College, whose house was now operated as an inn. Lula loved the elegant old bed and breakfast place, and she and Sailor slept late the next day, neither of them being in a particular hurry to find out what disastrous occurrence came next.

It was Lula who made the discovery a few minutes after they'd gotten home.

"Sailor! Come see these worms! They're all dead!"

"How could that be, peanut?" Sailor said, running into the backyard, carrying a letter in his right hand. "Thought you told me Beany was watchin' 'em."

"She musta left the hose on the rose bushes too long, and the water seeped into the worm bin and drowned 'em. Sailor, this is the worst!"

"Maybe not, peanut."

He handed Lula the letter.

"It's from Pace," she said.

Sailor nodded. "Go on and read it."

> Dear Mama and Daddy,
>
> I am just back from the trek and am writing to tell you the best news of my life. I have met a great girl, a woman I should say, from New York. Actually she is from Brooklyn which is about the same place she says. Her name is Rhoda Gombowicz and yes, she is Jewish. She is about the first Jewish person I have ever known to my knowledge. Rhoda is very beautiful with hair kind of like yours Mama and big brown eyes. Also she is incredibly smart. Sometimes she

talks too fast for me and I have to tell her to slow down but she doesn't mind my telling her that. She says everyone in New York talks that way which is one of the reasons she likes me so much she says because I don't. Any way Rhoda and I are in love now and I asked her to marry me when we were on a peak in the Himalayas. She said no woman would say no being proposed to in that spot so she said yes. The one problem is that Rhoda's parents won't let her marry a man who is not Jewish so I have agreed to convert to the Jewish religion. The only religions I know about are Baptist, Buddhist, and Bonpo, so why not? We will leave in a week for New York to meet her family and where I will find out what it takes to become Jewish. I will call or write to you from there. Rhoda says we should live in Brooklyn because that is where her family is. Rhoda is a mental therapist who helps people with their problems by talking to them not a physical therapist who performs rubdowns. You'll like her I know. She is 32 years old five years older than me and never married. Rhoda says if I want I can work in the diamond business with her father and four brothers. I told her I would wait and see about that part. Don't worry about me or anything. The next time you hear from me will be from Brooklyn!

Love, your favorite (and only) son,
Pace Roscoe Ripley

Lula looked up at Sailor but said nothing.

"What you think, peanut?"

"I can't think yet, Sail. I need a minute."

The telephone rang.

"I'll get it," said Lula, who carried Pace's letter with her into the house and held it in one hand while she picked up the receiver with the other.

"Hello?"

"Lula? It's Dal."

"Hi, Dal. How's Santos and Johnnie?"

"It was beautiful, Lula. I wish you coulda been there."

"Been where?"

"At the weddin'. Your mama and Marcello Santos was married this mornin' at three A.M. by a priest at Sister Ralph's. Santos died at ten past three. He was a happy old gangster when his heart quit."

"How about Johnnie?"

"That's the most beautiful part. Johnnie Farragut was the best man. He was strapped down in his bed and taped to a portable piece of equipment moved over from Little Egypt Baptist. After the ceremony, they rushed him back to the hospital where he had a kidney transplant operation. Marietta and I got word from the doctor two hours ago that he thinks it was successful. Doctor said it was a miracle they were able to locate a healthy kidney so quick. Came in on a private jet from Memphis, he said."

"And Mama? How's she holdin' up?"

"Woman's a rock, Lula. You be proud you're her daughter. She's with the mortuary people now, makin' arrangements for Santos's burial. She told me to let you know about ever'thin's gone on and tell you she'll call first chance after she's rested. How's things there?"

"Not quite spectacular as your news, Dal, but other than Beany lettin' the worms die while we was away, the big story is that Pace is gettin' married."

"Well, glory be! Not to one of them Hindu women, I hope."

"No, Dal, to a Jewish girl from Brooklyn, New York. Think she's kind of a doctor. He's movin' there from Nepal."

"You want me to tell Marietta?"

"Better let me do it. Mama's got enough on her mind just now. Give her my and Sailor's love and same to Johnnie Farragut. Thanks for bein' there, Dal. Love you, too."

"Been here all my life, Lula. Bye now."

"Bye. Take care."

After she'd hung up the phone, Lula read Pace's letter again, then put it down on the kitchen table. She looked out through the sliding glass doors into the backyard and saw Sailor standing next to the flooded worm bin smoking a Camel. A huge blue jay landed on the grass about ten feet away from Sailor. He flicked his cigarette at the bird and it screeched and took off.

"Ain't no way human bein's can control their own lives," Lula said out loud, "and ain't no way they ever can stop tryin'."

It suddenly occurred to Lula that she had forgotten to give Sailor a birthday present.

BARRY GIFFORD was born on October 18, 1946, in Chicago, Illinois, and raised there and in Key West and Tampa, Florida. He has been the recipient of awards from PEN, the National Endowment for the Arts, the Art Directors Club of New York, and the American Library Association. His novel *Wild at Heart* was made into a film by David Lynch. Mr. Gifford lives in the San Francisco Bay Area.